# KINGDOMS OF WRATH AND ICE

EDITED BY
LIZ DELTON & BENJAMIN THOMAS

Kingdoms of Wrath and Ice
Edited by Liz Delton and Benjamin Thomas

ISBN: 978-1-954663-11-4

Cover design by Liz Delton
Interior illustrations by Elise Berensen Meyer



This is a work of fiction. Names, characters, places, and incidents either are the product of the author's imagination or are used fictitiously. Any resemblance to actual persons, living or dead, events, or locales is entirely coincidental.

Content Guidance: This collection contains depictions of graphic violence, death, gore, thoughts of suicide, forced betrothal, and death of a parent.

Tourmaline & Quartz Publishing LLC
P. O. Box 193, North Granby, CT 06060
www.TourmalineandQuartzPublishing.com

# KINGDOMS OF WRATH AND ICE
### Liz Delton

Winter has always been a thing of mystery, darkness, and even death as nature itself dies off or hibernates for another year. The weather can be just as much an antagonist as the darkest villain; with its black ice, frigid frostbite, and endless snowdrifts to contend with. And though we think we have conquered winter with modern comforts, it still lurks in those dark months, its icy fingers ready to freeze, to crack the ice, to bury us in snow.

But there are kingdoms and realms without those comforts. Realms of fantasy, where curses abound, and beasts still roam. Where it's just as easy to become a hero as it is a villain, in times of darkness.

Just as we long to know what exists out there in the dark beyond the falling snow, or in the deepest of frozen lakes, we long to discover the inner workings of the villains in the tales we tell to keep warm around the fire.

And as the snow melts, perhaps we'll find a seed of hope...

# CONTENTS

# THE KELPIE
## by Andrew LiVecchi

THE KELPIE'S RAGE was in the beating of the waves, in the howl of the wind. She was in the lashing of the sea foam, reaching over the strakes with cold white fingers. She was in the forked lightning; the roar of thunder her hunted cry.

Connal leaned over the longship's prow, barbed spear in hand. Wind whipped his face, stinging his eyes with salt and snow, tugging at his blood-red hair. With his other hand, he gripped the stempost, fingers burning as the ship tossed, riding the storm like a wild horse.

"Pull!" he roared. His words fell into the wind and rushed back at him, joining the kelpie's stormwail. "Pull like your lives depend on it!"

Behind him, he could hear the heaving breaths of men at oars, the rhythmic splash of their catch. He turned his head a moment, fingers wrapped round the post. The men sang out a sailor's chant and pulled, the bared muscles straining on arms and legs. They were good men. Warriors all. Men who'd locked eyes with death and made him blink. They'd followed him out of his father's hall, loyal retainers keen for glory.

Yes, it was glory he'd promised them and vengeance also, for the lives of brothers drowned and devoured. Glory and vengeance both they'd find, here in the bowels of the storm, far from the jagged coasts of Cregeirann.

A flash of light and the drum of thunder. Above the black sea's foaming crests reared the horse's head and forelegs, riding the seas like a heathen prow, a goddess of rime and brine. There for a moment, then covered again in a darkening veil.

"Pull, lads!" he called out, his eyes fixed on the point in the darkness where she'd been. "The she-devil's there, in the black sea yonder. Pull, I say! Pull till the skin peels from your hands!"

The grunt of exertion was their only reply. The ship lurched, carving the ice-ridden sea.

"We've got her now!" he said, raising himself to full height and cocking the spear overhand. He wore no armour—too great a risk on the open sea—bore no weapon save the spear in his hand and the seax in his belt. A blade of kings, as his father had told him. "Pull me in closer and I'll stick her."

The ship tossed as a great wave struck it upon the starboard, casting up icy spray. He teetered a moment, crouched, and tightened his hold on the stempost.

Lightning danced across the sky, tearing the darkness like a beggar's rags. He saw it again, the horse's neck and dragon's body, clad in scales and fin. It looked upon him and snarled, baring a mouth of jagged daggers.

Connal snarled back, standing again at full height. He brandished his spear and howled into the wind. "I come for you, monster! I, Connal the Beastmaster, son of Craedon, king of the Iron Rock!" That was good, he thought. A beast should know the fame of the one who kills it.

The wail of the storm turned to laughter. He heard it on the wind's frosted voice, a woman's scornful laugh.

2

"Kill me, master of beasts?" she said. "You are far from the Iron Rock. This sea shall be your tomb. And that of those your pride has brought to ruin."

The lightning flashed again, revealing her at greater length, her body rising in coils from the sea. She rose and loomed over them, hanging there a moment twixt air and sea, beyond the reach of his vengeful spear. Then she fell, and the waters shot up in towering waves. The ship rolled and dipped to portside, filling with ravenous brine. Connal crouched low and stayed there. Another wave, born of her crash, soared to dizzying height, bearing down upon them.

"Hold!" Connal said, though he could hardly hear himself for the clamor of the storm.

The wave struck, smashing against them like a drunkard's fist. He heard the panicked cry of his warriors as two fell shrieking into the sea. The others hunkered down, shivering deep within the bilge.

"Farrion protect us," he prayed, "Lend your aid and calm the storm."

The waters raged but the saint was swift with his mercy. The ship held. They had weathered the worst of the kelpie's wrath.

"To oars," Connal said. "In again. Give me but one good shot and I'll have her spitted."

On they drove, beating against black rollers. The waves struck violently, yet the lightning held back, and his gaze could not pierce the darkness. He stood taller, tossing his head, the wet locks slapping his broad back.

She had taken her shot and missed the mark, and now it was his turn. She shrouded herself in darkness, shirking his hunting spear. The kelpie knew fear at last. Like any beleaguered beast.

He cried out into the darkness, a wordless, bloody song, battle cry of the islanders of those savage days before the coming of the priests. He heard the serpent's rumbling response, from deep within the darkness. A challenge.

"Hard to starboard," he said. "You'll not hide from me, sea-hag!"

Onward they shot like an archer's shaft, cutting through the black and frothing sea. Lightning fired the night sky and revealed her rising from the water, a black silhouette against a long line of jagged rocks.

Cornered at last and with nowhere to run. The warriors strove without command, quickening the pace of their clattering oars. The kelpie danced this way and that, holding the hunter in its baleful gaze, watching for his attack.

"Slightly to port, lads," he said. "We'll pin her against the rock."

The ship lurched to port and picked up speed, its prow aimed at the sinuous neck. Smooth as an eel she slithered away, narrowly avoiding the ramming motion. Then she hovered over the water, staring with wicked green eyes, head wagging in mockery.

The sailors cursed by the names of the old ones, Gaillag and Fearg, and stormy Drog. Yet Connal did not curse with them. Bounding from stem to stern, past the benches and bold companions, he cocked his spear arm, held her in his gaze. He saw her dance lithely, tossing her equine head. He felt the roughness of the ash against his palm, savoured the anticipation of the kill. Then he hurled it, bending as he threw, casting the weight of his body into the weapon. The spear flew through the darkness and the snow, over the foaming sea, into the kelpie's neck.

A shriek ripped from her body, louder than the thunder and the rain. The mare's neck twitched and wriggled, but the spear would not come free, gripping the flesh with barbs of iron. Connal had practiced that throw, years of tireless training on men of straw and forest animals. It would not come free.

The kelpie thrashed; its mocking turned to pain. A tail, long and thick like an adder's, launched from the water, striking madly at the surface. The sea heaved beneath the monster's rage, and the ship rolled unsteadily, driven on by the cord connecting spear to stem.

"We should pull back and cut the rope, my lord," said Olric, a grizzled carl, many years the king's retainer. He gripped the steering oar, arm trembling and straining with the pull. "A wounded beast's not to be trifled with. Like as not, the sea-witch'll pull us down to the wat'ry grave she's headed to."

Connal wiped the gathering water from his brows, blinked away the kelpie's tears. The cord was taut, a line connecting him to his prey. He saw her flailing, the blood leaking from the spear wound. He heard the thump of her tail on the ship's hull. A beast wounded. A beast at bay.

No, this was not the time for caution. He had spoken his boast in Craedon's hall, before the men and women of the Iron Rock. He had sworn by the name of God and the vengeful spirits also.

And Kierran too had sworn before the great assembly. Wolfsbane, men called him, a terror to Craedon's foes. He had proven himself years ago, in the haze of battle, where he'd earned a name by slaying Brecca's man-eater, the black wolf Duféel. Now his arms jangled with golden rings, signs of Craedon's favor. It was whispered that he would one day sit on the throne of Cregeirann. For blood alone was no assurance of rule.

No, he could not afford to hold back. Not while Kierran too roamed the seas, seeking for himself the kelpie's silver bridle, the token of victory. Not after Connal had given himself the name of Beastmaster. He would brave the thundering wrath of Gaillag herself to take that bridle. And pursue his quarry down to the gates of Lir.

"Keep her steady, Olric," he said. "Let no man lose stomach now. Put your backs in't lads!"

Olric nodded grimly and pointed them at the kelpie. Not a man grumbled as they fell to it, oars catching the water. The rope slackened as they drove on, and the ship rose and fell over the crashing waves.

Connal heard the kelpie's shriek, a rushing wind, stirring up the anger of the depths. Now was the time to press the advantage. He stalked to the front of the lurching ship and stooped to take up one of his warrior's spears. No rope secured it, no barbs protruded. Yet it was a good weapon all the same. He peered into the darkness and mouthed a prayer to Saint Urient, whose spear had taken the dragon Adrodeus. He cast his missile, watching it arc through the void, cursing as it fell useless among the waves.

"Bring me in closer!" he bellowed. His hands sought the woven cord, tugging it like a fisherman's line. He'd reeled in several feet of rope before he felt it tighten. Strength for strength, then. The hunter and the hunted.

"You weaken!" he taunted between gritted teeth, his sinews straining as he hauled in the monster. "You'll taste the bite of my dagger yet."

"Beastmaster," she said, her voice angrier and thinner than before. "The seas will smother you. And in Lir's sunken halls, I will devour your flesh."

And so saying, she rose from the water, arcing through the air like a hooked sea trout. Black mane fluttered in the wind, sinuous body hovering a moment over the water's surface. Then she plunged beneath the waves, and the waters whirled over the place where she dove. The rope flew through his hands, scraping and burning his skin, before wrenching free of his grasp altogether. The ship lurched forward, straining towards the whirling vortex. Cold, icy horror stabbed his heart.

"Back it down!" Connal said. "She's trying to drown us!"

Quick as an arrow's flight they responded, the warriors backwatering. Yet the ship did not reverse, though muscle strained and oar fell. They were drawn on by the kelpie's unrelenting pull, mere yards from the whirlpool. In a moment more, they would lie on the ocean's floor.

"My lord?" Olric cried above the chattering of starving sea-jaws. Water dripped from grizzled locks down a weathered face. His face was set and grim, yet Connal saw the glimmer of reproach in his eyes.

Drog take her. There was no time to cut the rope nor any hope of pulling against the inexorable current.

"Abandon ship!" he roared. As he mounted the strake and readied to plunge, he felt a twinge of guilt, having ignored Olric's wisdom. But there was no helping it now. It was done. He shrugged and dove head first from the ship.

 6

The water was cold. It punched him in the chest, squeezing the breath in his lungs. He fell an eternity in that watery abyss. In the darkness below the waves, blacker far than the night air, he knew terror at last. The chill hand of death round his throat.

He shook himself, clinging to life. His long arms cut through the water and his legs kicked gracefully. Swimming was as natural as breathing for this son of Cregeirann.

Connal's head crested above the sea, and he took in air in rasping gulps. He swam instinctively for the rocks he'd seen before by the thunderbolt's light. The waves and his strokes bore him quickly over the roiling sea, and soon his hands found rock: slippery, treacherous, but solid.

He mounted the shore and leaned back against the wet rock, panting with lungs afire. Quickly, he shed his wet clothes, sheltering them under the outcropping of rock. He hugged his knees to himself and shivered, the frigid air pricking his naked skin. Yet it was better this way. He'd known of men, hardened warriors, who'd escaped drowning in the angry sea only to fall ill and die on solid land, their sodden clothing an icy shroud.

So he sat and watched, shivering, waiting for the men of his crew. Yet no life stirred from the raging sea. No warriors rose from that watery tomb. He waited for God knew how long, and wept hot bitter tears. For his arrogance, good men had fallen, more flesh for the kelpie's feast. He had promised them glory and revenge, here in the icy sea, near the shores of the savage rock. Yet where was their glory now? And who would avenge their wasted deaths? He pulled up his knees and buried his head, weeping sorely.

Black night turned to gray dawn. The thunder quieted and the snow abated. The seas, murderous and angry, returned to their seething calm.

Connal heard the cry of the gulls, seabirds never far in triumph or in doom. He heard them and thought of home, of his father's thatched hall by the sea. Now, his mother would be awake, directing the servants, heating the stew-pots for the morning meal. He longed to be there among his kin, warmed by the hearth and tales of glory.

Unbidden, his father's wisdom sprang to mind. A man is known when life tosses him to his back, levels a spear at his throat. He is known when the Wyrd strikes him, weaving disaster into his life's thread. In the hall's warmth, he may boast, his cheeks hot with ale and mead, his heart full of men's approval. But when the drink has drained from his blood and the blade seeks his life, it is then that a man is proven.

Connal shook himself. Surely, he had drunk freely of the mead horn, had made more than his share of boasts. Under the haze of strong drink, he had fashioned himself hunter and beastmaster. Now without ship or crew, upon a strange land, he would prove himself, make good on those boasts.

The hunter picked himself up, dressing himself in tunic and trousers now mostly dry. He tightened his belt, fastening the seax there, and began his slow trudge up the stony beach, toward the sheer gray cliffs.

At the top of those heights, he saw at last the island's surprising breadth. Away for miles, the white fields rolled, reaching out to forests dark and dense, above which rose snow-capped peaks. And to the northeast, an astonishing sight: a tower rising from the earth, a mighty work of stone. His soul thrilled at this sight. There were people then, on this far-flung isle of the north, folk with craft enough to build the turret beyond. At once the crushing loneliness began to lift. Here was man where he'd thought only the kelpie reigned.

Connal sucked in a deep breath, shivered, and trudged on towards the tower, his gait quickening as his hope renewed. He walked for perhaps half an hour before a sound of a footfall spun his head round.

There, coming towards him, was a woman, dressed in a cloak of sable fur. She did not walk but glided, gracefully flitting over the clumpy, frozen heath. Her beauty dazzled him, long raven hair streaming in the wind, framing the lustrous white of her skin like the night sky, the moon. He stood speechless, feet rooted to the earth.

"Hello!" she called to him. Her voice, too, was beautiful, full of mirth and song. Her breath hung in the air before her, a delicate, fleeting mist.

"Hello," he said, raising an awkward hand. He'd not expected the island's inhabitants to be quite so alluring.

"What is your name, good sir? We don't often get visitors on this island." There was something familiar in the way she spoke. Something comforting.

"Connal," he said. "MacCraedon. From the Iron Rock."

"Connal." His flesh tingled to hear his name on her lips. She smiled, revealing a mouth of perfect, ivory teeth. "A pleasure." She slid gracefully toward him, and held out her hand. "I am Muireann, daughter of Eaghan, King of Brathadh."

He bowed and kissed her hand. "My lady." Her boldness struck him; no fear of the haggard stranger gripped her innocent green eyes. The folk of Brathadh must be strong, if even the maidens were this brave.

"So, Connal MacCraedon, what brings you to our island? And in such poor weather! Did you come alone?"

At her words, the sorrow welled within him again and he hung his head. "No, fair Muireann. I journeyed forth with a score of companions. Yet now they lie at the ocean's bottom, dragged to their deaths by my foolish pride and the kelpie's rage."

She laid a gentle hand on his shoulder. He raised his head, looking through blurry tears into her emerald eyes, brimming with pity. "The kelpie, you say?" her voice trembled. "That creature has plagued us year after year. My father has sworn vengeance, but still it defies him, preying upon the weak and the strong."

"I am grieved to hear it," Connal said. "I would gladly see your father, for I, too, have sworn to slay the beast."

She looked at him with eyes wide. "Oh, thank you, brave warrior! Long have we prayed to God and his saints for a deliverer. And at last he comes, washed on our shores an exile!"

His blood warmed at her words, his spirit soaring with pride.

Here now was the chance to redeem himself by saving this harried people. The shame of the retainers, the reproach of Olric would wash away in the kelpie's blood, in the adoration of King Eaghan and his beautiful daughter.

"Come, my lord," she said, dazing him with the flash of her black lashes. "I will take you to my father's hall."

On they walked, side by side across the heath. It was easy going here, the snow only ankle-deep. She told him of the kelpie's devastation: only recently it had attacked, hunting the men at their fishing, the women at their washing. There was no man or woman who knew not the loss of a loved one to that devil.

He nodded sadly at her tale. "It seems the monster has caused great suffering all across the West Sea. Even in my home."

He unburdened his heart to her, telling her of the kelpie's attack. The monster had come on the moonless night of Farrion's feast day, when all from carl to kern were packed into the benches, singing of ancient heroes and toasting the Worthy's name. The cup-maidens strode among them, giving drink to Craedon's warriors, reminding them of their duties, of the price to be paid for idle boasts.

And she, the sea-witch, lay in wait by Craedon's hall, disguised in the semblance of horse's flesh, one of several forms she was said to take. She caught the merry heroes as they wandered without the hall and dragged the staggering revellers down to the ocean depths. And when the horrid cry of one arrested them from their merrymaking, and they burst through the doors with swords and torches, there, by the fire's light they saw it, a mare no longer, but a monster, black as the night, a serpent with horse's head. They cast their spears at her and she fled, dipping beneath the waves. Many had wept then; his father had pulled his hair with grief, mourning the murder of his loyal soldiers.

"It was for this reason," Connal said, his voice nearly choking, "that I set sail in the deep of winter, with twenty of my father's best warriors. I swore by all the saints in heaven that I would destroy the beast and bring back her bridle as a prize."

10

She peered up at him, placing a hand on the curve of his bicep. "And so you will. I believe that you are a most powerful warrior." She gazed on before them in silence. Then she turned to him once more. "Can I confide something in you, my lord? Only, you mustn't think ill of me. Or my father."

"Never, my lady. You can tell me anything."

"The kelpie. I know what cave it haunts, here on this island. Some hunters from our village stumbled upon it months ago."

"Stumbled upon it? And they did nothing? What about Eaghan's warriors?"

She hung her head, the raven locks cascading over her face. "Alas. They were all afraid to face it."

Afraid? Anger boiled within him. What manner of men were these, their bones turned to water at the fear of a mere beast? Men robbed of loved ones, allowing their wives and children to sit beneath the shadow of monstrous death. To sit and enjoy their lord's favor, only to do nothing when the opportunity to serve arises. Truly, they were unworthy of this beautiful queen, this maiden with a warrior's spirit.

He turned to her again and saw her gazing upward, tears springing to her eyes. "Is something wrong, my lord? Please, don't look like that. I'm afraid you despise me now."

"Believe me, fair Muireann," he said, pressing her hand in his. "I could not despise you even to save my own life. Yet the warriors who have shrunk from their duty, leaving this monster to ravage the isles: them I despise."

She nodded gently. "Not every man can be strong," she said. "Not all are heroes like you, Connal Beastmaster."

He stopped and looked into her comely face, holding her hand still. A beastmaster: yes, that is what he had called himself, what he had shouted in his father's hall and into the wind of the storm. It was foolishness, a title self-given and unearned. He searched her glistening eyes, yet saw no trace of mockery in them. What was it then that galled him? He should be flattered by her attention. He *was* flattered.

"No, madam. They are not." And perhaps he should not fault them for it, not when his own quest had fared so poorly. Not while the title of Beastmaster was as yet a child's boast. "But I cannot count myself a great hunter until I have seen this through."

"You will," she said, her voice so warm and earnest that his self-pity faded. "I have faith in you, brave warrior."

"Muireann," he said, gently squeezing her hand. "Don't take me to your father. Not yet."

She looked at him quizzically.

"This cave you spoke of; you know the way?"

She nodded, her eyes widening.

"And will you take me there?"

"Yes, my lord," she said. "I will take you. Would you slay the beast?"

He looked at her long and hard, weighing his words. This was no time for bloated tales or exaggerated boasts. "I shall try, my lady. With all the strength that lies within me. Or die in the attempt."

She squeezed his hand in return and smiled up at him. "I am confident that before night falls, you will see a great terror overthrown."

Over the next half-hour they crossed the heather, pausing under the looming shadow at the dark wood's mouth. The trees stood in white and ancient glory, trunks no axe had touched, snow-laden branches wild and unchecked, gnarled oaks and proud elms, and aged willows creaking under the burden of time. The wind moved through the trees, whispering in heathen tongues, renewing a conversation millennia old. Connal halted a moment at the forest threshold, stunned by the forest's power.

"Do not worry, brave hunter," said Muireann, smiling her lovely smile. "There is nothing here to harm you. Just birds and squirrels." She took a step forward and he followed, unwilling to appear weak before her.

Darkness enveloped him. The air was heady with the scent of

12

moss and needle, bathed in the freshness of snow. Hidden birds sang out to one another, and the faint creaking of wind-rocked branches surrounded him. He felt his shoulders loosen and his pulse slow, as he took in deep lungfuls of pristine air.

They walked together in silence a while. Connal's eyes adjusted to the shade and he watched her, his heart thrilling at her every movement. He thought back to ballads sung by the winter's hearth. How the proud Lord Dernan cast eyes on fair Briana, sparking in a single moment the eternal fire of his love.

"Tell me, my lady," he said. "Are you... are you attached to any young man of these parts?"

"Why no, my lord," she said. Even in the darkness he could see her face redden.

That was good, he thought. Though how a lady as fair as she could have no lover was a mystery to him.

"And you, my lord? Are you unwed?"

"Yes," he said. Of course, there had been girls, noble and even common, who had caught his eye. Yet he had not considered marriage, had thought himself too young and free to fetter himself so. But it did not seem so unappealing now.

She smiled at him and he smiled too, feeling calm, quiet satisfaction.

Soon they plunged beyond the tree line, and Connal blinked in the sudden return of light. There stretched before him a long gray beach, comprised as much of gravel as of sand. And there, a squat gray rock, rough and unassuming, in which a small crevice opened to the dark within.

The kelpie's cave.

Muireann pointed a slender white finger towards the rock. "There it lies, my lord."

Connal paused, his feet rooted in the craggy sand. He listened to the tide's dirge, the waves slapping against the great rock, and smelled the sharp tang of the ocean's brine.

"You needn't confront it now, my lord. We could go on to the village. My people would love to meet the great hunter of Iron Rock."

"No!" he said too strongly. It was courage he needed now.

He took a step forward, mind reeling. Again, he felt himself galled. He had not earned her praise nor her respect. Did she know the outlandish boasts he had made to slay the kelpie, driven by envy of the Wolfsbane as much as by his father's honor? That brave men had followed him gladly on his quest, and drowned for his pride and envy? Would she look at him still with admiration and love if she knew the truth?

But the truth wouldn't matter, he told himself. Not if he made atonement now. He would descend into the darkness, to the kelpie's own lair, and in the bowels of the earth he would strike her.

Then he would show himself before King Eaghan, revealing the silver bridle that would hang in Craedon's hall. And in return for that favor, he would ask for Muireann's hand. She was a worthy damsel and would make a fine queen when Connal ascended to the throne.

He walked on before her, his gait quickening. They were at the mouth of the cave now. He put out his hand to grip the rocky ledge and pulled himself up. Something gave him pause. He looked back, and Muireann smiled at him with eager eyes. He waved to her and turned to his task. What lay beyond the threshold of darkness he feared to know. Yet her faith in him was heartening.

Connal crouched and stepped into the cave. It was dark within and nauseating. He sniffed the damp air, his nostrils filling with the reek of death. A heaving sickness rose within him, threatening to pour out of his mouth. He fumbled within the darkness, his hands scraping along rock wall. Down and down he went, feeling his way like the blind.

He heard a crunching sound beneath his boot, as of a twig snapping. He gave a kick and the object skidded along the rock, landing in the darkness beyond with a splash. There was water here at the bottom of the cave. And where there was water, the kelpie would be.

Connal cursed in Urient's name. If only he had brought a light. Why hadn't he thought of it before he subjected himself to the blindness of the cave, where even the hand before his face was hidden? He felt vulnerable here, a fish caught in the net. A chorus of echoes surrounded him, like the fearful whispering of the damned. He slid the seax from his belt and stood there, holding his breath, straining to hear over the thundering of his heartbeat.

Then a pale green light washed over him, eerie and accursed, as if cast by a spectre's hearth. He saw now the dome of the cave above him, high arched like a chapel. He saw the cavernous pool before him, deathly still. And there, to his horror, he saw the bones of many, white and gleaming, sucked dry of flesh, gnawed by equine jaws. A few sat in poses of mock-revelry, lounged about a slab of rock, their empty skulls grinning as if engaged in merry jest. And about them: the remains of countless victims, a garden of empty ribcages and chewed thighbones, skulls tossed carelessly in heaps, jawbones hanging precariously.

And there he saw the bodies of the freshly slain. Some lay half-eaten, limbs torn from soggy trunks. And there was one, with grizzled hair, his brow marked by an ancient scar. It was Olric, drowned under the waters of the Iarlir, his flesh uneaten. His wide, open eyes stared out at Connal, catching the light's green gleam. There was reproach in his dead-man's stare, a rebuke of pride and envy.

Connal gazed on this morbid scene with horror, a hand clamped over his mouth, stifling a gag. He heard a rustling sound and he turned to see Muireann there. No disgust wrinkled her brow. Still she smiled, the green eyes gleaming softly in the pale light's glow.

"Muireann?" he whispered. Chills ran up and down his spine.

Still she said nothing. Her green eyes locked on his, and her teeth were bared.

"You are not Muireann," he said, a statement more than a question.

"What do you mean, my lord?" Her voice was sickly sweet.

He swallowed. "These, these people. They're dead."

"Aye," she said, her voice hardening. She held his gaze, unflinching.

"Why?"

"Brathadh is no place for man," she said in a cold, distant voice that chilled his blood. "Yet man's avarice is so great, no land can satisfy him. And so, on and on he roams, scourging the earth with his cities, profaning the sacred groves and mountains of the Old Ones. And when we rise to fight you, you weep and pity yourselves. Tell me, 'Beastmaster,' would you kill to defend your home? Is that not what you've come for now?"

She stalked towards him and flashed the smile he no longer found lovely. "Well do it now, son of kings! My time on this earth is numbered. Hell's gates open wide to devour me. Finish the work your spear began." She held out her arms and tossed back her head, baring her white throat. The silver necklace glinted in the green light. "And take your prize."

Connal stood watching her, transfixed with horror. His veins filled with ice, his legs weakened as if beaten with staves.

"Do it, Beastmaster! Fulfill your boast!" She raised her head again and scoffed. "Or do you lack the courage to strike me thus?"

She writhed and wriggled then, transforming before him. A flash of green light blinded him, and he shielded his eyes. When he lowered his hand, she coiled before him as she had on the sea. A hideous creature, coated from neck to tail in black scales, the unnatural union of horse and serpent. Steam rushed from her nostrils, and the gaze of her green eyes weighed heavily upon him.

"Do you find it easier now, great hunter? Am I monster enough?"

Still he stood and stared, mouth agape, bereft of certainty.

She lurched forward, her tail catching and coiling round his right leg. She pulled him to her, kicking wildly at his head. He came to at last, the survival instinct aiding him, and he dodged the battering of her hooves. He felt a searing pain in his leg, as the serpent's tail clamped tight like a surgeon's tourniquet.

 16

Then he remembered the weapon in his hand, and he stabbed it against her scaly hide. Her skin was tough, yet the blade was sharp and plunged deep into her flesh. She squealed in a voice like Muireann's and he paused. Then he felt the force of a flailing hoof, grazing the side of his head, drawing his blood. He hardened himself then, plunging the weapon into her body. In and out the dagger slid, till at last her life came sighing forth, leaking from her wounds like a punctured wineskin.

The pressure on his leg subsided, and he felt her slip through his hands onto the ground beneath him. She was dead, the monster he'd hated and the woman he'd loved. And with her, the pale green light began to fade. In a few moments, darkness would descend. He reached down and ripped the bridle from her, and began his swift ascent. It was black again as he clambered up, but soon he saw the light of day once more. He moved more carelessly than before, catching and tearing his clothing on the cave's jagged walls, bruising and scraping his skin.

He stumbled onto the pebbled beach, falling to his hands and knees, still clutching Muireann's necklace. His heart beat wildly as he took in the sea air with violent tearing breaths. A feeling of doom flattened his spirit. He felt neither triumph nor exhilaration, nothing but the weight of guilt and death.

"Herriah's bones," a man said. "If it isn't Connal MacCraedon!"

He raised his head and saw that it was Kierran, standing tall and proud, hands on his hips, round shield on his back, the long wolf's fang hanging from his neck. About him ranged a band of grim and grizzled warriors.

"I thought you'd be feeding the fish right about now, Beastmaster," Kierran said. "We saw the wreckage of your ship coming in."

Connal said nothing, merely shook his head.

"So you braved the sea-storm, eh? Any of the crew survive?"

He shook his head again.

Kierran cursed quietly. "A shame," he said. "They were good

men. Ringbearers many of them."

"Aye," Connal said at last, his voice hoarse and raw. The image of Olric's vacant eyes rose before him.

"And the sea-witch? She escaped, I suppose?"

"No," Connal said. "I slew her. In the cave." He raised his hand slowly, revealing the glinting silver bridle.

"Gaillag strike me," the proud warrior said. "Is this a jest?" He motioned with his hand, and two of the warriors stalked forward, lighting torches as they entered the cave.

They remained in silence for some moments, Kierran standing, Connal still on his knees. The cry of gulls carried over the sea to him.

"How did you manage it?" Kierran whispered, scorn giving way to grudging respect.

"I wounded her in the storm. Then she came to me in a woman's form."

"Huh," the ringed warrior grunted. "That's some trick." The sea breeze blew over them, playing softly with Connal's hair. The warriors returned, their faces pale and sickly. Kierran looked to them and they shared a nod.

"Well I'll be damned," the hunter said, gazing incredulously at him. "I underestimated you, Lord Connal. Beastmaster." He held out his hand and Connal took it, rising stiffly from his knees. As if from a distance he heard Kierran's words, joylessly noted the awe in his voice. A fruitless triumph.

"There's a village nearby," Connal said. "King Eaghan's." And the real Muireann would be there too. "We should go to them and tell them they have no need to worry anymore."

"A village?" Kierran's brows arched. "We covered the whole perimeter of the island, lord. There is nothing here save for some ancient ruins, a tower crumbling into dust, crusted in ice."

Connal bowed his head, let the words wash over him. So that too was a lie. If there had ever been an Eaghan, ever a Muireann, they were surely dead, their bones adorning the kelpie's lair.

They stood for some time, silent and grim, both men watching

18

the open sea.

"I suppose you'll be wanting to go then," Kierran said. His voice held a coarse edge. "Your father'll throw you a mighty feast, I'd wager. What with the silver bridle and all."

Connal nodded and his gaze fell again to that trophy, still gripped tightly in his bloodied fist. Muireann's jewel. He loosened his weary hand, let it slip through his gory fingers to where it clattered against the pebbles. Then he walked on, past Kierran's astonishment, past the loose ranks of silent warriors, past the hooting of the gulls, on to the ship that would take him home.

#  Ashen Queen
by E. Seneca

BRIGID AWOKE WITH A JOLT, her hand flying away from the dried blood at her throat. It coated her entire arm, crusted and flaking, and her breath clouded the air before her as her thoughts swam, disjointed and broken. Why were her limbs so stiff and aching; why did a dull pain emanate from her very bones? It seemed as though she had been seated on her throne for a long, long time, but her memory did not cooperate, supplying her with only visions of darkness studded with slowly moving stars.

Shivering, she reached for her throat again, tracing the wide, jagged scab there and feeling flakes cracking along her scalp. Something thumped softly on the floor beside her, and in the dim silvery glow, she saw it was a frayed and moth-eaten rope, a pale mark left behind on her wrist.

A cloud of dust billowed slowly into the air, and as each tiny mote drifted, glimmering, into the light, images spattered across her consciousness like rain: the inexorable march of the troupe; the doors wrenching open; the shattering of glass; the tumbling of bodies upon the floor; the rough hands lashing her to the throne and the diamond-bright flash of the knife rising before it tore across her neck and there was only blackness.

Ah. So, she had outlasted them, just as she had hoped she would.

A smile split her cracked lips, painful as it was, and her bones creaked along with the chair as she levered herself to her feet. A wave of pinkish ash rose from her movements, slowly spreading through the room and bringing with it a modicum of warmth as it settled. Her knees trembled, weak after so long, but she stood under her own strength. Her eyes, dry from disuse, had adjusted to the meager illumination, and she saw that piled atop each other all around her were the featureless bodies of her soldiers, limbs twisted like broken dolls. Their glassy, staring gazes were all fixed upon the throne to witness the final terrible crime against her, and sorrow twisted her heart at their wretched expressions, at once desperation and agony, unable to fulfill their very purpose.

She had not the power to restore them just yet, but soon, as soon as she found some source of fuel. Gingerly she picked her way over to the window and brushed the curtain aside, blinking in the light from a waning half-moon reflecting off the fresh snowfall below the castle. No doubt beneath its pristine blanket lay ruined fields and razed buildings and butchered citizens, for all was perfectly, frightfully still, down to the laden branches of the thick fir trees lining the steps. Here and there, skeletons of the invaders and their horses decorated the drive, bones covered in snow. Years, she must have sat, awaiting the inevitable awakening, and she exhaled, watching her breath fade away, reveling in the sensation of merely being alive.

Perhaps they had taken her kingdom, but as long as she could yet open her eyes, she could rebuild it. And rebuild it she would, and make them pay.

Ice frosted his very eyelashes as Hans gazed up at the castle, gilding the tips of his fur collar with white. Dark, laden clouds hung over the hipped spires, the crimson tiles stark amid the pure landscape, the aged stone and glazed mullioned windows. Snow lay piled thick upon the sills and the parapets, edged with heavy icicles.

For all intents and purposes, the place appeared abandoned but for the whirl of pink circling the tallest tower. Such a hue ought to remind him of roses, of the most delicate blushes, of the gentle touch of a spreading dawn, but instead reminded him of blood in water, slowly diluting as it unfurled. He had no doubts that in some sense, it was sentient, and it was aware of his arrival.

As he approached the gates, loud snaps and crunches sounded from beneath his boots, too sharp to be the snowdrifts, and a glance downward showed him the shattered frames of broken bones, scattered among fragments of rusted armor. Hans paused, bending to knock some of the ice off to examine the emblem on the cracked helm, but it was not the one he sought: too recent. He replaced the skull with a small sting of regret that he could do nothing more for these abandoned remains, but their souls were long since gone and hopefully in a place of eternal rest.

The iron gates loomed overhead, and somewhere in the back of his head, a tiny voice quivering with apprehension whispered its doubts that he would succeed where the others had failed, but he had not come this far to turn back, not braved the annual blizzard only for his nerve to fail him at the moment of arrival. Bracing himself for the blow of the cold, he planted his hands and shoulder against the gate, and heaved.

The metal groaned in protest, creaking as it resisted, but he refused to be deterred, increasing the force until his muscles ached and his breath began to come short—then a salvo of cracks broke the silence as the ice coating the joints and holding the bottom to the ground shattered, and slowly it began to swing inward. He rocked back on his heels as soon as he opened a gap wide enough to pass through, then sidled inside.

Immediately, the back of his neck prickled, a wave of goosebumps sweeping over his skin through his numerous layers, and his eyes snapped up immediately towards the pinkish cloud. It had ceased its movements, now hanging suspended as it regarded him, no doubt as the intruder that he was. Hans stared back at it, the pit of his stomach twisting. He couldn't refrain from imagining it flensing his flesh from his bones in the blink of an eye, ripping all the warm tissues of his body before he could so much as draw his sword—but what good would it do against a swarm of ash so fine?

The ash shifted, condensing, and he tensed, hand moving to rest automatically upon the familiar hilt on his hip. Then, to his surprise, the ash appeared to relax, loosening once more into a swirling cloud orbiting the tower. Through the windows he could now see a single orange firelight, his gaze drawn instinctively towards it after such a long, frigid journey.

He exhaled a slow, staggered breath. So, she did not wish to destroy him just yet. Perhaps some greater, more amusing torture awaited him first. So be it; he was bound to see this through to the end.

Mustering up his courage again, Hans crossed what would have been the green, the only sound the crunching of his steps through the abundant snow banks and the wind whistling between the bars of the gate and the frozen trees. Perhaps at some point, statues and columns had adorned the grounds, but now they were but lumpy shapes, worn away by the bitter wind and coated in frost. They cast long, eerie shadows over the white ground in the mid-morning sun, misshapen and lumpen, and the light granted him little warmth as he slogged doggedly onward. Perhaps once, years and years ago, it had been verdant, but rumors said that even in summer, this place remained perpetually frozen.

It was difficult not to imagine the beauty that must have suffused the landscape before it was despoiled by ruin, and a touch of something akin to guilt brushed against his heart, though he had neither fault nor hand in this tragedy. A sense of desecration hung in the air despite the purity of the untouched snow, and he knew with a dreadful certainty that his presence was a trespass. No one had dared to disturb this place for so long, for more than frivolous reasons—and was his own reason, too, not frivolous in some way? Coming all this way, braving the long and arduous journey—but no, it was more than that, however much they had tried to convince him otherwise. Even now, he still believed it was worthwhile.

He tugged his scarf a little higher over his nose, for it seemed that with each step, the chill only grew stronger. The source of it, after all, was growing nearer, but as he passed certain lumps in the snow, it briefly intensified. He did not dare pause again to examine what lay beneath the uneven blanket, but he suspected that he was currently traversing an enormous grave.

Shuddering, he turned away, focusing on the steps rising up out of the snow before him, leading towards the enormous double doors emblazoned with the heraldry of the kingdom, veiled with ice. These, too, were shut, and the stoop was caked in snow that reached up to his knees. The body of the castle provided some meager shelter from the wind, and Hans reached for one of the massive handles, seeing no reason to knock when its master was already aware of his presence.

The metal bit at his fingers through his gloves, and he suspected he would need to break the frost sealing it shut before he could open it. He searched for a weak point, hands probing along the edges and the hairline gap between the doors. Reaching for the pick on the side of his pack with one hand, his fingertips skidded along the glassy ice with the other. There, a little above his head, the ice was thinnest, where the sunlight touched the longest. A few careful strikes, and it cracked and fell in tinkling shards, exposing the true color of the door for perhaps the first time in years, a faded and neglected red. He took hold of the handle again, and it rumbled and scraped as it slowly swung outward.

He nipped inside while he still could, pressing his back flat to the other door as he waited for his vision to adjust to the twilight of the interior. Being out of the wind was a relief, though the temperature within was not much different from the exterior, a deep chill saturating what he could see of the great flagstones and the thick walls. Out of the shadows above hung immense chandeliers besieged by cobwebs, their candles half-melted, and as he dared to pull his scarf down to his chin, the powerful smell of must assaulted him, nearly choking in its intensity. No doubt it came from the disintegrating rugs, the draperies, the tapestries with their heavy crumbling tassels. With no one to care for them, they were gray with dust, and through that same lack of care, it seemed there was no one to so much as watch the door, either.

As his eyes traveled downward, however, the reason for this was obvious: a sea of bodies covered the floor. Twisted and tangled in conflict, their limbs splayed out where they lay, fixed eyes staring blankly ahead. A frisson of horror passed through him as his gaze swept from one side of the hall to the other, taking in the carnage. It was only the lack of blood which kept the scene from being utterly unbearable, for although skeletons still clad in armor lay scattered, they were surrounded by deep, dark stains, their warm organs long since gone with only the scent of dust and decay to fill the air instead of rot.

But looking closer, Hans realized the skeletons and their armor had to be the remains of the human warriors, for those who still retained their skin and faces could not be anything of the sort, when they were so perfectly preserved in the stillness of the air but for a certain waxy sheen to their skin—presuming such a sheen was not in truth natural for their species.

In a way, those doll-like bodies were more unsettling than the remains of the corpses. Their limbs were so smooth and polished despite the enormous chunks which had been hacked out of them, and in those triangular gaps, nothing resembled flesh: only a gaping hole and horrid smoothness, like a lump of butter that had been cut

25

into. They did not appear to have muscles, or veins, or even blood, just that horrible pale flesh like porcelain and those glassy eyes. The thought crossed his mind that they were, in fact, nothing more than mannequins, elaborately and finely made puppets, but they bore no hint of wood grain beneath their tattered garb, and they were far, far too life-like to be artificial... surely? Tentatively, Hans lowered the pick in his hand, loosening his unconsciously tightened grip, and exchanged it for the familiar leather-wrapped hilt of the blade at his side. He would rather trek through another mile of waist-high snow than take another step forward, but he had little choice in the matter. If he wanted to obtain what he'd come here for, then he had to go forward.

But it was a matter of more than merely progressing. He had to search. Somewhere amid this sea of bodies lay his kin.

He swallowed, scanning the floor beside the walls for perhaps a candle or a lamp to grant him a little more light. As he picked up a cracked lantern from the debris and checked it for oil, an old and familiar guilt swelled inside him, one so clammy and icy that not even the tiny match flame dancing at his fingertips, bright and hot, could lessen. The thought of one of his own, however long ago, participating in this senseless, pointless slaughter was sickening, though he himself had nothing whatsoever to do with it. As the light bloomed around him, nothing but a meager circle of illumination that glistened off those hideous gaps in the fallen soldiers' porcelain flesh and threw sinister shadows into the empty sockets of the skulls, the feeling only grew.

There was nothing he could do to change what had happened, and these sins had not been committed by him, but they had likely been done for his sake, regardless of his not existing at the time. For the sake of hearth and home and all they held dear, the soldiers of the past had given their lives to protect the future generations from harm. Although then again, perhaps they had not done it for his sake at all, only their own satisfaction; any justification could be given to fulfill a raging bloodlust and a hatred unchained and irrepressible. And just as irrationally, he felt vaguely responsible, if only by association. But what powers did he have to make amends? This was a fool's errand, to be sure, and surely the only reason nothing ill had befallen him thus far was because his presence was amusing rather than offensive.

A soft hiss passed through the castle walls, and he froze, expecting the sentient ash to sweep down the curving stairs he could now make out at the far end, but it was only the wind, moaning softly as it blew through the open door. Hans shook himself, but the fear remained, heavy and thick and pulsing in his chest, as he approached the nearest skeleton. From beneath the fur around his neck, he carefully withdrew a half-moon pendant inlaid with glimmering stone, spider-webbed with a network of cracks. The faintest white glow emanated from its surface, and he observed it out of the tail of his eye as he gingerly nudged the pile of bones over with the point of his blade.

They broke apart in a cloud of dust, and beneath the rags was nothing but bits of metal, the remnants of armor and weapons. On to the next, then.

To disturb them thus was another thing that intensified the guilt, but there was no other way, and even if he wanted to bury them, the ground outside was too frozen, and it would only be a different form of disturbance altogether, and one that would draw ire. No, he simply had to continue, and leave this place with minimal traces.

Patiently, willing himself to ignore the fear, he moved from body to body, studiously refusing to meet the blank, staring eyes of the enemy soldiers, and trying not to think about the possibility of them springing up at any moment and overwhelming him. There had to be dozens upon dozens of them, a veritable army laying abandoned. But the further he went, leaving—despite his best efforts—a trail of further destruction in his wake, the more aware he became of a new feeling encroaching upon his guilt: the edge of sorrow.

An aura of wistful sadness hung over the hall, both in the pitiful bones that crumbled at the slightest touch, and the desperation in the bloodless, frightful faces of the puppets. There was no pain writ there, only the bitterness of failure. The old whispers of the soldiers who feared not death nor flinched at any blow passed through his mind, but he had never imagined they would look both so unsettling and so pitiable. He had imagined beings more immense, or a horde of berserkers—not these strangely human-like imitations, at once as mournful as they were eerie. They, too, deserved a respectful burial, yet he could not give them that either, only avoid touching them wherever he could, lest he somehow awaken them. If he was very fortunate, then he would find what he sought here among the wreckage, and then he could depart as he came and hurry on home before nightfall.

As he neared the stairs, however, his pendant gave a bright flare, and a distinct feeling of dread pooled in his gut. Hopeful, he stepped away, and to his disappointment, the light immediately dimmed. How foolish it had been to hope that this would end so easily—of course the man to whom the other half had belonged would not have been content to perish at the mere entranceway, just as the handful of survivors had recounted.

Hans steeled himself and mounted the stairs, holding the lantern high. Dust billowed into the air with his every step to the crunch of bones and the clack of metal, making him shudder. His grip on the sword tightened as his impulse to flee warred with the desire to press on, the paltry rays of slanting sunlight scarcely offering any comfort when they only showed him more destruction the higher he went. Every which way lay more puppets, and though he told himself firmly they were not alive, their eyes seemed to follow him, glaring at him accusingly.

He turned at a prickle on the nape of his neck, but they had not moved—or had they?

The further he went from the doors, the slimmer his chances of survival became. If they suddenly all rose just as he so feared—no, no. He couldn't think about it. If he did, then he wouldn't be able to continue.

The staircase forked into two more, and following the intermittent guidance of the pendant, he took the right-hand side, hoping against hope that each step would be the final one. The wind whistled through a few gaps in the walls, and faintly, he could make out a soft shifting and rustling, like that of sand. Did the ash care for trinkets, for things that were purely sentimental? As best as he could tell, the corpses had not been looted for their few bits of jewelry, but maybe the glow of the other pendant half would have caught its attention, though for what, he couldn't imagine.

He followed the glow higher and higher, into the deeper chill of the shadows and over more bodies; past the long cracks running down the walls and over broken glass and porcelain; around a bend and into a spiraling passageway whose intense cold rivaled that of the outdoors. A sigh whispered down towards him, setting his every nerve alight, and a few pinkish grains rolled from one roughly-hewn step to the next, skittering around his boots. He flinched away from it on instinct, but it merely rolled against the wall. There was no doubt about it anymore, this way led up to the spire he'd seen from the ground, and exactly where he wanted to go the least. But the pendant gave another pulse against his collar, so all he could do was steel himself and climb.

With each step, he shivered, and the tiny flame in his hands guttered as the wind rose in a moan from the depths, its tiny globe of light scarcely able to penetrate the thickness of the darkness dripping down from the tower walls, a physical force all its own pressing down on his shoulders. He felt as small as the flame, suffused by the gloom and surrounded by an immense, alien presence, dwarfing him with its power. He was nothing but a puny human, whose meager efforts could achieve nothing, whose bones would be dust just like all those who had come before him. He clutched the rusted handle of the lantern tighter, resisting the impulse to huddle against the curve of the wall. He had to keep going; the only way out was through.

The stairs seemed to stretch onward to infinity, a tiny window high above being the only sign of daylight. His breath grew short from the steepness of the steps, but he didn't dare slow down. He couldn't pause, lest he lose his nerve altogether. Even the glow of the pendant was a feeble thing, unable to provide more than the merest solace.

But eventually, he reached the peak. There he had to pause, doubling over to pant, lungs chilled by the temperature of the air. A small wooden door guarded the landing, its paint peeling off in long curls and hanging loosely on one hinge. The stone was stained with old blood, handprints layering the door frame. Hans reached out and held his hand over one such print, observing how it was the size of his own, then jolted back as he realized what he was doing. Foolishness.

He grasped the iron handle, and pushed the door inward.

Immediately, the smell of dust wafted out against his face, followed by the musty scent of dried flowers and clean, cold air. It was the taste of winter, crisp and biting, the temperature starkly different from the tower as bright, unimpeded sunlight smarted his eyes. It was as if he were outside, but in the sigh of the wind, all he could hear was the sinister rustling of ash, a sound that only filled him with dread, keeping him on the threshold. Then the dark spots dancing before his vision cleared, only for his breath to catch anew.

The circular room was a ruin, littered with skeletons and bodies much like the hall, with tables and chairs and fineries upended and smashed over the blood-stained floor. But nowhere was there more blood than upon the throne at the far end, where a deathly pale woman sat, her head bowed and the front of her dress soaked through with brown. It surrounded her in a wide pool, spattered over her arms and bony fingers where they rested, smeared through her flaxen hair and daubed over her dented crown. She did not stir from her position, but Hans stared hard at the thin skin of her neck, trying to discern a pulse, for, unmoving as she was, he had the distinct feeling that he was not alone. After all, if she was dead, then how would the castle and the surrounding land be buried in snow?

As if sensing this thought, one of her hands twitched, and a faint crackle from behind sent him ducking instinctively, an icicle whizzing past his head to shatter on the stone. Heart thudding in his ears, he glanced up at the woman, who slowly lifted her chin, opening a pair of frosty crimson eyes and revealing the crusted remains of an ugly gash across her throat that made the guilt swell up again, thick and choking, in his chest.

"Impressive," she murmured, "that you've come this far. But like the others, here you must perish."

The pink ash swooped inside through the open window, and another icicle formed over her hand, glittering with a reddish tinge.

"Wait!" he blurted. "Please, I didn't come here to fight you!"

She cut her gaze to his right side. "The sword in your hand says otherwise."

This was true, he had to admit. Reluctantly, Hans slid it back into the scabbard, conceding that it would be of little use regardless. He set down the now-unneeded lantern and held out his empty hands in a gesture of surrender.

With the same slow reluctance, the icicle disintegrated, though the suspicion—no, hatred—in her gaze remained. "I see. You are from the town, are you not? Your clothing looks familiar. Have you come, then, to parlay? To request that I not send the sweeping blizzard each year? That is what the other fools down at the gate came to do; at least, those who did not intend to ransack the remains of my castle—though the treasures that lay forgotten here, other than myself, are few. What? You shake your head? Then what could you possibly want? And why," her voice hardened, "should I listen?"

"I have not come here for the sake of violence," Hans said, and hesitated to speak the next words. "Although I know in your eyes I am as guilty as the rest, for the crimes committed against you are grave indeed."

The queen's eyes only narrowed. "Is that all you have to say? Crimes? What has been done here in my domain is nothing short of a travesty. You speak so lightly, so diplomatically of what was a baseless slaughter. Do not dare suggest otherwise—I witnessed it with my own eyes!"

A crackling halo of snowflakes coalesced around her head in her rage, several strands of her hair standing on end as she swayed to her feet. Hans retreated, and his back struck the wood of the door, solid and immobile. He wanted to grope for the handle, but with the temperature in the room rapidly dipping, his shoulder refused to move, and out of his periphery, a thin layer of ice snaked up his arm, slithering around his elbow and hardening with frightening speed.

"*Your* people came here," she snarled, advancing a step, ice blooming beneath her bare blue toes, "and *your* people *pillaged* and *ravaged* my country—for the mere sin of my existence; and you have the audacity to speak of it with such careless offhandedness." Another step, and another layer of red frost bled out. "As if you yourself have not trampled over this sacred land for your own selfish desires!"

Fear beating a staccato rhythm in his chest, he frantically shook his head. She stood so near now he could feel her breath tickling his face from above, lukewarm and coppery. Horrid visions of his blood being siphoned out danced in his head as the chill from his arm reached his shoulder, crawling towards his neck, and he knew that it would take only a sliver of exposed skin: a single wound, and the queen's powers would be able to draw out his vitality for herself, the very reason why they had attempted to destroy her in the first place.

"No?" she whispered. The snowflakes around her began to whirl as she raised a hand, covered in pockmarks like a moth-eaten curtain. Through the open window of the room, the cloud of pink ash swept inside, pouring into the dozens of cavities dotting her skin, filling up the flesh and returning home. Some of it drifted to the fallen soldiers, worming its way into their gaps. "What reason would anyone have to come here other than selfish ones?" She reached for his collar, and he shrank back, but there was no space left to even cower as the ice swarmed across his chest and down his other arm, sinking its invisible teeth into his veins. Although his heart thudded faster than ever, it felt as though his blood was slowing in his arteries, as if every droplet was congealing before it had even been spilled. He tried to move, but his unfeeling limbs did not obey, encased in a thick layer of white. The edges of his vision grew foggy as the clattering of the puppets filled the air, just visible beyond the queen's undulating hair as she loomed over him, crimson eyes blazing. But was it rage, or was it hunger?

He didn't know, and he couldn't tell. It was so hard to breathe, the air agonizingly frigid. His lungs prickled, as if crystals were forming inside them, and his breath itself felt cold against his face as he stared up at her, unable to look away, at once pleading and apologizing, for how was she wrong? She had done nothing except be undying, and for that, she had been judged unworthy of life and the prosperity she had worked to maintain. Who would not bear a grudge lasting as long as that endless lifespan? Who would not lash out with a deep and abiding pain at all of that accursed breed who dared to come near? Beyond the anger at the bottom of that red well was nothing but sorrow, the same sorrow steeping the entire castle, a sorrow that could not be soothed by words alone. The weight of it forced his eyelids shut, and upon their thin skin, he could feel swirls of ice forming, clumping his eyelashes together.

He had to explain, to tell her that he wished her no further harm, but he couldn't find the breath, couldn't find his voice, his thoughts growing sluggish and faint and buckling under the chill. *Cold,* they whispered, *so very, very cold;* too cold to breathe, too cold to live, too cold to exist much longer.

The slightest, smallest tinkle of metal, audible only for its proximity, reached his ears, and the tightness of the collar around his neck slackened noticeably; the freezing blow he had braced for never came. Tentatively, Hans cracked his eyes open, bits of frost breaking away. The queen still stood before him, but in one hand, she held the pendant, its gold stark against her papery fingers, its glow making her own paleness stronger.

"What is this?" she muttered. "Where have I seen this before?"

Seizing the opportunity, Hans jerked to the side with a salvo of cracking ice, and as he did, to his horror, the delicate chain snapped, leaving the pendant in the queen's grasp as he sprawled ungainly over the floor, nerves too numb to properly respond. "W-wait," he tried

33

to say, coughing through an aching throat. "Please—anything but that, don't take that." He reached for it, but the newly animated puppet soldiers started forth, brandishing their weapons, menace gleaming in their horrible unblinking eyes.

"I *have* seen this before." She moved it to the light, watching how it played over the stone and the opalescent reflections. "I am certain of it..."

Hope fluttered in his breast. Perhaps his death was inevitable, but at least he would have obtained what he came for. "Where? Here?"

"Be silent; my memory is long, and takes time." But no sooner had she spoken than did recognition come into her eyes. She turned, and from one of the puppets, took something from its hand, something that gleamed and glimmered and made his heart lurch in his chest, for side by side, it formed a perfect match with the one about his neck moments before. He struggled to his feet on aching knees, gaze riveted on the twin pendants in her hands. "Please— that's all I want; all I came here for!"

The queen did not move, continuing to observe the twin pendants beneath the light. Slowly, her red eye glanced back at him. "This?" she said. "You cannot possibly expect me to believe that."

"It's true, I—" Another cough broke his voice, and he leaned heavily on the wall behind him, shivering violently as his nerves awoke and the cold assaulted him. "It used to belong to my grandfather, and I—I wanted to bring it back home, that was all." He swallowed, and his voice came out small and awkward, for it was such a small, silly, pitiful thing. There was no reason at all for the queen to care about such a trifle. "My—my mother is growing old, and she said how much she wished she could have it to pass on to my sister who will be wed soon, as it was a family heirloom... yet lost here, she had no way of retrieving it, so I..."

He couldn't continue, throat constricted with both cold and fear. There was nothing more to be said, regardless. The pendant was all he wanted. Though he sympathized with her plight, there was nothing he could do to help her, even if he wanted to. Ultimately, as selfish as it was, what could he offer? He had nothing but his own life, and that he was not willing to give.

Silence filled the room, disturbed only by the shifting of the ash, slowly swirling around the queen. Hans couldn't bear to look up, to see the thunderous expression that surely twisted her face. The inherent foolishness of his entire journey pressed down on him, the heat of shame prickling beneath his skin.

Her voice startled him, cold and flat. "You traveled here for this alone?"

"Yes." Anticipating the next question, he added, "I—I came in secret, actually."

She made a noise approximating disgust, rightly so, and the next thing he heard was the rustle of her tattered dress and the clatter of the puppets falling to the floor. "You're a blithering fool," she snapped, marching towards him, and Hans lifted his head to meet her furious gaze. "You would abandon your family—risk life and limb—merely for this trinket?"

Internally he winced, for it sounded all so very idiotic phrased such, but it was the undeniable truth. Feeling that he had to reply somehow, he nodded. She snorted, whirling on her heel to sit back on her throne, and it was only then that he noticed how her legs trembled. Even after all this time, she was still weak. He watched as she rested her chin on her hand and glared out of the window, some of the ash rising from her arms and swooping out into the pale sky. The pendants rested on the knee of her frayed gown, winking in the light, and Hans did not dare hope that he would have them back. All he could do was wait, doing his best not to shiver convulsively.

The ice beneath his feet melted away, and the temperature seemed to warm somewhat, but not enough to keep him from shivering, and his clothes were damp, adding to the chill. He pulled his fur collar up over his nose, and some of the heat of his breath melted the frost from his face.

A sudden crackle made him flinch, and he looked down to see the water draining from his clothes, crystallizing into ice, and settling around the queen's pale feet.

"Thank you," he mumbled.

She did not answer immediately. "Many people have come here. Seeking riches, or to put an end to the blizzard, or myself; they are one and the same, after all. But never... for selfless reasons." She fingered the thin gold chains, winding them around her hand. "I never thought such a day would come, though that means little to you when you did not come to call on me for company alone." Before he could muster an answer, she held out her arm, the pendants swaying from her bony fingers. "Take your trinkets and return home. Do not set foot here again if you know what is best."

Tentatively, he stepped forward, hands cupped, and they tumbled into his palms. The glassy eyes of the puppets stared at him from beside the throne, motionless yet exuding a silent threat, and he was quick to stow the precious treasure deep into a pocket with trembling hands. Was she really just handing them over? He could hardly believe it. With more feeling now, he said, "Thank you very much, Your Highness. If there is anything I can do to repay you for your kindness—"

"You may leave, with all possible haste," she replied curtly. "Lest I change my mind on account of your dawdling."

Hans nodded and bowed, though the queen continued to stare out the window, her face unreadable. The door opened smoothly beneath his hand, though he could not bring himself to cross the threshold when his relief was tinged with something bitter, something which stayed his steps. Her words lingered in his mind, and he couldn't help picturing her stewing in rage, yet waiting for someone to appear without ulterior motives. Alone, surrounded only by skeletons and puppets. He glanced over his shoulder and saw she still had not moved. "If... you like," he said, words slow with hesitation, "I could come solely for your company."

"And what would you know, or care, about me?" she scoffed. "Do you not loathe me as all the others do, for both my blizzard and my inherent monstrous nature?"

He shook his head. "You've given me no reason to."

"Foolish child. Go, hurry home."

Disappointed but unsurprised, Hans turned back to the door—but as he did, out of the corner of his eye, the small flicker of a smile touched the queen's face for the first time.

# THE THIRD SON

## By Elise Berensen Meyer

THE LAST RAYS OF DAYLIGHT peeked over the Hryggur mountains and glimmered on the Ísjaka river as the funeral pyre was lit. Double moons, crafted from ice diamonds by Odin himself, began their ascent in the dark eastern sky; one gibbous, one crescent. The stars accompanying the lover moons' appearance began to wink out one by one as the fire grew brighter. Only a matter of minutes was necessary for the pyre to be ensconced in a brightness that overtook the twinkling sky and would soon overtake the mortal body of the king's advisor.

Queen Röskva stood closest to the stone ship that housed the pyre and would serve as a tomb, chanting sacred rights for the burning elf's soul. Symbols of Odin's great hall were carved in great detail along the side of the landlocked vessel and members of the Íslandian court stood around it; doing their best to appear solemn and heartbroken. Drek could not stomach the hypocrisy.

Turning towards the exit of the sacred burial ground, he muttered to himself, "That excuse for a male is never entering the sacred halls of Valhalla, no matter how fervent your efforts are, mother."

"What was that *bróðir?*" a tall figure asked, much too loud, while patting Drek on the back, much too hard.

"Nothing meant for your ears, Hallur."

"So solemn, little brother! Taking this quite hard, are we?"

"I am neither little, nor solemn. So you may quit your play at patronizing me," Drek answered, his latent anger undetectable in his disinterested tone. It was difficult to feel even a small amount of sorrow at the funeral of a corrupt elf that Drek had felled with his own hands.

"Oh, I apologize. I forgot you had reached the ripe old age of thirty-three!"

"You best shut that Loki-cursed trap of yours. You're causing a scene," Drek urged in a hiss.

"Yes, little brother. Best to save our scene causing antics for the feast," Hallur whispered with a conspicuous smirk before chasing after a group of lavishly dressed ladies of the court.

Drek's nerves simmered at the thought of the feasting he must, at the very least, show his face at. He hoped the insufferable event might prove useful for gathering more information on the corruption festering in his father's court, or his next three nights would be utterly wasted.

The surrounding crowd parted before the third born son of King Bryggur as he ventured away from the funeral rites. Drek's large stature, dark apparel, and aloof expression had that effect more often than not. A group of gossiping Jårls' wives didn't move upon his approach, however, and he took the opportunity to spy on their conversation.

"He truly insisted on a pyre? To be cremated is not so often done in these times!" one woman exclaimed.

The wife who seemed to hold all of the scandalous information smirked, leaving the group in suspense for a moment before spilling everything in a haughty tone, "Not only did he insist on a pyre in his death wishes, he became quite paranoid towards the end of his mortal life. He made his son swear a *blood oath*!"

The delicate elf women gasped all at once, their ring clad fingers fanning faces, touching foreheads, and patting hearts. It was quite comical; Drek's careful façade almost cracked in amusement.

"Yes! A blood oath of all things. He was terrified that if his corpse remained intact, he would be called upon by dark forces and become a member of the undead. A *Draugr*," the reigning wife whispered at the end of her revelation.

The ladies broke into a chorus of shocked chatter. Drek had suspected as much of the late Jårl though, so none of the surprise transferred to him. He resumed a more harried pace and left the court of Íslandia to their false mourning.

Three days. Three Loki-cursed days of feasting. Of looking sorrowful during sad stories he did not find depressing. Of laughing at jests he did not find funny. Of communing with courtiers he did not trust.

Leaving the revelers to enjoy their last feast day, Drek was on his way out of the great hall when he crossed paths with one of his servants turned street spy. To any passersby who happened to see the young elf walk past Drek while balancing a tray of spiced pear wine, it would seem that the prince and the servant made no contact. Yet, Drek walked through the behemoth doors into the front corridor with a note tucked into his large fist.

He opened the missive as soon as he walked through his chamber door and didn't bother relaxing into one of the plush leather chairs in the sitting room to read it. Heading straight to his dressing room, he decoded the message, letting his feet carry him along the familiar path. It related a lead that could reveal his next victim. No, he had decided not to think of them that way. Victim was much too personal of a word. Assassins used words like target, or mark. Those were better words. Words that separated him from the sordid deeds he carried out behind the crown's back. His own father's back.

Black training leathers hung in the back of his closet. They were nondescript and not unusual attire for a third born warrior-prince to own. However, when Drek donned them with a black tunic, boots, and a deep hooded cloak, he truly looked like what he had become. An assassin, but not one of those evil-worshiping members of the Order of Fenrir. They were the ones he was attempting to root out of his father's court, but sometimes you had to become your worst nightmare in order to fight it.

He dressed quickly, becoming like shadow itself as he slunk towards the balcony off his bedchamber. The well-used glass door made no noise when Drek pushed it open, just enough to slide beyond it. Taking care not to be seen, he crossed to the edge of the balcony, where a sturdy rope was attached to a baluster. The rope snaked towards the ground as he fed it through the railing. After climbing to the other side, he took the rope in his gloved fists and lowered himself, hand over hand, to the courtyard below.

The rope would be suspicious if any of the guards were to notice it on patrol. Drek held out his left hand, concentrated while making a few precise movements, and soon enough a small bird made of ice formed in the center of his palm. The miniature raven fluttered its wings as Drek blew magical life into the figurine. He commanded it to take the end of the rope and carry it back to the balcony. The tiny ice creation did as he bid, weaving between the ornate stone balustrades and coiling the rope on the balcony.

With a thought, Drek thanked his icy raven and dismissed it from existence. It would need to be conjured again when he returned, to retrieve the rope, but he had no more need for it at the moment.

From what information Drek had already gathered about the Order of Fenrir, the assassins never met all at once. Nor did they often meet in the same place. There was one leader, he knew that much. However, who that elf was remained a mystery.

Tonight, his sources led him to a lavish home in the heart of Ísborg, only a few miles south of the palace. Járls whose territories were a great distance from the capitol kept small, well-appointed residencies in town, much like this one. As Drek crept up the stone paved street, he took in the small mansion. Its number was carved into an intricate wooden sign by the front door. What it lacked in width, the building attempted to make up for in height. The roof, shaped like an upturned boat, capped the fourth story, and was ornamented with a large bear head.

It was like all the other homes in town belonging to members of his father's court, but Drek did not recognize this one in particular. He slipped into the cramped alley to the right of the building and called on his magic again. A thin layer of frost coated his body, cloak and all. The flexible coating turned from a frosty white to the color of deep shadow as Drek spelled it to take on the image of his surroundings. The illusion wasn't perfect, but every time he practiced the camouflaging magic it crept closer to making him completely invisible. In the dark, he was as indiscernible as a ghost.

The note had implied the Fenrirs would make a move on someone in this home tonight; fourth-story, third window on the west side. A fresh layer of concealing frost covered Drek's hands as he pulled off his leather gloves and slotted his calloused fingers into grooves scattered throughout the wall's stone facade. His bulky build wasn't exactly meant for scaling walls, but he made up for that with magic. Small ice platforms appeared where he needed to place his feet and disappeared as soon as he moved on to the next hold.

A matter of moments later and the rogue assassin was freezing the latch on the window, making it brittle enough for him to break as he forced it open. It wasn't a subtle move, but he used a cloud of icy air concentrated around the lock to dampen the sound. The glass moved noiselessly on its tracks; squeaky windows would not be acceptable in a house this dignified. Drek climbed through the opening, settled silently on the plush fur rug under his feet, and shut the window.

There was a form resting in the large four-postered bed facing

him, but he couldn't detect a rising and falling that would evidence the person was still breathing. Treading lightly, with sound dampening clouds around his boot treads, he made his way to the resting figure, keeping an ear out for any other nefarious persons that may be lingering. He prided himself on being the most dangerous thing in any room he entered, but when the Order of Fenrir was involved, he couldn't be too careful.

He reached to pull down the fur covering the bed when the cool bite of a blade tingled across his throat. Drek stilled, a layer of protective ice instinctually forming between his skin and the dagger while he cursed the imperfection in his cloaking spell that allowed him to be detected.

A husky voice whispered in his ear, "Come to murder some innocent pillows?"

The blade slowly moved away from his throat while he guessed at the identity of the phantom behind him. Once free, Drek threw back the covers to reveal a cleverly arranged mound of what was, in fact, pillows.

The phantom easily blocked his strike when he whirled around, wielding the knife he kept hidden up his left sleeve. The small throwing dagger was knocked out of his frost covered hand and clattered to the ground while Drek assessed his opponent. A dark cloak obscured the figure's body, a black cowl wrapped around the elf's face so all that showed were their eyes, but even those were cloaked in shadow.

"So you're the one who has been killing off courtiers associated with the Order." It wasn't a question. The information leading him here tonight was a trap.

"Yes," he answered. "And you have the pleasure of being next." His tone cut through the small distance between them, sharp as the long dagger he unsheathed while uttering the words.

He threw a backhanded slice at the Fenrir assassin's throat, hoping to catch them off guard, while simultaneously pulling another blade from his thigh holster. A metal bracer caught his dagger before it could connect, blocking a blow that would have been impossible for most elves to see coming. Drek seemed to have finally met his match.

The pair launched into a battle of daggers and bracers, strikes and blocks, arm locks and evasions. Every time Drek felt like he might gain the upper hand, the Fenrir slipped from his grasp or turned the tables completely.

Their dance led them towards the window he had climbed through. Hoping a ray of moonlight might allow him to see his opponent more clearly, Drek grabbed hold of his nemesis. Dragging them to the wall next to the glass and bracing his back against its delicately decorated paper, he attempted to peer into the folds of the assassin's cowl.

A dark layer of shadow was all that met his eyes despite the moonlight shining directly in the Fenrir's face. His opponent wiggled in his grasp, attempting to free themselves from the punishing pressure of his muscled arms. The movement made Drek all too aware of the body he had pressed against his own. The form molded to his sculpted chest was decidedly not male.

The force of slamming against the wall had caused his hood to drop. Tendrils of hair escaping from his styled braids fell into his eyes. He shook them out of his line of sight before realizing that the errant strands were a sign that his obscuring layer of frost had dissipated. The shock of realizing a woman was hiding beneath that cloak and cowl had made him lose concentration.

The veil of shadow concealing the Fenrir fell away, revealing eyes widened in the same surprise he felt.

"Who are you?" he asked.

His mystery nemesis narrowed her gaze, "Not now. I'll find you."

She slipped out of his slackened grasp, drew a shroud of shadow over her face, and disappeared out the window. A trail of fiery awareness was left behind where their bodies had been pressed together and it took Drek a moment to process what had just happened.

Shaking off the dazed feeling the Fenrir's abrupt exit had left him with, he remade his magical camouflage and followed the woman out the window. Although, when he touched down in the alley, the dark elf was nowhere to be found.

Midsummer Festival was in full swing and Drek was enjoying himself, for once. Perhaps the large fire in the center of the training yard was succeeding at warding off his more nefarious emotions. However, the ceremonial blaze did nothing to ward off the evil that was his two older brothers.

"Why won't you wrestle? Afraid to muss your pretty tunic, bróðir?" Hallur jeered while tugging on one of Drek's white-blond braids.

"He wants to look his best for all of the noble ladies he intends to woo tonight," Thrör goaded.

"Fine, I'll accept your challenge, Hallur." Drek had been heading to the fried cake vendor across the field. But after their relentless teasing, he could not pass up Hallur's dare and live peaceably with his brothers for the next fortnight. Besides, Drek wasn't there to chase women. There were none that he would trust.

Stringy, lithe muscles met Drek's corded bulk as Hallur rushed forward, attempting to put him on his back. The advantage of Drek's larger frame was that he could easily overpower his two older brothers when he had a mind to. Of course, he stood out against his more slender, quintessential counterparts. Something about the streak of Viking blood running through their line manifesting more in him.

Sand spewed behind Hallur's boots as he attempted to gain some purchase. Drek merely held his ground a few more moments, relishing his strength and this one advantage he had against his older, more essential siblings.

"Had enough, Hallur, or shall I embarrass you a little more?" Drek wasn't out of breath in the slightest, yet Hallur had begun to pant. His hot breath beat a staccato rhythm against Drek's ear where their heads were pressed together.

"I will best you"—*grunt*—"If it is the last—thing—I do!" A pathetic shove followed Hallur's sorry pronouncement.

It was best for Drek to put his brother out of his misery sooner rather than later. He let the weak maneuver move him back, and a garbled cry of victory escaped Hallur's lips at the small sign of advantage. It soon turned into the disgruntled sound of air being knocked out of his chest. The small space had allowed the larger elf to swoop in, latch onto his brother's upper arm, and throw Hallur over his shoulder.

A puff of dust clouded the training ring while Drek's satisfied laugh rumbled through his chest. Moaning from the ground followed a breathy cough and, feeling a bit sorry for how hard he had slammed his brother, Drek held out a hand. It was promptly slapped away, Hallur's pride a bit too stung to accept the proffered assistance. Well, if he was going to be so stubborn, Drek would leave him to it.

Dust was already settling to the ground as he turned towards the fried cake stand. Before he could take two steps, someone appeared at the edge of the ring as if they had emerged from the descending cloud of fine sand. He saw her eyes first. A pair of feline eyes that he would have been able to spot out of a crowd of one hundred thousand. The phantom who had held a knife to his throat, blocked every one of his strikes, and enraptured his thoughts unlike any other.

"So, you aren't completely useless in a fight." Her throaty voice floated and fleeted across the space between them, as if it was born of shadow itself.

"Surprisingly, it has been some time since I've found my equal in the training ring," Drek said, his voice suddenly lower than his normal tone, as he stepped toward his specter. His feet moved of their own volition, drawn to her as he was.

"Perhaps you have been moving in the wrong circles?"

"What circles would you suggest, my tantalizing specter?" He was but a foot away from her now. Gazing down into those remarkable eyes that were only a few inches below his own.

Instead of being shocked at his forwardness, his enticing nemesis seemed to enjoy the challenge of their wordplay.

"The darker ones." She smiled up at him, the curve of her mouth and twinkle in her eye becoming more tempting with every second he continued to stare at her.

"You mean, the *shadowy* ones?" She nodded. "I don't dance with wolves."

"Then, what would you call our little rendezvous last week? It felt like a dance to me," she purred while drawing his attention to her wrist.

She pulled on the long sleeve of her linen gown, the light lilac fabric slowly inched up to reveal a black tattoo. A wolf, the sign of the Order of Fenrir. The order of elves who were called dark for the nefarious gods they worshiped and the shadow magic they practiced.

The dark, twisting braids depicting the damning mark wove together in contrast to her light brown skin. Drek followed the strands of black turning and twining along her wrist until he felt sick. He had forgotten himself. A pair of gorgeous eyes and a strong yet alluring body had him flirting with this dark elf rather than slitting her throat where she stood.

Like the fluttering wings of a dove, the shadow elf's sleeve fell to cover her wrist again as she lowered her arm. Drek snatched up her hand, a little too quick and forceful to appear romantic, but hopefully no one was watching them closely.

"Be careful my prince, else your father's court should think us engaged," she practically growled while tightly closing her fingers around his.

The woman had quite a grip. Drek almost felt pressured to let her go, but held firm. He would not let her slip away from him as easily as she did last time.

"You're dressed as a peer of the court. Maybe I *shall* pick you as my wife. Although, I fear you would not return from our wedding travels alive." His threats did not seem to faze her. She merely rose one dark eyebrow, the expression one thousand words in itself. "Give me one good reason to not kill you here and now, shadow."

"Well, it would make quite a scene. One that would put a target on your back. You would be dead before you could trim the beard on that pretty face of yours in the morning. My immediate death isn't worth that, no matter how much you might *yearn* for it." The sultry lilt she put on the last sentence made it difficult for Drek to remember her death was what he should yearn for and not anything else.

Before the prince could suggest they move somewhere more private—so he could dispatch her, of course—the wolf in lady's clothing spoke again.

"If that is not enough reason for you to spare my life, here is another. You need me." Drek scoffed; she overestimated her physical allure if she thought such a thing would deter him from his true purpose.

Those dark red lips tilted in an amused smirk. "I meant, you need me to help you take down the Order of Fenrir and the rot it has spread through your father's court."

Her words felt like one of her punches to the ribs. If she was in earnest, this shadow of a woman was the answer to all of his cries to the gods.

"How can I trust you?" he asked with a hand on her waist, drawing her closer.

She whispered in his ear, as if they were some love-struck couple instead of mortal enemies. "Do you have a choice? You'll never make a dent in the Order without someone on the inside. Everyone you care about is in danger, including those spies you're so fond of. Without me, they'll be the first to have their throats slit."

A booming voice startled them apart before Drek could think of an answer, let alone utter one. It wasn't one of his brothers. For all their teasing they knew not to get in the way when there was a woman

48

involved.

"Daughter! Have you managed to catch the eye of a courtier so quickly?"

Drek turned to the man—recognizing him as a lesser Jårl from an obscure territory—and when the Jårl registered Drek as a prince his expression changed from congenial to stunned.

"Forgive me, my prince. I did not expect my Fjara to have been introduced to you as of yet," the man spewed while bowing in such a violent manner that Drek was worried the Jårl might smack his head on a knobby knee.

"No need to apologize. I am but a third prince, so of no more consequence than any other courtier here," Drek said with a nod.

Fjara, as her father called her, saved the man from further embarrassing himself by cutting in, "We were about to visit the fried cake stand, Father. Would you like to join us?"

"No, Daughter. I thank you for the invitation, but I will leave you young people to your frivolities."

The Jårl bowed and scraped as Drek held out an arm for Fjara. Her delicate hand, that he knew better than to think of as such, settled on his bare arm. The contact was almost enough to make him forget the dire nature of their acquaintance. Warmth like his icy self had never felt radiated from her touch, creeping up his arm and into his chest. This was a dangerous game they were playing at.

The smell of sweet cake fried in peanut oil and drizzled with fruit syrup and cream surrounded the couple as they moved through the crowd. After paying the vendor, Drek handed Fjara her dessert and walked by her side to the edge of the bonfire. Its great crackling covered up the fervent whispers that drifted to the prince's ears from the dark elf's painted lips.

They were to meet in the gardens below his balcony the next night, when the sun was on the opposite side of the realm and the moons glittered low in the sky. Agreeing to the arrangement, Drek looked down to take a bite of his cake. Before he could glance back up, the specter who had begun to haunt his life disappeared into the shadows cast by the bright blaze, her exit as quiet and mysterious as her appearance.

The lover moons, named for the great Mengloth and Svipdagr, shone down with delight on the couple who met in the shadows of a palace garden. The unnatural chill in the midsummer air lent Drek to believe the Norns were at work. Weaving the strands of his life on their loom made of bones, set upon the skulls of mortals.

The secrets passed from Fjara to Drek seemed to ring true in his mind. Or perhaps it was his heart that was leading him. At this point, it was too late to question his own judgment. He was in league with this alluring dark elf who had been recruited to the Order as a child and wished to break the bonds tethering her to their cause.

"If we are to root out this evil festering in our land, Drek, you must pretend to become one of us," Fjara suggested. Her hood was drawn low over the assassin's cowl covering her face, obscuring the eyes that Drek had not stopped thinking about for a week.

"How can I? I have assassinated at least ten people associated with the Order."

"That is exactly how one gains the notice of a secret society they wish to gain entrance to. All you need is my word. I will prepare you for an initiation meeting with the dark master, and then we can work on ruining their plans from the inside." Fjara pulled down her cowl and the shadows lingering around her visage disappeared.

She was a witch, knowing exactly what to do at what moment, forcing him to put an ever-increasing amount of trust in her. But her plan made sense, and the sincerity shining in her eyes was not easy for him to ignore.

"What must I do to prepare for such a meeting?"

Fjara's vulpine smile made an appearance. "We need to sharpen your hand-to-hand skills, for one."

An actual laugh, small and throaty, escaped her lips as Drek's large hands caught her waist and drew her closer. "I don't think my hand skills need any sharpening."

"I believe I have a few things I could teach you," she said softly in his ear. A shiver ran down his spine as she drew back and continued, "Other than basic assassin skills, you will need to present an affinity for shadow magic."

"That is a firm no." Drek stepped back, letting his hands drop. "My royal oath," he breathed out. There was nothing that could tempt him in breaking the vows binding him to Odin. In return for his faithfulness, Drek was blessed with stronger ice magic—a unique gift of its own—and he would be stripped of those powers and his honor if he were to turn to darkness.

Fjara's small hand, bearing precise callouses associated with the wielding of weapons, drew Drek's line of sight to match hers. "If it is your oath and ice magic you are worried about, there is no need. We do not draw on the shadows through devotion to Fenrir and his ilk. It is an element like any other."

Drek shook his head in disbelief. "I cannot listen to this."

"You can and *shall*," she said while forcing him to look back at her. Both hands over the pale whiskers covering his cheeks. "Yes, dark calls to dark. But we all have darkness inside ourselves. Does that make everyone evil?"

"I don't know what I am anymore. The things I have done, even if they were in the name of a good cause, they were still awful. There is just as much black in my heart as white."

"See, the darkness is already within you. Yet you have not broken any of your vows. That grayness within you is what you need for this magic." One of her thumbs ran a trail down his cheek, tracing a stray tear.

"Show me."

Weeks passed, the frequent clandestine meetings with his specter becoming the only thing in Drek's life worth looking forward to. Their time together was spent sparring—physically and verbally—and attempting to call up some shred of shadow magic within Drek.

He was becoming increasingly frustrated with his inability to conjure even a wisp of darkness. Fjara said she could feel the affinity in him with her own magic. She knew that this *could* work. The question of *how* was another monster entirely.

Haustblót was almost upon them. His fighting skills had improved more than Drek ever thought they could. Humility and pride both stirred in his stomach when Fjara informed him that his assassin skills were ready for his initiation meeting. Now, they only had to conquer shadow and their schemes could move forward.

While everyone else was milling about the palace courtyards, watching as people took turns gathering firewood from the stores and building up piles for the celebratory fires the next day, Drek was letting Fjara into his sitting room.

No matter how much Drek wished her visit was merely one of friendship, or even courtship, they had a singular objective. He must master shadow tonight. The leader of the Order of Fenrir was finally in town, and initiate meetings were the following day.

Ice formed in Drek's palm, building and twisting as he exercised his magic. The mass of frozen water finally settled into the shape of a rolling wave crashing over the shore. He handed it to Fjara before moving to stand by the fireplace. She regarded the ice sculpture, a faint trace of surprise washing over her controlled features.

"It's... my name." Her lips formed the words with reverence towards the small token he had gifted her.

"If you are the shore, then I am the waves of the ocean. Constantly drawn back to you, no matter what forces might try to pull me away." The words were affirmed as he stepped closer to his lady assassin.

"Drek, I have an idea of how we can get you over your magical block."

He stopped an arm's length from her, giving her the space to voice her proposal. However, she closed the distance between them. Setting the miniature ocean on a side table, her hands were then free to roam over his arms. They caressed the curve of his flexing biceps before grazing over his shoulders and resting on his chest. Her long fingers played with the ties on his shirt, slowly loosening them as if the widening gap between the laces was unintentional. Although Drek knew that this woman did nothing without great intention.

"I thought you knew how to help me with the shadow magic?" Drek laughed out. He attempted to cover up the shakiness in his voice with a confidently arched brow.

"You need to relax, Drek," she whispered as one of those tricky little fingers found its way inside of his shirt, tickling the spattering of blond hair trailing between his pecs. "You have been holding on too tight. If you just open your mind and let the darker side of you come forward, then your shadow should come forward as well."

A large lump formed in Drek's throat. He swallowed before saying, "You realize, if things go too far, my vow of faithfulness to Odin is broken."

"We don't need to go *that* far. Giving in to our most innocent desires should be enough." Her breath fanned over the shorn side of his head as her lips lightly caressed the piercing in his pointed ear. What had they been speaking of?

She laughed in that low, sultry way of hers. "We can save the deeper desires for when we are wed. There will be no breaking of vows then."

"Did you just ask me to marry you?"

"No, you implied it when you took my hand at the Midsummer feast, in front of your brothers and the sacred bonfire. I am merely accepting your offer now."

"You wicked woman."

He felt her smirk as she pressed a kiss to the side of his face. It was his undoing. One hand slid into her wavy black hair as the other gently grasped the sharp arch of her cheek, bringing her lips to his own. He lost himself in the feel of her, the silkiness of her long tresses, the softness of her curves, the firmness of her muscled torso, the way her lips slid against his. They fit perfectly. Their mouths moved together in an increasing fury, with the strength and wit of every sparring match and three months of built attraction.

A small gasp flitted from Fjara's lips. Her air trailing over his mouth, tempting him to trace the shape of hers. He gave in, his tongue softly caressing her full upper lip. The taste of strawberries and lime mixed with shadows and secrets overwhelmed his senses.

Fjara pressed her smiling lips to his. "Now, find where the darkness stirs inside you," she whispered against his mouth, taking his hands and drawing them to form a bowl between them.

A floodgate of emotion had opened within his heart. Hot on the heels of attraction and felicity, came hatred and despair. Drawing on the strength of his darker self, the part that had lied and maimed and killed, Drek attempted to give that essence life as an actual shadow.

Fjara raised their cupped hands. "Open your eyes, Drek."

Fear of failure coursed through him as he slowly relaxed his cinched eyelids and peered down. Fleeting between his fingers was a swirling pool of shadow, infinite possibility only awaiting his command to take form.

Shock, awe, and fear took turns commanding his voice as he spoke, "I did it. The only question is, do I still have my ice affinity?"

Keeping the shadow in one large palm, Drek pulled the other away from Fjara and silently prayed to Odin as he drew on his icy magic. To his great relief, frost quickly formed over his fingers, flowing swiftly up his arm and hiding it from view as he spelled it to reflect his surroundings. It was not at all diminished, as he had feared. The sleeve of ice felt more powerful than ever after using another type of magic.

"You're ready." Fjara nodded while taking a step back.

 54

"Let's make sure I can accomplish the feat on command. I would hate to make that kind of display in front of the Order. No matter how often I would like it repeated in private." His arm shot out, grabbing her waist and closing the distance between them once more. Now that Drek knew his feelings were reciprocated, he would never let her go.

The abundance of voices in the courtyard was beginning to dwindle by the time Drek felt confident drawing on the shadow magic.

Fjara slithered out of his arms, ever the elegant shadow, and moved toward the door. "I should go; we have an important day tomorrow."

"Stay, I need you."

"Drek." The way she said his name alone intoned all she could have said with several sentences. *Drek, I could be seen. Drek, we are not wed. Drek, you need your sleep. Drek, I know you are not an incomparable rake but you are acting like one.*

The answer to this was a simple one. "Then marry me," he said while following her to the exit.

"I have already said that I would," she answered with an arched brow.

Opening the door, Drek gestured for Fjara to lead the way. "Excellent, let's find Gothi. I'm sure he's still awake, blessing the wood for the bonfires tomorrow or whatever those of his ilk do the day before a feast."

He shut the door behind his lady and strode down the hall with purpose. Sure that her steps and mind would catch up with him momentarily.

"Drek, you cannot be serious," her voice sounded beside him. Quick and silent as she was, he had not heard her approach.

"We are on the cusp of a great turning point. The Norns are weaving and the gods are whispering. I will not risk marching into that den of wolves tomorrow without knowing that you are mine forever."

The animal within him purred in contentment when Fjara placed her hand on his outstretched arm. He would take that as her agreement with this brash scheme. Warmth that he only felt at her touch seeped through his thin shirt and made its way through his entire body. He felt alive, and Fjara's giddy laugh conveyed that her feelings matched his own.

They stopped at the royal treasury on their way out of the palace. There were dozens of extravagant rings that Drek gave his bride leave to choose from, but she picked a simple braided band with a moon on each end.

A small temple dedicated to Odin lay just beyond the palace's northern orchard. That is where they found the priest, preparing for the morrow's feast and the sacred rites he would perform. It didn't take much effort to convince Gothi to perform the ceremony—being a prince did come with certain liberties—and after fetching Hallur to be a witness, they were wed.

Drek slid the ring over Fjara's heart finger, pinching it so it cinched to a perfect fit around her delicate, yet deadly appendage. Silver and ice diamonds glittered as the moons kissed, but the simple beauty of the ring could not match the expression of happiness on his bride's face. Or the first kiss they shared as husband and wife.

A lonely estate lay on the outskirts of the palace's extensive grounds. It was currently vacant, sometimes used to house traveling dignitaries, and the perfect place for clandestine meetings of the Order of Fenrir. Drek stood outside the large wooden doors leading to the house's feasting hall. A great bear stared him down, its carved eyes boring into him as he absently stared at the blocked entrance. He was concentrating on keeping up the clouds of misty ice magic that allowed him to eavesdrop on Fjara's introductory conversation with the head wolf, Myrkrið.

A voice that seemed to come from a mouth hewn of stone floated to his ears, "You are sure he is loyal to our cause? The way he gained our attention could be seen as an audition or a declaration of war."

"He is most loyal, my lord." That was Fjara's voice drifting from the cloud.

"Bring him in, then."

The bear's face swung away on silent hinges and was replaced with Fjara's cowled visage. Feigned confidence laced Drek's persona as he entered the cavernous hall. A cloaked figure sat on a dark wooden throne atop a dais. Stopping at a respectful distance, Drek kneeled in obeisance, one fist over his heart and the other on his thigh.

"You may rise, Prince," the gravelly voice said from under his shadowed hood.

Drek wore no hood or cowl, he did not have that privilege yet, so it was easy to discern who he was. Although he was sure that Fjara had reported his identity to her unforgiving master long before this meeting. The silver wrapped around the ends of his braided hair clinked as he stood, free from the tight knot he normally tied at the crown of his head. He had a formal feast to attend later.

"You wish to join our ranks." It was a statement, not a question, so Drek made no move to answer. "Your status is as much a risk as it would be a boon to us. What makes you think you are worth it?"

Drek thought boldness was best used in these situations. "I possess magical skills incomparable to anything you have seen before, even amongst my own family. Surely you will not turn down an ally so close to the throne?"

"What if I told you I have an ally closer to the throne than even you are?"

Fear crept into Drek's carefully crafted mindset, but he didn't let it show in his expression.

"You *are* good." A laugh like stones in a tumbler rumbled from the dais. "Not even a flinch; I do quite like you. Yet, I have the throne in the palm of my hands and I find that I still cannot tell where your loyalties truly lie. You have a confusing aura about you, Prince."

"You cannot mean that the king, my own father, is involved with the Order?" Anger surged through Drek's body. The emotion rang in his ears, tightened a fist around his heart, and sped his breathing while eating his fear alive.

The cloaked figure cackled. "I have spoken no lies. What will you do about it?"

His decision was made in the sliver of a heartbeat. A skin of frost grew in the next sliver and Drek disappeared completely. His camouflage perfect in his heightened state of rage and heartbreak. His own father, betraying Odin and all the realm. This would be made right, Drek would make sure of it.

The intricately carved bear was blown off its hinges in an explosion of ice, and Drek was gone from the haunted hall before anyone could follow.

"You knew," Fjara whispered to the master she had hated all her life.

"Did you think I could not tell you were besotted with him the moment you reported his identity to me? Or that I could not see through you when you so hastily volunteered to root out the entity plaguing our order?"

Hatred, anger, fear. They all coursed through Fjara's veins, shaking her composure and freezing her in place. What would Drek do with this news? What would her master do to her?

"Go, child of shadow. See your prince ruin everything he ever loved. A king so wise and kind hearted as King Bryggur would not be in my pocket. No. But Thrör, he is the weak link in that chain of succession and Drek is about to put him into power."

Fjara wasted no words or time. She flew out of the ruined exit. Drek had to be stopped.

 58

The trek from the abandoned estate to the palace was not long. But, as Drek wrestled with the thought of his father being a traitor, the path seemed to stretch out before him, becoming a seemingly interminable distance between him and the truth. There must be some explanation, some proof of the king's innocence or guilt, and he was about to find it.

Silence spread through the palace's great hall as Drek burst through its doors. He left ice in his footsteps and an ominous cloud hung over his head. Across the room, a wolf assassin dressed in sheep's clothing was whispering in his father's ear. Drek had seen that same man leaving Myrkrið's meeting place not an hour earlier.

"Father, how could you? Colluding with assassins and letting their putrid shadows infiltrate our court!" Hatred and betrayal crushed the prince's battered heart as he spewed the angry words.

Before the king could answer or anyone thought to stop him, Drek shot an icicle straight through his father's heart. Shock rose on King Bryggur's face, but he was dead and fallen to the ground before it could fully form.

"No!" Fjara's cry rang through the room. She pulled him from the crowd gathering around his father. "This is all Myrkrið's manipulation. The King was innocent."

"No, he was colluding with assassins. The corruption in his court ran so deep. Even if he wasn't involved directly, someone who can keep the shadows at bay will be in power now." The shock of killing his own father led Drek to rationalization. The old king was guilty enough, or else the assassins would not have such a strong hold on the elven court. Even if Fjara was right, things would be better now, they had to be.

Thrör, his own brother, called for the guards to drag him away. Drek would not allow them to. He grabbed Fjara's hand, covered them both in concealing ice, and fled the palace, stealing food and cloaks from the kitchen on their way out.

They would be hunted like a fox in the woods, but they would survive long enough to fix this. Drek conjured the largest snow storm he could manage. A blizzard for the ages that would surely call up an early winter. It whited out the palace grounds and concealed the newlyweds' hasty escape to the Hryggur mountains. They could find shelter with the Dwarves—Drek had friends among them—then return when the time was right.

Trudging towards the faint shadow of mountains in the distance, Drek wondered at how *he* had become the one to be tracked by the king's guards when there was real darkness to be rooted out in Íslandia. Whether Thrör was his true nemesis or just another puppet for Myrkrið to maneuver, the third son of King Bryggur knew it was still up to him to sever evil's influence from the cosmos like the head from a snake.

Crying into the howling storm, he vowed to Odin, to any god that would listen, that he would rid the realms of the Order of Fenrir once and for all.

#  Grandmother Oak

By Benjamin Sperduto

TEMCHIN WAS WITHIN SIGHT of the cabin when he heard his father scream.

He dropped the armload of firewood and whirled around to see his father staggering through the woods, clutching his neck. The axe he'd wielded so powerfully only moments earlier now dragged in the snow behind him like an extension of his limp arm.

"Run, boy! Get inside!"

Temchin knew he was supposed to obey his father without question or hesitation, that any delay could mean death in the forest.

But when he saw the thing behind his father, he froze in place.

It was smaller than he expected, but it moved unlike anything he'd seen before. Not a beast, but not a man; rather some hybrid of the two. Although his father was running as fast as he could manage, the beast lopped after him without any sense of urgency.

Whatever it was, it was toying with its prey.

When its red eyes spotted him, the creature darted to its right and vanished into the darkness.

His father was only a few steps away when he drew up suddenly, his face twisting in helpless terror.

Temchin turned to see the beast reared up on its hind legs behind him. It had the head of a wolf, but wore a tattered red cloak smeared with mud and dried blood. One of its clawed hands shot out to seize him by the throat.

At that moment, he knew he was going to die.

"No! Please!"

The voice belonged to his mother, calling out from somewhere behind the monstrous wolf.

"We beg Grandmother's forgiveness, great one!"

Something about her plea caught the creature's interest. It loosened its grip and turned its head. Temchin saw his mother prostrating herself in the snow. She held out the strange necklace of bone and wood that she insisted hang over their doorway at all times.

"Please, great one," she said. "We did not know Grandmother Oak held sway here. Show us mercy on this night and I swear upon the old powers we will leave this place and never return on pain of death."

Temchin feared his mother's plea would be for nothing, that the beast would tighten its grip and tear him apart. But then it shoved him aside and moved towards his mother. It snatched the necklace away from her trembling hands and inspected it closely.

For a moment, the creature seemed to forget they were even there as it turned the necklace over and over in its clawed hands.

Then it turned and glared at Temchin's father.

"The axe. Leave it." Its voice was a coarse growl, but there was something vaguely human about it.

His father dropped the axe. As soon as it hit the ground, the beast lunged at him and yanked away the bloody scarf he'd pressed against the gash on his neck.

The creature pointed to their humble little cabin. "Burn this place and go. Or I will return to uphold our bargain."

With that final warning, it slipped into the night with scarf and necklace in hand, vanishing between the trees without a sound.

Temchin hugged his mother tightly and sobbed, letting out the fear that had built up in his chest.

"Wha...what was that thing?" he asked.

"No questions now," his mother said. "We must leave right away before it changes its mind."

After tending to his father's wound, Temchin helped his parents gather up what belongings they could carry and set fire to their cabin. Then they set out on foot into the cold winter night.

Grandmother Oak stood atop a barren mountaintop crowned by jagged rock. Her iron-like roots stabbed deep into the frozen earth, coiling around veins of ice to nourish her gnarled limbs. The harsh northern winds blistered her ancient hide, wearing away all color and any traces of softness. Nothing sprouted from her tangle of branches, which covered the hilltop like a great cloud of thorns.

Her twisted, bent form might have been something else many ages ago. Perhaps she had once been slender and beautiful before time, regret, and resentment wore her down and forced her to take root there upon the summit.

From her vantage point, she watched over the steep slopes leading up to her trunk and the fog-shrouded valley below. She heard the sounds of creatures skulking through the forests, smelled the vile stench of human settlements encroaching upon her domain, and felt the scorn of fledgling spirits that had yet to learn their proper place.

The chosen made the treacherous climb up the icy hill when Grandmother Oak called out to them. One by one, they emerged from the fog. Although they moved and looked like beasts, each of them wore close-fitting skins and masks of animals found throughout the mountains.

Badger. Stag. Bear. Eagle. Ram. Panther. Hare. Wolf.

They brought with them proof of their deeds, tokens of their devotion to Grandmother Oak's will.

Wings plucked from an arrogant fairy who dared to insult her.

The tongue of a forager who sought to taste the bounty of the forest for himself.

The head of a goblin who profaned the land with its heathen rituals.

These things and more they added to the great mound of trophies piled up around Grandmother Oak's trunk.

But they did not appease her. They only fed her seething anger, her unquenchable hatred for the impertinent wretches that refused to bow their heads to her majesty.

Wolf sensed something different about Grandmother Oak's displeasure when she tossed the bloody scarf upon the pile.

"What is this? I asked for the woodsman's hand and the head of his child."

"His axe is stilled, Grandmother," Wolf said. "And his seed will not take root in your soil."

"Why do you hate me so, Child? Has your Grandmother not cared for you since you were lost and alone in the wood?"

"Of course, Grandmother. I owe all that I am to your generosity."

"And yet still you wound me with this continued disobedience."

"No, Grandmother! You wished for the trespassers to be punished. They know the old ways and fear your power. Their home is ash, their iron rusting on the cold earth. They will not return."

"Then you have failed me. I wish for their warm blood to thaw the earth and nourish my lands. You will amend this wrong you have done me by hunting them down and finishing your task."

Wolf bowed her head. She dared not question Grandmother Oak, especially in the presence of the others. "As you command, Grandmother."

"Bear and Ram," Grandmother Oak said, "you will go with Wolf and see that she fulfills her duty properly this time."

Bear and Ram spoke as one. "Yes, Grandmother."

"Then go. And do not come before me again until it is done."

Wolf rose and turned to depart. Bear and Ram moved quickly to follow. As they left, Wolf's skin tingled, the way it felt when Grandmother Oak used her silent voice. Yet she heard nothing. Whatever was said was meant for the others.

Bear and Ram said nothing as they followed Wolf into the forest. They were younger than her by a season or more, but both were bigger and stronger. Ram's cloak had great clumps of wiry hair at the shoulders, but his mask's curved horns were large enough to keep his head from looking small between them. His boots were fashioned out of hollowed out hooves, which caused him to move with more of a trot than a walk. Bear's muscular body was buried somewhere underneath several layers of thick fur. He moved slowly and deliberately, his heavy mask rarely turning away from the path ahead.

Wolf could not recall what their faces looked like beneath their masks. It had been many winters since she'd looked upon her own features. The mantle of the wolf was a part of her now, bestowed upon her when she proved her strength among Grandmother Oak's children.

She supposed she'd had a name before Grandmother Oak's servants found her in the wood, much like the boy she'd spared yesterday. Perhaps even parents, as well.

Had she ever been alone? She'd never seen a child left to fend for itself, yet Grandmother Oak seemed to gather many such orphans from time to time. Most of them came as offerings from the bands of goblins dwelling throughout the hills. Wolf never questioned where they found the children before, but now she wondered if they were not so much "found" as stolen in the night.

They took the old trail down the mountainside, which was the fastest route to the valley below. The way was marked by huge stone monuments and altars left behind by the people who once made offerings to the old gods of the forest. Most of them had been worn down to smooth stone by countless winters, but some of them still vaguely resembled the powerful spirits they once represented.

The fate of the old gods remained a mystery. Only Grandmother Oak was old enough to remember the time of their reign, and she did not share her secrets willingly. On the rare occasions she did speak of them, she described only their arrogance and jealously, how they resented her growing power and sought to conspire against her.

Halfway down the mountain, the trail narrowed and snaked through a rock formation. There were etchings on the rock walls, far too worn now to be legible. Wolf always paused to look at the monument overlooking the mouth of the passage. Erosion had wiped away most of its features, but there was no mistaking the stance of a great wolf waiting to set upon unwary travelers.

She'd always felt a powerful connection to this place. But now there was something familiar about it. She reached for the necklace she'd tucked inside her garments, the one she'd taken from the frightened mother. Why she'd concealed it from Grandmother Oak, she couldn't say for certain, but it was almost as if she knew the very sight of it would have angered the ancient spirit.

The necklace consisted of several bits of bone and wood, each piece carved in the shape of an animal. She compared the tiny wolf carving to the monument looming above her. The resemblance was crude, but unmistakable. Sorting through the rest of the pieces, she saw other familiar creatures. A bear, a raven, a hare, and more, all of them representing one of Grandmother Oak's chosen.

One of the pieces was a flat chunk of wood with the image of a great tree engraved upon it.

Was that supposed to represent Grandmother Oak?

Wolf would have expected it to be in the center or at least bigger than the other carvings, but it was neither. She hadn't even noticed it when she first looked at the necklace.

"Wolf!" Bear said. "What are you doing?"

She quickly tucked away the necklace and turned to face Bear and Ram, who had stopped to stare back at her.

"Nothing," she said. "Keep moving. We're not far now."

The charred remains of the cabin weren't hard to find. Thin tendrils of smoke still rose from the ruins, and she could smell the ash from miles away. When the next snow fell, the ruins would be buried until the spring thaw.

Ram rooted through the wreckage, kicking over anything that remained partially standing. While he scattered the ashes and flattened the area, Bear took a closer look at the many footprints still visible in the snow.

A pack of goblins had swept over what remained of the homestead sometime in the night, probably hoping to recover some trinkets or shiny baubles left behind. Their footprints ranged all over, making it hard to distinguish which prints belonged to the fleeing humans.

Wolf could have pointed out the tracks leading south, but she decided to let her companion struggle. While Bear paced back and forth, she wandered over to the spot where she'd seized the boy.

The axe was still lying on the snowy ground, the blade covered with a thin layer of frost.

"This way," Bear said. "Come on, Wolf."

Wolf turned to see Bear and Ram heading into the forest. They were following the single file trail of footprints leading east, which clearly belonged to the goblins. She glanced at the family's tracks leading southward. They were faint, but not so hard to find that Bear should have missed them. He was stubborn, but not stupid enough to mistake goblin tracks for human ones.

Cautiously, Wolf fell in behind them.

She wondered if this could be a test of sorts. Perhaps Grandmother Oak told them to question her loyalty, to see if she would do something to protect the humans.

Wolf decided to say nothing for the moment, instead following them as they made their way up a steep hill in pursuit of the wrong quarry. The ground became rockier as they went, making it more difficult to follow the trail since the goblins took to the rocks whenever possible to conceal their passage.

When Bear finally lost them, he turned to Wolf and pointed up the hill. "Find the trail again."

Wolf considered telling him they were following the wrong prey, but decided to go along with the error. If Bear's mistake gave the humans more time to escape, the blame would not be hers.

She found the scuffs on the rocks left behind by the goblins' toenails and waved the others onward. "This way."

Bear and Ram followed. A gust of wind swept down the hill and she thought she heard the two whispering behind her.

The ground dropped off sharply to the right as they climbed, eventually giving way to a steep cliff that plummeted down to a tangle of thorn bushes and rocks far below. Wolf kept close to the edge, following the faint trail along the uneven ground.

She had to pause occasionally to find some faint sign of the goblins' passage. Each time she stopped, she heard Bear and Ram shuffling impatiently behind her.

The next time she slowed her pace, she didn't hear them at all.

Wolf glanced back. There was no sign of Bear or Ram.

Every muscle in her body tightened as she reached out with her senses.

She heard Bear's heavy footfalls before he lunged out from behind a thicket with a snarl. That split second of anticipation was enough for Wolf to leap aside and avoid being gutted by his claws.

But dodging Bear's attack left her off balance, which gave Ram an opening to charge with his horns down and smash into her back. The blow knocked the wind from her lungs and she tumbled to the ground. Her momentum sent her rolling over the cliff's edge, but she frantically scrambled to grasp at a root protruding from the rocks.

Wolf dangled there, suspended over the rocky, thorn-filled gorge below. Her chest burned and she felt her grip slowly weakening.

Bear loomed over her, snarling. "You betrayed Grandmother. You've become too weak to be among her chosen."

He reached down to rip away her mask, exposing her skin to the harsh winter wind. Strength bled from her limbs, and her senses became muted and muffled, like she'd been plunged into the waters of a deep, cold lake.

Ram joined Bear and snorted at her. "A real wolf would never have fallen for that track."

"She's not worthy of that name anymore. She deserves to die like the trespassers she spared."

Wolf felt her grip about to give way. "Please…"

"Mercy?" Ram said. "There is no mercy in the winter. Grandmother tried to teach you that, but you were too proud to listen. And now you die."

He stomped on Wolf's hands, sending her plunging into the gorge. She hit the ground hard and tumbled downward, rolling over rocks and through thickets before she struck her head and blacked out.

She remembered when Grandmother Oak gave her a name.

Her earliest memories were of the cold and the struggle against the other children. Nestled among Grandmother Oak's roots, they waited until her chosen returned to toss them scraps of food.

It wasn't enough to be the biggest and the strongest. The best scraps went to those who possessed strength, speed, and wits in equal measure.

Even then, though, she'd been different from the others. While the biggest of the children tried to overpower and intimidate the others, she understood that true power lay with the pack.

An act of generosity here and a show of compassion there was enough to form the earliest bonds. Grandmother Oak punished her for that, of course.

"The winter is harsh, child," she said. "You cannot suffer the weak to endure. There is no place for them among my chosen."

That night, she and her companions set upon Grandmother Oak's favorite when he fell asleep. They ate his flesh and painted their faces with his blood.

When Grandmother Oak saw what they'd done, she brought them before her and gathered her chosen around them.

"Who is responsible for this?"

She stepped forward and tossed the boy's half-eaten heart at the base of Grandmother Oak's gnarled trunk. "All of us. The pack is stronger together."

A gust of freezing wind rustled Grandmother Oak's branches. "No, child. This is your doing. The others are but followers trailing behind you. They are weak. Without your strength, they are nothing."

The chosen seized the other children and tore out their throats.

"But you... you are not like them. You are the wolf lurking in shadow, waiting for the right moment to strike."

The eldest of the chosen, Raven, stepped forward and held out a bundle of furs wrapped in a tattered, red cloak.

She took them and pulled the cloth open to reveal a wolf's head fashioned into a mask.

"Today," Grandmother Oak said, "you are nameless no longer, child. Now and forever, your name is Wolf."

"Is it dead?"

"Don't know. Looks dead."

"Big fall."

"Missed rocks."

"Trick. Clever, clever."

"Stick it with spear!"

"Don't touch! Don't touch!"

"Take to Grandmother!"

"No! Stupid, stupid. Anger her."

"It's breathing!"

"It moved! It moved!"

Wolf ached all over, like a massive bruise covered every bit of her flesh. But it was a dull pain, and when she rolled onto her back it didn't feel like anything was broken.

She opened her eyes to find a gang of spindly-limbed creatures with silver-speckled eyes gathered around her. Their rough skin was covered with patches of mossy hair, and their mouths were filled with several rows of jagged teeth. Each of them carried a crude spear with a tip fashioned from sharpened flint.

Goblins.

They jumped back when she sat up, a few of the braver ones leveling their spears at her.

"What happened to its head?" one of them whispered.

Wolf reached up to touch her face, but her hand now felt clumsy and heavy. She looked down at her thick gloves, which once felt like a second layer of skin to her.

"Other one took its face," another goblin answered.

"Made Grandmother angry."

"Let's take it back to her!"

"No! Stupid, stupid. Too old."

"Then kill it! Take back head!"

"No! No! Make her angry."

Wolf waved her clawed gloves at the creatures, which caused them to take another step back, trembling.

"Enough!" she said. Her voice sounded strange to her now without her mask.

When was the last time she'd taken it off?

She couldn't even remember.

"Bear and Ram. Did you see where they went?"

The goblins exchanged nervous glances before one of them, smaller than the others, spoke up.

"Went south," it said, gesturing with its spear.

The others glared at it, as if it had just revealed some long-hidden secret of their tribe.

Wolf got to her feet slowly. She unbuckled the straps that kept her gloves attached to her sleeves and pulled them away to reveal her hands. They looked small and soft, almost like those of a child.

"They'll be coming back," she said.

The goblins shuddered and chattered anxiously to one another, too many speaking at once for Wolf to understand.

"Quiet!"

Her voice wasn't nearly as frightening without her mask, but it was stern enough to startle them into silence. Their fear was predictable. Goblins could be found throughout Grandmother Oak's realm, and she despised them like few other creatures. Unlike human trespassers, however, she regarded them as a minor annoyance rather than a genuine threat. She dispatched her chosen to terrorize them and force them to do her bidding. Wolf didn't know how many of them there were, but she guessed there were several more bands like this one roaming the land.

One of the goblins wore a familiar necklace, which it had looped twice around its little neck to keep it from hanging down past its waist.

"You," she said, pointing to the necklace. "Where did you get that?"

The creature gestured toward the steep slope of the gorge. Wolf could see the path she'd left in the snow as she'd tumbled down.

Cautiously, the goblin stepped toward her, removed the necklace, and offered it to her.

"Sorry, sorry," it said.

Wolf took the necklace and inspected the carved pieces again. She scowled when she found the Bear and the Ram, but felt a knot in her stomach when she looked at the depiction of Grandmother Oak.

"Do you know what these are?" she asked.

"Old gods," the goblin said.

"Gone now," another said.

"Not gone, broken."

"Serve Grandmother now."

"How many of your kind have you lost to Grandmother Oak?" Wolf asked.

The goblins didn't answer right away, but then the smallest one spoke up again. "Many. Mothers. Fathers. Children."

"Grandmother is harsh," another said.

"Harsh like winter."

"We are weak."

"Punishes us."

Wolf waved her hand to quiet them. "Grandmother Oak lies. She is frightened. She fears what you might do together. She is old and blind and wicked."

The goblins glanced at each other, some of them lowering their spears and scratching their heads.

"Come on," Wolf said, walking in the direction of the ruined cabin. "Let me show you."

After some hesitation and chittering, the goblins scurried after her.

She found her way back to the cabin without much difficulty. Snow was falling again, covering most of the tracks except for the recent pair headed southward.

If she knew Bear and Ram, they would take the same path back. That would take them up the same winding mountain trail when they returned to Grandmother Oak, including the narrow, rocky pass that required them to walk behind one another.

"Now what?" one of the goblins asked.

"Must go! Danger!"

"Too close to Grandmother."

"Make her angry."

"Send chosen."

Wolf ignored them, instead trudging through the snow and shuffling her feet along the ground until she kicked something. She knelt and brushed away the snow to reveal the woodsman's axe. The metal blade had been sharpened recently and exposure to the wet snow only recently caused a few specks of rust to form.

She picked up the axe and turned to the goblins, who fell silent when they saw what she held in her hands.

"There is a pass up the mountain trail, the fastest way to the summit. We're going to go there and wait for Bear and Ram."

"What then?" a goblin asked.

"We kill them," Wolf said.

The sun had nearly set by the time Bear and Ram reached the pass.

Wolf watched their movements closely. They looked tired from the journey, their shoulders slumped and their feet barely lifting high enough to clear the snow.

Ram carried a wet sack bulging with three round objects, one smaller than the others. Wolf didn't need to look inside to identify the contents. She thought back to the terrified look on the boy's face, to the pleading eyes of his mother, who was wise to the old ways and rightly fearful of Grandmother Oak's wrath.

None of them deserved to die for their transgression. Grandmother Oak could have watched over them and received their offerings, but she was too rigid and deaf to the world and its many creatures. She wanted love and respect yet understood only fear and power.

Bear followed behind Ram. His claws were still bloodied, and he'd tied the wolf's head mask to his belt. No doubt he planned to return it to Grandmother Oak to prove the murder had been carried out. Soon she would gather another batch of wretched children under her roots and pass the mask along to whichever one survived the experience.

The thought of that angered Wolf. She would not let Grandmother Oak pass her poisonous legacy on to another unsuspecting orphan.

When Bear and Ram were about halfway through the rocky pass, Wolf gave the signal.

"Now!"

The goblins cut the cords that held back the logs they'd chopped down earlier in the day, dropping them directly on top of the unsuspecting chosen.

When the last one tumbled down, Wolf and her pack leapt out from their hiding places. One group of goblins stabbed their spears at Ram as he tried to push free of the logs, which kept him occupied while Wolf and the others fell upon Bear.

Wolf swung the axe down with all her strength to cleave into Bear's shoulder before he could push aside the trees pinning him down. While she hacked at him, one of the goblins darted in to snatch the wolf's head mask away from him.

Bear roared and thrashed his free arm around wildly, nearly gutting the scampering thief. But he couldn't stop it from ducking away and tossing the mask to Wolf.

She pulled it over her head and a rush of wild, electric strength coursed through her body. The world around her expanded; she could hear the rustling feathers of the birds overhead and smell the wet ash from the burned cabin in the valley below.

Bear became frantic now, desperately trying to push the heavy logs away, but the goblins kept jabbing at him with their spears to hamper his efforts.

Wolf stomped down on his free arm to pin it to the ground. She raised the axe high above her head and brought it down with all her renewed might to separate Bear's head from his body with one mighty stroke. His limbs went on twitching as she turned to confront Ram.

He'd managed to work his upper body free and seize two of the goblins. Wolf braced her legs and flung the axe at him. The blade struck him squarely in the chest, burying most of its metal head into his ribcage. She bounded over as he fell backward, coughing up blood. The goblins pinned his arms to the ground to hold him while Wolf ripped away his mask.

The face underneath was young, not much older than the boy he and Bear had ruthlessly hunted down.

Wolf grabbed the bag he'd been carrying and dumped the contents over him. Three heads rolled over his bloody chest and came to rest next to his.

"Please..." he said.

"Mercy? You should know better than to turn your back on a wounded wolf and its pack. But you're nothing but a stubborn sheep thinking only of its own stomach and doing whatever it's told without question. That makes you weak. And there's no place for the weak in the pack."

She looked to the goblins gathered around with their spears. Only a few of them dared to look upon her now that she'd donned her mask again.

"Put this wretched thing out of its misery."

The snow was coming down harder near the peak of the mountain.

Wolf knew Grandmother Oak's bitter roots would detect her footsteps well before she reached the summit.

The old spirit's brittle voice carried over the wind. "Wolf. You have returned."

If that fact troubled Grandmother Oak, she gave no indication of it.

Wolf reached the clearing at the summit and stood before

Grandmother Oak, who towered above her with the same stern, unchanging presence as ever before. How long she had been there, no one knew. Perhaps she was truly as old as the world itself, as she claimed.

But Wolf doubted that.

Grandmother Oak was ancient, but she was petty, vain, bitter, and full of deceit.

"Where are Bear and Ram?" she asked.

Slowly, Wolf approached her great trunk, stepping between the thick roots protruding from the frozen ground. "They sought to carry out your will, dearest Grandmother."

She took the sack hanging from her belt and emptied it over Grandmother Oak's roots, sending Bear and Ram's heads tumbling to the ground.

A gust of chilling wind swept over the summit.

"You think this proves your worth, child?" Grandmother Oak said. "These two are nothing. You are nothing, you faithless cur. There is no place you will be able to hide from my vengeance, no escape from the winter of your doom."

The goblins reached the end of the long trail behind Wolf. They gasped, shrieked, and howled at the dreadful sight of Grandmother Oak.

Another gust of wind lashed at them, throwing up a cloud of snow and ice.

Grandmother Oak laughed. "You think to strike some bargain on their behalf now? How low this petty sentimentality has brought you."

"No, Grandmother," Wolf said. "I didn't come back here to bargain with you."

She held out the necklace.

"There was balance here once. Everything in harmony. Until you decided to take it all for yourself. Isn't that right?"

Grandmother Oak snarled. "What do you know of it, child? The petty ambitions of petty spirits that fashioned themselves as gods of these witless mortals? None of them understood true power, not until I took it from them and bound it to my will."

Wolf nodded. "I understand, Grandmother. You taught me that much, at least."

She reached back and drew out the axe from where she'd tucked it beneath her cloak.

Grandmother Oak hissed as Wolf approached. "No! Stay back! I command you!"

Wolf swung the axe, driving the cold, iron blade into Grandmother Oak's great trunk. An ear-splitting shriek filled the air as thick, yellowish sap oozed from the wound.

"Stop! Stop!"

She swung again, widening the gash and forcing the axe deeper inside. The ground shook as Grandmother Oak's roots trembled.

"Please, child! No more!"

Wolf remembered how it felt dangling from the cliff while Bear and Ram stared down at her. She thought of the chosen slaughtering her first pack so many years ago on this very spot, of the helpless family that strayed too far into a bitter old spirit's realm.

She drew the axe back, thick globs of sap dripping from the iron blade.

"The winter has no mercy for the weak, Grandmother."

Wolf swung the axe again and again, hacking and chopping at the trunk until Grandmother Oak could do nothing more than whimper, her voice faint and pathetic on the wind.

Then the great tree creaked and groaned, unable to support its own weight any longer.

After one last, mighty blow of the axe, Grandmother Oak collapsed, crashing to the ground in a shattered mass of broken limbs. The wind died down, and an eerie silence fell over the mountain.

Wolf buried the axe as deeply as she could in what remained of the stump, driving it in almost to the handle.

She turned to the cowering goblins. "Leave this here. Let no one remove it, lest her power might find some way to return once more."

The goblins dropped their spears and groveled before her as she approached.

"Get up," she said. "The rest of her chosen still prowl the land. We will find them. Then, they will either turn their back on their dead Grandmother or they will join her in death."

They followed Wolf away from the fallen tree and into the darkness of the winter night.

# A Forever Winter

By Arwyn Sherman

"TELL ME AGAIN the story about the Snow Queen." Clara puts the hood of her cloak up, trying to block out the chill from the loose window. Her auburn curls poke out from the brown canvas and glitter in the light of the lone candle. Crude dark stitches line the hood.

Roan laughs, leans back into the pile of furs on his side of the room, and puts his hands behind his head. They're in the attic, a room they've shared since they were first taken to the warden. Two small kids jostled together with nothing in common but missing parents and a fear of the cold. They grew into the small space that was theirs, filled it up with gangly teenage limbs and whispered late-night stories. Clara's favorite was the tale of the Snow Queen.

"You know that one." Roan rolls his eyes. But it's all part of the game, the nightly ritual. The storyteller must be coaxed out, must feign disdain until the proper amount of begging has occurred.

"Please, Roan." Clara plays her part, bringing her safflower mittens together as if about to pray. "You tell it so well."

"Okay fine." Roan smiles, a glittering flash in the dim light.

*Many, many years ago, long before our parents, or even our parents' parents, were born, there used to be four seasons. Springtime, where everything rises from the mud and becomes vibrant. Summer, with its endlessly hot days and water-filled lakes. Autumn's brown leaves and cool mornings. And winter, the only season we know now. Which I don't have to describe, because we all know it well.*

*One day, on the very coldest night, a girl was born. No one knew it at the time, but she was born with the magic of winter in her. From her very fingertips, she could conjure ice, wind, and snow; anything that froze and was cold. Her village didn't understand her and was afraid; such is the way of most folk.*

*She was exiled when she grew up and could no longer hide. Hopeless, she went to the royal court for mercy and shelter. The king was immediately besotted with her beauty and asked her to marry him. The night before the wedding, she revealed her snow magic to him, wanting their matrimony to be based on honesty. She hoped he would respond kinder than her kin did. But the king cast her out and vowed to kill her if she ever returned. When she left, the king realized the danger he set forth and sent huntsmen to kill her. Instead of their return, a cold winter set upon the land and never turned to spring. They say it is the Snow Queen's punishment, and no autumn fire magic will undo the curse she has laid upon us.*

Clara sighs contentedly and pulls her knit blanket around her, settling into the bedding on the floor. Roan holds his hand out and the flame of the candle sinks into darkness.

"Was that good enough where you'll leave me alone?" he jokes, and she can hear the smile in his voice.

"Do you think the Snow Queen is still alive?"

"I don't think the Snow Queen ever existed."

"Then what about the seasons? How do we know they existed?"
"Because they exist elsewhere. But this is a kingdom of ice."

2

*Winter magic* is what they call it, the ability to call the frigid season into your fingertips. To cast it out into the world and make everything ice. Roan has autumn magic, bringing fire to his palm with a muted snap of his fingers. If the warden knew, he would send Roan to fight in the King's army and probably make a nice coin off the exchange. So, it is Clara and Roan's secret they keep together. Clara has winter buried deep inside her, coaxing icicles out of nothing and sending wind anywhere she wants.

This is Clara's secret that she keeps to herself.

Clara gains another secret when she is mopping the stone hallway on another frigid night, the moonlight guiding her movements. The warden is in the kitchen with his wife, his voice carrying out the partially open door. A chunk of light like a cut of cheese comes from the kitchen, interrupting the quiet dark of the hall.

"That girl is getting right up to marrying age." The warden's voice, low and gruff, creeps out of the room like an unwelcome rat. Clara stills upon hearing herself mentioned.

"Oh, surely not for a few more years," his wife says, timid as always. Clara can almost see her fretfully smoothing her dress as she speaks, her voice a soprano whisper.

Clara leans the mop as quietly as she can against the wall and slips over to the door to hear better. She stands against the wall, head tilted as close as possible to the entryway.

"Every day we keep her we lose money. I have someone interested, a soldier who came by a few weeks ago and took a little fancy to her."

"She does work for us. She's not a complete waste."

"Bah, barely enough to warrant the food we give her. And he's willing to pay us."

"Are you sure you can't wait another year? It is nice to have her for the potatoes."

"Woman, you don't know anything about keeping house. Let me be. The soldier gets her. He's coming in a few days to collect."

His wife is silent, as always. A battle barely fought and already lost. Clara holds a hand to her mouth, the rough yarn of her mittens pressing against her lips, the smell of nightshade and dirt still heavy on them. She thinks about leaving her little attic room, her talks with Roan, even the digging job she's assigned to, and her chest closes up. She can feel the need to cry, but it's almost as if her tears are as scared as she is, hovering at the back of her eyes. She slips away, making sure to put the mop and bucket back in the closet to hide that she was ever there.

If she is going to escape, they must not know she heard their plans. And escape she will, no matter what the cost.

3

She waits until Roan is asleep before untangling herself from her blankets. It's been two days since she heard the warden talking to his wife, and every passing hour she can feel the breath of this mystery soldier against her neck, a haunting specter that lurks in every stray thought. She thought about telling Roan, asking him for help, but every time she played that thought out in her mind, she only saw him giving up more for her than she was willing to ask of him.

He's blissful now, looking childish in his deep slumber, mouth slightly open, eyes covered by dark hair, the moonlight glowing against his umber skin. She pulls on thick leggings and a thick cotton slip before getting into her loose canvas dress she sewed from worn potato sacks. The stitches are dark and obvious, much like her cloak, which she puts on after slipping on her one sweater the warden's wife gifted her out of pity. It's cashmere, cream-colored with small, soft rose swirls embroidered at the neck.

Night is the coldest hours, dropping into a dangerous and windy freeze. Although Clara knows having winter magic makes her more resilient to it, she knows she is not fully immune, the speck of frostbite on her right pinky a permanent reminder of that.

Her thickly knitted socks are quiet against the wood floor as she takes the ladder slowly to not make noise. A quick survey to make sure the warden has not awakened, and then she is gone, slipping through the loose window and fleeing to the woods. A tiny speck against the dark night, becoming smaller and smaller until she is nothing at all. A darkness within the darkness, a body swallowed by the woods.

Clara's plan is simple—walk through the forest to the bustling inner kingdom. There, in the city, she is sure there is an inn that needs a maid or a blacksmith wanting a shopgirl. Somewhere she can tuck herself into and remain unmarried for as long as she wants. It wasn't the safest life, but it was something better than what was coming for her.

The length of the woods is unknown; some say it's infinite, others claim it's a mere mile. Clara hopes it's closer to the latter as she tromps through the tall snow. It's the light fluffy kind that sinks under her weight, making it double the effort to move forward.

Everything is quiet, save the occasional hunting cry of an owl and thump when a tree relieves itself of a clump of snow on its branches. Clara can taste the chill on her chapped lips, the air from every exhale sucking more warmth out of her. She continues to walk, the white fluff grabbing at her boots, weighing them down with every step. Misjudges her step and ends up in a deep patch, her foot sinking into oblivion, the snow coming up to her thigh. Clara falls with a soft *ooof,* the chill biting her cheek as she slips into the snow, the taste of dirt and melting water in her mouth. She can feel the snow rolling into her boots from the top, like icicle fingers running down her legs and pooling around her feet.

She sits up and turns, sinks deeper into the snow, which circles around her waist like a frigid lover's hug. When she tries to stand, the snow weighs her back down, pulls her into the ground until she's sprawled out helplessly. Looks up at the pinpoint stars, the sliced moon. Their light echoes enough off her breath so it looks like a half cloud rising from her lips.

What she wouldn't give for Roan and his ability to craft fire from nothing. She closes her eyes tightly and wills this thought away with only a single tear escaping. Every abled man in the city is drafted to the King's army, unless they have a coveted apprenticeship. There wouldn't be any opportunities for an orphan like him. If she had asked, he would have gone with her. But she would never forgive herself if he were discovered and drafted. The minute anyone is enlisted, it's a slow march to death in foreign lands.

Time passes. She becomes aware that she's losing touch in her fingers; her feet feel absent and heavy. Tries to clench her fist and feels like she's squeezing a lump of cloth. With a deep breath, she forces herself to sit up, then rolls to her knees and tries to stand. Her feet are foreign under her, blank from cold and unresponsive to her commands. She falls again, her hand catching her as she crashes back into the white powder.

A slow, ugly thought creeps into her mind. Uglier than regretting not bringing Roan. That the city may be too far away, that she may become a frozen corpse, hidden by layers and layers of endless winter. She would cry, but the exhaustion weighs her down and makes any strong reaction impossible. Instead, she sighs and contemplates how nice a nap would be, how she probably wouldn't feel that cold if she went to sleep.

Clara hears her first, a soft melody like a chorus of birds singing. So quiet she thinks she may be hearing a funeral song. Then she sees a small light, a few moments before realizing the woman isn't holding any lantern, but rather *is* the light, her skin so translucent it reflects off the snow. Her blonde hair is the color of sunrise at the very brink of dawn, the beige tendrils when the beginnings of the day are barely cresting night. The woman wears it in an impressive array of braids that circle her head like a crown; bits of gold spiral and jewels flicker with every turn of her head.

Her silk dress crunches as she kneels beside Clara, close enough where she can see the intricate gold embroidery along the edges. She smells of holly berries and fir, her hand warm against Clara's frozen cheeks.

"Oh, dear one," the woman murmurs. "You must come with me."

Before Clara can force her mouth to form words, she is scooped up and taken to a gilded sleigh pulled by two smoky-gray horses. She's wrapped in furs until she can barely see over them. The beautiful woman climbs in after her and gives her a tight-lipped smile.

"Who are you?" Clara finally musters the energy to ask as the woman clicks to her horses and the sled begins to pick up speed, the trees flashing past her in blurs of brown.

"I'm the Snow Queen," the woman says passively and gives Clara a look that can only be described as devilish. Even though she knows she should be scared, she feels a deep thrill of excitement as the sled barrels forward into the night.

4

The room is too quiet when Roan wakes, absent of Clara's usual mumbling and morning protests. The sun breaks through the window, casting light on an empty space where Clara should be. In their entire childhood together, she's never woken before him, and this space of empty blankets and furs unsettles him.

In the kitchen, there's no sign of Clara. Her mug and allotted slice of bread still sit on the table, waiting for her appearance as much as Roan is.

The warden hasn't noticed she's gone yet. It's not unusual for her to come downstairs after Roan. If Clara isn't here, and she's not upstairs, then she is somewhere that she probably shouldn't be. This realization turns the unsettled feeling in his stomach sour, the tea he's drinking curdling at the back of his throat.

The warden's wife looks directly at Roan, her blue eyes holding his in a way that's unusual for her normal meek demeanor. When the warden isn't looking, she takes Clara's mug and bread and walks out of the kitchen with a long, pointed stare at Roan that he interprets as a sign to follow. A few beats later, he does, slipping out of the house. The snow crunches under his feet as he makes his way past the greenhouse, along the wall, looking for the warden's wife.

She's tucked away in a small recess between the house and a shed. The smell of wet soil is heavy as he steps into the dark and skinny corridor. He can see her breath, faintly smelling of cream and lavender.

"He hasn't noticed she's gone," the wife whispers, "But I did; she left at high moon last night."

"Why didn't you stop her?" Roan says, a little too sharply for who he's speaking to.

"And do what? Force her back? You know, the warden is going to sell her off for marriage by the end of the week. She must of heard him talking about it."

Clara hadn't mentioned any of this to him, and there's a small prick of hurt that she kept this information from him. The wife pushes the staling piece of bread into his hands.

"She's probably already dead," the wife whispers. "You have a few hours before my husband figures it out. It might be good to make yourself scarce until he calms down; you know how he gets."

"I have to go after her," Roan says. "She might be in trouble."

"It's no use, you'll just get yourself killed."

"I still have to try."

The warden's wife doesn't have a response. Her large eyes just look sad as Roan turns away, walks to the back where he keeps his sled. He throws the wooden contraption over his shoulders as he crunches through the icy snow towards the woods. He knows when he returns the warden will be mad that he spent the day looking for Clara instead of working, but whenever he pauses to think about her, all he can imagine is the worst. Broken bones, stuck in a ravine, frozen. Clara, bent and irreparably cracked apart.

His pace quickens at this thought until he's practically running through the thick snow, the powder surging against his trousers like water against the bow of a ship. When he crests a hill, he throws his sled down in one fluid motion and jumps on, holding the rickety wood handles as it gathers speed. He looks at his surroundings as he barrels downward, trying to see her brown cloak, the small red cap she sometimes wears.

He is a blur through the forest, calling out Clara's name as he glides across the forest floor until he bottoms out at a plateau, coming to rest against a large evergreen. He leans against its girthy trunk and sighs, giving the area a glance over and finding nothing but green pines and snow.

A small crow hops his way to him, one foot touching the snow before quickly changing to the other. Its obsidian feathers glint in the mid-morning sun, its eyes dark but intelligent.

"Have you seen my friend, little one?" Roan asks, even though the likelihood that this is a talking animal is fairly low.

The creature proves probability is not in Roan's favor as it softly caws and cocks its head so one eye is directly upon him, but says nothing. It reaches its wings out as if to stretch them, shaking and reshuffling his feathers. Returns them to their usual spot, and gives himself another puff before settling in to stare at Roan.

He takes the bread meant for Clara out of his pocket and tears off a small piece, tossing it to the critter. She often feeds the birds with her morning slice, and he feels she would appreciate him offering the creature something.

It hops towards the bread, inspects it with one beady eye before snapping it up off the snow. Gives Roan an expectant stare. He laughs in spite of himself and offers it another bite, which the crow eagerly takes.

"The girl," it creaks, beak up to the sky as if forming words is a monumental effort, "the girl with the dark golden hair."

"Yes, yes that's her." Roan jumps into a crouch and looks at the now-talking crow. "Have you seen her?"

"Such lovely hair." Its voice sounds like a poorly played flute, windy and barely there. "Wanted to take some for my nest, like fine jewelry or nice roasted wheat."

"Is she okay? Where did you see her?"

"Snow Queen took her, wrapped her up like a present. To the castle she goes." The crow then lets out a large caw and flies for a few beats, sending its small body a foot or so into the air before settling down.

"The Snow Queen doesn't exist," Roan sighs.

"Yes, she does!" Another hop, "Yes, she does! And your friend is with her."

"Where?"

"The castle!"

"Where is her castle?" Roan's voice is hollow, not particularly trusting this crow and its stories.

"Go to the end of the woods," it croaks, "Take the road east. I will meet you when the sun rises."

Roan gives the crow the rest of Clara's bread. Before he was orphaned, his mother had told him that one must always be polite to talking animals. He wasn't going to turn his back on that now, even if she wasn't around to remind him. The crow jumps to the stray crumbs and snaps them up, giving Roan a perfunctory nod before leaping into the still winter air.

Another sigh, deeper this time. He stands. With nothing else but a crow's word, he decides his best course of action is to try and find the road it spoke of and go from there.

He brushes the snow off his trousers and sets off towards the end of the forest.

5

Now that the morning light was upon them and Clara was no longer on the brink of freezing, she could appreciate that the Snow Queen was incredibly beautiful. Sharp cheekbones and unfettered skin, her eyes sparkling like polished sapphires. Even amongst the brutish, hacked forest covered in snow, she is elegant. Her posture is like that of a true queen—straight and rigid. Her horses are equally regal, like puffs of smoke rearing in the frosty sun. Just looking at her makes Clara's heart beat uncomfortably fast, her palms sweating in foreign discomfort.

They ride in silence, the sled slipping smoothly and silently across the forest. Clara regards the Snow Queen with wide eyes and briefly wonders if she's died and this is just a very pleasant afterlife. How often had she wished for an incredibly alluring woman to whisk her away from her farm life drudgery? Too often to count, and now, here she is.

"You're not dead," the queen speaks, as if reading her mind, "you have that stunned look about you people get when they think they've crossed over. I promise this is not the afterlife."

"Do you often put people in the position where they think they've perished?"

"Ah." The Snow Queen smiles, her lips a deep red. "Normally they have, indeed, crossed over and I am not in the position to tell them otherwise."

"I see." Clara sinks deeper into the plush furs surrounding her, "In that case, where are you taking me?"

"My castle. It isn't much longer."

 90

Clara doesn't have a response, decides to take in the scenery they're riding through. She isn't sure why the Snow Queen has spared her, but isn't going to test her luck by getting annoying and asking too many questions.

A few minutes of silence later and the castle is upon them. They come to the large, ornate gates with golden swirls and opal inlay. The stone glints like a fresh snow cover, twinkling as the sled descends to the front. The horses whinny, their hooves prancing impatiently beside the glittering wall.

The Snow Queen lifts her right hand, her left clutching the reins, and unfurls her fingers. A ring of rainbow, the kind Clara used to catch against the wall when she played with the glass wind chimes her mother owned, splays outward. The air itself seems to shimmer before a gust of frigid wind blows through the gate and pushes it open. Once they are inside, she does a similar motion to blow them closed.

The courtyard is quiet, the sound of the horses' clopping along the cobblestones the only noise as they roll towards the castle. Gardens flourish around them—vibrant apples ripe for plucking hang heavy off trees, a bursting greenery of squash and beans. The air is pleasant and warm, an unknown feeling to Clara, who gets feverish and quickly sheds her furs.

"It's not winter here," she says as she looks up at the trees that explode with fruit.

"No, it never is."

"How?"

"I make the winter, and where I desire, I can make the absence of it, too."

"Then why make the rest of the kingdom a forever winter?"

"To punish them, of course." The Snow Queen clucks her tongue to still her horses. She steps out of the sled and offers Clara her hand, which she accepts, and allows herself to be guided to the ground.

The door to the castle is heavy oak, with rusted bolts and well-oiled hinges keeping it together. It's larger than both of them and shadows the entire front step. Despite its size, the Snow Queen pushes it easily inwards. Takes Clara's hand and leads her into a long hallway lined by floor-to-ceiling shelves. A long, red carpet runs down the length of it, and Clara makes sure to step carefully to not muss it up.

"Is there a name I can call you, unless you prefer Snow Queen?" Clara steps over a wrinkle in the rug.

"Elise," she says simply, "but only when we're alone and never in public."

"Okay... Elise. Why did you rescue me?"

"You're so full of questions, little one, aren't you?" Elise laughs and it sounds like a million little bells chiming at the same time.

She stops and whirls Clara so she's facing her. Reaches out and places a hand on Clara's heart. Even through her thick cloak she can feel the pressure, the warmth. Her heart is out of control, her lungs folding in on themselves until she can barely breathe.

"Because." Elise smiles. "You have the same magic as me."

6

Roan spots the main road as he breaks from the tree line of the forest. A swath of cleared snow that's turned to mud. He tries to pull his sled along behind him but it soon gets stuck, hiccupping over the rocks and sticky soil. He tries to carry it on his back, but after a few miles that becomes too much of a burden. Eventually, as his shoulders creak and neck pops with each step, he admits to himself that he must leave it behind. Finds a tree that's been split by lightning and tucks it into the empty space where the trunk parted.

Roan's chest restricts as he turns away from his sled. He swallows unexpected tears that spring to his eyes. The sled was the last vestige of his life before the warden, and watching it lay there, soon to be abandoned, twists a shard of grief that is buried deep in his heart. He remembers his mother giving it to him, her cheeks rosy and flushed, eyes filled with pride as he took it outside and flew down the hill by their cottage. And now it is nothing more than a chunk of wood nestled in the crook of a dead tree. Roan forces himself to take a breath and push his distress down until his face is placid.

Roan walks until the sun starts to set; the road alight with light orange like stained glass. He looks back as if he can track the starting point of his journey, how far he's come. Sees only his set of footprints squelched in the mud. When Roan turns back, he is stopped by a man standing in the middle of the road. He's large and brutish, covered in grime and soot. Old furs cling to his body, held together with waxed twine and luck, a large sanded club in one hand and a knife in the other.

The moment Roan stops, he is surrounded. Everyone in the group appears like the first man, unwashed and filthy like they've slept in the mud. All of them have weapons, some sharpened wood spears, others antiquated guns with rust that blooms like wisteria vines along the edges.

The man gives Roan a blackened smile and proclaims, "In case you haven't figured it out, you're being robbed."

"I don't have any money," Roan says.

"Well, that is just too bad," the man says, his gut giving a slight bounce as he grabs Roan's arm. "We don't have much use for penniless folks on the road here."

"Wait." A girl steps into the circle, leading a spotted horse behind her. She looks related to the man, same brown hair, dark feral eyes that hop around like they're constantly assessing the world. She has a singular, thick braid that comes around her shoulder and hangs to her waist, a dress of crudely stitched furs and canvas. She points a slender finger at Roan and states, "I would like him."

"Daughter, we can't just keep everyone ya fancy," the man sighs and turns to the crew.

"I would *really* like him," the girl says loudly before her father can speak again.

The man groans, gives Roan an eye roll as if to say, *daughters, what can you do,* and waves his hand at the rest of the crew, dismissing them.

"I guess we're taking you," he says, and Roan can only nod.

Roan rides with the robber girl. The crew move as one through the woods, abandoning the main roads and going into the depths of the forest. At first, Roan tries to not touch the girl, but eventually the ride gets too bumpy and he wraps his arm around her waist. The patches of fur feel smooth against his wrist, her canvas-covered shoulders scratchy against his face. She smells surprisingly pleasant, like wood smoke and berries.

"You'll like it here," she says. "It's not so bad; we have a good cave that you can keep dry in."

Roan nods, unable to speak. Even though he's behind her, she seems to accept his response and reaches back, slowly stroking his jaw with her hand.

"I'm looking for my friend," he manages to stutter out.

"That's too bad." The robber girl shrugs, her whole body rolling with her shoulders. "You're one of us now. Which means you aren't going anywhere."

7

The dining hall has high dark ceilings with painted stars that twinkle like the actual night sky. A long table made of dark wood takes up the length of the room, a single centerpiece filled with candles sits in the middle but is otherwise bare. There's a warm fire that burbles softly at the head of the room.

Clara tries her best not to stare as she walks in, the soft warmth coming over her in gentle waves with every step. Elise comes up beside her, a brief hand on the small of her back that sends trills up her spine.

"I'll teach you," Elise says, "your magic. You've kept it hidden, no?"

Clara nods, her cheeks reddening at Elise's soft cluck of disapproval.

"It's okay." She takes Clara's chin in her hand. "You had to survive."

Clara nods again and her heart swells with the Snow Queen's touch. She doesn't know how long she's been at the castle. It feels like forever, basking in the eternal spring and pining after the frigid but kind queen. They spend every moment together, Clara laying across the lounge couch as Elise reads her fairy tales, gathering lush vegetables from the garden plots, dining on fancy meals her invisible staff makes.

"Winter is in your heart, and all you have to do is call upon it to do your bidding. It will become your dearest friend—and the closer your heart is to it, the more you will be able to do."

Clara unconsciously puts her hand on her chest when the Snow Queen speaks. Can feel her unruly heart beating under her palm, always quick and erratic whenever she's near Elise.

"Here." Elise guides them to sit on the bench by the long table, takes a metal goblet filled with water and sets it by Clara. "Ask it to become ice."

Clara stares at the tepid water rolling against the side from the momentum of being put down. A single ruby inlay beams on the side like the center of a sun. She stares at the liquid and thinks as hard as she can, begs it to become firm, to harden upon itself like clenching fists until it's immutable ice. A small film appears across the top, spider cracks throughout. Clara asks it to become colder, harder. It tightens slightly but does not go farther than the first inch of water.

"A lovely beginning." Elise claps her hands in delight. "You'll be powerful in no time."

"I fear offending, but I have a question," Clara says.

"Go ahead with it."

"I don't mean any harm, but what's the point of keeping the kingdom in eternal winter? It is a rough life to live in."

"To punish the King." Elise wraps a strand of Clara's hair in her finger and whirls it into a curl. "For banishing me when I needed help."

"That was centuries ago, the King is long dead."

"But his heirs remain. And so shall the winter until the last of them die."

"And the rest of us? That have to live with muted lives?"

Elise shrugs. "Revenge always has a cost."

"One you're not paying," Clara snaps before she can think twice. Elise gives her a sharp look, and Clara swallows in fear.

"Tell me." The Snow Queen's lips curl in disdain. "Do you love the King so much you'd fault me for destroying his corrupt system?"

Clara thinks about the castle that sits to the west, the vibrant balls run by unpaid labor. The legions of captured boys playing soldier to gain more land that quickly succumbs to winter. Her own lack of choice, being trapped between playing servant or being married off. The drudgery of surviving in the hard corners of the world. She looks at Elise, her eyes hard and fiery as if she can watch Clara's thoughts cascade downwards.

"The winter affects everyone, though," she whispers half-heartedly.

Elise leans into Clara, her lips grazing her ear. "If you want spring, then make sure the line of King Eljred is dead."

Clara turns her face so her lips brush Elise's and, overcome with the intoxicating smell of berries and fir, kisses Elise softly.

"I could do that," she says without thinking, only imagining the bliss of finally seeing a warm sun.

Elise kisses her again, her thick eyelashes fluttering against Clara's cheeks.

"We could," she says, "together."

## 8

The robber girl has an oversized goat that is almost as large as the horse she stole from the nobles. She ties both of them up at a wooden post at the mouth of the cave carved into the mountain. Roan follows her to a spot at the far end, piled in furs and a quilted blanket. The girl plops down and takes some flint, tries to spark her lantern into bearing light. After a few unsuccessful attempts, Roan leans over and touches a flame onto the wick.

"Autumn magic." The robber girl grins. "I knew there was a reason I liked you."

"It's a secret." Roan brings a finger up to his lip and smiles conspiratorially, though he knows robbers are less likely to talk to recruiters of the army than he is.

"Cross my heart," the girl giggles delightedly. "We're going to have so much fun."

Roan's heart skips a beat, a memory of Clara dancing in his mind as the robber girl pulls him into the lump of cloth. She curls up on her side and Roan mirrors her so they are face to face.

"You know I have magic, too," she whispers.

"Oh yeah? What's that?"

"I can make anything I want return to me."

"Really?"

"Robber magic." Her grin glints in the firelight. "My goat? No matter where it goes, it will come back the minute it is able."

"Impressive," Roan says, and the girl seems to blush at his approval.

They sit in silence for a while. Roan can feel the girl contemplating every curve of his face, the way the firelight dances across his angular nose.

"I have a deal," he says.

"A deal? I do love those."

"You want me to stay here. And—" he swallows before lying, "—I want to stay here, too. But I would be happier if I knew my friend was okay. What if I took your goat and found her, and that way I could return to you once I was done."

The robber girl turns so she's laying on her back and takes a few moments to think. A deep sigh turns into a softer one before she sits up.

"Under one condition."

"Which is?"

"You must kiss me first."

Roan startles and isn't sure what to make of her proposal. She is pretty enough, even with the mud smeared across her delicate nose and splattering of freckles. He wouldn't mind kissing her, if he's completely honest. Especially if it would get him to Clara. The robber girl looks at him expectantly.

He leans in and grazes her lips. She runs her fingers through his hair and pulls him into her, pressing into his soft lips. She tastes like maple syrup and ginger. Before he can fully register what's happening, she's pulled away with a wry smile.

"Go then," she shoos him, "take my goat. Remember to return to me."

Roan nods and gets up, forces himself to take a few steps before running to the head of the cave. The goat looks perplexed as he unties it, letting out a soft, sleepy *baaaa* as Roan leads it away. He almost feels bad for not planning on returning.

The crow swoops in and lets out a victorious *CAW*.

"I thought you were stuck forever!" it cries.

"You're here," Roan laughs joyously, "I thought I'd seen the last of you."

"Never! I lead you to the queen!"

And in the night, the crow flies just above Roan, guiding him and the unfortunate goat through the winding hillside until they reach the same ornate gates that he can only imagine Clara once stood before.

"How do I get up there?" Roan looks up, defeated.

"I take you," the crow says, grabbing the shoulders of Roan's coat in either claw.

Roan didn't think it was possible, but the crow lifts him to the very height of the wall, where his stomach turns at the sight of how far up they are, and gently brings him down. At this point, the goat trots off, figuring it is no longer needed.

He barely notices the gardens, or the trees, as he runs towards the castle.

"Clara!" he calls out, "Clara I'm here."

Instead of Clara, though, he runs into the Snow Queen, who emerges onto the veranda from inside. She towers over Roan, who stumbles back to behold her. Tall and menacing, in a long silk robe the color of grayed snow and starlight. The small quartz pieces in her hair sparkle as she takes the steps down to the garden. Roan's mouth goes dry and he tries to swallow as she approaches.

Clara appears behind him and visibly brightens at seeing Roan. She runs past the queen to him with her arms out and they embrace.

"It's been such a journey," he weeps, "but you're here. And alive."

"How did you manage to trespass into my land?" the Snow Queen's voice is cold.

Roan goes to point to the crow but, being the smart creature it is, has made itself scarce.

"I do not like trespassers," the queen says and slowly takes her front steps one by one until she's in front of Roan.

"I-I apologize," Roan stammers, "I had only a mind to make sure Clara was safe."

"She's perfectly fine."

"I see that. Thank you for caring for her."

"Please don't hurt him." Clara turns to the Snow Queen, fear visible in her eyes.

The Snow Queen doesn't acknowledge Clara's plea, raises her hand, and unleashes a blizzard. The icy gusts push Clara back, her face hit by the chill as she stumbles into the tomatoes. The grass at the edge of the walkway wilts under the unexpected cold.

Roan's eyes are wide as he looks at the impending storm charging his way. His autumn magic erupts from inside him unbidden, the force of survival overcoming any other instinct. At the last moment, Roan is able to throw up a wall of fire, so hot the mint plants he is beside begin to curl and die. The blizzard melts around him, turns into wet soil at his feet. He faces the Snow Queen, his breath gusting in pants that are visible as they hit the cold air. Positions himself with his palms out to prepare for another strike.

Clara runs to Elise and throws her arms around her neck, whispering every frantic plea she can think of, dissolving into sobs. The Snow Queen looks to her, then meets Roan's gaze with hardened eyes.

"Autumn magic always succumbs to winter," she says, "but I have distressed my precious Clara enough. I will take one thing from you, then let you leave."

Roan is too scared to ask what she means and remains still as she detangles herself from Clara, walks to him and places a hand on his forehead.

"In my time of isolation, I've learned many types of magic," she says, "including the magic of memory."

By the time her palms have left his skin, Roan has no recollection of Clara.

He looks at the two women, confused, not sure how he ended up in this strange palace. One of the women screams, a painful wail that makes him run from the grounds in terror. The large gate blows open as he reaches it and before he can think twice, he's running through the forest.

Back to the robber girl. Because she, too, had placed some of her magic in him.

# 9

Clara turns to Elise, her face contorted with tears and rage. A slight wind picks up, pushing through her hair like a caress. She doesn't know if it's Elise's magic or a natural current which enrages her further.

"You stole him from me," she screams, "he was my best friend and you took him."

"I had to."

"No, you didn't! You don't have to do any of this, and yet you insist on it. Because you're *selfish*," Clara spits the last word out in disgust.

Elise's eyes are wide and, for the first time since Clara met her, she appears at a loss for words. She reaches out fruitlessly, but Clara is gone, running towards the forest with a forlorn cry.

By the time she is out of the gates, which are still blown open, there is no sign of Roan. Just a thick wave of snow and evergreen. She pauses and surveys the landscape, eyes squinting against the reflection of the sun off the white, rolling hills.

"Roan!" she screams, but only hears her echo and nothing more.

She begins to run again, unbeknownst to her in the opposite direction of her friend. She runs until the woods become unfamiliar. The land warms, and she stumbles into a small square of lush greenery and warmth.

A patch of spring. An apology.

# How the Sea Witch Lost Her Heart
### By J. D. Trebmal

## CHAPTER 1
## LILJA

WHEN THE TIDE WENT OUT, Lilja stepped down on the ice to test its strength. No cracking. Perfect. The wind rushed over the frozen harbor and cooled her face as she sawed through the ice. She had chosen a spot near a small bluff on the shore to cut the hole. Here there would be room underneath to enter the dark cavern created when the water rolled back to the ocean on this Jultide, the lowest of low tides. It only happened once a year, on the winter solstice.

Moonlight illuminated the vast sheet of ice like a silver lake, hiding the receding water below. "Tovin would never be this brave," she muttered.

She discarded her saw on the upper beach and slipped into the hole, careful not to crack the edge of the suspended sheet as she passed through it. Beneath, the whistle of wind was gone, replaced by dripping echoes. The air was pungent with seaweed and ocean creatures. She wrinkled her nose and tried not to gag. A chill seeped through her clothes. Something ominous and mystical. Lilja pulled her wool cloak tight around her, tugging on the reindeer-hide belt she'd won from Tovin yesterday.

Her playmate had lost the fancy belt to her in a game of Bones and Shells. They weren't supposed to play games of chance. Only grown-ups were allowed to gamble. But Tovin had smuggled out his father's set and Lilja wasn't one to turn down an opportunity or a scheme.

Today's scheme, or opportunity, depending on how one looked at it, included gathering mussels from below the ice, a practice that had been outlawed during her grandparents' generation. Too many harvesters had not returned to the surface before the tide came in.

Lilja knew how long to stay under, though, and she was not afraid. The ice would not break today. It was as strong as her resolve. The village festival would start soon, at midday, for a few hours as the sun slid across the horizon. She was determined to bring the most mussels to the contest and win her family their own reindeer pack. Pappa's chest would swell so large his tunic would split. Mamma would be furious at Lilja for going under the ice, but she would forgive her after she won.

Lilja pulled a candlestick and match from her tunic pocket. She wedged the candle between some rocks and lit it, its flame dancing and casting shadows in every direction.

Sea lettuce drooped flat and soggy against the sharp boulders in the sand. Along the crevices, mussels lined the cracks, their valves closed tight as they waited for the ocean to return. She pulled out her knife and began prying them from the rocks, their tiny threads clinging to the stone surface like stubborn infants to their mothers. Unlike babes, however, the mussels would never return to their birthplace. Instead, they would be cooked with whale fat and salt flakes for the Jul feast. Lilja's mouth watered.

Her bag was only half filled when she noticed her candle waning. She had taken every mussel in the shallow part of the cavern. If she wanted to return truly triumphant, with a bulging bag, and the surety that she'd beat Tovin in the contest, she would need to venture deeper under the ice. She looked again at the candle and licked her lips. There was time if she hurried.

She grabbed the candle and picked her way around huge boulders covered in slimy, green and red seaweed. Her boot splashed in a tidepool. She stepped around another pool. A dark shadow flitted under the water—a cod frightened by the unfamiliar light.

The candle wax dripped over her mitten, reminding her that her time was limited. She must find another hoard of mussels or make her way back to the opening with what she had. Lilja set her lips together and went on.

Around a boulder that towered overhead, she found what she was looking for. A wall of mussels crept up the boulder like a glistening, black tapestry.

"If only I'd come here first," she said.

"Who's there?" A melancholy voice, more beautiful than she'd ever heard, vibrated through the cavern and into Lilja's mind. She whirled around but saw no one. "Who comes to mock me in my misery?" the voice moaned.

Lilja searched the nooks and corners surrounding her. A splash! Behind a huge boulder.

Lilja gulped and peered around the rock. A wide, shallow pool lay hidden there, and something, or someone, writhed in it.

She aimed her candlelight at the creature in the pool. The orange flame illuminated a young woman's face, pale, almost translucent. Stringy sea moss clung to the sides of the face and covered bare shoulders and a bare chest like a clothing of thick spider's web. Eyes, as big and round as sand dollars and green as the Bifrost, stared back at her. A silver-green tailfin splashed again in the pool. Lilja's mouth dropped. She knew of these creatures. They stole men from their boats and brought only bad luck to villages. Their beauty would steal your heart, she'd been warned. This creature wasn't particularly beautiful, Lilja thought, but she was, without a doubt, a mermaid.

## ELVI

Elvi muttered curses as she thrashed in the pool. It had been too shallow for her to get a proper gulp and now she was almost suffocating. Her sisters had warned her about drifting too close to the shore during the solstice tide. Why had she been so curious? Why had she wandered off from the deep to see if the rumors were true? To see if the water really was sucked back under the ice as the ocean slurped it up. If she had listened to her sisters, she'd be helping them prepare for the Jul ritual, stringing pearls for the love dance or preparing urchin delicacies for the feast.

Instead, she would miss the feast, miss the rituals, miss seeing the new husbands to those who had claimed unmarried fishermen from their boats. Jul was the only day when husbands were allowed out of the home caves. Elvi was too young for a husband, but she enjoyed the spectacle nonetheless. It reminded her that once there had been a husband to her mother. Her mother had died when Elvi was very young, from a harpoon to the chest, right through her heart. And her father, unable to live underwater without his wife, disappeared. If her mother was still alive, she would have kept Elvi from making such a foolish trip to the shore.

Now, Elvi would die too, not from a fisherman's spear, but from her own folly. How had she been so unfortunate to seek refuge in a pool no deeper than her thumb? She peered at the human, one of the young girls, gawking at her with ice-blue eyes through a flame-light. Elvi wasn't sure what to think of this human. She'd never been so close to a female one before.

Her sisters had warned her not to converse with them, although they were as capable of understanding a mermaid's mind language as the males. Females were tricky and selfish and immune to mermaid beauty. And worst of all, if one saved you, you were bound to them for the remainder of their short-but-not-short-enough lives. Elvi wasn't sure how that bond worked, but she had been told to avoid it at all costs.

Elvi tried to sip another gulp, to help her think clearly, but the water only wet her lips, taunting her. She pushed through her desperation and concentrated on the girl. Could she use her somehow, without invoking a life bond? Then the idea came to her. What if she made a bargain with her? That would not elicit a bond.

"Do you like wishes?" Elvi used her most bewitching voice.

The girl's eyes narrowed. "How do you speak without moving your mouth?"

"Nevermind that." Elvi shook her head. "Do you want a wish?"

The girl, unmoved, folded her arms. "I didn't know mermaids granted wishes."

Elvi huffed. This human was denser than she'd expected. "We do... occasionally. I will give you one wish, if you'll carry me out of this pathetic excuse of a pool and back behind those rocks. I saw a deep divot back a ways. I'm sure it is still filled with water."

"Why can't you wish yourself there?"

Elvi groaned. She would die before the girl took the offer. Her throat was already bone-dry. "I can't work magic on myself, only on others."

The girl pinned her gaze on Elvi with a hunger only a greedy human could muster. "One wish?"

"One wish, nothing more, nothing less." Why did this human take so long?

The girl looked down at a bag slung across her chest, bulging with the pillaged shells of a hundred black mussels. She glanced at her waning flame-light, her eyebrows knit together. What was she thinking? Elvi wondered. Did humans think?

"Mussels," the girl spouted. A mischievous gleam flickered in her

eyes. She licked her lips. "I want to win the mussel contest." Her lips curled into a wry smile. "That'll show Tovin. I might not best him in arm wrestling, but I *can* beat him. Not only at chance, but at skill too."

Elvi was relieved. The wish, being rather small, would only cost her one or two days from the end of her very long life. She would merely put an enchantment on the girl's bag to never empty until she won. "Granted. Now take me to that divot where I can wait out this infernal low tide in comfort."

The girl gave Elvi her flame-light to hold and scooped her up, with more ease than Elvi had expected. "Over there." Elvi pointed to a path between boulders. The girl complied, staggering slightly under Elvi's weight. Being carried by a human was so degrading.

"Where is the pool?" Beads of moisture appeared on the girl's brow.

Elvi looked around but couldn't adjust to the yellow gleam shining back at her. Her eyes were not used to flame-light. She held it away from herself and squinted. The floor was smooth and bare. Where was that divot?

"Deeper then." Alarm filled her as dry air burned her throat. She must have passed the divot farther back than she'd remembered. How far back?

The girl did not move.

"Go!" Elvi demanded. Her chest tightened. She must have water soon or she'd choke.

"The tide." The girl's round eyes were fixed on the flame-light. "If I go much farther, I won't be able to get out before the tide comes in. I'll drown."

Elvi coughed. "I must have water now." She fought the burning and thought of a solution. "Keep going. If the water catches you, I'll grant you a second wish, one that will turn you into a mermaid long enough to swim to shore."

The girl nodded in agreement. *Good,* Elvi thought. *Still a bargain, of sorts.*

Soon, they were so deep beneath the ice, it was merely a frosty memory above them, the flame-light barely reflecting off its glassy surface.

"Here it is," the girl huffed as she lowered Elvi into the refreshing pool of water. Elvi dove below the surface, drinking the cold liquid and quenching her scorched insides.

"Ah!" She sighed, bobbing up to the girl and smoothing her silky hair off her face.

A rumble vibrated through the cavern. The girl's face grew stark with fear.

"Don't worry," Elvi assured her. "I've already cast the enchantment. When the water arrives, you will sprout a fish tail like mine and swim yourself and your bottomless bag of mussels to shore. We have dealt fairly, you and I."

Elvi's words appeared to quell the girl's fear. She turned to retreat back to her land, but it was too late. A sloshing gurgle echoed around them. Then, ocean water rolled in, dousing Elvi in her pool. It hit the girl at the waist and knocked her down.

"Oh!" the girl yelped as water washed over her. She thrashed to pull herself up, sputtering. The flame-light disappeared, leaving the cavern in the blue darkness Elvi was accustomed to. Icy water wafted past her. She hardly noticed. Her attention was rapt with the satisfying transformation of the girl's legs into a shimmering fish's tail. A tail as green as her own. And flipping through the water with true grace, not awkward human strokes.

Another wave crashed against the rocks and boulders, filling the cavern higher and higher. The ice roof was closer now. Elvi felt peculiar. She bobbed at the surface, watching the girl. But her own tail felt stiff, only bending in one or two places. And it had the sensation of being two tails, each one moving in its own independent direction.

Elvi's heart plunged. She gulped a huge gasp of air, air that didn't burn. The water hit her face, choking her. She dipped her head below, her blood growing cold. The salt water stung her eyes. Her

beautiful fish tail was gone. In its place were two bulky, fleshy, horrific human legs.

If Elvi had been able to, she would have cried out. The ocean had almost reached the top of the cavity, leaving only a small gap for Elvi to gasp for breath. The cavity grew dark as her own eyes lost their ability to see through the blackness. How had she been so dumb? So wrong? How had she forgotten her sisters' lessons? The ones that told her changing a human's body came at the cost of your own.

The gap below the ice was gone now. Elvi had no more air to breathe. Her insides burned all over again. She knew she could not hold her human breath long enough to swim to shore. She struggled to kick her legs, to swim without a tail. It was futile. Despair gripped at her with its deadly tentacles. Her chest threatened to burst. Her head pounded with pressure and panic. She was going to die. And die as a human!

## LILJA

The sea water tasted delicious to Lilja. She flipped and turned and darted between rocks. She could see in the darkness as if it were day. The ocean was a playground, not the fierce creature she had always known it to be, taking and giving with the same waves. She wanted to stay underwater for hours, skip the silly Jul feast. But wait! The lure of winning the mussel contest was stronger. She began searching for the direction to her hole near the shore.

A figure caught her eye close to the iced ceiling. It was jerking and fighting the water. It was the mermaid, but her tail was gone. In its place were two pale legs. She was kicking them in short, useless motions. Her green hair had turned brown. Her eyes were squinted closed and her cheeks were puffed. She was holding her breath.

Lilja's heart skipped as she realized what had happened. The mermaid had turned into a human as Lilja had turned into a mermaid. Poor thing. She probably didn't have any idea how to swim without a tail. And swimming with a tail was so easy. Lilja flicked hers and swam toward the struggling figure.

The mermaid smashed her face against the ice, but there was no air left. Then she began to sink. Her stilted strokes no longer kept her at the top.

Lilja let out a bubbled gasp. The mermaid would surely drown. Her heart ached for the creature. A creature who had been so generous. Had given Lilja so much, for such trifling favors. She darted toward the mermaid and wrapped her arms around her waist. She searched for the hole in the ice.

There! Light streamed through the ice in one spot near the shore. She swam faster. Finally, they were near the bluff. Lilja thrust the mermaid through the hole, flopping her down on the upper beach.

In moments, the mermaid's tail returned. Lilja felt her own tail disappear. Her legs were back, along with the frosty chill of the wind. At least her clothes came back too and they were dry. Lilja laughed. "I didn't know you would turn human. Good thing I was there or you'd have drowned. Can a mermaid drown?"

The mermaid gave Lilja a baleful glare and began dragging herself toward the hole where water now sloshed through.

"Why are you so angry?" Lilja asked. "If I hadn't arm wrestled Tovin so much, I might not have been strong enough to save you. You should be thanking me."

The mermaid gasped. "I must get to the water."

Lilja sprang to her feet. "Let me help you then." She reached for the mermaid's arms.

The mermaid jerked away and hissed. "No!" She looked like a bedraggled jellyfish as she groped for the opening. "You've done enough. You saved my life, that is true, but now..." She reached the water and slipped in, submerging for a few seconds.

When she reappeared, the sunlight glistened on her wet moss hair, orange light shrouding the green. "Now we are bound, you and

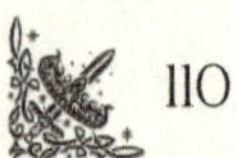

I." Her voice rang through the open air like a withered breeze. "Bound for a lifetime."

## CHAPTER 2
## ELVI

Elvi swam with an anxious heart to the meeting spot she had agreed on with Lilja. This would be their fourth year meeting on the Jultide solstice. Over the years, Elvi had learned to tolerate, and even like, granting Lilja's annual wish. The first year, Lilja wished for a bigger house for her family, with all the comforts to protect against the harsh winter. And a lavish barn and large pens for the reindeer herd she had won from the mussel contest. Elvi gave these things begrudgingly, but she gave them anyway. She had learned from her sisters that her heart would turn to ice if she refused the wish.

The second year, Lilja wished for prosperity for another—Tovin, the boy who Lilja talked of often. This wish softened Elvi toward the girl.

On the third year, Elvi took joy in giving Lilja her wish of wealth for the whole village. The girl's charity ran deep as an ocean trench. Her sisters had been wrong about human girls. She wasn't selfish at all. Elvi smiled as she swam through the frigid waters toward the shore.

Their normal meeting spot was the deep divot that Lilja had taken Elvi to in her moment of need four years earlier. But some years the tide wasn't low enough to meet under the ice. Those years, like this one, they would meet above through a hole that Lilja would cut.

The ice covering the bay was thicker than usual. Lilja would have a time cutting through it this year. But she must. They would commune at the winter solstice, just as the sun rose. Then, Lilja would ask something of Elvi, Elvi would grant it, and they would go on their ways.

But Elvi was nervous. What would Lilja wish for this year? Wealth for the whole North Country? The bigger the wish, the more of Elvi's last days it cost. While she was impressed at the generosity of the girl, Elvi hoped for once she would wish for something small and personal. Lilja deserved it, didn't she? And Elvi didn't want to give up a whole year of her life over this bond.

Elvi swam harder. Her sisters would delay the Jul ritual till she returned, but they wouldn't delay it long. Then Elvi would see the husbands and be jealous for the last time. This spring would be her turn to claim a husband. She was finally of age. And her sisters had complimented her on the beauty that had only recently blossomed on her translucent cheeks. She was sure she would lure a handsome man into the depths where they would start their own family.

The rock that marked the meeting spot was in sight now. The blood in Elvi's veins coursed faster as she approached. A light hovered overhead, moving on top of the silver ice like a burning moon. A flash of metal broke through. The saw. Lilja was here.

## LILJA

Lilja worked hard to push the saw through the ice. Sweat trickled down the back of her embroidered tunic. She pulled her heavy furs and mittens off, wishing she had her family's team of servants to cut the hole. But Elvi had told her not to tell anyone of their bond. And she enjoyed having this secret. She enjoyed that the village had no idea how they'd been so blessed. She enjoyed that she had the power to take it all away if she chose. Fortunately for them, she had other plans.

She grumbled as her arms burned. If only the tide had gone far enough out today, she'd be able to walk below, get her wish, and return before the first course of the Jul feast was over. She straightened, catching her breath. Her bracelets jangled as she stretched her wrists and arms. The rings on her fingers flashed gold in the coming light of sunrise. She was no longer accustomed to working hard to keep herself fed and warm. No more chopping wood for the fire. No more milking the goats till her hands ached. They had servants for such work now. And she could no longer win at arm wrestling with Tovin, but... she no longer wanted to.

Finally, the hole was cut. The ice bobbed freely. Lilja grasped the ice pick she'd brought and plunged it into the floating piece, heaving it out of the hole. Elvi's glistening face popped through as the first rays of sun glowed like fire on the horizon. Her soggy green hair dripped over her shoulders like candle wax.

"Perfect. You're not late." Lilja breathed with relief. She would need to hurry to get back to the village in time for the best part of the Jul festival. The part when the girls danced and claimed their husbands.

Elvi's smile was warm despite her ghost white skin and pale blue lips. Her large eyes watched Lilja with anticipation. "Good Jul to you, dear Lilja."

Lilja laughed. Elvi was always so formal. "Good Jul to you too, Elvi," she replied.

Elvi nodded. "I trust last year's wish was successful?"

Lilja shook her head, pulling her furs back over her shoulders. The wind chilled her sweaty body. "The village is *too* prosperous. Your charm on the land worked too well. Now, families from all over the North Country are flocking to us like geese. And they bring their beautiful daughters to steal away our men. Steal away Tovin to be exact. He told me last year that once we were sixteen, he would marry me. But now he is distracted by all the beauties that keep moving in."

Elvi frowned and her eyes darkened. "So your wish this year is to take away the village wealth?"

"No," Lilja gasped. "It's much easier to live comfortably when all around you share it. No. I have a better solution in mind."

Elvi's face grew concerned.

Lilja drew in a deep breath, confident her wish would fix all her problems. "My wish this year is that you make me beautiful. More beautiful than any other girl in the village. Make it so that if other girls move into the village, I am still more beautiful than them." Lilja was proud of herself for thinking of that last contingency.

Elvi stared at her with round eyes and a dropped jaw. Why did she look like that? It wasn't a big wish. Small compared to blessing the whole village with riches.

## ELVI

Elvi's heart sank like a wrecked ship. Lilja's wish was small, yes. But it was for her body. If Elvi granted it, she would have to give up her own beauty. And not for only a few moments like when she turned Lilja into a mermaid. For the rest of Lilja's life.

Could Elvi give up her beauty so soon after she gained it? No. It was finally her time to claim a husband, and she would never lure a fisherman into the deep without her beauty. It was all a mermaid had when dealing with human men. What was she to do?

The thought of killing Lilja and ending the bond right then darted through her mind. She pushed it out, with the guilt that came with it. Besides, if Lilja died at her hands, her heart would turn to ice, just as it would if she didn't fulfill the bond. She must wait for Lilja's natural death for the bond to end. Elvi's stomach twisted into painful knots. If she couldn't claim a husband, she would never have daughters of her own.

"Hurry," Lilja said, breaking through Elvi's conflicted thoughts. "The sun has already risen and the Jul feast has begun. I must get back before the Dance of the New Brides begins or Tovin will choose another girl and I'll lose my chance at him forever."

Elvi scrunched her eyebrows together. "Wouldn't you rather be wed to one who favors you without a spell? There must be other suitable men in your village." Elvi wondered how many of them would be claimed for husbands by mermaids come the spring fish harvest.

Lilja stomped her foot down on the ice, sending a crack splintering toward her from the hole. Elvi eyed it warily. "I only want Tovin. And he promised me he'd marry me... before those treacherous minxes arrived."

Elvi dipped into the water to wet her throat. Another approach would be needed to shake Lilja from this too-heavy-a-price wish. "Remember when I turned you into a mermaid?"

Lilja nodded, her face pinching in annoyance.

Elvi pressed on, hoping Lilja would be as compassionate as she had been generous with her wishes. "Just as I lost my mermaid form when I gave you one, I will have to give up my beauty if I grant this wish."

Lilja wrinkled her nose. "But you have no beauty to lose. I'm sure you won't mind."

Elvi's stomach tightened. Her hope for compassion dwindled.

Lilja crossed her arms and peered at the orange light of the sun. "Come now, give me the wish. I must leave for the village now or I'll be late for the dance."

The water swirling around Elvi seeped through her like a bitter current. How could she have been so wrong about the girl? She wracked her mind for a way out of this wish. For something better she could offer Lilja. She had an idea.

"Instead, let me give you a much better husband than Tovin. He is not worth the cost. And from what you have told me, he sounds like a shallow fool whose affection is as fickle as the tide. He is a child, a lag-about, spoiled by the riches you wished for him. Let me send you a real man. A chief. A king. Someone who has earned his rank and wealth."

For a moment, Lilja's eyes gleamed. Elvi's heart lightened. She had found a way to keep her beauty, beauty that was only apparent to fishermen, not silly girls. But Lilja's face grew stern and determined. She licked her lips. "No. Tovin is the only boy for me. I must have him. Make me the most beautiful girl in the village. That is my wish."

Elvi gulped a swallow of sea water, but it was not refreshing. Her eyes stung as if urchin needles pierced them. She looked at her reflection in a polished medallion Lilja wore. Her heart ached for the beautiful face that stared back at her. A face she had only just grown into. But Lilja would not be deterred.

A lump formed in her throat as she took in a last look at her beloved face—her luscious hair, her round eyes, her perfectly formed nose, and her seductive cheekbones and lips. Finally, knowing she was out of time and ideas, she closed her eyes and said, "Granted."

Her heart plunged to the deep darkness below her. When she opened her eyes, a poxed, scarred face with a crooked nose and beady eyes with bags like oyster shells looked back at her from the reflection. Her hair had turned to black ooze, her lips thin and purple, and her cheeks sunken and hollow. Her dreams of a husband and being a mother were carried away on Lilja's radiant face.

## CHAPTER 3
## LILJA

Four years later, Lilja regretted her wish.

It had broken her heart into a thousand tiny pieces. She plodded through heavy snow to the frozen bay, clutching the ice pick till her knuckles were white as pearls in the darkness. The full moon faded into the coming dawn as she crested the hill beyond the village. The tide would be extra low when she got to shore. Her spirits were lower. They roiled between rage and agony, in an abysmal slurry of sorrow.

Tovin had left her. Left her and their child. And ran to the arms of another. How could she have been so stupid? She should have wished to be the most beautiful woman in all the North Country—

no—the world. Then he would never have found that hussy.

Or, she shouldn't have wished for him to become chief last year. Then he would have never left the village and met *her*. But he'd been so restless and ambitious. Lilja knew he would find a reason to go to other places, other villages, regardless of his chief position. She'd hoped being chief would give him pause to cheat. It didn't.

She had even used a wish to bear him a child their first year of marriage. His daughter. Her daughter. Thinking it would be enough to keep his attention on her. They named her Ostara for the Spring, for she was born on the equinox. Lilja had sung her lullabies and coddled her and raised her to the young toddler she was now. And where had he been? Off gallivanting with the trollops and teases of the village, and finally to those in other villages. He only returned long enough to revoke his chief position, all for another woman. Lilja's wealth and beauty had not been enough. Her child had not been enough. She had not been enough.

Lilja tripped as a sob escaped her. Tears froze like rivers on her cheeks. The silvery crust of ice at the shore was blurry as she plunged the pick in with a sickening crunch. Lilja grunted as she yanked it out and plunged it in again. All her anger flowed through her arms as the ice cracked and broke and fell away below in the pocket of air. She realized after she'd chewed a sizable hole that she'd failed to check the ice's strength. No matter. She didn't care if it collapsed and crushed her.

She wiped the tears from her face with her chapped hands and lowered herself into the cavity. It was quiet below. Only the drip, plop, drip of water left behind by the tide echoed through the icy halls of the ocean. The odor of fishiness slapped her across the face almost as hard as Tovin's betrayal. She struck a match and lit her candle, grateful she'd remembered to bring them. She would never find her way to Elvi's pool without some light.

Her head throbbed as she passed mussel covered boulders and clusters of drooping seaweed. The candle warmed her cheeks and nose. She breathed and felt a trepid sense of calm settle over her. She did not know what she would wish for this year but she had to come nonetheless. The bond compelled her to come; she had no choice.

It angered her that she was forced to make a wish every year. Wishes that had brought her nothing but pain. If only she'd been strong enough to resist coming. Resist wishing. And now she was here again, under the ice, driven to wish.

As she stepped between glistening rocks and around small puddles in the sand, she tried to think of a wish that would get her away from here for good. A wish that wouldn't end up being a curse. She wanted to wish for the bond to break, but Elvi said it wouldn't work. How else could she get out of this wretched pact? She would only have until her candle reached the halfway mark to decide, then she'd have to head back to the surface before the tide came rolling in and drowned her.

A spark of an idea flickered at the corner of her mind. She tried to ignore it. It was too horrible of a thought. But was it? It would surely break the bond and end her suffering. Gradually, the idea wormed its way in front of her vision. She grasped at it, clutched for it, grabbed hold of it. Her love for it grew stronger with every step forward into the darkness. By the time she had reached Elvi's pool, she was serene with resolve to execute the idea.

## ELVI

When Elvi reached the deep divot moments before the tide receded, she was a shell of a water spirit. Nothing more than a fading cloud of ink from an octopus. She was ugly. She was barren. She was lonely.

Lilja's wishes had taken everything from her. She now knew why her sisters had warned her against becoming bound to a human girl. It had cost her more than a few days off her too-long life. It had cost her all the happiness that would have made that life livable. Now her only joy was to watch Lilja's daughter from behind the rocks during the summer months when Lilja brought her to the beach to play.

She felt the emptiness in her womb like a hollow oyster with no pearl to offer. When Lilja had wished to bear a child, and no child had come, Elvi had given it to her. She knew, now that she would never claim a husband, that she would be childless for eternity. It wasn't much of a sacrifice at that point.

But the next year, when Lilja had asked for the voice of a songbird to sing to her daughter, the daughter Elvi would never have, Elvi had granted the wish for the child. Now her own voice was the rasp of an eel. Fitting for the sea hag she had become. At least the child would have the music of the ocean.

Last year's wish had not cost Elvi much. Only a few weeks off her life, which she gladly gave. But a pit grew in her stomach as she worried what Lilja would ask for next. What would this year's wish cost?

She lay waiting, dejected, in the pool of the deep divot. A yellow glow penetrated the dark, quiet cavern. Lilja was here.

When the girl approached, her ravishing beauty stunned Elvi, as it did every year since the wish was granted. Lilja's formerly round face and plump cheeks had given way to high cheekbones and an angular chin. Her soft eyes had become piercing and alluring. Her previously thin lips were now full. She was beautiful by human standards.

"What is your wish, Lilja?" Elvi flinched as her own croak of a voice ground against the cavern rocks.

"What, no greeting?" Lilja's voice, its melodic lilt empty of vigor, stabbed Elvi's chest with longing. "Nevermind." The girl's eyes searched the cavern with a haunted gaze. "This will be our last meeting."

Elvi's mouth went dry. What did the girl mean? What was she scheming now? And why? She waited for Lilja to speak, too afraid to draw the plan out of her.

But she didn't speak. She perched herself on a low rock and crossed her arms in front of her, watching the flickering dance of the flame-light with dull interest.

"What is your wish, Lilja?" Elvi repeated, hoping to get whatever horror the girl had in store for her out of the way quickly.

Lilja sighed. Her shoulders sagged. She kept her eyes on the flame. "I have no wish this year, Elvi. I have nothing to want, nothing to love, nothing to live for."

"You must have something you can wish for. Something small and trifling would do. Your flame-light is waning. You must make a wish soon. Wish for a new piece of jewelry. Or a toy for Ostara." Speaking the babe's name was like a knife in Elvi's heart.

Lilja closed her eyes. A glittering tear rolled down her cheek. "Ostara," she whispered. She opened her eyes and focused blankly on the flame again, tipping the short stick so that it dripped on the sand. "I will miss her laugh. Her smile."

Elvi's spine tingled. What did the girl mean?

"I should have brought her with me. Then we'd be together. Now, she'll be given to another family, I suppose, after they realize I'm dead. Probably as a servant."

Horror struck Elvi. "What has happened? Why are you talking like this?"

Lilja's eyes turned to Elvi, as if seeing her there for the first time. "You are ugly, aren't you?"

Lilja's words stung but Elvi pushed them aside. The tide would return soon. Lilja must head back to shore now. "Make your wish, before it's too late."

Lilja's face turned to stone. "I have no wish this year. Those loathsome wishes cost me my life, my love, my heart. It is shattered, you know. It has turned to ice and cracked into tiny shards. Tovin has betrayed me. He drove an ice pick into my chest and I am dead." Lilja dropped her flame-light on the sea bed and buried her face in her hands. Her wails carried through the cavern like a bellowing gale of wind.

 120

Elvi's heart raced. If Lilja drowned below, the bond would be broken and Elvi would regain all she had lost. Her beauty, her voice, her hopes for a husband and daughter would be restored. She pushed down the bubble of jubilance that threatened to rise in her. What would become of Ostara? Lilja's precious daughter would be tossed about on the waves of chance. She would never know love. She would become as miserable and ruined as her mother.

Elvi's heart longed to help the little girl, the daughter of her loneliness. She wished she could save her from growing up motherless, as she had done. If only she could heal Lilja's heart. Fix the wrongs she had done to her, indulging her over the years, spoiling her.

This was all her fault. If she hadn't been so foolish to come to the seashore all those years ago, she and Lilja would never have ended up in a life bond, and Lilja would have been free to struggle like any other human. But the wishes had protected Lilja from the buffeting winds of life. They had sheltered the girl from the harsh waves and now... Lilja was turning to death as an escape from the storm that had come.

Elvi's guilt threaded through her like the arms of a kraken, stinging her at every nerve and limb. She had to fix her mistake for Ostara. Fix it for the little girl. Fix it for Lilja. "Think of Ostara," she pleaded with Lilja. "Go back to her. You don't have to make a wish, just go!" Her own words cut through her like sharp rocks. Was she willing to let her heart turn to ice for Lilja? For Ostara? Yes! She was desperate now. The flame-light, while managing to keep burning as it lay on the ground, was dangerously small. The tide would return soon.

Lilja ignored her plea and continued to weep. Elvi wrung her hands at the inconsolable girl. "Please, Lilja. Tovin was never worth all you gave him. He's not worth giving away your life. He's not worth making your daughter motherless." Elvi's voice wheezed as she cried for the girl to run. Run for the shore.

Her pleas went unheeded. Lilja's shoulders sank lower as she sobbed into her arms. Elvi's heart beat so loudly she almost couldn't hear the rumble of water threatening to return. Her heart! Her heart was not broken. Her voice, her beauty, her chance of being a mother was gone, but her heart was still beating, still loving, still whole. "Wish for a new heart, Lilja! One that is unbroken."

The girl's sobs quieted. Her blue eyes rose, rimmed with red.

Yes. She would take it. She was not past healing. "Wish it, Lilja, quick."

With a haunted look on her face, Lilja spoke. "I do wish for an unbroken heart. But it isn't possible." She resumed weeping but that was all Elvi needed.

She gulped a large swallow of water, wanting to take more time, to feel for the last time, to love once more. But the tide was coming. There was no more time. She closed her eyes, a tear escaping. Its warmth trickled down her cheek. She knew it would be the last one she ever shed. Her heart pounded as she cast the spell.

The hollowness inside her came suddenly, as if a bubble had popped. Her mind could almost recall... what it felt like to love... like a dream drifting away as she awakened... until finally... it was gone... a memory... and then... not even that. The longing in her womb disappeared as well, and she forgot. Forgot why she was in this pool, staring at a human whose tear-streaked face looked at her with confusion.

## LILJA

Elvi stared back at her from the pool with an air of indifference. What had the mermaid done? Lilja had not meant to make a wish, but she felt the change, the enchantment. Where her heart had been broken and splintered, now it was whole and full of love. Love for Ostara. Love for herself. What had she been thinking—wishing to die? She wanted to live. She wanted to return to her daughter and hold her in her arms and kiss her plump cheeks. That was all she cared about now. Tovin was a distant nightmare. He was nothing.

The candle she had dropped had barely enough wax for her to pick up and hold. The echo of waves crashing jolted her. She gasped. She must run. Run before the cavern filled with water. She looked toward Elvi but the mermaid had dropped below the surface of her pool. Something had changed. Something had ended. The bond was broken.

Lilja ran from the pool, her senses keen and alert. Her eyes stung from crying but they were clear. The sloshing of water echoed behind her, sending her speeding forward, dodging rocks, splashing in puddles. Her heart pounded strong and hard as she dashed ahead of the tide. She breathed salty air as she panted. She stepped into a deeper puddle, wetting her leg up to her knee, but she didn't stop. She must get out. She must get back. She must live.

Lilja made it to the hole in the ice right as the water lapped up against her ankles. She scrambled through to the surface, the cold wind biting against her wet legs and chapped hands and face. But she was alive. And she was healed. Elvi had healed her. Elvi had given up her heart so Lilja could live. Her love for the mermaid swelled and made her weep again as she trudged through the snow to the village. To her daughter.

Many years later, on a cold winter evening, Lilja sat in front of a fire.

"Amma," said Lilja's smallest grandchild. "Tell us again of the mermaids."

"I want to hear about the Sea Witch," said her oldest grandchild. "I heard she lurks in a cave in the deepest part of the ocean, and only comes out to steal young children away." This girl loved striking fear in her siblings' hearts.

"I heard she's as ugly as a hagfish and evil as the undead," another grandchild chimed in.

Lilja laughed then scowled. "You children shouldn't believe everything you hear. The Sea Witch does none of that. She is lonely... and empty." Lilja sighed, remembering. "She once loved more than you can imagine. And it cost her everything." Lilja shook off a tear and sniffed. "Now off to bed, little ones. Your mother and father will be back from the Jul festival in the morning."

"Sing us a lullaby, Amma." The youngest child yawned as Lilja tucked him in.

"Yes, Amma. We love to listen to you sing." Another one rubbed his eyes.

"Alright my loves." Lilja sang. She sang a song of the sea, of sorrow and sacrifice, of love, and her heart was warm.

# ELEMENTAL
## by Lily Manning

THE RINTUZA MOUNTAINS stretched across the continent, casting an ancient shadow and imposing a subtle rule over the countries unfortunate enough to neighbor them. Their towering peaks, half-hidden by an eternal frosty mist, dared any mortal to attempt to cross their inhospitable terrain.

Terrain inhospitable, perhaps, to everything but the aptly-named Rintuzan crocus.

And so, for the first time in seventeen years, Moria found herself face-to-face with a flower.

The small yellow bud had only just uncurled, exposing its fragrant belly to the harsh ice storms of its mountainous home.

Moria was not as young, as sweet, or as brave as the small blossom, and she curled in the snow before it like a dying fern. Shivers had taken hold a while ago, and they now wracked her body, shaking her to her core. Moria's eyes and nose ran even as the salty fluids froze to her face. She'd hoped to catch a whiff of the flower beside her, but the snow-laden wind carried its fragrance off before her frozen nose could even hope to attain a hint of the sweet scent.

The freezing wind pierced her lungs with every sharp breath, and Moria feared her throat would shatter if she tried to call for help. Not that her feeble plea would do much good—the storm would swallow her voice just as the snow now seemed to swallow her body.

Voices murmured on the edge of her consciousness, and she found herself drifting away from the storm. She briefly worried that the flower would be lonely before the world fell to black.

Avondale was situated at the edge of the Rintuzas' foothills, twenty miles south of the base of the nearest mountain. Some considered this a safe distance, and some knew better.

While the sun shone in the south, the north was clouded and quiet, and the looming summits cast long shadows that reached out like claws toward the village.

No one came to the town from the mountains; the few remote villages that hid in the cracked precipices preferred to wallow in their solitude. But Avondale was thriving, nonetheless. Hunters loved to winter there, thanks to its close proximity to wild hunting lands. During the summer, the few passable trade routes between the lands north and south of the Rintuzas were opened, and Avondale was one of the first towns waiting to welcome the Northerners and their merchandise into the south.

The town was also equipped with a rather large garrison—they were an extra measure of security between the unfamiliar northern traders and their equally unfamiliar customers. The untamed foothills provided an excellent location to train cadets, and this ensured there were always extra soldiers at hand for the restaffing or transportation of prisoners to the isolated, stone-hewn fortress of despair known as Morcliff Prison.

Altan rode directly for the garrison upon entering Avondale. He had questions for the captain of the guard.

He sensed the man waiting behind him as he tied Mila to the hitching post, and so met the heavily armed, balding soldier's glare with one twice as withering as he turned.

"Take me to Captain Carrick."

The soldier snorted. "Boy, you don't—" he stopped himself abruptly as his gaze met Altan's icy gray one. His eyes flicked in quick succession to Altan's colorless white hair and the scar that traced his jaw, wrapping under his ear and behind his head. The guard cleared his throat, amending himself. He dipped his head. "Wraith. The captain is this way."

Altan hated that name. *Wraith.* Like he wasn't fully human, wasn't fully *there.* Just a ghost, watching from the shadows. Which, to be fair, was exactly what he did. Most of the time.

But he still hated it.

Carrick looked up as they entered, and gestured the guard away. As soon as the oak door shut behind him, the captain nodded at Altan. "You got here quickly."

Altan didn't say anything. It's not like there was anything else he could've been doing. He lived mission to mission. Carrick knew that.

The captain sighed. "Sit, Altan. I bet you're tired."

Altan draped his cloak over the back of the offered chair and sat. The burns between his shoulder blades stung, and he didn't lean back into the seat. "I'm not."

"Tea, Altan?"

"No." Altan's gaze flicked around the room, impatient to get to business. Overfull yet neatly organized shelves lined two of the walls, and a large window offered an impressive view of the gray dusk behind the captain.

"I've had a room prepared for you. Why don't you get a good night's rest? I'll have someone rub Mila down, and we'll discuss more to—"

"*Enough,* Captain," Altan snapped. "My horse and I are fine. I need the details on my target, and then I'm going to leave."

Carrick knew why Altan was here, knew he had a job to do. The old man's welcome of Altan only made things worse when Carrick wasn't there. Kindness was short-term. The void it left was permanent.

Carrick's lips drew into a thin line, and Altan could see him make a decision.

The captain drew out a sheaf of paper and handed it to Altan. He leafed through it, reading the information as Carrick relayed it orally. "Moria Maddock. Forty-one years old. She was serving out a life sentence until she escaped three days ago."

Her file was filled with page after page of accounts of her crime. Altan skimmed it, but he didn't waste time over it. It wasn't his concern what she had done, only that the Sovereign wanted her dead for it. There were startlingly few personal details about her life on the sheaf; nothing he could use to his advantage.

"Any relations?" he asked, still digging through the file.

"No, none that we're aware of. Her husband and infant died as a result of her... misdeed."

"Friends?"

"Maddock has been locked away for the past seventeen years. I don't think she retained any of her friendships."

Altan set down the sheaf. "How did she escape?"

Carrick sighed. "I suspect she may have had inside help. She was inexplicably out of her cell, unsupervised. By the time any of the guards noticed, she was already outside the walls. It was snowing heavily, and they weren't able to follow her. She killed one of ours on her way out—choked him to death with his own scarf."

Altan's lip curled. He would find the rat and kill him. A man who betrayed his brethren—people who trusted him with their lives—deserved to be put down like a disease-ridden rodent. He was no better than the criminal he'd set free.

There was just one thing bothering him.

"How do you know she's even still alive? It's midwinter. Not everyone's as apt to this weather as I am."

"We don't. But we need to be sure. She can't run free."

128

Altan nodded, mostly out of reflex. He'd find Maddock in the mountains, dead or alive, and return to the Sovereign with her head.

Altan stood and slung his cloak over his shoulders. He had everything he needed, and there was no reason to linger. He'd been trained to do things quickly and efficiently, and that's exactly what he'd do. Altan wouldn't risk the anger of the Sovereign by dragging this mission out.

Carrick stood as well and crossed over to one of the bookshelves. After shuffling around for a moment, he pulled a carved box from the second-highest shelf. "I have something for you."

When Altan didn't immediately approach, the captain looked up. "Altan, please. It was brought over by the Northern traders late last summer. I was going to give it to you over the solstice, but..."

"I was indisposed at the time," Altan finished. He looked pointedly at the door. "I need to leave now."

The dark circles under Carrick's eyes made him seem older than he was. "I know, but—here." He drew a small, round leather case from the box and handed it to Altan.

"It's a compass," the captain said as Altan flipped open the lid. The compass face was off-white and inlaid with onyx that traced the shape of a compass rose. It was simple in design, yet expertly crafted. Altan had no doubt it was of the finest quality. The needle quivered and settled as he held it stiffly in his hand. He'd done nothing to earn it.

"I already have a compass."

Carrick set the box back in its place on the shelf. "I'm sure you do. But it never hurts to have a spare, especially in the Rintuzas."

Altan snapped it shut. "I can't."

"It's a gift," Carrick said, resting his hand on Altan's shoulder.

Altan flinched.

He immediately regretted it. Carrick dropped his hand and something akin to concern entered his eyes. Altan hated it.

He shoved the compass into his pocket before the captain could say anything, and turned to leave, but paused as Carrick spoke.

"Altan, are you sure you don't want to stay at the garrison tonight? It's already dark out."

Altan turned around, sure his eyes were betraying the fact that yes, he did want to stay. He wanted to stay in Avondale forever and never return to the Sovereign, never be sent out week after week, month after month, *year* after *year* like some dog carrying out his master's bidding.

He avoided Carrick's gaze. "I can't."

The captain finally nodded, giving up. "In that case, good luck, Wraith."

"Don't," Altan said, opening the door. "Don't call me that."

As Moria drifted back to consciousness, several feelings hit her at once. Firstly, her toes were burning. Secondly, she was covered by something large, heavy, and fuzzy. And thirdly, a soft, constant clicking floated on the edge of her hearing.

She tried to throw off the fuzzy thing, but it only collapsed around her body even more. It was a blanket, she realized. Moria fumbled around, searching for the edge. She finally found it and threw it off herself. She blinked. The room was dark and warm, and the glow of a fire illuminated it gently.

"Hey, hey, hey," a voice crooned from behind her. "You're fine, but you need rest."

Moria's head whipped around. A woman who couldn't have been much older than Moria herself sat cross-legged in a wide oak chair, knitting away at a long, vibrantly yellow scarf.

The woman smiled. "I'm Ada."

Moria blinked, hard. The last thing she remembered was lying in the snow... *freezing* to death.

"How—" her voice was dry and raspy. She cleared her throat. "How did I survive the snow?"

 130

"You nearly didn't," Ada said, still knitting vigorously. "Your face and feet were covered in frostbite."

So that was the burning in her toes, Moria realized. They were still thawing out.

"What were you doing up here, anyway? I thought Flatlanders steered clear of the Rintuzas. Especially during winter."

Moria nearly scowled at the woman's bluntness. "That's none of your business."

The knitting needles kept clicking, "You were frozen like a teardrop in January when I pulled you from that snow. I think you owe me some kind of explanation." Ada's smile found its way onto her face again. "At least tell me your name?"

Ada's open face made Moria want to trust her. By the stars, Moria wanted so much to be able to trust her.

"It's... Laura."

But her trust had been misplaced and murdered before, and Moria wasn't going to take that risk again.

"Well, Laura," Ada said, "Unfortunately, you're stuck here for a bit. The storm has the whole area buried."

If Moria was unable to get out, then anyone trying to find her would be unable to get in. A small grin tugged at the corners of her mouth, the movement foreign on her face.

"I hope that doesn't mess up any plans," Ada continued.

"I didn't have any."

One of the room's walls rustled and opened and a child ran in, through what Moria realized was a flap to another, brighter room.

"Mama, I need you."

Ada sighed but smiled. "What do you need, Sonya?

Sonya was small and blonde with wide brown eyes and barely reached knee height as she tugged at her mother's skirt. "I need you."

"For what?"

"I *need* you."

Ada picked her daughter up and looked apologetically at Moria. "Excuse me, but she *needs* me. You're welcome to come out if you

want. There's breakfast."

As she said it, the mouth-watering scent of sweet oatmeal reached Moria. She hesitated only a moment before following Ada to the kitchen. There was no reason to reject the woman's hospitality.

The kitchen was a spacious affair. The log walls had been chinked tightly—the warmth from the crackling fireplace stayed in the room, heating it wonderfully. Animal skins were tacked tightly across holes in the wall to let in light, and Moria suspected they were taken off in the summer to allow for airflow.

Ada set Sonya down at the low table and beckoned Moria to sit before she filled three bowls with oatmeal.

Moria found the sweetness overwhelming and slightly repulsive, but she was sure it was only because she wasn't used to it. Either way, she finished her bowl long before the other two, and she easily accepted the second helping that Ada offered.

"So," Moria's host said once they were finished, "Now that we've got you back on your feet, we need to figure out how to get you home."

Moria's jaw tensed slightly. There would be people looking for her by now. She didn't want to risk being caught by leaving too soon.

If Ada noticed, she gave no sign. "My husband should be home in a day or two. He'll know which trails are fit for travel. You're from Avondale?"

Moria ignored the question—she had a much more important one of her own. "Where's your husband coming from?"

If he was anywhere civilized, there was a decent chance he would have heard news of her escape. Even worse, he could know her face, especially if Morcliff had already gotten posters up.

"Jari's trading with the only place we can reach during these months," Ada said, unaware of the noose Moria felt tightening around her heart.

"Morcliff Prison."

Morcliff Prison. Altan could feel the darkness that shrouded the place. There weren't any of the usual smells of death, since everything was frozen, but a general mood of despair and dread hung over the massive stone fortress, a mountain in its own right.

They'd ridden through the night, and a bloodred dawn had started reaching through the cracks of the Rintuzas. Mila was beginning to get skittish as they finished the last leg of their journey, climbing the long, bare avenue that led to the iron-gated entrance.

Altan patted her mane reassuringly and told her in a steadying whisper that this wouldn't take long.

The gatekeeper was new, a fresh-faced young man who had obviously drawn the short straw on dispatchments, and he refused to admit Altan.

At first.

However, after a few infuriating minutes of arguing and intimidating glares, the gatekeeper rolled the portcullis up to grant Altan entry. He didn't miss the gatekeeper's dirty look as he passed through the gate.

Once inside, Altan gave Mila's reins to a stablehand who assured him she'd be well looked after. Satisfied, Altan headed immediately for the warden's office.

Altan had to take a preparatory breath before he stepped through the warden's pinewood door. Warden Miretta held grudges even better than his brandy, so it was little wonder he hated Altan, but he wasn't even subtle about it. At least Altan didn't have to take his orders from Miretta; he was thankful Carrick was the highest ranking officer in the area—even if it did make for an extra stop in Avondale.

Altan entered Miretta's office. The warden looked up from his paperwork, and a scowl flashed across his face before he replaced it with a sarcastic smile.

"I didn't know the Sovereign was sending his favorite little killer.

I would've sentenced a few prisoners to death to give you something to do."

"I'm not your executioner, Miretta."

"Well, you may not be *my* executioner, but..."

Altan ignored the slight. "Give me the details about the escape *you* allowed to happen, and I'll get out of your flea-infested hair as soon as humanly possible."

Miretta snorted. "Says the elemental."

*Who's definitely not human.* Altan had learned long ago that what was unspoken was just as important as what was.

*That* was what infuriated Altan. This obsession people had with labeling him as *other.* Every time someone looked at him like he was some monster, avoided eye contact, refused to speak directly to him...

Altan could feel the beginnings of an icicle forming in his hand.

"Calm down, Wraith," Miretta said in a tone that was anything but calming. "There's already plenty of snow around here. You don't have to make more."

Altan dissipated the icicle. His jaw tensed, but he didn't react otherwise. Miretta wanted a response, and Altan wasn't going to give it to him.

"Give me the details of the escape."

Miretta settled back in his chair. "Yes, yes. I'm sure Carrick already told you everything, but here's my superior recounting: four days ago, we found one of our men strangled to death with—"

"—his own scarf. I know. Tell me something I don't."

Miretta rolled his eyes. "We locked down and searched the prison, but Maddock was gone. One of my men thought they saw footprints leading Northwest, deeper into the mountains, but the storm swept in, and by the time we were able to go outside again, any trail she may have left was gone."

"Carrick mentioned a rat."

The warden drew a sharp breath. "Yeah."

"Have you figured out who?"

"Andrej Nian. He's been here for the past six years, and I never would have thought..." his voice trailed off. "But everything points to him."

"Where—"

"We have him in lockup, but he's not talking."

That was problematic. Northwest was a very vague direction to follow, especially considering that Maddock most likely got turned around in the snowstorm and was no longer even headed that way. Altan needed to know if Maddock had any safe houses or hideouts in the mountains, and where her destination was. And since he couldn't question the criminal herself, Nian was the only other person who might know.

"Take me to him."

"Wraith, there's nothing we haven't tried. You're not going to get anything from him."

"I doubt that, Warden. You've only had him for a few days. So lead the way, or I can explore your prison myself. I don't care which."

Miretta grumbled some choice words but rose to his feet and pulled open the door. "Come on. It's a long walk."

"Hello, Andrej."

The man's face was bruised and scabbed over with dry blood, and he stared out silently from his one unswollen eye at his interrogator.

"Just so we're clear," Altan continued, forming a small icicle and twirling it in his hand, "I'm going to kill you if you don't tell me what I need to know." He placed the tip of the icicle at Andrej's throat.

"There'll be no 'keeping you alive because you have vital information, blah blah blah.' If you won't tell me, you're useless. And if you're useless... you're *dead.*" On the last word, Altan shifted his hand and stabbed Andrej in the shoulder, eliciting a rough scream from the man. Altan dug the icicle deeper into his shoulder.

"You have until tonight."

Jari returned home the next evening, hauling a sled full of provisions. Sonya ran out to meet him, and he scooped her up in a hug, greeting his wife the same way. Ada met him with a kiss and the promise of a warm dinner.

Jari turned to Moria. She took an involuntary step back. His face was ravaged with claw-mark scars, and his eyes were a grayish-white—blind. He tilted his head. "A guest?"

How did he know she was there?

"Yes," Ada said. "Laura somehow got lost in the storm; I found her while I was checking on the goats."

Jari smiled. "Good thing. Nice to meet you." Moria shook his extended hand.

Jari turned around and wrapped his wife in another hug, this time muttering something in her ear. Ada wasn't nearly as good of a whisperer as her husband, and Moria heard every word of her reply.

"She's not a convict, Jari."

Moria froze. If he knew—

The man spoke again, and something flitted across Ada's face, gone as quick as it had come.

Ada clapped her hands, but a shadow of doubt had begun creeping over her face. She hurried them all inside. "We'll discuss more over fondue, I'm sure you're both hungry."

As they moved to the kitchen, Moria wondered at Jari's deftness of movement. He pulled out a chair easily and sat down.

Ada handed Jari a fork and uncovered the fondue pot. Steam rose from it, and the sweet yet savory smell of melted cheese filled the room. Moria dipped a chunk of bread in the pot, covering it in the gooey sauce.

"How was the trip?" Ada asked once they'd all set the steady rhythm of dipping and eating.

"Oh, you wouldn't believe." Jari's body seemed to come to attention, matching the excitement in his voice. "Someone escaped a few days ago."

Moria froze mid-chew.

Ada tried to look surprised. "What?"

"Some woman... Maria Maddock, I think?" He turned to face her, blind eyes searching. "How'd you get lost in the storm again, Laura?"

"I..." Moria couldn't let them find out. She wouldn't go back to Morcliff. Her eyes flitted to Sonya, and the lies rolled off her tongue. "I was collecting the crocuses. It was my daughter's birthday." She buried her head in her hands. "I didn't know about the storm."

Ada was suddenly all compassion, reaching across the table to hold her hand.

"We'll get you back to her, okay?"

Moria nodded, slightly guilty about pulling the woman's heartstrings.

Jari sighed. "I'm sorry, Laura. It's just... dangerous, having a convict run around like this. Especially one as dangerous as Maddock. Someone came up for her. From the capital, I think."

Moria squeezed Ada's hand, and she squeezed back, just not for the same reason. This was bad. If the Sovereign had sent someone after her... "Who?"

"Some kind of assassin."

Moria swore silently but kept a blank face. "Any particular one?"

"They called him the Wraith. Apparently, he's been at the Sovereign's beck and call for a few years now, and he's damned good at what he does."

"Killing."

"Yeah, killing." A strange look crossed Jari's face but was gone as soon as it came. He resumed his excited energy. "I think he's elemental."

Moria closed her eyes and took a breath. This was getting worse and worse. Elementals were rare—the only one she'd ever known had been slaughtered at her feet—but they were powerful. Each could manipulate a facet of nature—flora, ice, metal... the list went on.

"Wait." She opened her eyes and looked at Jari. "How could you tell? You're..."

"Blind?" Jari smiled. "It's a good question. I don't know how to answer it, though."

"These mountains are ancient," Ada said, a hint of reverence creeping into her voice. "They practically have a soul of their own, and living here, we've had no choice but to recognize it."

Jari nodded. "There's something up here, all right. And whatever it is has forced us to realize it. And once you start feeling those kinds of things, that sense stays with you." He shrugged. "The Wraith had the same natural sense about him, I guess." He paused contemplatively before continuing. "Anyway, he found the guard who'd helped the prisoner escape."

*Andrej.* Moria didn't want to hear what came next.

"The Wraith killed him. I didn't *see* anything..." Jari laughed at his own joke. "But they said he froze the blood in his veins, then snapped his head off like an icicle from a roof."

Elementals couldn't do that—their powers weren't unlimited. But they could do *other* things. The rumors may have been exaggerated, but Andrej was dead. Moria was sure of it. A nauseating mix of rage and dismay battled in her stomach.

Rage won.

Moria would kill the Wraith.

Altan didn't really know where he was going. The guard had been thoroughly unhelpful—he didn't know nearly as much about Maddock's plans as Altan had hoped.

The snow was deep here, and Mila had been high legging it for a while. She was getting tired.

Just as Altan was debating whether or not to give his horse a break, voices cut through the mountain air, shattering the silence.

They were muffled by the snow at first, but as Altan drew closer, it was obvious that they were looking for someone.

"*Laura!* Jari, where could she have gone?"

"How would I know?"

Altan could see them now. A middle-aged woman and a man, presumably Jari, with a ravaged face.

"Did you check the barn?" Jari continued. "She may have just..." his voice trailed off, and he turned around to face Altan. "Hello, Wraith."

Altan started. How could this blind, secluded man know who he was?

He shook off his doubt. He didn't have time for cryptic isolationists.

"I'm looking for Moria Maddock."

The woman had come over, eyeing Altan with distrust, and Jari turned to her. "Ada, *that's* what it was. Moria, not Maria."

Altan didn't know what they were referring to, and he didn't care. "Have you seen anyone come through here?"

The woman, Ada, responded with her own question. "Have *you* seen anyone, Wraith? Like a woman lost in the woods?"

"Have you lost someone?" Altan couldn't see how anyone who actually lived here could get lost. Didn't they know their own home?

"She was a guest."

"A guest," Altan repeated. He didn't think these people got many guests so deep in the Rintuzas, especially in the winter. He only knew of one person who could've been through this way. "What did you say her name was?"

"I didn't."

Altan sighed. Why were Rintuzans so difficult?

"Then tell me."

"It was Laura," Jari answered.

"An alias. You two were harboring an escaped criminal."

Ada gasped. Altan scanned the area, half expecting an ambush. "Which way did she go?"

"No, Laura couldn't have..." Ada trailed off, seemingly unsure of what defense she could give Maddock.

Altan didn't have time for this. "Some people lie and harm carelessly, and she's one of them. I need to know where she went."

"I don't know!" Ada told him, an edge of panic in her voice. "We've been looking—"

A strong wind blew past them and swallowed Ada's words, stirring up the fresh snow into a small flurry.

The gale kept going, dragging a trail of snow behind it. It seemed to curve around the ancient spruce trees, finally fading from view as it ventured deeper and deeper into the forest.

Altan looked back at the couple, who had fallen silent.

"She wants you to follow," Jari said slowly.

Again, Altan didn't know what the man was rambling about. But he had no leads, so this was as good a place to look as any.

He dismounted and handed Mila's reins to Jari, hoping the man knew how to handle a horse. "Watch her."

As Altan followed the disturbed trail of snow the wind had left, the trees rapidly grew larger and thicker. The sky was soon reduced to a smattering of bare patches in the canopy, and the forest sank into a soft gray glow. The forest seemed infinite; Altan could no longer see the treeline.

Snow blanketed everything—tree branches sagged under the weight of it and the only hint of undergrowth was the small bumps in the white landscape.

It was silent. The wind was gone, there were no animals, and the snow absorbed any other sounds. Altan's heartbeat was deafening.

But despite its apparent emptiness, the forest seemed full. Bursting even, with something. Something that hung in the treetops, that wound its way through the tangled branches and kept vigil. Something that thrived beneath the depthless snow and watched and waited.

Altan called an icicle to either hand.

And the trees melted away.

The clearing must've been half a mile across, a blemish on the wooded expanse.

Moria stood in the middle, waiting.

The Wraith glided silently over the snow, directly toward his prey. Her.

Moria tightened her grip on the knife in her hand, hidden behind her back.

He came closer. A hundred feet. Fifty. A dozen.

He stopped and threw down his hood. "Moria Maddock."

Moria tried to conceal her surprise at his age. He was a *child*. Certainly beneath twenty.

But he was also an elemental. His white hair had a strange shine to it, like there was ice trapped in the roots, and his slate eyes blazed out at her, oddly familiar.

"Wraith."

He remained expressionless. "Then you know why I'm here."

"Yes." She could see twin daggers of ice glistening in his palms. He took a step forward, and her gaze darted to the tripwire now only a pace or two from his feet. The movement was slight, but he noticed.

The Wraith knelt and cut it before looking at her again. "You really thought something like that would stop me?"

"It was worth a try."

"You're only delaying the inevitable."

He lunged forward, blades at the ready. Moria jerked out of the way as the icicle passed an inch above her face, leaving a chill in its wake.

She drew her own knife and stabbed at him, but he twisted out of reach.

Before Moria recovered a defensive position, the Wraith kicked her hand sharply, sending her knife flying from her already-cold fingers. It sank into the snow and out of view.

Moria bolted.

He chased after her silently. She was close. So close.

Once they'd reached the treeline, Moria jumped over the coil of rope she'd laid out earlier and spun around. The Wraith was intent on her and stepped right into the trap, which snapped tight around his ankle and pulled him up, dangling him two yards above the ground.

Before he could try to swing up and cut the rope, Moria drew a second knife from the folds of her clothes and held it against his neck. He stiffened.

"Drop your knives."

After a bit more pressure from the knife at his throat, he did.

This man—this *boy*—had killed Andrej. Murdered him.

"You killed someone," she hissed.

"Really?" The Wraith's face was as impassive as ever. "I had no idea."

His indifference was infuriating. She cut savagely across his face, leaving a dripping trail of crimson from his nose to ear.

He drew a sharp breath.

"You have *no* respect for life," Moria snarled. "You're a monster."

The Wraith glared at her through the blood dripping into his eyes. "I'm not the one in prison for murdering my own child."

Moria stumbled back from the words like they'd been a physical blow. "How—"

She couldn't finish the sentence. That night had been full of mistakes, but she wasn't the one who killed Altan.

She hadn't murdered her baby.

Moria shut her eyes against the image of Altan, his small, soft face torn and bloody. "You don't know anything."

142

Moria took a breath and hefted her knife. It was light in her hands, intended for chopping tomatoes in Ada's kitchen. She'd kill the Wraith, then leave. Head North, probably. She was used to the Rintuzas by now. She could make it.

She stalked forward. The time for talking was over. The Wraith watched her closely, then tilted his head, exposing his neck. He knew what was coming, knew he couldn't get out of it.

Moria stopped short. A thin scar ran along the Wraith's face, tracing the exact same path as Altan's injury.

Something tightened in Moria's gut. There was no way it was possible. Altan *couldn't* have survived.

Unless...

She stopped. For some reason, Maddock just stopped. Her knife fell limp in her hand, and she stared at his face, not quite focused, as if trying to recover a forgotten dream.

Perfect. Altan formed another icicle and twisted upward, slicing through the rope with the crystalline blade. His ankle, which had twisted as the trap had taken hold, gave out as he landed and he sank into the snow with a gentle *thump*.

He surged back up again, ignoring the pulsing throb in his foot, and wiped the blood from his eyes. This mission had already dragged on long enough, and she was *right there.*

As he closed in on her, Maddock stumbled backward. "Wait, stop!"

Altan didn't. Maddock dropped her knife. "Stop!"

What game was she playing?

Altan rushed forward and tackled her to the snow, pinning her in a headlock. "Any last words?"

"Altan, please." Her eyes bore into his, warm and brown and... familiar?

"Who *are* you?" he snarled. But his grip on the knife wavered, prompted by some unconscious instinct. "How do you know my name?"

"Because I *named* you, Altan."

She wasn't making any sense. The *Sovereign* had named him.

"I don't know what—"

"Altan." She pried the icicle from his hand. "I thought I'd lost you. Don't you remember?"

He didn't. Not anything solid, at least. But something was worming its way through his chest, spreading doubt.

Again, she met his eyes. They were honest, pleading.

"I'm your mother."

And those three words opened a floodgate. Distant sounds and smells surged through his mind, and at the center of it all was a presence. Her.

He sank into Moria's arms, into the unfamiliar comfort of an embrace.

"Come with me," she whispered. "You don't have to do this anymore."

Altan had been waiting his whole life to hear those words.

# THE DARK KING OF TIME

## By Tina Capricorn

*I WAS A MAN. ONCE. Now I am more than that, but less than a ghost. My name is lost to me. All that I am is the ice.*

A frozen wasteland lays before me, unfurled far beyond what my eyes can bear to see.

I look down at my feet, numbly aware I have been trudging through the snow and ice in a steady stride. My boots are dark gashes against the white of the slush, their peat-brown complexion contrasting with the ice.

Blinking away snowflakes and ice crusted to my eyelashes, it is impossible to discern my progress. I glance behind me. The expansive, empty white is the same in every direction. I've lost count of my steps marking how long and how far I've walked, the numbers blurring in my mind. I only register this horror by wrapping my cloak tighter, my expression unchanging, my mouth stiff and immobile.

I flex my palms beneath my cloak. A strange, prickling emptiness haunts me. Something has been taken from me, and I have been exiled here—wherever here is. Yet I still sense a glimmer of... power. Life. Somewhere in this frozen place, it beckons to me, and I have been following its trail since I could discern it. I walk, numb, not quite alive but unable to die.

I pause, my cloak clutched close, my breath visible in the air. The landscape and horizon are unchanged; a reliable, empty plane of snow and ice. The sky is veiled with clouds, ashen and writhing in furious streaks from gray to periwinkle. The ice is the cruelest, a blinding white that stings my eyes. I squint, about to resume walking, and that's when I see it.

A rainbow beam of light streaks above the ground. Before I know what I'm doing, I kneel, placing my hand to the ice. There is a stretch and pull at my forehead as I frown with concentration, my face unused to changing expression.

A prickle of energy breaks through the numbness of my cold palm. I still, thoughts clamoring in my head. I know, with every kernel of my being, this is some kind of... gateway. It leads beyond this ice, beyond this endless frozen nothing.

I look up, squinting at the sky. Inhaling deeply, I am somehow still starved for breath. The air is thin as well as cold, and I am thinning with it. This ice is my exile, my tomb, if I could die.

But now I have found an opening, a small fracture in the vast white.

"Only those with the blood of Eterna may pass, and they pay the blood price," I heard myself say aloud. My eyes widen. Those words. I hadn't known them a second ago.

I glance down at my hand, and something innate, as simple as breathing, pulls at my consciousness. I glance up, and the gateway is more obvious. Oscillating rainbow light shimmers in a circuitous pattern and grows brighter.

A flicker of an image erupts over the disc of gate light. A memory of *mine*, of a time long before, blazes like a shooting star as the image

146

appears. It is a woman, her hair red like blood with golden ochre skin that shimmers against the bleak landscape. Her eyes bore into me, verdant green. A memory is awakened in me, of singing by firelight, as I called down the Moon, as my mother had, and as no man had before.

*I was a human, once. A human with power.*

The realization causes me to hold my breath, and my eyes burn as I resist blinking, not wanting this lost memory to end.

I feel my lips moving as I stare at the wavering light of the gateway. The image of the woman stares back at me. I hold my hand up from the ice, leaning towards her, as if to catch her in my grasp.

But she and the light disappear and my hand remains empty. I shudder.

"Eterna." The sound of my voice is foreign. Tears spill hot from my eyes and freeze on my cheeks. I fall forward onto my knees, gasping for breath as the cold sears my lungs. Squinting, I try to follow the thread of memory in my mind, but like a passing shadow, it is gone. My past returns to its muddled gray state.

I pound the ice.

More hot tears bleed down my cheek; they fall, frozen and pebble onto the icy ground. Wiping my face, I blink a few times, staring at where the light of the gateway had been. Testing my power, I place my palms on the frozen ground once more and the light of the gateway returns, making a colorful pattern on the blank backdrop of ice. The image of the woman does not reappear.

I retract my hand and the glimmering circle vanishes. Another certainty bombards my frozen senses.

There is life on the other side of the gateway. I can sense it, almost taste it on my cold tongue—*power and blood.*

An old hunger stirs inside me. This dark need to consume causes me to shudder. I cannot give in to that. I must remember who I am, as I remember who I love.

"My beloved Eterna." I choke on a sob.

An image of blood on stone flashes before my eyes. I inhale

deeper, grimacing and flaring my nostrils. Instead of disturbing me, it heightens a clenching need that even the ice and thin air fail to cull. I press my palm onto frozen ground again and the gate reforms. I bend my chin up, sniffing the air.

*There is more than a little power and blood on the other side; an entire kingdom exists beyond this gate,* my hunger goads me.

"But should I enter? Who would welcome me?" I ask the ghostly landscape around me.

The rainbow colors of the gate ripple in a concentric pattern, never pausing or changing.

"Do I deserve welcome?" I ask, a small part of me hoping for confirmation that I deserved the cold, the desolation.

I look down at my trembling palm pressed against the slushy tundra. My pallor is blue-gray like the sky above me. I was a man, once. Now I am... I don't know.

Before I can acknowledge what I'm doing, I press my hand deeper into the ice covered tundra. As my palm makes full contact, the gateway transforms into a glass door with a knob. The power beyond its threshold beckons to me like a siren song.

"Eterna." My voice echoes in the empty, cold horizon. No one is here to listen.

I shudder and the ice breaks beneath my hand.

"I am yours, Eterna." The doorway of the gate brightens and levitates, approaching me, ushering me across its threshold.

Its heat pierces me like a thousand blades; the only tether to my sanity in this void is the name of my lost love, repeated over and over on my lips.

It is warm.

I feel... warm.

I hear a fire crackling nearby, and feel the heat of the flames on

my exposed skin.

I open my eyes, adjusting to the dimness of the room. The gate light still burns on the back of my eyelids.

"You're awake, stranger from another time." A deep voice rumbles from somewhere close by in the dark room. I do not respond.

I fumble weakly, my hand palming a bucket next to the bed. I lean over and vomit into it, as it was evidently left for this purpose. I look up, my vision blurry, searching for the voice. I see nothing, my surroundings appear only dimly.

*Nothing will ever be light enough again,* I think with terror. At this moment I would rather be in complete darkness. I lean over and vomit again.

"You were in the Feranivis," the voice says after my heaving and coughing subside. "None survive out in the wastes for long."

I wipe my mouth with the back of my hand and glance down. I gasp. My skin is gelatinous. Even with my shabby eyesight I can discern black veins—or where my veins should be—visible underneath the moist sheen of skin without pigment or opacity; like I was beginning to disappear.

"Most become a walking corpse. The magic there thins you out, until you become... nothing."

I still can't identify the speaker. I blink as tears fall down my cheeks. I touch them, attempt to examine them between my grotesque fingers. Even with my feeble eyesight, I can see my tears are hideous—black and oily, gritty and viscous.

"What is wrong with me?" My hand trembles, and I lie back, staring at the ceiling of this place.

"Your body is ridding itself of the toxins from Feranivis. It's a miracle you survived at all. There is little oxygen there, so your skin is starved. That is why it has changed."

"I am a monster," I whisper, looking into the fire. "I should have never come here."

"Perhaps."

"If I could become ash, I would float on the wind—Eterna and I would be reunited." I close my eyes and reach towards the fire, extending my hand.

"NO!" he shouts, but I have already submitted myself to the flames.

When I open my eyes again, I discover my vision has returned somewhat.

I glance down at my hands. One is bandaged. Color is beginning to return to the other, but my complexion is still a corpse-like gray.

I look up at the ceiling to distract myself and realize I am inside an ancient underground library. There is no source of natural light, or windows of any kind. The ceiling has intricate geometric patterns carved in a repeating circle that become stone balconies, winding and delineating the levels of the open interior of what must be a vast cave. It makes me dizzy to count the floors, so I close my eyes.

I take a deep breath, attempting to calm myself. *This is good. My vision is returning.*

Curiosity gets the better of me and I try to sit up. I see across the sprawling stone floor there are many hearths like mine in the circular cavern. Every fireplace contains a similar arrangement as the small nook I am currently in. Bookshelves crowded with abundant tomes are arranged in such a way to make each hearth almost a room unto its own. There are comfortable chairs and small tables with carafes and mugs. Only a few possess a narrow bed like the one I occupy.

"Do you have a name?" a familiar voice asks, the same voice as before. A figure finally comes into view, appearing around a bookshelf that creates one wall of my particular parlor by the fire.

He looks to be a human man, except his large stature and preternatural movements are fluid, like moving water. He is impressively tall, with wide shoulders covered by a long gray cape.

The cape is stitched with blue and silver thread, which, from observation, I sense is enchanted.

"You are a Blood Orphan," he says with conviction.

My nostrils flare in surprise. He recognizes what I am, even if I do not.

He gives me a warm smile. His black hair dusts his shoulders when he tilts his head, observing me. He has a regal gaze, arching black eyebrows framing ice-blue eyes. He exudes powerful magic that is familiar and strange all at the same time. My heart trembles a little in my chest.

"And your power, when you had it, was in *beginnings.*" He cocks his head to one side again, his hair swaying over his gray caped shoulder. "Time-magic is radiating off you in waves, dissipating away from you." He pauses, frowning.

I don't react, not intending to give anything away. He nods, realizing I won't respond, and steps forward. He sits next to me in a chair beside the narrow bed.

"That bandage doesn't even need to be there." He indicates my hand. "You were barely burned. Strange that you are almost resistant to Nexus-fire."

I hear him speaking, but I am transfixed as I glance at my hands again. My complexion is more opaque, but a ghastly color. The black veins of Feranivis' magic crisscross my skin in a winding pattern.

"You are healing remarkably well. But that is to be expected of a Blood Orphan." He arranges his gray cloak behind him on the chair. "Or do you prefer Old One? Most prefer that term now. Less dramatic." He sniffs.

I stare at him, silent. The firelight plays against the spine of the books on the shelf next to him, dark gashes flickering against orange light.

"You were exiled to Feranivis?" Not a statement, but a question. He is trying to be polite, but my silence is answer enough.

He smooths his pants while he sits back in the chair, crossing his long, lithe legs. He wears tall boots that are silver blue, polished to a high shine; they reflect the firelight.

I blink at him, keeping my expression neutral.

"I do not need magic to deduce these things about you, timeless stranger. Only someone with lineage dating back to the ancestral planes of Aeor-Eterna itself could trespass the First Gate, and only someone with the blood of the goddess could survive wandering about Feranivis." He pinches his chin, his blue eyes transforming to indigo, deep and full of power. "You called her name when you put your hand in the Nexus-fire, and yet you were barely singed." He shakes his head, smiling a little. "Not every Blood Orphan has her power, and the ones that do are called..." He waves his hands in the air, gesturing at me.

I squint at him, realizing he has paused, and is waiting for me to give him my name. I can't give him something I don't have.

"What may I call *you*?" I say instead.

"You do speak." He raises an eyebrow at me. "Not many would survive Feranivis to then cast themselves into a Nexus-fire. You must have a great name."

I shake my head. "I do not know it."

"You may call me Guardian of the First Gate." He makes a dissatisfied grunt and recrosses his legs.

"Guardian of the First Gate," I repeat the meaningless title in my mouth. "I do not... remember my name. Feranivis kept that."

"Then we are at an impasse." He studies me. Firelight twinkles in his eyes as he watches me, and a surge of power—his *magic*—flows around the room, cocooning us together in this secluded underground library. His distinct magical scent of cedar, fog, ash, and sunlight makes my nose itch.

"Even timeless strangers that can use the First Gate must have a True Name if they wish to remain here." He bows his head and steeples his fingers, elbows propped on the arms of his chair. His blue eyes have a hint of steel gray as they survey me.

"The First Gate?" I ask, not feigning interest. "I know nothing of a First Gate, just as I know nothing of my name."

"The Gate that ended the Future War," the Guardian replies, frowning. I gasp involuntarily. My mouth dries up at the mention of the Future War. My skin chills, and the roaring Nexus-fire flickers a little in the wide hearth.

"You should not use that term." I lift my chin. "There is bad magic attached to it. Can you not sense it?"

The Gate Guardian leans forward in his chair. "Sense what?"

"It is... blood-magic. Elder magic." My gaze challenges his, and a hunger inside me stirs. Blood-magic—the dark power the Elders possessed, also inflicted this hunger on me. Blood-magic can also revive me, perhaps even sustain me—and my broken body knows it. I salivate, glancing at his neck.

The Guardian's expression softens. "Relax, Old One. The Elders were banished long ago. They remain, dying forever in the Breaking of the Light. They can never escape. The Future War was long, long ago."

I stiffen. There is a cold clarity deeper than the chill of Feranivis at the thought of the Elders and the Future War. Images of a woman chained to a stone and my body soaked in blood flash before my eyes. Then the image of the Gate Guardian sitting in front of me returns. I shiver and clutch the blanket spread over me tighter.

I glare at him. He is a fool. For such a potent magic wielder, he somehow does not sense this dark magic attached to those ancient words. I have to make him understand.

"Do not use that term. It is theirs and has their magic attached to it—their magic is still *entangled* with this world."

The Guardian frowns, his shoulders tense. His hands remain steepled over his crossed legs. The fire in the hearth pops, scattering ash into the air.

"The goddess banished them there, in the Breaking of the Light, a dark hole in a yawning, empty cosmos. Do you question Eterna?" He raises a black eyebrow at me.

I stop breathing at the mention of her name. "Eterna?"

"The goddess. She is named after the ancestral planes that created her, Aeor-Eterna. The Elders renamed the ancestral planes when they conquered it, as you must know..." He let his words trail off, watching me.

I hiss at him, the power of this place stirring at the mention of her name, washing over me in a warm wave. "They *conquered* her?"

"The Elders are usurpers, time travelers from another universe. It is what they do. They have an... insatiable hunger." He strokes his chin. "You know nothing of the history of the Blood Orphans, though you are one. Perhaps Feranivis took more than your name."

"How?" I ask, the burn of anger in my throat. "How did they find her? Eterna controls time, it is impossible—"

He raises an eyebrow. "You know much about the goddess, except how she fell."

I blink, the image of a woman chained to a stone flashing before my eyes again. I glare at the Gate Guardian, jealous of his knowledge and my lack. What am I without my memories?

"It was her love for a mortal. The Elders used him to manipulate her, and in the end, the mortal betrayed her."

I shake my head, inconceivable grief constricting my chest. "He betrayed... the goddess?"

"He sacrificed her to the Elders on the Stone of Time." He sighed, glancing at me. "I have pity for him. Though he had power, he was a thrall of the Elders in the end—given their blood and their cursed hunger, he was forced to do their will."

I shake my head, covering my face with my hand.

"The mortal saw what he had done and created the First Gate— rescuing all of the Blood Orphans enslaved by the Elders on Aeor-Eterna during the War. The First Gate brought them here." He gestures to the library behind him. "Where we have thrived for generations, forming nine kingdoms across space and time."

I am silent for several moments, thinking on what he has said.

"You are peculiar, timeless stranger, besides being nameless, you also do not know our oldest story—the legend of Eterna and Vin—" He stops himself before finishing and stares like he is waiting for

some bad news, but then his expression lightens.

He stands, rolling the cape off his shoulders, and walks the few steps between his chair and a small table with a thermoregulated carafe and several cups next to it. He pours two cups of a steaming liquid and walks to my bedside.

"I cannot remember…" I shake my head, willing something of my past to surface.

He puts the steaming cup down at another small side table between the hearth and my narrow bed.

"That is regrettable." His brows relax as he takes a long sip from the mug. "If you cannot tell me your True Name, you cannot stay."

I stare at him, unable to respond. Will he really send me back to Feranivis?

"We welcome all." He paused, giving me a long look, his eyes unreadable. "Even those that fought against the sovereignty of Aeor-Eterna during… the time you do not wish me to mention. But you must tell me your True Name." His blue eyes are soft, and actually quite beautiful. But a tingling sensation causes me to look past him and his riveting stare, to the library behind him.

The books have a collective presence about them. When he mentioned my beloved Eterna earlier, I felt the power of this place. There is something in the books here. They are almost alive with ancient power and history. I inhale deeply, my insides burning with remembered channels of magic.

Like claws grating over flesh, the library's power presses into me—but I can't hold on to any of it.

"Where am I?" I ask, clenching my teeth.

"The Nexus Archives."

"This is a place out of time," I say, and see confirmation in his eyes even though he doesn't answer me audibly.

He glances behind him, to the library. He can sense the shift in the magic from the books, as it reaches out towards me, but he isn't alarmed or surprised by it.

Hushed whispers, layered over each other, emanate from the

books, and they begin to visibly glow with energy. The color is a dark gold, rich and layered with flecks of ochre and electric streaks of white.

I nod, the magic of the books prickling my flesh, entrancing me with my lost magic.

Finally, he answers. "It is as you say. This place is a crossing all the realms share."

I reach for my cape, which is white and folded neatly at the foot of the bed. I pant from the exertion of merely placing it around my shoulders. I have magic flowing through me, but my body has still not recovered.

"Feranivis still affects you," he says with relief in his voice. Why is he relieved I am still weak?

"My magic is gone." I grimace, a twinge of regret catching the breath in my throat. It had been true before, but somehow hearing myself say it is worse.

"I know." The Guardian's eyes soften at my admission. I bristle at his pity.

Determined, I remove the blanket from my lap and turn in the narrow bed, placing my feet on the ground. Even this small amount of movement taxes me. Examining my clothes as I catch my breath, I see I am dressed in white pants and a loose white tunic.

The Guardian stands. "You were exiled to Feranivis." It is a statement and not a question anymore.

I still, not wanting to acknowledge it.

The Guardian sighs again. "As impossible as it seems, I believe you have been wandering in the wastes since the First Gate fell, which for my kingdom, has been thousands of years. In others, even longer."

I gape at him. Thousands of years? The Gate... fell?

"How could the Gate be 'fallen' if I used it?" I ask.

"Gates are intrinsically tied to their creators." His eyes widen as if he just solved a riddle.

I stare back at him, the firelight playing across his smooth skin.

He doesn't blink, just stares at me, his ice-blue eyes boring into me. I can feel the magic in his stare, piercing me with a thousand reminders of what I no longer possessed.

A chill creeps up my spine as I wonder why the Nexus Library maintains a Guardian for a fallen Gate...

"You had so much magic once." His eyes glow, a silver-blue ring of power highlighting his irises. His power prickles over my skin. "Your power was in *beginnings*. But also Gates. You created Quantum Gateways through time. And when you were human, you were the only male to ever possess the power."

"Say my name," I plead. "I know that's your power. You are gifted with Naming. Besides that, you know who I was before Feranivis. Say my name!"

The Guardian shakes his head. "You have no name. You belong to the wastes."

"Who am I?" I grasp the sheets between my fingers and wring them. I cannot stand, I can only yell. I have forgotten who I was. Forgotten everything but the ice and what my blood cannot deny. This connection to Eterna, to all that happened. It can't be erased, or purged from me—not even by Feranivis, not even without a name.

The fire blazes instead of dimming, the magic of the books flaring with it.

"What happened to me?" My voice cracks. "Can you at least tell me that?"

"You were split." The Guardian nods, his ice-blue eyes assessing me. "Heinously. There are magical scars. You were cut so deep you will never retain magic again on your own. I see the power of the Elder Volumes in the library call out to you, and yet the time-magic flows right through you, like a stream, confirming this. You are not him. You are what is left."

"Split?"

"By the Gateway, when it fell." His face remains neutral, but magic seethes around me. The fire blazes higher in response to the clashing of our power, causing me to perspire. If it had been another

circumstance, I would have rejoiced in being warm enough to actually sweat. Instead, my sweat turns cold, as my body reacts to the immense amount of time-magic flowing through it from the library.

"Who wrote these books?" I shiver and jut my chin towards the closest bookshelf. The books jolt on the shelf from my attention.

The Gate Guardian stares at me, rolling his shoulders back as more of his magic unfurls in the small space before the hearth, attempting to shield the books' energy from me.

"You have known my name since I came through the Gate!" I protest.

"Perhaps."

"You cannot dispose of me in Feranivis. I will resist. I still have power. The library is full of *my* magic." My eyes widen as I say it. It's true.

I attempt to stand and manage to stumble over to the closest shelf, my shirt cool with sweat as it billows at my back. "Their magic is attracted to me."

"The King of Time wrote those books—the Elder Volumes. You are *not* him," he says, using a formal title instead of a name. I feel the finality of what he says, and his magic brands me as the monster that I am.

Truths begin to clear things in my mind, like removing a layer of dust from a mirror. I know with certainty: I am a troubling remainder. I was never meant to survive. These were my books. I wrote them. I was the King of Time—and now I am what is left of him, after the First Gate fell, after the War ended.

I rest my palm on a book spine. The magic coils like golden thread, winding over my arm and wrist before fading away, unable to attach; it flows back into the books.

The truth sings in my blood as I touch the spine of another tome. My heart shudders as I feel almost unbearable hope.

"What has been split from me, my spark, my magic, is not lost— it exists, somewhere." I mouth the words, scarcely believing them.

The Guardian nods and gestures to the surroundings we are both

ensconced in.

"If existing in a corrosive time loop is existing, then yes. Eterna's magic, Aeorian magic, cannot be destroyed. Our sparks are eternal, in that way." His blue eyes ripple with power.

"Eterna." I am numb, and his voice sounds distant as my frantic thoughts drown out his words. "What happened to Eterna?"

His brows draw up in an expression of pity, but this time it's not for me.

"She is... scattered between Quantum Gateways. She exists only as time-magic and blood-magic now."

I feel the truth of what he says in my blood and my bones. She is gone and yet she is *everywhere.*

Her magic permeates this place, and I know I would find that to be true in all the kingdoms connected to the Nexus Archives. She is scattered through their blood and their time. Her sacrifice created an abundance of life here.

I look at the Guardian's steel-blue eyes. I decide to tell him the only thing I know is true.

"We are *Bound,* Eterna and I. She is Sanguine-Laeth—"

He growls, as if what I've said is somehow sacrilege.

"The One of Many Names is all of ours, as we are hers. We are bound to her as she is to us. We are the heirs of Eterna's sacrifice—"

"And mine." My shoulders tense.

The Guardian's posture becomes rigid. He unsheathes a sword; its black blade glitters with... blood-magic.

"You must return to Feranivis, or I will slit your throat here in the Archives."

I study his sword, my hunger piqued by the blood-magic dancing on its surface like inky smoke.

"The goddess is *mine.*" I bare my teeth—but before I can react, his blade is against my neck.

His power is a smothering magic, the color a miasma of blue. As his magic washes over my senses, it confirms all he said is true. This is no human magic wielder—he is a descendent of Eterna. His blood hums with her power that is, for me, still lost in time. She is scattered, her magic in him and the others who dwell here in the Nexus Archives.

I shudder with anger. She is *mine*.

"I would spare you because you created the First Gate." He looks at me with shimmering blue eyes. "And you atoned for your betrayal, as you said, with your sacrifice and leading the Blood Orphans out of the Aeor-Eterna after the War. But you are a shell of that man, a ghost—nothing more. It was a mistake to heal you, but I had to know for myself why the Gate Guardians remain."

My eyes become hot and my fists clench. The sword's blade presses into my neck before I have a chance to reply.

The tip crumbles across my skin like it was made of dust. I stare at it, blinking with shock. He slowly withdraws the ruined sword from my neck, his hand trembling.

His broken sword edge glitters blue in the dim hearth light, the blood-magic in the blade seeping into me, strengthening me.

I touch my neck with curiosity, my eyes never leaving his. There is a bit of grit where the sword tip crumbled. I smear it away.

His mouth remains open, still not recovered from his blade disintegrating. I can sense his power thrumming with alarm beneath his skin; a quick, constant cord of fear and confusion.

Sensing that I finally have the upper hand, I reach towards him and grasp the rest of the blade in my hand. I jerk it towards me, the action almost collapsing me back against the closest bookshelf.

The metal crumbles in my hand and I vibrate as I absorb the last of the blade's blood-magic.

I inhale, hearing the books on the shelves rattle in their places as more of their magic is drawn to me. I won't be able to retain it after I leave the Nexus Archives, but I understand that while I am here, I can direct it.

"You know my name. But I don't know yours. I compel you—" I reach towards him and golden strands of power swirl around his neck, forcing the words from his throat.

160

"My name is Stian Grá Gael, Guardian of the First Gate, and King of the Harborym." He withdraws his hand, dropping the ruined sword, which is only a jagged hilt now. "I cannot let you pass!"

I inhale again, ripping the blue magic he has cocooned us with into myself. Gold and blue strips of light coil around my body. He grunts in pain and clutches the chair for support.

The energy sears through my veins as it passes through my body, banishing the last of Feranivis' cold magic—but I will be forever marked.

I look down at my hands. My skin is more blue than gray, but remains ashen like a corpse.

Without my spark, I will never truly be revived.

In terror, I snarl at Stian, unable to think of words. All my color has been leeched from me, as has my magic. Why?

"You bathed in the blood of the goddess," Stian growls, answering my silent question. "You betrayed your Sanguin-Laeth, the most holy beloved, and sacrificed her to the Elders on the Stone of Time!" He squirms, attempting to escape my magic's grasp.

Tears sting my eyes. I wipe them away with the back of my hand. He is right. I bathed in her blood. Despite this, my empty fist rotates as I tighten my magical cord around his throat.

I speak through clenched teeth, feeling my magic seethe through me with certainty. "It was the cost of opening the First Gate, and the only way to... end the War. Without it, your ancestors would never have escaped." The books across the library shake with this truth. "We lost *everything* you gained—"

I watch as Stian reaches into his cloak and pulls out a dagger, slicing through the magical knots I have woven his power into, connecting it to mine. I recoil from his attack but advance on him anyway.

Stian's face blanches as we both realize returning me to Feranivis will not be successful. I am inundated with power in the Nexus Archives, where time is unfettered and a library of my ancient magic is hidden in text.

I relish it, my stolen magic flowing through me, reverberating in my empty spaces. It doesn't fill me—I'm not whole. I'm far from whole. The magic caresses the rough scars of my creation, the hollow inside me where I was split in two, highlighting all that I am missing. It is bittersweet.

The library shudders, and I see others in this sanctuary are noticing the heavy magic swirling around us in our nook by the fire.

"Come with me," I command Stian.

"Never—"

He grits his teeth as he attempts to run at me with the knife from his cloak, but my magic encircles his limbs again like a golden web, keeping him anchored in place.

"It wasn't a request, Stian." I twist my wrist in the air, and he is forced to his knees before me. The golden threads of my power stretch back his fingers until they break. He screams and drops the knife. It falls to the stone floor with a quiet clink, barely heard above the din of the whispering books.

The other Guardians that serve with him are almost to our hearth. The prickle of Eterna's power is perceptible within them all. The books' whispering has become deafening; I can see the other Guardians' lips moving but I do not know what they are saying. Casting their own magic, no doubt.

From one of my Elder Volumes, I finally hear the thread of the spell I was hoping for. I repeat its words out loud.

Every last creature, save Stian, falls to the stone floor at once, their magic surging from their bodies in long sinewy ropes of power that fly through me and into the Nexus-fire.

"I will purge this world of every last drop of her power." I feel a smile tug on the corners of my mouth.

"Please, spare them—" Stian croaks out, lifting his head from my magic's crushing grasp. He looks at me, weary.

"No."

My hands twist again and the cord of magic connecting me to each of them snaps. Sparks of light obscure what I have done, but the

smell of their blood and eviscerated flesh is palpable.

Stian lets out a fierce cry and manages to move his hands into fists, gathering his magical energy. Indigo and turquoise light swirls around us, causing books to fall off the shelf and the fire in the hearth bank down to embers.

"You would not be here, were it not for all that I have lost!" I respond, siphoning his magic through myself and into the fire, causing him to stagger backwards in surprise.

His blue eyes meet mine when he grabs the chair for support. I have almost depleted him entirely, and still he fights. It's admirable.

I reach for him and touch his forehead. His eyes glaze over, his body becoming rigid. Despite paralyzing him with my power, he manages to flinch under my touch. His arm is warm, like the fire, and his magic flutters under his skin. I salivate. The hunger I have been cursed with stirs.

I bite into his neck before I know what I'm doing, the hunger taking control of me. I feel his power and blood course into my mouth. Stian sways and leans against me as I drain him. He is weak, but tries to pull away from me. I keep him in my grasp, my hands rippling over his body greedily.

Finally, when I have satiated my blood-lust, I place him gently on the couch by the fire.

"Ah, yes." I wipe my mouth on the back of my hand. His blood coats my tongue like honey. "You will be a great tool for the plans I have." My eyes settle on him. With him, I would find all with Eterna's power, and take back what is hers.

My eyes warm and crackle with light and it reflects off his pale, smooth skin. Already I know I cannot part with him. He could be the source of my power as I search for Eterna through time.

As well, he is the first person I have met in thousands of years. That alone makes him significant to me.

*Claim him*, my venomous hunger whispers. *Mark him as yours.*

"I will not pursue your kingdom Stian, if you sever all ties, renounce the Harborym and give yourself a new True Name to serve me—"

He flinches as I lean into him, whispering close to his face.

"Look at your library, Stian. This is the fate of all who have Eterna's blood." I grasp him by the back of the neck, his blood and power strengthening me. I turn his head towards the grisly sight of the dead Gate Guardians. "I will destroy *every* creature that possesses her magic. Whoever benefits from my loss. I can smell the Aeorian magic in this place. All the beings here that deserve to die." I turn, looking across the library. The corpses of those who were alive moments ago lay lifeless in pools of blood on stone. I suppress a shudder at what I have done and turn his head back towards me. "Is that what you want me to do *to you?*"

"I would rather die than help you," he mumbles, his blue eyes hooded but unwavering.

*Feranivis could bring him to heel,* the dark hunger in me whispers.

I nod, knowing the true terror of the icy wastes. He would gladly serve me, to escape that place.

"Perhaps you need to cool off in Feranivis and think about this," I say decisively. I haul him to his feet, dragging him to the fire. "The hearths here in the Nexus Library are no mere fires, are they? They are Gates as well. Very clever to keep me cooped up next to one while you had your existential crisis on Gate Guardianship."

I hadn't stood next to the hearth yet, so I hadn't really appreciated how large it was. Carved out of granite, with a winding, intricate design and runes carved on its stony exterior, this Hearth-Gate of the Nexus Library was three handspans wide at least and as tall as Stian—when he could stand upright.

I lean my head next to his and inhale. The scent of cedar and fog are almost gone, his magic almost depleted.

"You were a fool if you expected me to *return* to my exile." I say into his shoulder. He doesn't respond and I shake him. He is like a doll in my grasp, all long and lean muscle. His head lolls to the side and I can't help myself, baring my teeth again, I latch onto his neck.

This time he screams. I am taking something vital from him now, his core spark, the essence of his magic, into me, through his blood, something he can never recuperate. His power and blood fill me—

*Now I can give myself a True Name*, I think as I as split his magic away from him, severing something intrinsic inside him.

I am wounding him, as I have been wounded.

But I will heal him, as he healed me.

He begins to shake in my grasp, and I feel how close he is to death. Still, my teeth and mouth won't let go of their connection with his skin. My eyes water with how heavenly he tastes; his blood and magic are like nectar.

Finally, I let go, gasping. His blood dribbles down my chin.

Without hesitating, I bite my wrist and offer it to him. He refuses.

"You will die without my blood. We are not in your legend of Eterna now. This is real, I have taken all that the goddess gave you, and more. It is impossible to survive without your spark—isn't that what you said?"

His head falls to his chest. "Even stripped of my magic, I will never submit—"

I smother his mouth with my wrist when he speaks; the despair in his voice, despite his brave words, is sweeter than his blood. He grasps my wrist with his teeth slightly, drawing our now mixed magic into himself. His body wants to live, even if he does not.

But then he releases his latch and spits the blood on the ground like a petulant child, defying me and himself.

"Stubborn." I haul him into the hearth and before the Gateway.

The flames part as we cross the bright threshold and I feel his power simmer inside me, his blood soaking into my thirsty veins. My eyes are hot and glowing, reflecting off his black hair.

"You are right, Stian. I am no longer who I once was, the mortal—the betrayer." I stroke his hair, damp with sweat, the heat of the Nexus-fire almost intolerable for him. I want him to feel this heat before the cold of Feranivis. "Thanks to you, I Name myself. I am

*Chronos, the Dark King of Time.*" I press my bleeding wrist to his mouth again. He doesn't bite down, but he doesn't close his mouth or turn away. My blood and our mixed power drips into his mouth. He will need every drop of this after I abandon him in the icy wastes. "And you are *my great power, my sword—Vladimir.*"

"No—" He sputters, weakly turning his mouth from me, tears streaming from his eyes. His body is slack, an almost empty weight in my arms. Feranivis might kill him before he submits. He is that stubborn. "I will always be Stian," he finishes with a whisper.

"Perhaps," I say, using his old refrain against him. "But with your great power exorcising the land of Eterna's sacrifice, the goddess will return to me." I hold up my wrist, letting the Nexus-fire cauterize the wound. The time-magic of the fire laps over my skin until not even a scar remains.

I look down at him, his blue eyes changing as my power, my hunger, takes hold of him. His now amber eyes travel to mine as he feels the Elder's blood-magic take hold.

"From now on you will be Vladimir Lazarus and you are *mine.*"

I toss Vladimir through the Gate, to Feranivis. The flames surround him in blinding rainbow light until he disappears.

I step out of the Nexus hearth, looking up at the soaring levels of books in the Nexus Archives, wiping my empty hands together.

"It would seem I have some reading to catch up on."

# The Winter Queen

## by Jan Marie Reynoldson

THE WINTER QUEEN STOOD TALL and proud on the parapet of her palace of ice and gazed over the snow-filled mountain valley that was her realm. She reigned over this mountain chain and its long valley from mid-fall to mid-spring. She allowed the queens of the other seasons to move through her realm as she slept through the warm months of the year, but it was clear to all that this mountain valley was hers to rule. Her high walled palace with tall spires of ice stood near the top of the tallest mountain. To anyone passing below, the palace seemed like a part of the mountain glacier on which it rested.

Frost covered her white gown in lacy patterns and fur-like hoarfrost lined the collar, cuffs, and borders. The gown lifted at the edges, like the front of a blizzard, and the silky strands of her long, white hair swirled around her pale face at the touch of the North Wind, her companion. Her eyes, the color of a winter sky, pierced through the blowing snow to focus on the sight far below. She was the Winter Queen. Everything in her realm was rigorously white; yet, below her, bright colors dotted the snow of the valley floor.

Spring was months away. She had banned colors in her realm during the winter months. The colorful forms moved over the even snow, leaving tracks that marred the purity of her realm. She was furious. Humans had come to her realm.

"We can drive them away," whispered the North Wind in her ear. Then he moved to stand beside her. His long, white tunic and mantle whipped with his growing fury.

The Winter Queen raised an arm in anger and called forth a blizzard. She swung her arm around and the snowstorm raged down the mountainside. She and the North Wind swept the people away, pelting them with wind-driven ice crystals as they fled.

Now no creature moved in her realm. It was pure white and even again. The Winter Queen sighed, and the snow stopped falling. The North Wind swirled up to stand at her side. All was still. Silence reigned once more, and the Winter Queen felt at peace. Over her realm lay the peace of winter slumber, of deep sleep.

The Winter Queen stood on the parapet of her palace, as still as a pillar of ice, and savored the silence of her realm. She stood for days, for weeks, in complete silence. Sometimes the North Wind stood beside her or embraced her; other times, he swept silently over the mountains and down the valley. Her mind slept, like the hibernating forest animals. She dreamed, but even her dreams were soundless. Northern lights, woven from her dreams, danced silently across the night sky.

A tinkling sound disturbed her sleep and brought her out of her dreams. It was not yet time for the melting of the icicles. The sound was not natural. The Winter Queen awoke abruptly. Bells jingled through the frosty air. Humans had returned to her realm. They moved across the snow-covered valley in colorful horse-drawn sleighs. Small, bright bells strung into the harnesses rang out merrily at each movement of the horses. The people in the sleighs laughed heartedly and sang rowdy tunes.

The Winter Queen raised both arms in wrath and brought them down with force. A vast avalanche rumbled like thunder down the mountainside to crush the invaders of her realm. The roaring avalanche made the land tremble. Death screams of people and horses pierced the air. She could feel their terror before they died, and she smiled contently. The rolling masses of snow covered them all. When all was still, she made the snow fall until her realm was even and silent again.

No creature made a sound in her realm. The Winter Queen sighed, and the snow stopped falling. All was deathly still. Silence reigned once more, and the Winter Queen felt satisfied with her revenge. Over her realm lay the peace of death.

The North Wind came down from the mountaintop and stood beside her.

"Come, my love, let us go to rest. I am out of breath, and you are pale and tired."

"Men have come to disturb me."

"I know. I have seen them wandering the valley. Colonies of men are spreading across the land. We could not keep them for long from this magnificent valley."

They looked down over their realm. The Queen of Spring was making her way up the valley, melting the snow as she went. For weeks, they watched her progress from the balcony of their bedroom. Every now and then, the North Wind would blow, just for fun, and the Winter Queen would send snow flurries. They prolonged the season beyond its usual time, but they could not hold onto the valley forever. Their time was ending this year.

The compacted snow of the avalanche was the last snow to melt. When the twisted limbs and heads of men and horses began to appear, their terror still frozen on their faces, the Queen of Spring fled down the valley. Carrion birds led the surviving men up the valley to collect their dead.

The men stood huddled, looking up with fear at the white mountain. The Winter Queen could hear their pleas to her to take pity on them next winter, but she had no pity and sent a snowstorm to flay them. They did not leave, though. They knew they had incurred her wrath, and they sought to appease her by building great pyres with the broken sleighs to burn their dead.

The blazing flames only served to infuriate her. Fire was the enemy of Winter. It could withstand even the North Wind. The Winter Queen and her companion howled their fury, but the fierce wind they sent down onto the group of men only whipped the flames higher. The men stood in a tight group with their funeral pyres between them and the wrath of the Winter Queen and the North Wind. Though their laments brought her joy, their presence at the foot of her mountain disturbed her and their fires inflamed hateful revenge in her heart. The icy crystals she flung from her hands finally drove them away, but their fires remained and burned throughout the night. By the light of the embers that still glowed at dawn, the Winter Queen narrowed her eyes and vowed that she would do all in her power to keep men from her valley.

"If they wanted to appease my anger, they should have taken their dead up the flanks of this mountain and thrown them into the crevices in the ice. Then I would have been able to look on the terrified faces of their dead for all eternity and take pride in my revenge on them. Instead, they have denied me of my prey by burning the bodies. They have robbed me of my revenge. They have insulted me, not honored me. They have earned my eternal wrath."

The North Wind looked at her as she spoke. Her face was dark with anger. Her heart was black with desire for revenge. He would have spoken a warning to her about the corruption that was growing in her soul, but he knew she was too angry now to listen to his words. He sighed and turned away. She had always been quick to anger, but peace had always returned to her heart once her anger was spent.

The men did not return in the days that followed, and neither did the Spring Queen. The Winter Queen laughed. As timid as she was, Spring might not return to the valley this year. Until their anger passed, the Winter Queen and the North Wind raged with snowstorms and blizzards until the Summer Queen peered into the valley. Then they retired to their bed to sleep throughout the summer and the beginning of fall.

The Winter Queen and the North Wind began their show of force long before the Autumn Queen left the valley. She tried to hold her place, but the North Wind stripped the colorful leaves from the trees and blew them out of the valley. No bright colors were allowed in the valley under their mountain palace. Snow fell early that year and continued to fall all winter and long into the spring. The Winter Queen filled the valley with deep snow, making it impossible for men or beast to move over the land. The North Wind blew all the seeds off the bushes. The grasses were covered in deep snow. No bird or animal came to feed in their realm that winter. Nothing moved in the valley.

When the Winter Queen and the North Wind saw the Spring Queen trying unsuccessfully to melt the abundant snow, they laughed and went to bed early. The Spring Queen would be busy until summer with the amount of snow they had left in their valley.

They slept soundly and heard nothing through the thick icy walls of their palace. They did not hear the glad singing of men in the valley that year, but they saw the new fields and gardens in the mouth of their valley when they awoke midway through fall. They stood on the parapet of their palace and stared in shock and horror at the sight of men working to reap an abundant harvest from their fields.

The Autumn Queen looked up at them as she moved her hands over the trees, causing the leaves to color under her fingertips. She was solemn in character and did not laugh at them, but a hint of a smile played at the corner of her mouth.

"With the abundant snow last year, the river ran strong all summer long. The men were able to increase the number of their gardens and, with the water irrigated from the river, their plants flourished even on the hottest of summer days. They have even built homes just outside of the valley. They thank and praise you for the abundant snows. You have brought fortune upon them after the hardship they suffered the past two winters."

The Autumn Queen had not done well to anger the Winter Queen and the North Wind with her words. They declared battle on autumn and brought hard frosts that threatened the last of the harvest. The North Wind and the West Wind, the companion of the Autumn Queen, warred with each other in the narrow valley, sending the icy crystals of the Winter Queen and the colorful leaves of the Autumn Queen swirling around the fleeing farmers. In the breaks between battles, the men took away the last of their produce and took refuge in their homes outside the valley. The valley was empty once more.

The Autumn Queen and the West Wind retreated, and the mountain and its valley were once again under control of the Winter Queen and the North Wind. The Winter Queen raised her arms to bring an abundant snowfall to her realm, but the North Wind stopped her arms before they fell. She turned on him in fury, but he spoke to her in strong, firm words.

"The abundant snows give men what they need: water in the spring. Stay your hands this winter. Let no snow fall upon our mountain or in its valley. Without snow, they will not have enough water in the summer to irrigate their crops. Their food plants shall wither and die. Their wells shall go dry. Without water, man cannot survive. They will leave this valley and we will win the battle without having to lift a hand."

His words encouraged the heart of the Winter Queen.

"You are right, my love. I will not give them what they want. But if we do not let them know that we still rule here, they will move into our realm. Fill the valley with your strongest breath and I will freeze everything. Let us chill men to the bone this winter."

The North Wind nodded in agreement and blew hard over the

valley for the rest of autumn, while the Winter Queen brought hard frosts. He blasted the valley with frigid wind all winter. He blew away the fences the men had built around their fields. He blew down the sheds they had built to keep their tools and sent the pieces rolling down the valley all the way into their little village. The North Wind did not stop or let up the force of his gales. He raged all winter and well into the spring.

When the East Wind came with the Spring Queen, another battle ensued. There was no snow for her to melt, but the Spring Queen found it difficult to nurture the plants back to life without the snowmelt. The Winter Queen did not send snow to the valley that spring, but she sent frosts that withered flowers and burned the new buds black. The howling North Wind flattened any plant that tried to rise and stripped the frozen flowers and buds off the trees. He and the Winter Queen held against spring as their forces allowed, but they were weary from their efforts all winter. By mid-spring they gave up and retreated to their palace on the mountain.

The brays of oxen, the sounds of metal on rock, and the shouted orders from mouths of men disturbed the sleep of the Winter Queen and the North Wind in mid-autumn. They went to look out from the parapet of their castle and stared in shock at the sight of men hauling the last fruits of their harvest away from fields at the foot of their mountain.

"Your plan was a good one," noted the Autumn Queen as she colored the leaves on the trees in the valley. "The men labored hard this year with little water in the river for their crops and their beasts to drink; but the wells were still full of water from the snows of previous years, and they survived. During the summer, they noted that there was more water in the mountain springs than in the river along the valley and they decided to plant half of their crops here. A handful of families established a small village here. I am afraid that you will have to live with their presence in your realm from now on."

Furious, the Winter Queen and the North Wind blew frosty winds and snow down onto the men below, but the oxen did not suffer from the cold and the men were dressed warmly. The men knew how cold this mountain could be. They knew the wrath of the Winter Queen and the North Wind.

The Autumn Queen and the West Wind fled to lower altitudes and let winter take the mountain valley earlier this year. The men took refuge in their homes. The North Wind and the Winter Queen howled against them with all their force, but the men had built sturdy houses and stalls far enough from the mountain slopes to avoid avalanches. The snow piled high, but this did not bother the men. They knew that water would return to the valley come spring.

The Winter Queen and the North Wind hurled their fury until almost mid-winter. Then the North Wind stopped to catch his breath.

"This is pointless. The men are well prepared. Our fury in years past has taught them how to survive. It has made them resourceful and prudent."

The Winter Queen nodded worriedly. "What can we do to convince them to leave?"

The North Wind shook his head and shrugged. "Now that they have taken hold, there is nothing we can do to force the men to leave our valley. When humans make up their mind to stay in a place, they will stay until they decide to leave. The harder you beat them, the more stubbornly they will stand their ground. Men are stubborn, but they are also lazy. They work hard when they need to, but they tire of it soon enough. They want an easy life, but life here in this dark and cold valley will never be easy for them. They will tire soon and leave. We must only be patient."

The Winter Queen snarled in anger. "I am not patient. I will not tolerate their presence here. There must be something I can do to get rid of them."

 174

She turned away and went back into their palace. The North Wind would have followed her, but she was angry, and he knew he could say nothing to calm her. He flew away up onto the mountain to wait until her anger passed.

Days later, from the top of the mountain, the North Wind heard singing voices rise from the valley. The villagers were merrily celebrating the Winter Festival. Worried that the singing would disturb the Winter Queen, the North Wind returned to their ice palace. He searched every room, but the Winter Queen was not there. He thought she must be lower in the valley, to whip up a massive snowstorm to punish the noisy villagers, but the skies were clear and sunny.

Not knowing where else to look, the North Wind blew down over the village and was surprised to see his companion in the village square. Disguised as a woman in a festive cream-colored dress, she was handing out winter treats to children and adults from a gilded box that hung around her neck with a bright red ribbon. The Winter Queen felt his presence and glanced up, smiling into the gentle wind. She laughed merrily and handed out the last of the sweet treats to a group of elderly women. The Winter Queen smiled with gleaming eyes as she watched the villagers, young and old alike, popping small, white cream puffs into their mouths. They begged her for more, but her box was empty.

"I will be back tomorrow," she promised. "I shall go home at once and work all night to satisfy your desires."

"The festival will last another two days. Can you please bring your winter treats every day of the festival?"

The villagers begged and pleaded with her, and she laughed.

"I would be honored to return every day of the Winter Festival to offer them. Now I must hurry away to make more. I will be back tomorrow, I promise."

As soon as she was out of sight of the village, the Winter Queen loosened the ribbons that bound up her long white hair in tight braids and it tumbled loose with the aid of the North Wind. She brushed her hands over her embroidered dress and the creamy cloth gave way to the frosty lace of her gown. The North Wind lifted her up into his embrace and carried her back to their palace.

"It pleases me to see that you have made peace with the men in the valley," he whispered into her ear as they stood on the parapet and watched the sun set behind the mountain. He laughed gently. "It is fitting that you have gone to them during the Winter Festival. They worship you this time of year."

The Winter Queen laughed, but her mood disturbed the North Wind. "Yes, they worship me, but I have not forgiven their offenses to me. I have discovered a way to take my revenge on them."

The North Wind pulled away and looked at her, perplexed at her words.

"I do not understand. You seemed so happy as you gave them those treats."

She laughed. "Of course I am happy that they are eating them with such gluttony." The sun disappeared behind the mountain crest and the sky darkened rapidly.

"Come with me. I will show you my plan for revenge."

With dread in his heart, the North Wind followed the Winter Queen into the palace. She led him to the room of spells where she worked her magic. The North Wind stood in the doorway, his arms tucked around his sides, as the Winter Queen set the gilded box on a block of ice in the center of the room. She wove her arms and hands in intricate patterns as she intoned her spell:

*Let my desire for revenge be sweet*
*I weave a spell of death into each treat*
*For each of these sweets they shall eat*
*A year of life shall be taken away*
*Heed no plea, from my plan I shall not sway*
*I care not for the future, come what may*

She repeated the spell incessantly, and at the end of each refrain,

176

a sweet miniature snowball formed in the air and fell into the box.

"What are you doing? Have you gone mad?" cried the North Wind, but her spell deafened her to his pleas. He tried to rush into the room to stop her cruel plan, but her spell froze him in the doorway. He could not stop her. She would have her revenge, come what may.

"You are condemning innocents to death. Your plan for revenge will taint your soul."

The cries of the North Wind could not penetrate the effect of her spell. He turned away, horrified. She had already taken decades of life from the villagers that day, and he was powerless to stop her plan for revenge in the days to come. He could try to stop the villagers from eating her deadly sweets, though.

The next morning, the Winter Queen left the palace on an ornate sled, laden with a huge, gilded chest full of her magicked treats. The North Wind tried to blow her off course, but her spell would not allow for interference. When that effort failed, he sped ahead to the village, raging through the streets. The people were outside celebrating the Winter Festival, honoring the Winter Queen. They fled from the North Wind, but not to their homes. The entire population of the village took refuge in the long hall they had built for public gatherings. The North Wind could see them peeping out of the windows, anxiously awaiting the Winter Queen. He could see their enthusiasm as they spotted her speeding down the mountainside on her sled, her gown flowing behind her like wind-whipped snow.

The North Wind tried to block her sled with a wall of wind, but she cut through it without even disturbing her hair. She steered the sled straight toward the door of the great hall. The people, seeing her coming, opened the door as she approached. With pompous air and festive flair, the Winter Queen entered the building on her sled, hardly slowing down. Cheering loudly, the villagers closed the door quickly behind her and the festivities began.

The hall was well-built with huge logs, solid walls, and a strong timbered roof. It was immune to winter storms and fierce winds, and even more so with the Winter Queen inside. The North Wind could not touch her, or the people who begged for her treats. He sighed in despair for the consequences of her perverse plan and retreated to the mountain.

The Winter Queen returned at sunset. The fatigue of pulling the sled up the mountain could not dim the satisfaction on her face. She smiled broadly as she gazed at the whiteness of the mountain snow. She looked up as she approached the palace and saw her companion on the parapet watching her. Her smile grew larger, and she waved to him with the innocence of a child. The North Wind frowned in disapproval, but she did not notice in her satisfaction with her plan for revenge.

The Winter Queen left the sled below and came to join the North Wind on the parapet to watch the last colors leave the sky. The gilded magical chest had returned to its original size, no larger than a jewelry box. She hugged it like a child to her breast as she spoke of the wonders of her day.

"The villagers love me. They worship me."

"If you are glad that they love and worship you, why are you killing them?"

"I am the Winter Queen, and this is my kingdom. There is no place for humankind in the kingdom of Winter. They will not leave, so they must die."

"Who will worship you when they are all dead?"

She laughed. His words made no sense.

"I do not need anyone to worship me. I am the Winter Queen, not a goddess. Now I must make my treats for them." She laughed again, turning back for one last comment.

"Can you imagine? They begged me to return all week long. They wanted to extend the Winter Festival for another four days. In that time, they could eat enough to end all their lives this winter." She sighed with regret. "It is too difficult for me to continue that long, though. It will be hard enough for me to make them tonight. I told them it was tiring for me to do this for them and that three days of festivities were enough."

"No one is obligating you to do this," the North Wind reminded her. "Do not waste your precious energies on these people." He tried to put his arm around her to pull her into his embrace, but she jerked away, pouting disappointedly at him.

"I promised them I would return with more than I brought today. Would you have me break my promises?"

"I wish you had never made them," he muttered.

"I do not break my promises and I do not go back on my word," she said.

Then the Winter Queen turned her back on him and hurried to her spell room with her magical box. The North Wind turned away to watch the stars appear in the sky. He hoped with all his heart that her spell would end with the Winter Festival, and that she would forget this folly over the next year.

The North Wind hardly recognized his companion as she left the palace the next morning. Her long dress, though still lined with white, was bright red in color. Her long white hair was rolled up into a bun, and she wore a long red cap on her head. She loaded a huge, gilded chest onto her sled, which became a sleigh with a snap of her fingers. The Winter Queen called two reindeer from the forest and harnessed them to the sleigh with bright red trappings, covered with bells. The North Wind could not believe what he saw.

The Winter Queen climbed onto the sleigh and shouted a command. The reindeer leaped forward, pulling the sleigh down the mountainside, bells tingling frenetically.

The North Wind shouted before she was out of sight. "You have become the thing you hate most!"

Furious, the North Wind refused to stay where he could hear the festivities of the villagers. He flew to the other side of the mountain and stayed until his anger calmed. Winter was ending when he returned to their ice palace. The Winter Queen was standing on the parapet looking over her realm, and he came to stand beside her, hoping that her anger had passed. She spoke to him as if he had never left her side.

"Look, they are burying the last of the elderly villagers. All the old people have died this winter. Two families have left the village for good, and they swore as they left that they would spread the word about the curse on this valley. Men will no longer come here. My plan for revenge is going exceedingly well. I shall continue to make my treats for those remaining until they are all dead."

The North Wind saw that her soul was already corrupt beyond recovery. He shook his head in pity at the loss of her honor.

"I will have no part in your folly. I am leaving. I will find a purer Winter Queen."

She brushed him off. "If you will not share my desires, I do not want you here."

The North Wind left at once, flying away over the mountains to the north. The Winter Queen was not disturbed by his departure. Her heart focused only on her plan for revenge.

The Spring Queen did not come into the realm of the Winter Queen that year. She stopped at the mouth of the valley, shocked at the sight of so many graves and repelled by the smell of death in the air. The crops planted that spring by the remaining adults matured poorly and yielded barely enough during that timid summer to keep the remaining villagers fed through the winter. There would not have been enough food if the last of the adults had not died at the end of harvest.

The Autumn Queen watched children bury their parents and her tears fell over the valley. The leaves on the trees did not turn bright colors that year. They turned gray, molded, and rotted off the trees. The trees and plants rotted under her tears. The children remaining would have despaired and run away, but the Winter Queen came early that year and covered the valley with clean, white snow. The children were happy to see that winter had returned. They loved to play in the snow. They loved the Winter Festival. They loved the Winter Queen. They had food to eat in the storerooms. They still had cows for milk and chickens for eggs. They were the proud inhabitants of the valley of the Winter Queen, and they would never leave. They would stay there for the rest of their lives.

The Winter Queen stood alone on the parapet of her palace at dawn on the last day of the Winter Festival and watched the last boy in the village bury the bodies of his brother and sister. These two had died during the night, after burying the last of the children the afternoon before. The children had eaten dozens of her treats in the first two days of the festival. She smiled with satisfaction. Now there was only one. This was the dawn of the last day of man in her realm.

The Winter Queen did not need her sleigh today. She did not change into the red dress and cloak that she now wore to the Winter Festivals. She took the small, gilded box with her treats and drifted down to the village on a light snow flurry. The boy looked up at the sight of the first snowflakes and then he saw her, brilliant white and sparkling, floating down like a snowflake to stand before him. He sighed in wonder and awe.

"I told them. I told them that you were really the Winter Queen, but no one believed me. I was right, though, wasn't I?"

The Winter Queen smiled. "Yes, you were right. I am the Winter Queen, and you are in my realm."

Despite his grief, the boy stood before her and bowed deeply.

"I told those that left this valley that they were wrong to leave. This is the realm of the Winter Queen, and it is an honor to live here. They didn't believe me, though. They didn't want to stay."

"Why did you stay?" Her voice was as hard and sharp as ice. The boy misunderstood her accusation. He thought it was a test of his loyalty.

"We stayed because we love winter. Those who left dreaded it. The first snowflakes of the year always make us happy. We smile when we see the designs the frost makes on the windows of our homes. This valley is magnificent when it is covered with snow. The Winter Festival is the best, though. We look forward to it all year. We look forward to seeing you and eating your delicious treats."

The boy looked down at his dirty hands and bent to wipe them in the snow. He did not see the disgust in the eyes of the Winter Queen as he dirtied her pure white snow. The boy stood and ran his wet hands over the back of his pants. He looked up at her then, shyly.

"You are so beautiful. I told them that you were not pretending to be the Winter Queen. I told them that you were really her. I am glad that you came here to see me today, even though I am all alone now."

"It is the last day of the Winter Festival," she said with a sly smile. "I saw that you were all alone and needed comfort. I have brought my treats for you." She extended the box out towards the boy and smiled wider as he licked his lips. She opened the box and he peered inside. He was disappointed.

"There are only two," he pouted. He took one, though, and ate it slowly, relishing each tiny bite until it was gone.

"You know that I am the Winter Queen. These treats are magical. I can make as many as you want to eat."

The boy smiled broadly as he reached for the last one in the box. "I knew they had to be magical because sometimes they are rich and filling, and other times they are light and airy."

The Winter Queen smiled ironically. A year of life was not the same for everyone. She closed the box and tucked it away into the pocket of her white mantle.

"You are all alone now. Do you still want to stay here?"

The boy nodded between bites. "We were talking about this last night. With all the food in the storerooms of all the homes, we could survive two years or more without worry. We would not have to leave this beautiful place." He paused, looking at the last bite. His voice was sad now. "They died during the night though, and I am all alone." His voice drifted off. He did not eat the last bite.

182

"Do you want to leave, like the others?"

The boy looked up in shock that she would suggest such a thing.

"No, especially not now that I know you are really the Winter Queen." He popped the last bite into his mouth. "With all the food, I could survive three years, maybe more. I will stay here."

The Winter Queen smiled. "Then you will need more sweets."

She took a step back and began swirling her hands, pulling magic and snowflakes from the air. The Winter Queen intoned her spell:

*Let my desire for revenge be sweet*
*I weave a spell of death into each treat*
*For each of these sweets they shall eat*
*A year of life shall be taken away*
*Heed no plea, from my plan I shall not sway*
*I care not for the future, come what may*

The boy paled as he heard her words and took a step away from her.

"They were right. The people who left said there was a curse on this valley. It was impossible that so many young people were dying. It was your spell. You made us die before our time." His voice trembled in a mix of fear and anger. His whole body trembled, but he did not have the strength to run away.

"Humans invaded my realm. You had no right to live here. Will you leave now that you know the truth?"

The boy thought for a moment. "You took away the years of my life, like you did with the others. If I went away, how much longer would I live?"

The Winter Queen laughed. "What did you answer before when I asked? You said three years, maybe more. You ate two treats. So you have one year left, maybe more."

The boy gulped. "Even if I leave now?"

The Winter Queen nodded, smiling wickedly.

The boy took a deep breath and squared his shoulders. "Then I will stay. If I have only a year or a bit more of life, then let me live and die in a place I love."

Now the Winter Queen smiled proudly on her loyal follower.

"If you do not wish to have your body torn apart by carrion birds or wolves, then you should dig a grave for yourself."

The boy froze in fear, but only for a moment. He angrily grabbed his shovel and dug a shallow grave beside those of his family. The effort tired him, though, and wore away the last of his strength. The Winter Queen grinned as she watched him work.

When the boy sat down beside the empty grave, too tired to stand, the Winter Queen leaned down over him and offered him the treat.

Forgetting the death spell in his fatigue, the boy reached out thankfully to take it. Weak and shaky after his effort, the boy popped the whole cream puff into his mouth. When he felt the last of his strength flowing away, he remembered.

"Three years," the Winter Queen whispered into his ear.

"Maybe a bit more," the boy answered, but he fell back into the grave he had just finished digging. He tried to drag himself out, but his life was slipping away too quickly.

"Three years, no more," the Winter Queen laughed in triumph.

The boy was under her spell, though, and could not hate her even now.

"I will never leave this valley," he promised with his last breath. "I will stay with you forever."

The last human in her realm died then, and the Winter Queen exulted in a swirling dance with snowflakes, until her sight fell upon the boy. He had died with his eyes open, and he seemed to stare at her accusingly.

The Winter Queen did not want to see him or any human ever again. Though she was never one for physical labor, she picked up the shovel and scooped the earth from the mound into the grave until it completely covered the body. Then the Winter Queen lifted her arms and called down a heavy snowfall; but her hands and her gown were dirty with earth, and the snow that fell was the color of a winter grave.

Furious, the Winter Queen returned to her palace on the mountain and tried to wash away the filth; but try as she might, she could still see traces of dirt under her fingernails. Her beautiful dress was irrecoverable. In fury, she threw it off the parapet, and it plummeted to the rocks below like a dying swan.

She trembled with rage as she slipped into a clean tunic. She looked for the North Wind. He could calm her with his embrace. Then she remembered that he had left. The Winter Queen listened for his voice, but the valley and the mountains were silent.

She broke the silence, calling for him desperately from the parapet; but he did not answer. There was not even a hint of a breeze. She was stunned. He had truly left her. She screamed in rage, her cries echoing from the mountainsides. She filled the valley with agony and despair.

She remembered his words to her: *you have become the thing you hate most.* He was right. She felt filthy and smelled of death. She found herself disgusting.

Shamed, but still proud, the Winter Queen stifled her cries and turned away from the hateful valley, now empty and silent. She left the parapet and wandered the halls and corridors of her palace but found no peace; they were empty and silent. She could feel the trail of filth she left behind her. She had to clean the stain from her hands, from her soul.

The Winter Queen wandered over the mountain slopes, searching for streams to wash in, but they were either frozen or dried up. She remembered the well in the village and went there to wash. The mud around the well only dirtied her more. She had defiled herself by her interactions with humans. She would never be clean again.

Resigned to her fate, the Winter Queen looked around the empty village. She had imagined she would be glad to be rid of the humans, but she felt nothing. The village was as empty and ugly as her heart.

The children had lived savagely in the past few months. They had not taken proper care of the animals, which had escaped from their pens to find greener pastures down the valley. The fields were abandoned. The village had fallen into disrepair and ruin. There was no color, no life, no sound, no warmth.

Disgusted by dirt-brown snow and gray mold, the Winter Queen went through the homes of the villagers and found colored scarves, shawls, and blankets. She draped these over the open doors and windows of the homes and over the tombstones. Disturbed by the silence, she went through the stalls and found all the bells that had hung around the necks of domestic animals or adorned the harnesses. She hung these on the walls and doors of the stalls, over the fences and in the trees around the village.

The Winter Queen stood back to judge her work. The colors lifted her heart a bit, but everything was silent and still. She wished that the North Wind would blow over her, even in anger, but the air was heavy and still. It pressed on her, choking her, and she ran from the village to climb her mountain in search of cleaner and lighter air.

As she approached her palace, the Winter Queen was stunned to see cracks and fissures in the ice walls. The stains she had left earlier had corrupted the purity of her palace and had weakened its integrity. As she watched in horror, her palace crumbled to pieces before her eyes. Chunks of ice detached and fell crashing at her feet or tumbled down the steep slopes of the mountain. Distraught by her loss, the Winter Queen fled down the mountain and returned to the only place left to her.

She fell to her knees near the graves just outside the village and wept. She wept for hours, or for days. Time had no meaning anymore. She knew that the Queen of Fall had not come to her valley that year and she knew that the timid Queen of Spring would run as soon as she saw the empty village and all the graves. Life would never return to the valley. It would remain dead all year, gray and brown.

Out of the corner of her eye, the Winter Queen saw the colored cloths moving slightly on the tombstones and she heard the distant tinkling of bells. She looked up, hoping to see the North Wind returning to her, but she was alone. As she looked around, the colored cloths fluttered like wings of birds, and the bells rang merrily.

Then the Winter Queen remembered the last promise of the dying boy: *I will never leave this valley. I will stay with you forever.*

She was not alone. He was here; they were all here, she knew it. The spirits of every life she had taken were here now to haunt her. They would be with her for eternity. She was their queen.

Resigned to her fate, the fate she deserved, she stood and wandered through the empty village. The spirits followed her joyfully, as the villagers had done before she had taken their lives. The colored scarves and shawls swirled in a dance around her as she passed, and the bells rang joyfully.

Her long hair was now gray and her face was grim. Her gown, woven from the ash and the dusty remains of her victims, swept over the barren earth of her hollow victory.

She was the Queen of Death.

She was the thing she hated most.

# GLACE NOIR
## By Kimberly Grymes

IF THE PEOPLE OF DORIAN REMEMBER my birth name, they don't use it. They only know me now as Glace Noir, the underwater creature that lives in the south-side cove along Lake Grogan. I know this because every now and then, someone will come to the water's edge and call to me, begging me to end the everlasting winter cycle I've cursed the kingdom of Dorian to live.

"Glace Noir, please release us from the endless winter," they plead. I find it amusing that more recently they've started adding, "Or at least let us die," to their pathetic requests.

My answer is always the same, regardless if I let the messenger live or not. I tell them, "When you release me, then I shall release the kingdom." I can't help the cackles that escape, echoing throughout the cove and mocking their request for freedom.

To be honest, this whole you-curse-me-and-I-curse-you thing is quite ridiculous, and it wasn't my fault to begin with. Dorian wouldn't even be in this predicament if the people would only stand up to the one person who can really end their misery. Their beloved ruler—my brother—King Philip.

I wasn't always this fearsome creature cursed to an underwater prison. And just because I cannot recall how long it's been since I've walked dry land, that doesn't mean I've forgotten my life from before.

I will never forget.

Never.

# THEN

Dorian's downfall began long before I was born. When a lonely king, pressured to take a wife from one of the surrounding kingdoms, fell in love with a commoner from the north. Being from the north may sound harmless, but the people of my mother's village were widely known for their mysterious and unearthly powers. The southern kingdoms feared the magic my mother's people possessed, so they banned anyone from traveling beyond the snowy borders leading into the northern lands.

But my father, King Sebastian, went anyway. He was known for his stubborn ways, doing whatever he deemed beneficial for *his* kingdom. "It is my kingdom, and I shall rule as I see fit," he would say to anyone questioning his orders. In secrecy, he'd told me that the real reason he wanted to travel north was because he was curious to know if the rumors were true—if there really was magic. It was during his first visit to the snowy lands that he fell in love with one of the northern commoners—my mother.

The two were married within six months, making her Dorian's new queen—but by title only. It took a long time for the people of Dorian to even glance her way. Not until years later, when she gave birth to me and my twin brother, Philip, did they begin to accept her into their hearts. But only as the mother of their future heir, not as their queen.

Our mother might have come from the frigid north, but her heart was warm with love for her family and the kingdom. She never minded the whispers or the fake smiles. She was just happy they were smiling.

I wish I'd paid more attention to the signs of my brother's discontent. Maybe if I'd attended court more often and mingled with the lords and council members, but attending court was boring and swallowed up the whole day. To me, that was valuable time I preferred to spend with Mother, reading her books about the history of her people and learning how to use the magic that flowed through my veins.

While I kept to my books, Philip spent his days following Father around, trying to take an active role in running a kingdom. Father indulged Philip's keen interest because he was a kind man who loved his son. Though, whenever I was nearby, Father would single out my opinion on matters of the kingdom. Philip would offer his solution, but Father only cared to hear what I had to say. This angered my brother, but I always mistook it as sibling rivalry.

Then one day, Mother pulled me aside and warned me to be mindful of Philip's temper. We were getting older, and his childish tantrums had festered into something dark.

She explained to me, "You might have been born on the same day, but you came into this world three minutes before Philip. You, Celeste, are the rightful heir—not him. So please be careful."

I didn't believe her. Philip was my brother, and we were family. He would never go so far as to hurt me just for the crown.

For many years, we continued in our daily routines. Philip kept his distance, which was fine by me. I rarely attended court, spending most afternoons with Mother in the northern tower of the castle. I'd reread her old spell books and practice the ancient language of the north. Mother would praise me on how my casting abilities were beyond what she could do when *she* was twenty years of age.

Then one day, things took a turn for the worse. I'd been so

consumed by my studies that I hadn't realized Father had grown extremely ill. The last night we spoke, the night he passed away, he asked me one thing. "Please, Celeste. Promise me that you'll give Dorian the attention it deserves. Don't run away from your duties as their future queen. Be strong, stand tall, and show them the powerful ruler I know you can be."

Father's death was hard, but it hit Philip harder. My brother wouldn't even look at me after that night, as if it were my fault Father had died.

Over the next few days, the lords of the royal court rallied against my mother. They said it wasn't right for an outsider to rule over Dorian, especially one from the northern lands. Their anger and disapproval spread like wildfire throughout the kingdom. Farmers, fishermen, blacksmiths, bakers, and others all joined in protest, saying the king's wife had no place as their queen. Afraid for her life, our mother made a deal with the lords to step down and allow King Sebastian's next of kin to take the throne—me.

I only agreed to become queen to alleviate the tension the lords had created with the citizens of Dorian. And it seemed to work. Everyone liked the idea of me becoming their next queen. Everyone except Philip, which I didn't realize until it was too late.

I'll never forget the morning of my coronation, because it followed the night of my mother's murder.

I awoke to Philip standing over my bed. His expression was like stone, as was his delivery. "She's dead. Mother's no longer with us. Now, get dressed. It's your big day." His words took some time to sink in. He explained the culprit had escaped the castle grounds before anyone realized she'd been killed. Then, while I still lay in my bed, in a daze from the news, he turned and left.

The loud slam of the oak door jostled me to my senses, and, wasting no time, I hurried to dress myself. The last thing I wanted was to face my ladies-in-waiting, or anyone else for that matter. I didn't want their sad eyes burrowing into me, or their condolences weighing on my already heartbroken thoughts.

It was all too much. First losing Father, and then Mother. And to top it off, later that day, I was expected to pledge my loyalty and devotion to Dorian as their new ruler—a birthright I had no desire to fulfill. I needed to get away. If only for a brief moment to regain my composure before standing in front of everyone at court.

So, I retreated to the one place I knew would bring me closer to her—the cove.

Our castle had been built atop a shallow cliff overlooking Lake Grogan, and at the base of the cliff was a small cove. At first, it was impossible to reach, until Father commissioned quarry workers to chisel out a stairwell for better access. When the stairwell and pier were finished, he reserved the cove for his beloved wife and children. It was Mother's private sanctuary. A place she could go whenever she needed to escape the chaos of the castle.

It was exactly what I needed.

I grabbed my blue cloak and rushed down to the lowest level of the castle, deep beneath the rocky hillside where the entrance had been carved out at the base of the cliff. A chill hung in the air outside, as if winter wasn't ready to let spring have its turn.

My boots sank in the cold sand as I raced across the beach toward the wooden pier. The second I stepped onto the first wooden plank, a strong wind rushed at me, lifting the fabric of my cloak into a fluttering ripple. It felt as if the wind were trying to lift me up and away, helping me to escape my troubles.

When I reached the end of the pier, I fell to my knees and released the tears I'd been holding. I pounded my fists against the wood, then pressed both hands flat to the pier. The frost on the wood felt good against my heated skin. The cool relief shifted into a subtle vibration, making my palms tingle. It was as if the frost were reminding me of the magic running through my veins.

Leaning into the wood, I opened my mind to the magic of the north. Mother once spoke of how the more powerful casters could communicate through thought, no matter the distance. So, when a cluster of faint voices in the back of my mind grew louder, it only startled me for a brief moment before I stopped crying and started listening. Their collective voices whispered inside my head, encouraging me to seek revenge for my mother's death. *"It might have been one hand that killed your mother, but the kingdom plotted as a whole. Punish them all! Give them something worse than death."*

"No," I cried, shaking my head. "I can't... I won't!"

Now, looking back, I cringe when I think about how naïve I was during my days on land.

Lifting the skirt of my dress, I moved closer to the edge of the pier. A layer of ice stretched out over the water, butting up against the rock wall that enclosed the cove from the rest of Lake Grogan. The morning sun peered through the narrow gap. Out in the distance, the waters of the lake glistened, while the waters within the cove remained dark. With one hand, I reached over the side of the dock and brushed away the thin layer of snow covering the white ice. Then I pressed one hand to the surface and whispered the ancient words of the northern people. Like a flower blooming in spring, the opacity of the ice faded, expanding outward and providing a crystal-clear view to the waters below. A family of fish swam by, piquing my curiosity at how any creature could survive such freezing temperatures.

I sat there, letting the world beneath the water distract me from the ache in my heart. In that moment, I wanted to stay there forever. I never wanted to be queen. I only wanted to live a happy life with my family and learn how to embrace my heritage. At that moment, I decided I was going to march into the royal courtroom and tell my brother he could have it all.

"Celeste!" Philip called, interrupting my thoughts.

I leaned up and faced my brother. He stood on the beach with a line of royal guards behind him. Five on each side, standing at attention. Their gazes stared out past me.

"Sister, I need you to come here," Philip called again.

"Has something happened?" I asked, unsure of what this visit could mean. Why had he come to the cove with a protection detail?

When I didn't move, he lifted his chin and straightened his stance. A passing breeze caught his hair, momentarily pushing back the wavy black strands that curtained his face.

I remember there wasn't a hint of humor or kindness in his expression, only determination. The naïve girl I was couldn't help but wonder what I'd done to anger him.

So I stood and brushed my hands along my dress, straightening out any creases. I didn't realize I was in any danger until Philip stepped onto the pier. From beneath his cloak, hints of white light gleamed along the hemline.

*He's going to use magic on me.*

You see, I wasn't the only one who possessed the magic of the northern people; Philip did too. He didn't practice as often as I did—or so he wanted me to believe. But I knew he'd been practicing in secrecy. It amused me to watch him without him knowing. I guess I'd always hoped he'd set aside any ill-fated feelings for me because of the crown and remember our childhood friendship. To value our shared culture over politics. But seeing the stone-cold stare in his eyes that day as he approached me on the pier, I realized there was nothing between us. He only saw me as an obstacle in his way to the crown.

I offered him a kind expression, hoping to give myself more time to think of a way out of this mess. "If you're upset with me for wandering outside the castle without an escort, then I apologize. I needed some fresh air, that's all. I shall return shortly."

Philip paused, halfway out onto the pier.

The silence between us lingered, as if he were trying to find the right words to a delicate conversation. Meanwhile, the magic in my core stirred and the voices of the north returned, warning me, *"He's here to end you."*

I feared they were right, but to what degree? There was no way Philip would actually kill me. He wasn't a murderer.

My heart raced as he lifted his hand from beneath his cloak. The tips of his fingers illuminated with a bright light. "Celeste, daughter

194

of King Sebastian and princess to the Dorian kingdom, I curse you to never set foot on land again. I bind you to the cove waters for eternity. No man, woman..."

"Philip, no! Please!" I pleaded, but he didn't stop.

"...or child shall free you from your underwater prison!"

My gaze shifted from Philip to the icy water surrounding me.

*"Your time is running out, Princess,"* the voices in my head whispered. *"You know what you must do."*

Philip paused in his incantation. "Celeste! I'm sorry about Mother. If it eases your mind, she didn't feel any pain." Then he closed his eyes and continued chanting the binding spell.

I couldn't believe what he'd just confessed. The sound of his voice faded, replaced by the pounding of my heart. A cold, tingling sensation coursed through my veins. When I glanced at my hands, the tips of my fingers had turned white. Frost crystals sprawled up my hands, wrists, and arms in an intricate lattice pattern. The power inside me pulsed, syncing with my raging heart. The northern magic was right. They must *all* be punished.

I lowered my head and whispered a counter-spell.

"Oh, no you don't!" He raised his other arm, and with both glowing hands aimed at me, he shouted, "I claim your magic, Celeste, as my own!" He reached out and began pulling an invisible rope—a tether that yanked at my insides.

"No!" I screamed, holding on to my magic. I had no idea where he'd learned such a spell, to steal the power of another. It was nothing Mother ever shared with me or anything I'd read of in her spell books.

*"Ticktock, ticktock,"* the northern magic whispered in my mind. *"Your future is inevitable, but you can still claim your revenge. But you must hurry."*

"Don't take my magic, Philip! It's all I have left of her!" When he didn't falter, I acted. I looked to the sky, and with all my strength, I gathered whatever magic he hadn't stolen from me yet into my core. Then I called out to the magic of the north, "Let my final spell's worth be equal to the love and devotion I have for my mother." Dipping my chin, I stared at Philip. "You, brother, may claim my kingdom, but only until the curse you've bestowed upon me is broken. Let this kingdom be enveloped in snow and ice, and frozen in time for as long as I am a prisoner to this cove." Bowing my head, I spoke the ancient words, casting the spell that carried out my wishes.

A ball of light the size of an apple shot out of my chest. Instead of flowing toward Philip, the last of my magic flew upward into the sky and exploded, raining down as a flurry of thick snow.

It took a few seconds for Philip to notice the snow because he was still reveling in his newly acquired power. "I'll handle the weather after I've finished dealing with you." His ruthless expression finally broke, and a wide grin appeared. "Now, off to your prison!"

From the palms of his hands, a burst of wind rushed at me, lifting me from the pier and tossing me over the side. As I was thrust backward, I stared up into the falling snow and thought, *This is far from over, brother.* My body slammed into the ice, shattering it like glass. I wriggled my cloak free from around my neck as my body sank deeper into the dark, icy waters of the cove. The corset of my dress pinched at my skin, and when I glanced down, the satin fabric had changed to shimmering scales. The skirt of my dress clung to my legs, twisting tighter and tighter until they were bound together and layered with large, iridescent scales. At first, I struggled to swim, but then a wide translucent fin unfolded where my feet should have been, allowing me to regain my balance. The long sleeves of my dress vanished, exposing the now bluish-green skin along my arms. My face and hair seemed untouched by my brother's spell that had changed me into something a fisherman might catch and cook.

My lungs burned and I couldn't hold my breath any longer. When I opened my mouth, cold water coated my throat and filled my lungs. At first, I thought I was drowning, but then I exhaled, and inhaled. There was no pain, and it felt as natural to breathe in water as it had in air.

196

I blinked several times and my eyes adjusted. The midnight world beneath the water was no longer daunting, but beautiful. There were rock formations, plant life, and a variety of aquatic creatures swimming and walking along the lake floor.

*"This is your curse—your prison for eternity,"* the collective of voices echoed in my mind.

"How can I still hear you?" Using my tail fin, I spun in circles, seeking out their presence. "I thought I lost all my magic."

*"One can never completely lose their magic. It's a part of you, and as long as you're still alive, then so is your magic."*

"Then I can fight now." I looked up to the surface.

*"No. You're too weak. Let the kingdom simmer in their new prison."*

"My spell worked?"

*"Indeed, child. Indeed."*

A shadow emerged over the broken edges of the ice above. With a flick of my tail, I swam closer, but not to where I'd be seen. It was Philip. His distorted appearance lingered over the pier's edge. I waited until I heard his footsteps pounding the wooden planks of the pier before getting a closer look. Carefully, I raised the top of my head from the water. Being able to cross the water's surface meant I could still interact with the world above, at least. Webbed fingers with long, pointy nails clutched the edge of the broken ice. The beach was empty, and a dusting of snow had already covered the sand.

For a second, I thought Philip had left with his guards, but then he shouted into the air, "Whatever you think you've done, I shall find a way to undo it. This is my kingdom now! Do you hear me? Dorian is mine!"

He stomped along the pier and trudged up the beach, never looking back as he disappeared through the carved archway of the cliffside.

I let go of the ice and floated to the depths of my new prison. My body sank until it hit the sandy floor of the cove's bottom, causing a cloud of murky water to surround me. It was at that moment I decided I wasn't going to be the foolish little girl anymore.

"If it's a monster he wishes me to be, then it is a monster he will get."

That was the last time I saw Philip. Over the years, he's never returned to the cove, and only sends expendable messengers, because he knows even in his triumph—he's lost.

# Now

I'm barely awake when a man's voice calls to me from the world above. "Glace Noir!"

Rolling over in my bed of silt, I hide my head beneath one arm, hoping the man will come to his senses and leave before... I hate thinking about the bloodshed, even if it is who I am now.

Time means nothing anymore. The sun rises and sets, as does the moon, but the seconds and minutes and days never move forward. Surrounding the kingdom, so I've been told, is a magical barrier of snow. A nonstop blizzard so thick and high that no one can see the world beyond it.

"Are you down there? I have a message from the king."

*Of course I'm down here, you daft idiot,* I think while glaring up into the open waters. My gaze drifts to the green moss growing in the cracks of the rock wall surrounding me. I built the makeshift home during the first few months of my imprisonment. Those nights were some of the hardest. I slept alongside the wall I built, pretending I'd fallen asleep in Father's study, against the stone wall of the castle.

"Glace Noir!"

*Ugh, fine.* With an eye roll and a forceful whip of my tail, I push off from the cove floor. Cloudy water swirls within the enclosed circle of my home as I shoot upward into the open water. Even with the sunlight glimmering along the surface, the world down here is shrouded in an everlasting midnight blue. Arching my back, I stretch my arms over my head, grazing my fingers along the tip of my tail fin. I do a quick spin, shaking any remnants of sand from my hair before swimming toward the shoreline.

En route, I rip out a handful of pondweed and nibble on the ends before reaching the shallow area of the cove. I've never ventured up to the beach. Too risky. Instead, I prefer to lure my prey out onto the pier. I dive low beneath the pier, ignoring the skeletons that have piled up over the years at the base of the wooden posts.

Coming to the other side of the pier, I lift my head out of the water, but only to the bridge of my nose. I watch the young man searching the waters along the shoreline. He looks like most, with his shabby locks sticking out beneath a wool cap, an old scarf wrapping his neck just below his thick beard, and tattered patches mending a heavy coat. I laugh when the idiot loses his balance and stumbles out into the water. He's barely in past the top of his boots, and yet he screams and splashes water everywhere in his pathetic retreat. Halfway up the beach, he spins, frantically patting his body down as if I were a leech and I've latched myself onto him.

After seeing enough, I close my eyes and draw on the magic of the north. I'm supposed to be reserving it, but I can't help the bloodlust of the creature I've become. Silently, I call upon the magic for a simple glamor and an enchanting voice to help lure him. Previous encounters have taught me that approaching people as the aquatic creature I am scares them off. I've tried ignoring the lust inside me, but then I end up doing more than just drowning them. So, this is the price I must pay each time my idiot brother sends a poor soul to the cove with one of his messages.

When the glamor spell is complete, I peek around the support post. "Hello?" I say with a fragile voice. Appearing weak and nervous helps the illusion. "What do you want?"

The man stops scrambling about, and when he spots me, moves closer. At the water's edge, he tugs off his wool cap and holds it to his chest, flattening his hair with his free hand. Eyes wide, he says, "You *are* as beautiful as they say."

I give him a small smile, as if following a script in a play. I just want to get through all of this as fast as I can, so I dunk beneath the water, skipping past the monotonous small talk. They all ask the same questions— *"What's it like being a lake creature?"* or *"Will you please free the kingdom?"* or *"Why does no one age?"*

The second I disappear, he starts yelling after me. "Wait! Don't go! I have a message from the king!"

I couldn't care less about the message unless Philip were here to say it to my face. But he's not here, so I'm forced to listen to yet another pathetic attempt from one of my brother's expendable cronies.

"I'm over here!" I call out, resurfacing on the other side, a bit farther along the pier.

The man hesitates, but only for a second, as if he's trying to resist—but he can't. Twisting his cap in his hands, he shuffles onto the pier. I swim backward, stopping at the end of the dock.

He follows, though his gaze is focused on the open waters below.

When he reaches the end, I ask, "What's your name?" Each word from my glamored lips keeps him entranced.

Crouching to one knee, he tells me, "Griffin."

"Nice to meet you, Griffin."

He glances toward the beach, then back to me. I know he's under my spell, yet something has him distracted.

"Griffin, is everything okay?"

"Yes. I, uh... I haven't been completely honest with you."

I sink my shoulders beneath the water's surface, a strange tightness pulling at my skin. I can't remember the last time I felt nervous—caught off guard—and by a simpleton. Every time Griffin turns and looks at the beach, I do too. What is he looking for?

Twisting his cap, he sucks in the frigid air before asking, "I

know you won't release the kingdom of your curse, but I was wondering—"

"I will tell you," I interrupt, "what I tell the others begging me to end the kingdom's curse." I can't help the venom in my tone. I'm tired of being blamed for their misery. "Warmer days will return once my brother releases me from this prison. He is the one responsible, and he is the only one who can undo all of this."

Griffin's brows pinch together, and he licks his chapped lips before leaning closer. "Your brother? He's responsible for the curse? Not you?"

I nod, my nose dipping into the water. I don't want to expose too much of myself in case there is a threat somewhere waiting for a vulnerable moment. A moment I refuse to give them.

He slips the wool cap over his head and stands. Abruptly, he spreads his arms wide to the sky and shouts, "Thank you, for hearing our prayers!" Eagerness has replaced his anxious nerves, which confuses me. "Where can I find your brother? I must speak with him."

"My brother?"

Griffin looks down at me, a smile stretching from ear to ear. "Oh, Glace Noir. This whole time, we thought it was you. King Philip said it was you who cursed the kingdom. But it was your brother! Ha! Wait—" He freezes on the dock, mid-excitement. "You said you've told this to others?" I nod, and he continues, "And then you..." He gestures to the water with his eyes. "...kill them?" I nod again. I've never lied. I may entice and lure people out to their deaths, but I've never lied. He shuffles from one corner of the dock to the other. "But why? Why not let them live so they can confront your brother? That would help you too, would it not?"

I slowly glide beneath the water to the corner Griffin has moved to while answering, "It would, but you're all so devoted to Philip. You helped him plot against my mother. I will never forgive any of you for that."

"Your mother?" Griffin narrows his eyes. "Philip? Like King

Philip? You think he's your brother?"

Griffin's words strike hard. Has it been so long since I've walked on land that they've all forgotten about me—their beloved princess?

"What is my name?"

The man glances over at the beach, then back at me. "Glace Noir."

"No, that is the name my brother, your king, gave me after he turned me into this monster and imprisoned me in this cove." I pause, letting that bit of information sink in. "My name is Celeste, and I was to be queen of Dorian. Philip is my brother—my twin— and was born three minutes after me. He wanted the crown, and I was in his way."

Griffin shakes his head in disbelief. "It can't be true. Why would he let this nightmare continue? You're saying he could've ended it all this time?"

"I am. Now, I want to know what you meant when you said you weren't being completely honest with me about having a message from your king."

Our conversation has drawn out longer than any other. Usually by now, I'm done and back in my home as another body sinks to the pile of bones beneath the pier. But I'm curious to know what he's hiding. I'm also giving him the benefit of the doubt because I find it interesting to learn that my brother has somehow misled the people to believe I was born this way, and I'm nothing more than a terror on their kingdom.

"Well," he starts, then turns to wave a hand toward the beach. "If you weren't going to end the curse, then I was going to ask you for a favor."

"A favor?" Movement catches my attention from the carved doorway in the cliffside. A woman steps out holding a young man's hand. He looks to be fifteen or sixteen years old.

"If you won't, or can't, end the curse, will you please give us peace like you've given the others?"

I stare at him, then at the woman leading the young man out

onto the pier. The boy stops several times, but then moves after the woman whispers something in his ear.

"What is she telling him?" I ask Griffin.

"That it'll all be over soon."

*Peace through death?*

I let myself sink below the water's surface to take in the bones piled up beneath the pier. I stare at them, and even though they are only bones, no flesh, I can tell they're smiling. They're free. I never gave it much thought that killing them would also release them from the curse. The curse that's meant to punish them for supporting Philip.

Well, that ends today. I'll find another way to appease the cravings of the creature inside of me. Returning to the water's surface, I see the woman and the boy standing next to Griffin.

"Take me first," the woman says, stepping out in front.

"No. I don't think I will," I say with a cunning smirk. "Instead, I think we can help each other." They glance at one another, puzzled looks crossing their faces.

Griffin moves closer to the dock edge. "So, you will break the curse?"

I nod, and they hug each other and cheer. The end of the pier jostles, and they all freeze, hoping not to fall into the icy waters.

"But I wasn't lying about not being able to break the curse. The only way the everlasting winter will end and time will resume is for my brother, your King Philip, to release me from this underwater prison. To restore my human form and allow me to take my place as Queen of Dorian."

"He won't agree to any of that!" the woman shouts.

Griffin holds out a hand, trying to calm the woman, before facing me. "She's right. There's no way King Philip will ever do any of that. He'd probably kill me and them—" he gestures to the woman and boy, "—for even leaving the cove alive."

*"They need to prove their loyalty to you,"* the magic of the north whispers in my mind. *"All of them."*

"One moment," I say, then dive. My tail fin splashes up into the cool air. With lightning speed, I race to my makeshift home. Inside against the wall is a small, smooth white rock with red veins. I found it long ago and kept it as it looks like blood running through ice; a reminder of how much I hate Philip for killing our mother.

*"Oh, yes, that will do,"* the magic of the north coos. *"You've got just enough magic stored to make this work."*

Cupping one hand over the top while the other holds the stone, I close my eyes and squeeze. "Let this stone be a collection of truth for all who pledge their loyalty to me, the creature who lives beneath the icy black water of the cove—the true ruler of Dorian. Once every citizen of Dorian pledges their loyalty, let this stone weaken and immobilize the man who has cursed me to this prison." The veins within the stone glow red before fading.

I flick my tail and launch myself up into the open waters, swimming back to the pier. Griffin and the others are there waiting.

"Here," I say, reaching upward, handing the red-veined stone to the man.

He hesitates but takes it. "What do I do with it?"

"Go and tell my story to everyone in the kingdom. Have them pledge their loyalty to me, their true queen, by touching the stone of truth. But be warned, if they are lying or being deceptive in their pledge, the magic of the north will know and end their life right then and there."

"And once everyone has touched the stone and pledged their allegiance to you, then what?"

"Then rest the stone on my brother's chest while he sleeps. The stone will do the rest. Once Philip is incapacitated, bring him to me." I can't help but smirk. I've waited a long time for this moment. For a plan to overthrow Philip and get my revenge for what he did to me and our mother.

Griffin drops the stone into his pocket and nods. "I'll make sure everyone knows the truth about who you are and what King Philip did to you. You have my word, Princess Celeste."

They turn and leave. The kingdom's fate in their hands. Warmth swells in my core, filling me with hope as I sink below the water's surface.

Months go by after my encounter with Griffin, and I worry the plan has failed.

*"Have patience,"* the magic of the north tells me, trying to ease my growing concerns. *"You'll be walking with two feet before you know it! Then you'll be Queen Celeste of Dorian."*

My mind begins to drift, and I'm on the verge of a deep sleep when I hear my name echoing above. I jolt upright and shoot into the open waters, swimming straight for the pier. Cutting through the surface, I search the night for the person calling my name. Moonlight glistens along the surface, and I see the beach is filled with people. There's a small crowd standing at the end of the pier. I slowly approach, cautious not to get close enough to be captured and killed.

"There it is!" someone yells. Boots pound the wooden planks until all eyes are on me.

"She's not an it." A familiar voice rises above the murmurs, and Griffin pushes to the front of the crowd. He sets the lantern he's holding onto the pier, then crouches. "Princess Celeste, it took a little longer than expected, but the stone worked. I remember you. I don't know what happened or how I forgot, but the more people who pledged their loyalty, the more I remembered you from my life before the curse."

I swim closer. When a wave of gasps erupts, I know I've gotten close enough. Even Griffin's mouth gapes. "You look different," he says, white puffs of breath filling the air around his face. "What happened?"

"I used a glamor to hide my true appearance. It's easier to lure curious people out onto the pier if they're not scared of me."

"Easier to drown!" someone shouts from behind Griffin.

"Easy, there!" Griffin says over one shoulder. "We're all on the same side now."

Clenching my sharp nails into my palms, I refrain from climbing up onto the pier and piercing them into that man's flesh.

*"Breathe, Princess. Breathe,"* the magic of the north says in my mind. *"Bloodshed will only make them run—and then what? You'll be left in permanent isolation."*

*"Fine, fine,"* I silently respond. *"I won't claw out anyone's eyes, unless they force my hand."*

"Did you finish the job?" I ask.

Griffin stands and waves a hand over his head, calling for something to be brought forward. The pier is only a few feet wide, but with so many people it's hard for me to see what they're doing.

A broad-shouldered man with a bandage wrapped around the top of his head sets down an unconscious man. No, wait... He's not unconscious, because the man's glossy eyes are open wide and staring right at me.

It's Philip.

I look up at Griffin. "You did it!" The creature in me stirs for what's to come—revenge. I've never wanted anything more than to make my brother pay, and now that day has come.

The man with the bandage around his head takes a few steps back. "What happened to him?" I ask, pointing a webbed finger at him.

Griffin glances back at him, gives him a nod, then turns to tell me, "Well, you said the stone would know who was involved in your mother's murder, and it did. There were... some men—" he pauses, "—that refused to pledge their allegiance. We had to use brute force to restrain them." He rubs one hand along his beard while shaking his head.

"You touched the stone to them?"

Griffin nods.

"And they failed. The stone knew."

206

Griffin nods again. "I don't know how, but an invisible force swept through the castle and attacked the men, slicing open their throats right in front of us."

"I'm sorry you had to see that, but they got what they deserved. Blood for blood." My heart races with panic as I realize the stone has punished them in the same way Mother died. Glaring at Philip, I swim closer. "Is that how you killed her? With a blade to the throat? You said she felt no pain!" I wipe the tears streaming down my cheeks. "You may have turned me into a hideous lake creature, but it's you, brother, who was born a soulless monster!"

I look up at Griffin, and ask, "Where's the stone?"

He fumbles in his coat pocket until he finds it. The red veins glow with energy, fueled by the pledges of everyone in the kingdom willing to follow me. When he hands it to me, all the power within flows from the stone and into my hands, recharging my magic.

I gasp as my insides burn with the magic of the north. My time as an underwater creature has been filled with ice and darkness, and for the first time in a long time, I feel a renewed sense of who my father wanted me to be.

Philip releases a loud groan, drawing my attention to his face. He's unable to move his muscles, so his words come from the back of his throat, barely coherent. "You haven't won yet, sister." For a moment, I think he's trying to say something else, but then I realize what he's doing. A faint glow of magic is forming in one of his bound hands.

*Tsking,* I say, "I don't think so. It's time for you to atone for what you've done."

I plunge underwater. With the stone in one hand, I speak the words to unbind the curse placed upon me. The last of the red-veined magic seeps into my skin, and I let the stone fall to the lake floor.

*"Forgive them. Forgive them all and your curse will be broken,"* the magic of the north tells me.

"I don't know if I can."

*"You must. They've pledged their loyalty to you. Now, finish*

*breaking the curse and accept them as the people of your kingdom."*

"Fine, I forgive them." And with those words, a whirlpool spins me faster and faster, launching me up and out of the water. Everyone at the end of the pier parts as I land in the center. Dripping wet, I lie curled up mere inches from my brother.

Griffin rushes to my side, pushing back strands of black hair from my face. "Princess Celeste, are you okay?"

Lifting my arms and pushing myself into a sitting position, I say, slightly winded, "Yes. Thank you, Griffin." I hold out my hands and he helps me to my feet. My actual two feet. I stumble, and the man with the bandage around his head catches me. I press my hands against his chest, eager to regain my balance and put some distance between us. I'm not used to physical contact, except for when a poor soul is fighting back, trying not to die, as I pull them to the lake's floor. But this man, or any one of them for that matter, isn't trying to kill me.

"Sorry," I say, then turn to face Griffin. "And thank you for believing me."

He gestures to their former king. "And him?"

"His punishment shall be equal to his crime." I get down on both knees and place my hands on his chest. Philip's eyes are trembling, silently pleading with me, but I ignore him.

I also ignore the northern magic speaking in the back of my mind, warning me to be careful. *"You are human again—time has resumed. All is normal and yet all is the same. The creature was not all Philip's doing. The creature was in you all this time. Be mindful of the bloodlust."*

I know exactly how I'll handle the cravings. Quietly and discreetly, and with elegance like a queen. But first... I plunge my still-sharp nails into Philip's chest. His only reaction is his eyelids opening to their fullest.

Everyone behind me gasps and steps away. I don't care that their eyes are on me. This is my moment to make him pay, and I want every second to last.

Whispering, I cast Philip to live an eternity in an underwater prison. The same prison he'd sentenced me to. After I withdraw my hands from his chest, blood dripping from my fingers, I roll him off the pier and into the water. The last part of my spell is an exchange, his eternal life as a prisoner to the northern magic for the curse I placed over the kingdom to be broken. To end the everlasting winter.

"Let it be," I say to the sky.

*"Let it be,"* the magic of the north replies within my mind.

I can't help but smile as the collective laughter echoes in my mind, because these people have no idea what's to come. Of the creature they've just freed and promised the throne. I'm no longer that naïve little girl.

Now, by day I'm Queen Celeste of the kingdom of Dorian, and by night, Glace Noir will come out to play.

# IMMISTAR
## By Paul Williams

Cᴌᴀᴠᴇ ᴘᴇʀᴄʜᴇᴅ ᴀᴛ ᴛʜᴇ ꜰʀᴏɴᴛ ᴏꜰ ᴛʜᴇ ꜱʜɪᴘ, wishing that the captain would fall overboard. He spoke to her as a passenger and not a superior, supplementing idle prattle with idiotic safety instructions. His twelve-strong crew rowed below, pushing the oars in perfect symmetry. Pew was with them, stroking his violin in a tune she did not know. She regretted hiring an elf musician and a dwarf crew.

Then the rational part of her brain returned. Dwarves originated in the snowlands and were skilled navigators. Few others could survive long periods at these temperatures. Pew was the only archer, and the only living being, who had ever killed a giant. A monster who wandered across the borders of the snowlands into an arrow. One small perfectly crafted weapon from a harmless tree.

The oars, from a tougher tree, stopped. There was no explanation. Then, the scratching on the violin ceased. The captain pushed a greasy finger through the bottom of his beard and onto his lips. Clave waited. The captain pointed. She looked at the piles of snow that covered the shore on either side. Within the white canvas, two small black dots moved, then disappeared.

The captain tapped his foot on the deck. The oars started. Pew came up the ladder.

"What was it?" he asked breathlessly.

"The eyes of a bear," she said. "I think."

"You think right," said the captain. "Hundreds in the snowlands. Hunt by sound. Can hear a fish moving under the ice, so your clumsy feet tramping around will bring them all out."

"You are paid to guide us through such dangers," Clave reminded him.

"I'm paid for two weeks," he said. "Two days out, two days back. Ten days waiting in between if you last that long."

"If we don't, you won't get paid for the return."

He shrugged. "Not by you." Laughing, he spat over the side and flicked his fingers for them to go away. Pew and Clave retreated to the top of the ladder. There was nowhere for private conversations. She would not normally talk to elves, unless interrogating them, but they were preferable to dwarves.

"Dwarves are so rude," she complained.

"Can you blame them? Centuries of oppression. They are not as forgiving as elves."

"Nor as greedy," she said.

He blushed. "A human killer would demand at least twice my fee."

"Have you ever killed a bear?" she asked.

"In truth, lady, I have never seen one."

The answer did not surprise her. Few in the kingdom had reason to go to the snowlands. The rivers from Aleshala to Breoma flowed quickly, and the connecting road was maintained with regular patrols of soldiers and waystations with blacksmiths and restaurants. Anyone crossing the snowlands risked death from the cold before they considered the bears and giants and whatever else might lurk here. Nobody took that risk.

Until now.

Three weeks ago, Clave received a summons from the king. No explanation or warning. A soldier arrived at her office and demanded her presence. She went immediately, leaving an underling in charge of the day's court proceedings. The commissioner's castle in Aleshala was directly behind her office and the king's palace was behind that. As official buildings would always be targeted by terrorists and rioters, this design gave the king two layers of protection. Clave grew up in the shadow of the commissioner's castle, wondering what it would be like to occupy it. Listening to stories about people working hard to improve their social status. Telling herself that she could live in a castle one day. Everyone else wanted to smash down the regime. She wanted to earn what was theirs and make it hers.

After the security rigmarole, where she punched a soldier who tried to search her, Clave was taken to the royal office. An underground room at the back of the palace, with one ventilation slit, a few candles in secure holders, and a throne where the king rested his feeble back on lavish orange cushions.

The king provided wine, his best, in a large glass. The servant then returned with a chair. Usually, visitors stood, since they were only welcome for a short duration. "You continue to impress me," purred the king.

"I continue to do my duty."

"And it is noted. The commissioner's role is due for renewal. I am thinking of a replacement."

In the king's six-year reign, the longest in history, there had been three commissioners. All male. None with her talents or qualifications. The king looked at her keenly. She feigned surprise. "Your Majesty, I am not prepared for such an honor."

"Your readiness will be tested," he said. "Later today you will receive a file on a wanted criminal. A terribly depraved individual who considers himself beyond the laws of our land. I will announce the new commissioner in three weeks. Bring me Immistar before then."

"Immistar?"

"Did I not say?"

It was a rhetorical question and a challenge. She would either deliver Immistar or die trying. Death was for others. She had persuaded herself to accept that and now never questioned. Others—like the failed current commissioner. She passed him on her way out, bowing and wondering if he knew.


The file arrived. The charges were false and irrelevant. Like most of those she read. The easiest way to get an opponent arrested was to accuse them of tax evasion. All such charges had to be answered by the suspect. The law was specific. Once in custody, confessions and payments followed. The allegations against Immistar from an unstated source were that business owners, specifically the owners of fish restaurants, paid him for protection. The charges were collected by goblins. Clave knew that there would be an intermediary, as goblins did not work directly for giants. In a world where all businesses were affiliated with different local gang leaders, none would testify.

The king had helpfully provided a copy of the original treaty, which was just readable. It had Immistar's print on the bottom. Clave recalled the salient details from school. The two human settlements expelled the giants to the snowlands, guaranteeing their safety for eternity. The school textbooks did not mention the small print. Clause eight, section two, said that all those who signed had the right to investigate suspected cases of tax evasion in each other's domains and to remove individuals implicated in such cases to their own territory for trial and punishment, if convicted.

All of Clave's cases ended in conviction. That was due to her preparation and a judiciary appointed by the king to carry out his orders. In the six months between Immistar's arrest and trial, Clave would move into the commissioner's castle. Already she could imagine dwarves painting her walls and replacing the drab furnishing. She would hire additional security, possibly the lycanthropes, and pay them extra from her own salary to keep her independence from the king.

She glanced at the barrels and chests that the dwarves brought to trade with Immistar. The law forbade dealings with known criminals. A law she now broke in pursuit of a bigger target. The king would remember that and use it against her if he wanted.

The dwarves stopped rowing when the moon came out. They had paused a few times when the captain saw bears close by. Now the journey was nearly complete. In front of them was the ice. The boundary defined in the treaty where the temperature changed to freezing. Some said a spell limited the power of the sun, others credited an underwater god with freezing powers. It looked as if a great carver had reached down and planted a sheet like a wall. A small passage led to the shore and was just wide enough for the boat to fit. The captain signalled. Six dwarves jumped overboard and began pushing the boat from behind, with the captain on deck shouting directions. Shivering, the dwarves obeyed. Slowly the boat turned and slid into the gap. The dwarves now all jumped onto the ice and pushed the boat forward. There was no space for the oars. The dwarves moved as fast as they could, flicking their feet around to stay warm.

"It ensures that our arrival is known," said the captain. "The bears are used to hearing the movement of the dwarves at this time. They will not investigate. In the morning, they come for our cargo. By then, there will be a small hole in the boat that takes up to ten days to repair."

"Do they not guard the entrance?"

"No need."

The boat stopped where the water ran onto the snow. The captain indicated for the crew to start unloading the cargo. The dwarves ran, taking smaller items first so that their frozen fingers would not drop anything heavy. Clave disembarked. She was shivering, despite the thick coat she had bought at the goblin markets. It was supposed to be wolf but smelled of dog. The trader awaited trial. The covering did not prepare her for the extreme drop in temperature or the freezing crunchy snow that cut through her boots. Pew seemed unaffected. "There was a time when elves hunted freely here," he remarked. "My grandfather fished in the waters, making holes in the ice."

"Yet you've never seen a bear."

"There were only a few of them in those days."

"How many now?"

"At least five hundred," the captain informed her, laughing. "They have Immistar's protection."

The treaty did not allow hunting in the snowlands. Immistar's lands.

The cargo was piled up. Clave still resented not being able to ask what was inside or to check documentation. One by one the dwarves headed back to the ship, leaving her and Pew alone on the snowy beach. When planning, she had expected the dwarves to take her straight to Immistar. Now it seemed she had to find her own way. No point in waiting for the bears to collect the cargo, as there would be too many for Pew to kill.

"We do not move at night," said Pew. "Lady, it is too dangerous."

"You can see," she said. Elves had perfect night vision. "Be my guide."

"My grandfather only fished in daytime. Not because of bears. There is something else. A beast that lives below the snow and hunts at night."

"The dwarves did not mention this."

"Perhaps they are safe in their boat. Come, there is a cave up there."

She followed him, slowly. As the night came in, she could only just see his blond hair glowing in front. Her footsteps extended his prints, bringing extra snow over her feet. It was a treacherous climb, silent except for their heavy breathing. As she struggled for grips, she wondered how many people had fallen. Death was for others. Not her. Then, her hand pressed against a wall, and she knew they were under cover. Pew pushed snow across the entrance, building it right up. She could not see enough to help. When finished, he spoke proudly, "There are small holes for breathing. Sounds we make here will not carry to the bears unless one is right outside. You need to sleep and not snore. Lie with your face down. I will make sure you are awake when the bears come for the cargo, and then we follow them."

She did not appreciate him taking charge. "They will hear us."

"Not above the noises they make carrying the cargo. It is our only chance."

Unconvinced, she rolled over and tried to sleep. It should have been easy after limited opportunities on the boat. Instead, she worried about making sounds, and Immistar's reaction. She had carried out several arrests, but never alone. Always in a team of four, armed and able to call on reinforcements if there was any resistance. Here, she had an elf and a team of dwarves, who would only do what they were paid to do, and she technically had no authority over them.

"Respect," she muttered. "Respect the land, its inhabitants and the treaties they signed." In her youth it had been a prayer for many. Now, as trade supplanted the fear of conflict there was a natural respect for the people of Breoma, Aleshala's traditional enemy, and an economic acceptance of the species that lived under human rule in both kingdoms.

"Respect," repeated a muffled voice. "Respect."

Clave sat up. She reached out a hand, catching a glimpse of Pew's hair. He quickly covered her mouth.

"Respect," came the voice again. It sounded male, whispering louder than before. She heard something shuffling through the snow. A lizard, she imagined. Then came a gentle tapping, a hissing, and the voice said clearly, "Immistar will see you in the morning. Respect."

The shuffling came again. Pew kept his hand in position for a full five minutes. She wondered why he had not shot the visitor, then lay back down and this time, slept.

Sunlight woke her as Pew removed the snow barrier. It had ascended almost to the top of the cave wall. He motioned for her to move forward quietly until they stood on a ledge looking down. She had not realized how far they had climbed the previous night. The boat below contained the tiny figures of the dwarves with rings of smoke rising from their cigarettes. Further along, eighteen bears collected the cargo, standing upright, and piling it in their open paws. On all fours they would be invisible. Each was the size of two humans, muscles bulging in arms and legs. Their faces were covered in white fur which extended over their ears. Their paws had three claws, retracted now for carrying the cargo, and not visible in their footprints. She estimated a value of six hundred for each skin plus a hundred or so for the meat. Perhaps Pew could kill one before they returned as an extra gift for the king.

After the bears collected all the cargo, evenly balanced in their deadly paws, they turned and began retracing their steps back to Immistar's castle. But they were heading right towards Clave and Pew. Towards the cave. Clave crouched as low as she dared, holding her breath as the enormous creatures trudged past the remnants of their nocturnal barrier. They smelled of fish, slime, and sweat and were all grunting heavily. Pew was right. The footsteps of two small beings would not be detected.

She slid out after him, slipping and almost falling. The bears did not turn. The path went down then up and around a slope. The wind blew past, not dispatching fresh snow but redistributing the existing surface. Clave stepped into the footsteps of the bears, sinking, and forced to take enormous strides. Pew followed, needing three times as many steps. For an hour or more they trudged, the sun mocking them with false promises of heat. Clave's skin cooled and she twisted her face to avoid the wind's deposits.

The path went uphill, and a huge mountain loomed over them. She grimaced at the thought of climbing it, then saw the first bear going around to a ledge overlooking a valley. Directly below them was a frozen moat. The path led to a bridge across the moat, held up by icicles and only suitable for one being at a time. The drop to the moat was probably twelve feet, and she suspected the ice below was thin enough that a heavy creature could pierce it should they fall. The bridge led into a castle, built of stone with a single storey and tower. It was the size of six human castles, dominating the valley yet unseen behind the protection of the mountain range. Immistar's palace in the center of the snowlands. A castle that, even in this incongruous setting, competed with those in the castle in Aleshala.

When the last bear was across the bridge, Clave stepped on. She tried not to look down or across at the tower, sensing someone watching her. Claw marks showed where each bear had dug in for extra protection. The bridge was slippery. Pieces of uneven snow and ice littered the way ahead. No handrail.

Clave was halfway across when she heard a shout. A bear was returning towards her. Its movements jolted the bridge. She half-turned, wanting Pew to shoot. Instead, he waited, arrows hanging uselessly from his belt. The bear grunted furiously and opened its mouth. She jumped.

She doubted that death was for others as the moat drew nearer. There was an almighty crack, then she plunged underwater into temperatures that made the previous night seem like a heatwave. Gasping, she reached out for the hole she had made, trying to pull herself back on land. A white shape filled it. The bear had jumped too and somehow not cracked the ice further. He held out a paw.

"Go," said the voice from the night. Below her. Somehow, reaching out from the icy depths where nothing could live. "Respect."

She took the bear's paw. It pulled her to safety and then she collapsed into the warm smelly arms.

Clave awoke staring at the moat. It took her a minute to see that she was inside the castle. Looking down through the window of the tower just like someone—or some *thing*—had looked up at her. The ceiling seemed like the sky, and the window was a long narrow slit without protection against the elements. It sloped down with a funnel that ran through the driving snow and descended into the moat. It reminded her of the slides that children made, except it was wide enough to host six horses. There were two other windows, designed the same.

Clave pulled herself out of the chair she sat in, a comfortable seat with a cushion, and pushed off the blanket. Pew was on the other side of the room, not moving. He pointed at a chain that attached his leg to the wall. His arrows were gone. The room was huge, with a table and chairs that reached to her head. As she got up, she saw there was a lever at the side of her chair that had reclined it down. She pushed it back and it rose to the level of the table. At the far end of the room was an archway.

Then Immistar walked in. He was three times her size but seemed even bigger. He had a heavy moustache but no beard and wore nothing except a loin cloth. His scalp was bald. A hand without a thumb reached down and hovered above Pew who tried to escape, but banged his head against the chain. Immistar laughed.

"The treaty indicates hospitality," said Clave bravely.

"My servants saved you from certain death. I have provided comfort and a meal is being prepared. Your ally, in contrast, carried weapons and the fame of slaying my brother. I think it reasonable to restrain him."

"I did not know it was your brother," said Pew.

"How many giants do you think there are left?" Immistar said. "Four came to the snowlands. I am now the only one. Two perished in the first month. I embraced the lifestyle, respected the conditions, and now I have a new brother." He took two strides across the room, raised an arm, and waved out of the window. The ice cracked. A hand covered in ice broke the surface and waved back. Then it descended and the ice reformed.

"Magic," hissed Pew.

"No, it is the science of beings more powerful than you and me. Magic is what you used to kill my brother." Immistar hovered an arm over Pew again. The giant smiled. "If not, please correct me. Tell me of his dying moments. Tell us."

Shivering, Pew said, "I would not want to disrespect the spirits of the dead."

"Your deceit is disrespectful. My brother was already dead. I know because I killed him. He did not agree with my alliance, wanted it to be just me and him. I made a different choice and returned him to the land beyond the snow where his body might join the soil as our custom dictates." Immistar's voice became menacing. "You saw a chance to make a fortune as a skilled hunter. To tout your services, give talks and become the first elf celebrity."

"No," said Pew.

Clave saw that it was true. She had interviewed enough people to know the signs of falsehood. It was her fault for being conned. Like everyone else, she accepted the story at face value. Believed that a wandering elf musician killed a giant.

Immistar gave Pew his bow and two arrows. "Prove your skill," he challenged. "Shoot me. One arrow in the heart. That's how the story goes, isn't it? That's where you stabbed him and put some animal blood on the arrow to make it look convincing. Now, kill me. Make the legend real."

For a second, Clave wondered if Immistar wanted to die, then saw the cleverness of his plan. Pew hesitated. He lifted the bow and looked at the arrow.

"No," she said. "If you attack him, he is allowed to kill you."

"She knows the treaty," chuckled Immistar. He eyed her more

carefully, she felt with more respect. "I pledged not to attack anyone unless they threatened me, and I can only kill them if that threat is to my own life."

Pew put the arrow down.

"You are wise," continued Immistar. "Come, let us eat."

In her career, Clave was used to extraordinary eating habits but had never seen anything like Immistar's table. It was set at human height with six bears standing upright, chairs for the guests, and a huge throne at the end accommodating Immistar. There was water and wine, the latter tasting as good as the king's and evidence of smuggling, plus different types of fish—some roasted and others raw, served with tiny sea vegetables. The centerpiece was a tray of meat.

"What animal is this?" asked Pew, taking a mouthful.

"Dwarf," said Immistar.

Clave stopped eating, hoping she had misheard. Immistar continued munching, then waved his fork upward. The crew of twelve dwarves came in, chained together with a bear pulling the end of the chain. Immistar casually lifted the chain, spun the dwarves around and then hurled them out of the window.

They went up in the air, swinging in different directions then plunged down onto the ice. As it broke, the ice hand came out and grabbed them one at a time, separating them from the chain and popping them into a mouth that emerged two feet away from the hand. It was the mouth of a giant, like Immistar's, except no teeth were visible.

Death was for other people. Dwarves. Clave tried to hide the fear that was biting her.

"They betrayed me," said Immistar. "I count that as a threat."

"I do not threaten you."

He laughed. "You seek to put me in a jail so you can live in a palace." He picked up Pew's chain and spun it thoughtfully. Then he dangled Pew out the window and secured the other end to the table leg. Pew hung shivering in mid-air. "I assume our business is private," Immistar said to Clave. The bears retreated, leaving food uneaten.

"There are rules around confidentiality." Clave knew she had to stay calm. If Immistar wanted to kill her he would have done that first. Pew and the dwarves had wronged him. She had not.

Death was for other people. She gazed at Immistar and listened intently.

"I have read your rules as well as the treaty. You may regard the snowlands as being isolated, but I have suppliers that bring me everything I need from both the human lands."

A network of suppliers, she speculated. It was forty years since the treaty was signed. The giants were abandoned to the snowlands, creating a boundary which the humans respected. Until now. She realized the king had probably drawn inspiration from Pew's alleged giant-slaying, giving him confidence to make this move. Thinking that Immistar was weak, and not knowing about the ally underneath the ice.

"Then you know what brings me here?"

"The king wishes to end the treaty but dares not attack me. So, he seeks an answer in the clauses. You wish to arrest me for tax evasion."

"I was asked to bring you in for questioning."

"And if I refuse, you have the power to arrest me?"

"Yes," she said confidently.

"But that would abuse my hospitality and be seen as a threat. If I resisted, would you use force?"

"I would not endanger my own existence," she said. Standard response. Sometimes tax agents died in the line of duty, earning a state funeral attended by the king, or more commonly, his representative. Death happened to other people. Not Clave. She sometimes envisaged switching allegiance at knifepoint.

"Not even for your king? Or your career."

She deliberately drank more wine. "Tell me about the creature under the ice."

"So that you may prosecute him?"

"Has he committed an offense?"

"Living without registration is an offense. So is what you term magic. He is the original inhabitant of this land."

"Why did I not know of him?" she asked, thinking of school and the lessons on the treaty. They mentioned the time before, when the four giants lived like outlaws, and when dwarves, goblins, and elves all lived in their own separate domains.

"Because your history starts with your emergence and conquest," Immistar said. "In the beginning there were dwarves, giants, and one other. A cross between a lizard and a giant. We respected it. The dwarves saw it as a predator and pest who had to be removed. They found an enormous stone wedged in the bottom of the seabed and built a chain. When the beast was sleeping, they fixed one end of the chain to its leg and the other to the stone. Now it could only roam a fraction of its territory. The dwarfs abandoned that area. There, its lifestyle was unchanged for centuries and it was forgotten by the dwarfs. But we hadn't forgotten. We searched the snowlands and made contact before agreeing to the treaty. We became friends, for want of a better word. Now I protect his land with the help of the bears, and he has vowed to protect me. If your king or the other humans brings armies, he will sweep them all away." Immistar swept the cutlery and plates, along with Clave's wine glass off the table. "With that agreement, I guarantee to keep the treaty. You have your land. I have mine. There is nothing for you here."

"I cannot leave without completing my duty," she said. "If you choose to resist then I will report that, and the king will respond as he sees fit."

"I chose to answer your questions," he said. "If the answers are satisfactory, then there will be no arrest. That is your law, is it not?"

"Yes," she said.

"And a creature who admits tax evasion may evade punishment

and further sanctions by paying the amount due or naming others?"

"Under certain conditions," she said, intrigued.

"The dwarves bring me goods," said Immistar. "And information. I pay them with fish, some of the rarest are lucrative delicacies."

"That explains the restaurant links," she realized. Breaking the rules of disclosure. She blamed the wine. It wasn't the only broken rule. No scribe was keeping a transcript.

"Dwarves sell to goblins, elves, their own kind, and kings," Immistar went on.

"The king buys your fish?"

"The dwarves sell his wine. Is that taxed? I don't believe there is a royal exemption. Arrest your king—or are you as corrupt as he is?"

She tried to keep her face passive, staring defiantly at him. Letting him make assumptions whilst she calculated how to turn the situation to her advantage.

Immistar unhooked the chain and pulled Pew back into the room. "You leave now," he said to them. "The only trade I offer you is this palace and the snowlands, in exchange for the king's head."

The bears escorted Pew and Clave across the bridge. The sun was beginning to set. Clave looked back to see Immistar at the window. She nodded a farewell.

"You have failed," said Pew. "You are returning empty-handed."

"And you are returning to disgrace."

"Only if it is mentioned."

"I will not be party to your continued deceit."

The bears turned back, leaving them alone on the treacherous path. "There is only your word," said Pew sulkily. He was right. A court would convict him because of her reputation. The court of public opinion expressed in tavern and newspaper gossip might take

a different view. Might believe Pew, until he was prosecuted. Lying to an official was technically still treason.

He pointed an arrow at her like a spear a pained expression on his face. "Walk across the edge."

She shuffled her feet, digging them as deep as she could, then bent and hurled snow at Pew. Ducking, he pushed the arrow at her. She knocked it away with her hands, slipped, and fell backwards. Pew leaned over her.

"Please promise to stay silent."

Death was for other people. Clave nodded as best she could, sat up, then pushed Pew. He shoved her back. "Then die." Pew rolled her towards the edge. She reached out, grabbed the arrow, and felt herself falling. There was a rumbling like an earthquake. She was flung up and across, landing on an even pile of snow. Around her, the landscape jolted. A giant ice hand was in the air, holding Pew, then it descended back under the ice. She ran after it, fell again, and slid until her body broke the ice for the second time in less than a day. It was darker and colder. She was prepared. She pushed her arms out, swam, and called with her mind. "He's mine." The arrow was still in her hands. Up ahead was a flash of green. She couldn't hold her breath much longer. The green was the scales on a lizard's leg. Extending through the sea like a tree growing from the bottom. Attached to the leg was a chain. She levered the arrow against the chain and pushed down.

"I can free you."

A freezing hand lifted her up. She blinked and somehow found herself beside the boat where they had arrived. Pew's body lay next to her, stabbed through the heart with his arrow. A voice echoed in her head. "What makes you think I want to be free?"

It took Clave four days to row to Aleshala. She began before remembering about the hole the captain said the bears would put in the boat, and scrambled around looking for it whilst still in the ice. Not finding anything, she prodded the boat forward, then into the open sea. Her arms ached and she saw double. She slept for an hour at a time, sometimes in sunlight and sometimes at night. After each rest, she changed oars and position. A wind could have blown her off course, but it was not a stormy season. She also felt that there was a presence guiding the boat. Something beneath the waves deterring predators. Providing the extra strength needed to keep moving.

At the harbor she went straight into the tavern and demanded a bed. The landlord recognized her before she spoke and evicted a paying couple. She remained in bed for a whole day, then ate, washed, and changed attire before heading to the king's chambers. This time there was no need to assault the guards as they allowed her through without comment.

"Where is Immistar?" demanded the king.

"I will take you to him."

He glared at her. "I will not go to the snowlands."

"Per the treaty, you must answer the charges of tax evasion that he has levelled against you. Failure to do so results in the treaty being invalid."

"And allows me to invade," said the king. He rubbed his hands. "One giant. My army will find a way."

"He's not alone." Clave explained about the creature. "The dwarves imprisoned it in its own lands. It doesn't want to leave, but it will protect Immistar and follow him."

"Then we will destroy that too," decided the king.

On her way home, Clave stopped at the marketplace and bought some curtains. She chose two designs, one for the commissioner's castle and one thick enough to withstand the harsh winds of the snowlands.

 226

# DON'T FEED THE BEASTS

## By William Rigsby

*SHOULD ANYONE FIND THIS LETTER, I want you to know that I would do it again. I owe nothing to Icanthia or the King, and least of all to the High Governor... but should the worst happen, I leave this account to whoever finds it.*

When I arrived in the Northlands, what the King called *Icanthia*, I had nothing. Like most sorry sops that end up at Larsport I was hoping to strike it rich. I like to think that I am smarter than the average sop though, so I didn't sign up to join with the miners or loggers. Instead, I joined the High Governor's Icanthian Royal Guard. Which may sound like some fancy army with matching uniforms and plumes in their helmets, but let me assure you, they were mercenaries of the lowest order.

I had military experience, served for eight years in the Hillmarch Royal 13th, and that was enough to get an officer's position.

Lieutenant Morgan Forscythe, and damn was I proud of it. The only trouble was, I had no idea what I was walking in on. See, at the recruiting office, they tell you about all the opportunities that await in the Northlands. They say it's basically guard duty, but everyone gets paid like generals because of all the gold, silver, old wood and black marble that pours out of the frozen continent. You don't have to be a miner or logger slaving away for some useless speculator. As long as you've got some know-how with a sword, then you have a place in the High Governor's personal army. What they don't tell you is that all the devils in the abyss wouldn't touch the Northlands with a ten-foot pole.

The Northlands are infested with the worst kind of monsters you'd use to scare kids with at bedtime. If you are from Hillmarch, or some other petty kingdom in the south, then everything I am about to write is going to sound insane, but I can assure you over my probably already dead body that this is a true account.

My first week, the High Governor, a slimy piece of work named Hather Mortenmier, assigns me to a town called Iron Hill. Iron Hill wasn't remarkable, just a mining town on the periphery of human territory. Well, a few days in, a couple of the newest recruits get into a fight about something stupid. Some locals have gathered around to watch, but it's not your usual fight crowd, you know, egging them on to gut one another. Instead, they are pin-drop silent, just staring wordlessly. Soon enough, one of the recruits lands a monster right hook into the other's nose and he falls back into the snow clutching it. A faint gasp and murmur rises up from the onlookers and they start to leave. When he pulls his hand away from his nose, sure enough, the thing is leaking blood like a river over a cliff. When the crowd sees that, they erupt in every direction.

A potbellied man in a baker's apron runs to me gesticulating wildly, palpable fear behind his eyes, "Officer, officer! Get your men together quickly!"

"Why?" I chuckle. "It's just a scrap, his pride is hurt worse than

his nose, I guarantee you."

A woman screamed at me, her mess of black hair obscured a face ashen with fear, "You don't know. The blood; he's bleeding, you fool, they are coming!"

The humor of my own wit is strangled by the panic on her face, and I say, "Who's coming? What's it matter if he's bleeding a little?"

"Did you just come off the docks at Larsport, you half-wit? They smell blood; get your men together, they are coming!" this latest from an old man, spittle spraying as he shouted.

When I was a kid, I had heard stories of the first men to journey to the Northlands. They were brave heroes who fought off great beasts, six-legged bears, huge carnivorous moose, the fearsome Yetis, and great cannibalistic giants. Until that moment, that's all they had been, stories, for the great heroes to vanquish.

That's when I saw it; it must have been thirteen feet tall, with huge claws, covered in matted white and black fur, roaring like the unholy anger of the gods. A Yeti, real and in the flesh, coming in fact for *my* flesh. Only there were no heroes here, just me, twenty or so armed mercenaries playing soldiers, and a village full of terrified miners.

I started screaming orders at the top of my lungs, fear ripping at my heart as my mind desperately tried to reconcile the great beast tearing down the mountain. The trouble with mercenaries is they won't die for king and country; no honorable death protecting innocents. Only coins buy their loyalty, and it's hard to spend your money when you are dead.

In the end, it wasn't my brilliance that saved the village, it was the quick thinking of some locals. They slaughtered some of their chickens and threw them out into the woods while we evacuated the people.

"It'll work if it's just the one; if there are more... well... we'll just hope there aren't more," the potbellied baker said, his eyes distant as the last of the villagers fled.

Iron Hills had to be abandoned for a full month afterwards in order to give time for the creature to move on, and even when the time had elapsed, a full sweep of the area had to be done by the Royal Guard.

Iron Hills would prove to be the best possible outcome. The worst of all days were the 'Expansion Expeditions'. Orders would come down from on high that just outside of human territory was some spectacular deposit of gold or other valuables, and it was our sacred duty as the Royal Guard to make it a safe place for humans to live and prosper.

Humanity had carved its niche in the Northlands out of a stretch of grand rolling hills and plains; the edges of that plain were bounded by thick oldwood forests and enormous mountains. Tradition held that all of this had once been forest, and that the great heroes of old had simply carved out the plains by force of will, but that never sat right with me. The forest was too old, too evil. It had been here long before man, and would swallow them up in the end. It always seemed to me that the forest was growing—quietly, slowly—and when you weren't looking, it was testing the edges, probing for weakness.

None of this, however, would stop the High Governor and his pursuit of new untapped wealth in the wilds. So, the Guard would be rounded up and sent out to one of the border towns to prepare our expedition.

The worst of these expeditions was near a town called Neardevil. Situated along a river that was frozen more often than not, it looked out into the untamed woods. Neardevil was one of the few walled towns in the Northlands, as well as one of the few to have a permanent Royal Guard garrison present.

Before I tell you about the expedition, I should explain something. The Northlands were never some properly uninhabited wasteland, void of civilization. The civilization that was there just wasn't human. The Trömde are small and humanoid in shape; from a distance, they can be mistaken for children, but upon closer inspection, they often have long white beards, and conical heads that they keep hidden under long fur hats. They were here long before the first man set foot in the Northlands; some even remember those days firsthand. Their villages are often nestled deep in the thickest tangles of the woods, untouched by the beasts that surround them. Rumor is that their blood has no smell, though no one would test this. No worse luck than offending a Trömde.

Whenever an expedition was sent out, it was often because a Trömde would report a find in unclaimed territory and offer to reveal it in exchange for some favor that the expedition would do en route. There could be anything as simple as assisting in the repair of a local Trömde bridge, to strange and arcane rituals that were beyond human comprehension.

Before the expedition from Neardevil, I had more than a few run-ins with Trömdes. They tended to be odd in mannerism, speaking in questions, chewing oldwood bark, and pushing their long hats out of their eyes. When push came to shove, however, I would trust a stranger Trömde over any mercenary in my company with anything.

Anyway, back to Neardevil. The expedition was issued an order by the High Governor himself and read:

*5th Company of Royal Guards to begin an expedition to the site of the black marble deposit presented by Mr. Bröjild Hjarg, in exchange for services rendered under the Guards duty assisting with: Pest Control. The site is to be secured, cleared, and a sizable sample is to be extracted for evaluation.*

*Signed,*

*His Royal Majesty of the*
*Hillmarch's High Governor of Icanthia,*
*Hather Mortenmier*

A few things about this order were immediately out of the

ordinary. The first being that black marble was extremely rare. After decades of extraction from the Northlands, gold had lost some of its luster as the standard of wealth. The peak of nobility now used pieces cut from black marble, which not only was unique to the Northlands but was also only ever found in extremely small quantities. The word *deposit* indicated amounts large enough to warrant a full mining operation. The second thing that was odd, was the duty we were to be assisting with: *Pest Control.* In the Northlands, that meant getting cozy with the cuddly creatures of the woods.

The last thing was the name which presented the find. I was familiar with all the Trömde that were willing to work with their new human neighbors. Those that hadn't already started working with us could charitably be described as *unhelpful,* and uncharitably be described as hostile. Before departing from the High Governor's stronghold of Hraston Castle, I checked the records and my suspicions were validated. There was no record of a Bröjild Hjarg ever offering information before. Unfortunately for me, I was still only a lieutenant, and my opinion was deemed 'inconsequential' and the expedition left Hrastor Castle for Neardevil anyway.

Winter had just begun to show teeth in the Northlands, which didn't mean that the snow was beginning to fall—it meant that the snow was three feet deep on a good day. Drifting off the marked roads would lead you into snow drifts twice as deep as I was tall. Lucky for me, kernrose grows well in spite of the cold here, so my pipe was never empty, and soon my cheeks were warm from the gentle puffs.

Our company was about 150 men of varying experience under Captain Hikkom Barenbutton—the men mostly called him Captain Bar. He was all right as captains go, not too arrogant, power hungry, or stupid. He did have a weakness though; he felt the need to prove his competence often. It probably came down to being the fifth son of a noble nobody had ever heard of, out here trying to gain the respect he never got at home. Validate the man's orders and you'd be in his good graces the rest of the day.

When we arrived in Neardevil a few days later, I caught my first glimpse of the mysterious Bröjild Hjarg. He was average looking enough for a Trömde, I suppose. His face was even more wrinkled than usual, and his teeth were blackened from years of chewing oldwood. He was talking with Captain Bar and gesticulating excitedly with his spindly arms. It's always hard to tell if a Trömde is angry or simply excited, yet to me it always looks like they have a scowl, rain or shine.

I got my second chance to look Hjarg over at the officer's meeting later that night. The location of the black marble deposit had been marked on a map and we were discussing potential routes over the terrain, but no cartographic expedition had ever been sent out in this direction before. Another lieutenant by the name of Leana Firdottir recommended taking several weeks to map the area and get a lay of the land, when the doors to the room burst open.

"I apologize about my lateness, Guardsmen," Hjarg said. "I was detained by other matters you would not understand." His voice was rich and deep, like that of a kindly priest comforting a mourner. "There is, however, no need to delay, as I am quite capable of guiding the company to the location of the marble. The cartographers can wait. I am more than enthused to answer any topographical questions you may have later, but first, the matter of pest control."

There was an uncomfortable shifting in the room. Everyone had seen their fair share of action; Firdottir herself had been a part of the defense of Dardontown when a great pack of hromsbears had descended upon it, but no one in the Guard would seek it if they could.

"Yes, about that, Mr. Hjarg," Captain Bar said. "The High Governor was scarce on the details about the nature of this pest control. Would you mind enlightening us?" Captain Bar's words were careful and precise, but he clearly wasn't thrilled with the idea.

"Of course!" Hjarg said jovially. "A nest of woodwyrm has been discovered between the Trömde village fo Allmö and the site of black marble. While normally we would take care of this problem ourselves, the first moon of winter is arising, which precludes us from partaking in violence."

Some of the tension let out of the room. Woodwyrms were ugly furry snakes around ten feet long, but weren't particularly dangerous to humans, at least not in comparison to the other beasts. Woodwyrms were stranglers. That meant no blood, which meant the rest of the Northlands fauna would hopefully stay home.

The rest of the meeting progressed uneventfully through the discussion of terrain and encampment locations. Soon, we were packing again and crossing over the frozen river into the wilds. The trees overhead were heavy with snow, making the trek beneath feel like we traversed a never-ending cave with specks of light like islands in the sea.

The journey to the wyrm nest was eerily uneventful. The snow crunching underfoot and clanking of metal were the only sounds as the march deepened into the woods. Eventually, the woods broke into a clearing. We made camp and began digging in. Still, there was the quiet of anticipation. The wyrm den was about four miles from camp; we would travel light at daybreak, armed with large, forked poles and hefty bearded axes. The night passed in uneasy tension, broken only by the crack of dawn.

The wyrm nest was a large and ugly thing. A twisted pile of carcasses scattered around a clearing pocked with man-sized holes. The way to flush out woodwyrm is to pour oils down into the pits. The oils burn woodwyrm skin and drive them to the surface, where they can be pinned by forks and then diced by the axes. It's back breaking and disgusting work, but at least it isn't particularly dangerous if you have a team that knows what they're doing. Importantly, the blood of woodwyrm is thick and green, which doesn't attract the attention of the other beasts of the old wood.

The day progressed with clinical efficiency.

A thought gnawed at the back of my mind. This nest of woodwyrms was not particularly large or belligerent. They are mostly a danger to unguarded livestock, and as far as I know, the Trömde don't keep livestock. Why take us here to clear out a pest that isn't pestering? Why trade away a kingdom's ransom for a minor inconvenience?

Soon the last of the wyrms was exterminated and we returned to camp. Much of the apprehension of the journey had seeped out of the mercenaries with the day's work. All that was left now was to secure the black marble and we would all be paid handsomely.

We set out the next day for the marble deposit. We should have seen the signs. No snow hares darted before us, no birds chirped from the trees. The trees themselves had their snow shaken from them, and there were deep furrows in the freshly fallen snow. As the sun reached midday, we crested a small hill. Just over the hill were huge chunks of black marble, scattered as though some giant had smashed a black marble vase upon the ground. These pieces of marble were several stories high and as wide as a house, some broken into pieces, and others still intact.

Orders were issued, and soon a line of wooden stakes was hammered into the ground around the site. It wasn't until we began examining the marble itself that consternation began to grow. This wasn't some naturally occurring deposit of marble. This had been cut and moved here. The worst discovery, however, was made by one unfortunate sop who stumbled while walking through the maze of marble and reached out a hand to steady himself. The edges of the marble were sharp as steel and he sliced open his palm. The cry went up across the company, sending chills down spines.

"Fresh blood!"

Chaos erupted as guardsmen scurried to their positions carelessly, some slipping on the smooth marble, some running into others, and still others simply brushing past the sharpened marble. All of them gashed open ever so slightly. Not enough to warrant injury in any civilized part of the world, but here it may as well have been a death penalty.

The first horn sounded from the north side of the encampment. Three long blasts, a hromsbear. Six legged and freakishly muscular, the hromsbear hunt in packs, able to run with their hind four at full gallop while their front slash forward at the fleeing victim. I ran towards the horn when a second and a third sounded, the horn calls mingling across the encampment. Goredeer—like huge carnivorous moose—and Yeti were descending on the camp as well.

I sprinted towards the officer's tent to find the captain screaming orders to anyone he could find. He spotted me.

"Forscythe! With me, gather any men you can find!"

I followed him, grabbing anyone who looked like they didn't know where to go, and we pushed our way to the top of one of the hills. When we crested the hill, we saw below four hromsbears pacing at the edge of the woods, watching us with cold red eyes gleaming behind matted white fur. There was an oddness about them, they seemed to be straining forward, eager to charge up the hill, but something rooted them in place.

The same story came from across the camp as various creatures of the woods gathered along the edge of the tree line. But they didn't charge. What were they waiting for?

An eerie silence fell on the camp as hours passed. Soon the sun began to dip low and the light faded. Torches were called for, but the darkness lay so thick that they seemed to do little but keep my eyes from adjusting to the dark.

Then it happened all at once, deep in the darkest pits of the night, the cry went up that they were on the move. Sure enough, the sounds of screaming men started to echo around the piles of strewn marble. The detail that sits in my mind was the face of the captain issuing orders to the men around him, bold and brave. He shored up the defense and braced the boar spears. It was all going so well; one bear had been felled without any major casualties.

Then it was all over.

One of the bears took six boar spears straight to the chest without stopping and tore into the captain. It's hard to describe the next few moments without visceral words like *mangle* and *pulp*. Suffice it to say, no one would recognize the poor sod's body. I retreated with what remained of the men to the tent camp where a second line of defense had been set up. With the captain dead, command fell to myself and two other lieutenants. Three of us in total stood together shouting for the mercenaries to give their lives for the profit of some fat piece of manure holed up in a warm castle. I realized the hopelessness of our task before the others.

"We have to pull back and make for Neardevil; we can't hold here, there's too much blood. This place will be swarming with them before next day," I shouted over the din.

"They'd follow us, and Neardevil would be swamped as well, we can't risk it," Firdottir shouted in reply.

I looked around, hoping for a solution to drop from the heavens to save us. Instead, it came from hell. We had gathered the camp in a tight circle of bristling spears to keep the hromsbear and goredeer at bay. In the center of that circle was the medical tent, where the wounded were being treated to the best of our ability.

My first mission in Iron Hills came back to my mind, and I knew what needed to be done. I called one of the least scrupulous guardsmen over to me.

"When I give the signal, go to the wounded tent and order the surgeon to open the palms of all the wounded. Tell him if he refuses, I'll feed him to the hromsbear personally, but if he does it, then maybe the rest of us can escape with our lives." He nodded and held out his hand. I dropped a purse into it, and he made his way to the center.

At first, the other lieutenants were aghast at the idea, but all of them had seen it before. The only way out was to leave less troublesome prey behind. I'll never forget their cries as we pulled up the defensive line and pushed west back towards Neardevil, abandoning the tents laden with the unfortunates. We fled madly through the woods, with only a vague notion of where we were headed; it was only by sheer luck and panic that we managed to find the river and follow it back to Neardevil. No one spoke to, or even looked at me. They knew I was the one who had made the call to save their lives, but even to mercenaries, the wanton sacrifices of comrades weighed heavily on the soul.

I might remind you here though, I myself was a mercenary with loyalty only to coin—but you can't get paid if you're dead. The story spread, and soon I was a leper without leprosy. On the long march back to Hraston Castle, not a single word was spoken to me. It was better that way, better to not have to think and only to march. When we returned, however, the silence that had enveloped me was shattered as I was summoned to give a report to the High Governor.

He sat in his audience chambers with all the pomp of a king, but the appearance of a fat drunkard, with a silver laurel wreath perched on his head, and a cup of wine in hand. His cheeks were red from the drink and his blonde and gray hair fell about his face in disarray.

"Lieutenant Forsythe," he said curtly. "I understand you were present at the death of Captain Barenbutton? Inform me of the manner of his death."

I tried my best to relate the events leading up to the disastrous defense of the marble site with stuttering nerves. I hadn't had the chance to talk through anything with anyone or rehearse events, so it came out as a jumbled mess.

Governor Mortenmier nodded sagely as I spoke, and then said, "It would appear to me as though the job which you were contracted to do is unfinished. I understand that the untimely demise of Captain Barenbutton is an inconvenience, however, the Royal Guard does not employ you to simply turn tail at the first casualty. The revenue available at the site you described is worth more money than your entire company, and I simply will not stand for it being wasted because a few lazy mercenaries couldn't be bothered to kill a few rugged beasts. Now, I am not without understanding, and as a recompense for the death of Captain Barenbutton, I am henceforth promoting you to acting captain for the duration of the expedition." He smiled, deeply pleased with himself, no doubt.

"The duration of the expedition?" I said dumbly.

"Yes, Captain, you will take the men of your company and the

remaining lieutenants and you will secure the marble site, as ordered originally. Mr. Hjarg has informed me it will be quite easy to retake if the proper effort is put in," he said genially.

"Did he now? Then I should go speak to him about our next course of action," I said, grinding my teeth.

"Indeed, I will allow you to rest the night here, but you depart tomorrow morning," the governor said, waving a hand.

I wandered the halls of Hraston in a daze, unsure of where to even begin, but then I spotted him. Mr. Hjarg stood waiting for me at the end of the hall, eyeing me like a prospective horse buyer, but with no warmth to speak of.

"Come, Captain, I wish to have a word with you."

The next day, the company of men, still haunted by the previous day, saddled up with fresh provisions and, heads hung low, made their way out of the castle back towards Neardevil. Each time I made the trek to Neardevil, the journey felt longer and colder. The snow is heavier, the wind howls more forlornly, and the men are quieter. Neardevil was much the same as we left it, though it too had caught the air of despair and was quiet as the grave. Scouts were sent out into the woods to see what condition we had left the black marble site. They returned within an hour.

"They are coming this way; we never even made it as far as the site," the gruff, bearded, scout captain spoke softly, helmet gripped in white knuckles.

"Get the men to the walls then," I replied in a tone much the same. "Rouse anyone who's bedded down; we are in for a long night."

Soon enough, there they were—a line of demons straight from the abyss, once again champing at the bit to be released from the edge of the woods onto our small camp. This time, though, I was ready. Barrels of boiling oil were brought to the walls, and we began pouring them onto the frozen river below. The charge began and they tore across the clearing onto the river. The first few hromsbears that were fastest made it across the river, but once the main body of them were on the ice, it cracked, and they were sucked underneath into the dark current below.

The ones that made it across, however, were more than enough of a problem to deal with. Their claws tore as they hauled themselves up the side of the wall like enormous spiders. Soon enough, they were over the top tearing into the Guard. The fight lasted all night, but in the end, four hromsbears lay dead in exchange for twenty-seven guardsmen.

After the battle, the air amongst the men had shifted. That night, I called a general meeting to discuss the operation to retake the marble site. A man in a sergeant's uniform stepped up once quiet had been called for.

"Captain Forscythe," the sergeant said. "I have been speaking with some of the men, and we decided that our lives are not worth the Governor's pocket book. We will go no further. We wish for you to join us along with the rest of the Guard. No amount of coin is worth our lives."

He sat back down, and a murmur of approval rippled through some of the soldiers.

"What you are proposing, Sergeant, is desertion," I said. "It's mutiny. Tell me, how do you propose we get paid if we leave the High Governor's service? You want to start scratching rocks in a mining town?" I sneered. Clearly, they had not been expecting resistance from me on this—I mean, I had been there at the site when our camp was ripped to shreds; I was the one who the High Governor ordered to lead our suicidal march back into the woods.

The sergeant stood again and stammered, "Morgan... you can't send us back out there. We won't go. It's suicide."

"It's *Captain,* and you'll do as you are told, or you'll be treated as a deserter. Am I understood?"

He sat slowly, the anger in his eyes palpable.

I turned towards the rest of the company and spoke. "Once one of you can find someone who will pay more than the governor, I'll

be the first one to sign up. Until then, this is my company, and you'll do as you are ordered, or so help me, I'll feed you to the beasts myself."

The march to the marble site was uneventful, and upon arrival, the stink of corpses wafted through the fallen marble slabs. It was somehow an even more brutal scene than I remembered. I gave orders to go nowhere near the slabs of marble, and simply to secure the site. Reports came to me that creatures had been spotted in the woods some ways off. I kept the news to myself, no sense frightening already flighty mercenaries. With the defenses set up, we saddled back up and began to make our way back towards Neardevil.

I passed an announcement back to the rest of the troops as we marched.

"We will proceed directly to Hraston Castle without stopping at Neardevil for much-needed time off. I will ensure that bonuses are distributed for your bravery."

After the long and miserably cold journey to Hraston, we arrived, and I was brought to the audience chambers of the High Governor.

"Captain! I knew you would be more than capable of achieving the goals I set for you. You have been most admirable; I have graciously decided to make you a permanent captain in recognition of what you've done. Mr. Hjarg has informed me that there was a spot of difficulty with the morale of some of the troops. I trust that you will deal with them as deserters."

"Thank you for the promotion, sir. I will have them dealt with shortly. I also promised that the loyal men would receive a bonus for completing the mission. I trust that will not be an issue, considering how many samples we brought back with us?" I said respectfully. In response, the Governor began to laugh.

"Oh Captain, you overstep. There will be no bonuses. In fact, we are going to go through some necessary cutbacks in terms of wages. You understand, of course, but I am afraid the budget just can't handle the current wages. It won't be an issue though; we still pay more than any of you sword-for-coin lot can get anywhere else. Now, go deal with the deserters. You are dismissed, Captain."

I simply nodded and turned to walk out.

That night, the deserters were gathered and executed. It was a brutal affair, and if I was to pick what I regret most, it would be their deaths.

Afterward, I stepped outside of the walls of the castle. Mr. Hjarg stood outside waiting for me. Behind me, a cart filled with the bodies intended to be taken away and buried to keep the creatures away from the castle.

"This will be more than enough, Captain. Thank you for returning what was once ours. You have my gratitude," Hjarg said gravely.

"Don't thank me; he just couldn't afford the bill anymore, and you could. Shall we get started?"

We scattered the bodies around the castle. I looked up to the empty guard towers. All of which had been assigned to a now dead deserter. When the job was done. Mr. Hjarg handed me the reins to a cart loaded with black marble and nodded as I headed in the direction of Larsport.

I never found out what exactly happened at Hraston Castle. I do know that the creatures of the wood had followed us from the black marble site, and that the deal Mr. Hjarg offered me included words like "vengeance" and "extermination". I hope to never find out.

I made it to Larsport, hired a ship, and returned at long last to the Southlands. I was wealthier than I could have ever dreamed. Especially when the black marble stopped flowing from the Northlands. Soon everything stopped flowing from the Northlands. They said the beasts had retaken the lands and that no man was safe to set foot on the cursed continent ever again.

As I finish this letter, I will say again that I regret nothing. I have a beautiful home, a family, and more wealth than I could ever

spend, even if I was determined to.

...But every year the snow comes a little earlier, and stays a little later.

# COLD REVENGE
## By Maria Carvalho

GRIAC BALANCED THE BASKET-LADEN pole across his shoulders as he settled onto his mare, enjoying the beauty of the newborn morning. He drew in a deep breath, savoring the air's aroma—a mixture of flowers and meadow grass—and looked over at his mother riding beside him. Asha gazed off into the distance, a dreamy look on her face. She was no doubt thinking about the upcoming celebrations. Tonight's harvest feast would include pies made from the jasoba fruit they were on their way to gather, just as they did every year. There would be music and dancing, and Griac would be allowed to stay up extra late.

Isahr's three small suns shimmered low to the west of the clear emerald sky as they followed the path through the sleeping village, the rows of silver-flecked stone cottages reflecting the morning light. Although few people were up yet, Griac was not surprised to see Jinec already heading down toward the seaside; their priestess was tireless in her efforts to protect the citizens of Meligo. The small land mass was surrounded by golden seas that dominated the rest of the world, save for Drozuc—a frigid wasteland on the opposite side of Isahr.

As they rode past the village in companionable silence, the terrain became increasingly steep; the lush fields gave way to outcroppings of gleaming niej rocks covered in garlands of blue-blossomed vines. Rainbow-colored lurzim birds, clicking and whistling cheerfully, kept them company on the trip. They soon arrived at the grove of towering onyx trees, whose clusters of clear, hexagon-shaped jasoba fruit glittered in the brilliant sunlight.

While the horses drank from an adjacent stream, mother and son set to work, looping some of the lidded baskets onto their belt hooks before heading to the trees.

"Be careful, my birne," Asha said, as she did every time.

"I always am, my ammita," Griac replied with a smile as he began to scale one of the grand trees. When he reached the top, he took a moment to savor the sweeping views, then focused on detaching the fruit clusters from the thick branches, tucking them into the baskets with a practiced hand. Asha did the same on a nearby tree. As they worked, the spicy scent of the wood mingled pleasantly with the sweet smell of the jasoba fruit, and the nearby waterfalls provided soothing background music.

They were nearly finished when Griac's tree started lurching back and forth. Digging his fingers into its rough bark, he clung on tightly as it swayed in the gusting wind.

"Hold on, Griac!" called Asha.

"I am—make sure you do, too!" Griac called back, tilting his head to see that she was hanging onto a branch near the top of a tree. Then he heard a mighty *crack* and watched in horror as the branch was ripped from the tree, a look of terror on Asha's face as she plummeted with the branch to the ground below.

"*Ammita!*" he cried, scampering down the tree as fast as he possibly could. The wind had stopped as quickly as it had started.

Running to where Asha lay, Griac let out a cry when he saw the stream of bright orange blood running from her nose and mouth, her eyes wide with fear as she lay pinned beneath the massive bough.

"Can't... breathe..." she gasped. Frantically, he attempted to leverage the tree limb off her, but it was far too heavy for him to budge.

"*Help!*" he screamed. "Anyone! Please help us!"

The horses whinnied in agitation, but no one else could hear his cries.

"I'm sorry, Ammita—I can't move it!" he cried in anguish.

"It's okay... my birne," she whispered, her eyes closing.

"No!" he yelled, desperately trying to summon every bit of strength inside him to free her from the branch.

Without warning, an intense tingling—like acute pins and needles—surged through his fingertips, followed by a warmth that spread from his fingers throughout his entire body.

What in the world was happening to him? Before he could process what was going on, the land began to shake violently, the jasoba trees swaying as a huge boom reverberated through the air.

And then it was over. The odd sensations Griac had experienced were gone, the terrain still and quiet again.

But the land had changed. In disbelief, Griac stared at the enormous chasm in the ground, which started just past where he knelt and stretched as far as he could see towards the village below.

Looking back at his mother, he found that the bough had been dislodged. But he knew it was too late. Asha was completely still, and when he touched her face with his trembling hands, her skin felt oddly cool.

Cradling her body, he closed his eyes and sobbed.

Jinec directed a stern glance at the jeering crowd that had gathered at the water's edge as she and the boy approached. The noise level dropped in deference to their leader, but occasional cries of "Put him to death!" continued to ring out. Griac, pale and gaunt, didn't seem to hear them.

The priestess had been mystified when the ground started to shake on that fateful day; part of her daily work was to imbue the land with enough strength to protect it against such phenomena. When she saw the jagged chasm running down the hill from the jasoba grove, she had no doubt that an earthquake of that magnitude could only have been caused by the use of the *wairua* on a scale far exceeding her own power. But who could have done such a thing? And why?

Like her mother and countless generations before her, Jinec's ability to channel the *wairua*—the stored energy of ancient stardust that lay within Isahr's many metallic niej rocks—made her the leader and protector of Meligo. She had always believed that there was something unique about the physical makeup of her family that allowed them to use the *wairua*, for no one outside of her lineage had ever shown any sign of being able to use that power. Yet now, someone had clearly done just that, and at a terrible cost to her people.

As she had helped attend to the injured and provide comfort to the grieving, Jinec had been stunned by the scale of the destruction. Upon learning that Asha and Griac had not yet returned from their fruit harvesting trip to the grove, she had ridden the fastest horse there, fearing for their safety.

When she'd found Griac and the mortally wounded Asha, her heart had broken for the boy, who would now be an orphan, his father having died when Griac was only a baby. She assumed the earthquake had caused the tragedy with the branch, but after she brought the inconsolable boy back to her cottage and coaxed him into sipping a bit of soothing herbal tea, Griac had tearfully relayed the details of what transpired in the grove. Jinec had tried to hide her shock as he described the tingling in his fingers and the spreading warmth inside him that immediately preceded the ground splitting open—exactly the sensations that she experienced every time she channeled the *wairua*. In that moment, Jinec had understood that, as unbelievable as it seemed, the boy had been responsible for the devastating quake.

But how could that be? She'd been about the same age as Griac—not far away from becoming a young woman—when she had first developed the ability to use the mysterious power, but it had taken years of training before she learned how to draw the energy from the niej rocks and direct it to influence natural elements whose physical makeup made them responsive to the *wairua*, such as water, land, and air. How could he have unwittingly unleashed so much power? And what else might he be capable of?

Although her heart went out to the poor child, she had to do what was best for her people; it was her responsibility to protect them. The fact that he had not intended to cause harm was of little consolation to the villagers who had lost their loved ones. Even if she were to start training him now, there were too many uncertainties, and she would not risk any further loss of life. She would have to send him away quietly, not disclosing to anyone that he was responsible for what had happened until after he was safely away.

But Rolyi, the village gossip, had seen Griac go into the cottage with Jinec and positioned herself under a window to eavesdrop. Word that the boy was behind the earthquake that had brought so much death and destruction spread quickly, along with the villagers' fear and anger. Jinec knew she needed to act quickly, before they took matters into their own hands.

Now, as she guided Griac into the small boat loaded with food, drink, and blankets, he didn't resist, folding himself into the vessel and staring out at the sea.

"I am sorry, child. I wish there was another way," Jinec said softly, barely able to keep her tears in check as she stepped back onto the shore. Griac kept his gaze fixed on the endless waters.

Closing her eyes, she stretched her arms out in front of her, feeling the surge of the *wairua* as she pulled it into her. Soon a strong wind began to blow, pushing the boat further and further out into the shining golden sea. That wind, combined with the countertide she had in place to help prevent flooding and tidal waves, would allow the vessel to catch the current that would carry it across the vast ocean to Drozuc.

Only one group of Meligons had ever made the journey there, many generations ago. The brave explorers had discovered it during a mission to learn if there was any other land on their small planet. After arriving at the lifeless land of icy darkness, which they named Drozuc, they did some exploring and made high-level maps of the barren land. When they eventually returned home, the group reported that the only other land they had found on Isahr was not fit for habitation. No one had been back since.

Knowing that Griac would have to live out the rest of his days in such a desolate place filled Jinec with sorrow. But there was no other solution.

As he stared at the vast ocean before him, Griac was numb, save for the ache in his heart that he'd felt since losing Asha. He hadn't been able to eat or sleep; whenever he closed his eyes, he saw the look on his mother's face when he had failed to save her. What had happened after that—the physical sensations he had experienced, the subsequent gash in the land that had taken the lives of seventeen villagers—had been a complete mystery to him. But he knew the two were connected, and when Jinec gently explained that he'd inadvertently caused the tragedy by somehow tapping into the *wairua*, he had wanted to die. It was a relief when she broke the news that he was to be exiled; his own people hated him, but not as much as he hated himself. Whatever hardship lay ahead, he deserved it.

Griac pumped a fist in triumph when he discovered the ditow ensnared in his trap. Few of the docile sea creatures came this far east, and catching one was cause for celebration.

Although the hour was still early, the distant trio of suns was already starting to sink beneath the horizon. In the last of the meager light, Griac pulled the homemade net from the ice-encrusted water onto the frozen shore and looked with disdain at the pathetic dark-skinned animal, whose amber eyes were fixed on him in terror. Pulling out the long knife he'd painstakingly carved from stone, he plunged it into the creature's mid-section, enjoying the way it screamed and frantically thrashed its flippers as its lifeblood poured out. He let the ditow suffer for a while before growing bored and delivering the fatal strike.

His bounty in tow, he navigated the slick gray ice until he reached a path cutting through the deep onyx snow, following it until he arrived at a mountain of niej boulders. Although it was nearly dark, he expertly scaled its craggy face until he reached the cave that was his home.

Pulling off his face mask and several outer layers now that he was out of the incessant wind, Griac set about dissecting his catch. Years of practice had made him an expert on how to make use of every part of the animal, from its skin—perfect for clothing and bedding—to its teeth and nails, which he used for tools and put on the bottom of his boots for traction on the ice. He would ration out the meat—a delicacy compared to the fish he typically subsisted on.

In those early, desperate days after he first came to this land of nearly perpetual night, he never dreamed he would survive for this long, let alone thrive. He had ached for his mother and all he had lost, agonized over what he had done. He had nothing to live for. Alone in the punishing environment, he had lain down on the icy coast and stared up at the stars, which seemed to shine more brightly on Drozuc than they ever had in the Isahrian sky. He knew he would soon drift into a final sleep, and all the pain would be over.

And then he'd heard something: barely audible, like a whispering on the wind, so faint at first that he thought he must have been imagining it. But the sound had grown louder, an insistent murmuring that piqued his curiosity. Forcing himself to sit up, he strained to hear until he began to make out the words:

*Griac, your journey is not at an end. You are at the beginning of the path you were meant to take. Trust in yourself and in the* wairua. *You are meant for greatness.*

He'd looked around wildly, but there was no one there. Was he hallucinating? He shook his head, trying to clear it, but the voice continued—a mingled whisper, like multiple voices all speaking at once:

*There is so much power waiting for you here—a power far beyond Jinec's. You will learn how to use the* wairua, *to pull it from the niej rocks that dominate this land, then control it. You must picture in your mind what you wish to happen and make it a reality. It will take time. And once you have mastered it, you will return to Meligo and show that pathetic witch what true power is. You will make her pay. You will make all of them pay for turning their backs on you. And all of Isahr will be yours.*

"Who are you?" Griac had called into the inky air, but he was met with only silence.

The voice must have been a figment of his dying brain, for the words were pure madness. He was no one. His use of the *wairua* had been a fluke, and had caused great pain and suffering. He wanted nothing more to do with it.

But the voice had continued on, telling him how unfairly he had been treated by Jinec and his people, that to exile an innocent boy who had just lost his mother and hadn't meant to cause any harm was unspeakably cruel. It said that the worst offender was Jinec—pretending she was being merciful by sending him away, when in truth she could not stand the thought that she might not be the most powerful person in Meligo.

The more Griac listened to the persistent voice, the more the words resonated with him. He had thought himself guilty, thought Jinec's actions were warranted, but now he was beginning to see the truth: she had been jealous. That was why she had refused to teach him, instead casting him out. It was inexcusable. A spark of anger smoldered inside him, and with it came a newfound sense of determination.

He would do as the voices had directed: learn how to use the power he didn't understand, right the wrong that had been done to him. For the first time since that terrible day when his world had changed, Griac started to think that there might be a future for him after all. Perhaps he, like the stars above Drozuc, would shine more brightly in the darkness.

Spurred on by this new sense of purpose, he had found the strength to get to his feet. Dawn had just broken, its weak light casting a faint glow on the ice-flecked water, offering a glimpse of the slate-colored fish that dwelled there. He had previously dismissed the thought of trying to catch them—he had no way to do it—but now it occurred to him that this could be a chance to try using the *wairua*.

Griac walked to the water's edge and concentrated, remembering what the voice had said: he needed to pull in the energy from the surrounding rocks that lay under the sable snow and picture what he wanted to do with it. Extending his arms out, he focused, trying to draw in the *wairua*. Then he imagined the fish swimming towards him, beaching themselves at his feet. Though he tried for a long time, it was of no use; there was no tingling in his fingers, and the fish kept their usual distance.

He thought about the things he knew Jinec could do: keeping the seas calm, strengthening the land, influencing the skies to make the weather favorable. Never anything involving manipulating another living creature. Perhaps, he realized, the power only worked with nature-related elements.

Refocusing, he tried again. This time Griac felt the tingling in his fingers that he'd felt on that awful day in the grove. For a moment, he hesitated, but then his resolve intensified. The pins and needles sensation grew, the warmth he'd experienced once before spreading down his arms and legs, providing welcome relief from the numbing cold.

Moving his hands in a circular motion, he pictured the ocean swirling in front of him, imagined the energy flowing from the rocks into his body and then into the sea. To his astonishment, the water started to churn—slowly at first, then increasingly faster, pulling the fish into it and then spitting them out onto the icy shore, where they wriggled helplessly. He laughed in exhilaration. He had actually done it! And if he could bend the water to his will, what else could he do?

The voice had been right. He was going to become more powerful than Jinec, and she had known it. That was why she exiled him, alone and afraid. Oh, how he would make her regret that decision.

As the long, dark days passed, his smoldering anger began to burn hotter; thoughts of how he would return and exact his revenge spread through his mind like a noxious weed. He was going to teach the priestess, and everyone else, a lesson, returning to Meligo in triumph. How sweet it would be to see the look of shock on their faces! He would enjoy making Jinec in particular suffer, let her know how it felt to be at his mercy, just as he had been at hers. How woefully she had underestimated him. How they all had! He would punish everyone who had treated him like a criminal.

By the time he grew into a man, Griac had learned to harness and control the power that lay within the rocks. He quickly abandoned his early attempts to calm the wind and raise the temperature; it took far too much energy to make even a dent in the brutal environment, and he needed to build up as much power as possible to make the return journey to Meligo and carry out his plan for revenge.

In the ceaseless cold and darkness, he focused on honing his abilities, using the *wairua* only for basic needs like catching the fish he needed to live. As his mastery of the power increased, so did the hatred in his heart and his thirst for revenge.

Occasionally, he would hear the voice on the wind that had first spoken to him on that life-changing night. It whispered of how well he was doing, how powerful he was becoming, how he was going to make Jinec, and all of Meligo, sorry for what they had done.

Jinec walked down to the sea, unable to shake the sense of foreboding she'd awoken with after having disturbing dreams that she was lost in an icy darkness, engulfed by a bitter cold that cut her to the core.

Standing on the silver-pebbled shore, she looked at the calm seas stretching to the malachite horizon, breathing in the perfumed air as seabirds swooped and called. Multihued fish were visible in the clear, golden water. All was as it should be.

She shook her head and smiled. Perhaps she was becoming paranoid in her old age.

Shielding his eyes and squinting in the still-unfamiliar light, Griac felt a rush of adrenaline as he spotted the coast of Meligo in the distance. He was wise to have stored up such a vast amount of power; the journey had required great strength, but he still had more than enough power to carry out his plan.

As he approached the coastline, he easily reversed Jinec's counter-tide, directing the waters to push him to the empty shore. Scrambling onto the land, his legs unsteady at first after being at sea for so long, Griac took a moment to rest and look around. How strange to behold this land of his youth, whose shimmering seas and argent shores he'd seen only in his dreams for so long. It was all as he remembered, yet so very different, the vivid colors and heady scents assaulting his senses, the overwhelming warmth making him dizzy.

It seemed like paradise, but this perfect world was stained by betrayal, rife with the stench of injustice. He couldn't wait to turn it into an icy wasteland. Whether any of its inhabitants would be strong enough to survive the change was not his concern. They were all to blame. He was almost giddy with the anticipation of doling out his long-overdue justice.

Griac began striding up the path he'd last walked as a terrified, grief-stricken boy. He remembered it all so vividly and yet it almost seemed as if it had happened to someone else. The flood of memories only heightened his sense of betrayal, intensifying his anger. His fingertips tingled with the need to unleash the rage and power stored up inside him. But he had to be patient for just a little longer. First, he needed to find Jinec.

As he entered the heart of the village, people yelled in fear, the sight of the stranger sending them running. They had no idea that the visitor with the wild ebony hair and bone-white skin had once been one of their own.

Hearing the cries, Jinec emerged from her cottage, gasping as she beheld the tall, oddly-dressed figure. She knew his identity at once. Her premonition had been right after all.

Walking confidently towards her, Griac didn't stop until he was so close that Jinec could smell the stench wafting off him. His appearance was shocking. It was not simply that he had grown into a man; he looked much older than his years—no doubt from the toll the Drozuc environment had taken—and his unruly hair and beard gave him the look of a wild man. But it was what she saw in his eyes that concerned her the most. The drastic change in him was clearly not limited to his appearance.

The villagers gathered around the two figures, keeping a safe distance.

Griac smiled, a menacing grimace revealing decaying teeth almost as black as his hair—and, Jinec was quite certain—his soul.

"It's been such a long time, Jinec. Happy to see me?" he asked, noting how she'd aged in his absence. Her hair was nearly white, deep lines etching her face. Although she was tall, he towered over her. She had always seemed so grand when he was a boy, but now he saw she was nothing but a weak, frail old woman.

"Griac. I am pleased that you are alive. But you know as well as I that you were not meant to return here. Why have you come back?" she asked, drawing herself up straight and trying not to betray the fear she felt rising inside her.

"Oh, I think you know exactly why I'm here, *priestess*," he growled, and a chill much like the one she'd experienced in her nightmare ran through her.

"Enlighten me," she replied, her voice barely above a whisper.

"To be the new leader of Meligo, of course," he said nonchalantly, eliciting gasps from the crowd.

Griac chuckled at the reaction, looking around at the villagers.

"Oh, don't worry—once you get used to the dark and cold, you'll love it!" he said. "That is, if you survive."

Jinec started to raise her hands in an attempt to summon the *wairua*, but Griac struck her hard across the face, sending her reeling to the ground.

Wiping blood from her mouth and nose, Jinec managed to sit up, her head spinning. "Your quarrel is not with these people, Griac," she said. "It is with me alone. It was *my* decision to send you to Drozuc. If you must take your revenge, take it out on me. Leave the rest of them out of it—they are innocent."

His face contorted into a sneer. "Innocent?" he hissed. "Do you think I've forgotten how they all acted like I was a criminal? How some of these—" he gestured to the villagers, "—*fine citizens* were calling for my death? They are all as guilty as you—you, who saw fit to sentence a boy who had just lost his mother to a life of isolation and hardship because of an accident! How could you have been so heartless?" he demanded.

"Do you think it didn't tear me up to send you away like that?" she asked. "Or that I haven't wondered countless times whether there was something else that I could have done? I had so many other lives to protect! I had no choice."

He rolled his eyes, waving a hand dismissively. "Oh, such a martyr, so worried about your people. Or perhaps you simply could not stand the idea that someone else was able to use your precious *wairua*!" he spat. "You felt threatened by me! You wanted to be the only one with the power so that everyone would continue to worship you—and only you."

Jinec started to protest, but he cut her off. "Enough of your lies. It is time to do what I came here for. Time to set things right, to fulfill my true purpose. Really, I should thank you for helping me realize my full potential."

As she struggled to get to her feet, Griac delivered a brutal kick to her ribs. Jinec cried out in pain and fell back to the ground, eliciting a laugh from him.

"I could kill you now, but it will be so much better to let you watch as your domain becomes mine, to see your people suffer because of your selfishness," Griac said.

He raised his arms towards the sky, hands extended, and closed his eyes. The jade sky darkened as heavy clouds gathered. A wild wind whipped across the land, the temperature freefalling as he used the full force of his power to pull in the frigid air from high above.

Lurzim birds called out in alarm and flowers curled in at their edges as the villagers stood frozen in place by fear. Griac savored it all. The look of pure shock on Jinec's face as she lay there, defeated and bloodied, was the best part. Revenge was every bit as delicious as what he had envisioned. It was all going exactly as he had planned.

From behind him, a boy's voice rang out. "I'm scared, Ammita!"

Griac whirled around to see a small boy burying his face into the neck of a young woman whose arms were wrapped protectively around him.

"It will be okay, my birne," she said soothingly, although there was naked fear in her eyes.

In a flash, a vivid image of Asha flooded Griac's mind, along with memories of how safe he had felt with her and how kind she had always been to him. The force of the flashback took him by surprise, momentarily interrupting his concentration, his arms dropping a bit.

Seeing her chance, Jinec willed herself to stand and reached her hands up to the sky using all the power she could muster.

Before Griac could react, a bolt of lightning shot from the clouds and struck him in the chest. A look of confusion crossed his face as he collapsed to the ground.

Jinec cautiously knelt down beside him, but she knew he was dead. The clouds were already lifting, the wind settling down to a gentle breeze as the temperature rose. Hugging one another, the villagers cheered and cried with relief. It was over.

At Jinec's insistence, Griac was buried next to Asha, in spite of protests from some people. She hoped the gods who decided on a person's fate for the afterlife would consider the true soul of Griac to be the pure, innocent boy he had once been rather than the monster he was driven to become.

# CROWNS OF SWEETGRASS

### By Cherie Lynae Cabrera Suski

THE KING'S SORCERER dragged his blade across the child's palm, making the same neat slice he'd left on dozens of girls in the last six moon cycles. The little one screamed, and her governess cooed as he caught the blood in his chalice.

"When will we know the results?" The child's father paced, his armor creaking. He didn't spare a glance for his daughter as her governess carried the crying child from the room.

"It could take a few hours." The sorcerer sprinkled a fine powder into the chalice and stirred it with his finger.

"And the betrothal?"

"If she proves to be the strongest ice wielder of her generation, she will marry the prince." The sorcerer dropped a stone into the liquid, dipping his finger into the chalice.

He paused, his breath becoming clouds. Frost covered his body, and he yanked his hand back.

"Argh." He collapsed into a chair, holding his ruined finger. The blackened flesh quivered from where it hung on the bone. "That's never happened before."

Up and up and up. Juniper shaded her eyes as she searched the battlements of the castle of Troms. Soldiers in furs milled about. The sun turned them into black figures, punching holes in the sky as they paced. Her father's hand clamped onto her shoulder.

"Enough daydreaming. Stay sharp while you're here."

Bruises bloomed under his fingers.

"Yes, Father."

"Use concise words. The less you say, the better."

"Yes, Father."

Juniper folded her hands into her skirts and followed General Silverneedle. Sweetgrass tickled her ankles as she walked, the vanilla scent calming her. She recited the mantra her governess taught her. The four tenets of being a noblewoman.

*Obedience, silence, strength, and... I can't remember. Obedience, silence, strength, and...*

She covered her mouth. "Ivy?" she hissed her governess's name, adding a fake cough to the end. She waved her hand at her side, knowing Ivy would be a few steps behind her. "Ivy."

"Silence, girl."

"Yes, Father."

They joined her father's men, their procession falling in line. Flanked by soldiers, Juniper marveled when their march echoed off the mountain walls cradling the castle. She worked the velvet of her skirts, her fingers both pale and delicate against the azure fabric.

"Daughter," the general said after they passed through the grand castle doors. "At my side."

Juniper tripped and would have fallen if Ivy's hands hadn't

braced her. She mouthed '*thank you,*' and received an encouraging nod. With the grace of a goose, Juniper stepped into her place.

The Cryoky Royal Guards stood at attention behind a woman dressed in fine brocade and a royal herald.

"General Silverneedle, bless the Mountains you arrived safely." He bowed low. "The king and queen wish to hold counsel. Can Lady Violet, the King's niece, escort our future Princess? She is to meet Prince Alder."

Juniper arranged her face into a mask, holding back the nervous giggle that built in her chest.

Lady Violet's shoes clicked as she stepped forward and curtsied. Her eyes lifted to Juniper's father. "May she take her leave, Lord?"

General Silverneedle nodded.

"Follow me."

Juniper hesitated. "May my governess join us?"

"Mountains, child." Her father blew out a puff of air. "Ivy, see to it Lady Silverneedle does not ruin her betrothal upon first meeting the prince."

"Yes, milord." Ivy curtsied low and fell into place behind Juniper.

Juniper took solace in the sound of Ivy's heavy gait behind her. She had no expectations for this introduction, though her lady's maids swooned every time her summers with the prince came up. Ivy often shooed them from the room, reminding them of Juniper's short twelve-summers of life.

"Lady Juniper." Violet's chestnut hair fell in curls down her back, ending at her wide hips. "Are you excited about meeting my cousin?"

"Yes, Lady Violet, I've been waiting seven summers." Juniper traced the silver line on her palm, a constant reminder she would marry the prince and one day be the queen of the Cryoky.

"You must have some incredible gifts to be chosen."

*My gifts?* Juniper glanced back at Ivy as she struggled for an appropriate reply. Ivy smiled, her corpulent cheeks lifting. "I can't do anything impressive yet."

"I guess I couldn't at your age either."

Juniper heard the smile in Violet's voice.

"Our family matures into their gifts later than yours. My father was fifteen-summers. My mother made it to her seventeenth-summer."

"I wish I had that problem." The pearls of Violet's veil blinked as she shook her head. "The later your coming-of-age, the longer your betrothal. I would love to put off marriage for a while."

Ivy's history lessons came to mind. *Betrothals among the Cryoky are not official until both children survive their coming of age. The more power, the more dangerous their transition to adulthood.* The thought made Juniper's blood run cold. She didn't want death or marriage.

The sounds of steel meeting steel greeted them as the guards pulled the doors open. Juniper drank in the scene. A teenage boy and a young woman sparred in the room's center. Their white tunics stuck to their chests as they blocked and lunged. Their bodies showed their discipline with every movement. His, a sum of firm angles and straight lines; hers, subtle curve upon subtle curve.

*Obedience.* The fighters' arms moved with practiced thrusts.

*Silence.* Their lips sealed against any sound.

*Strength.* Their swords sparked with the power of their blows.

*Balance.* They followed through with their attacks and fell back in turns.

*Yes. Balance. The last value is balance. Obedience, silence, strength, and balance.*

A mask covered the top half of the woman's face. Her lips

screwed up in concentration. She'd shaved the side of her head in the Pyrona fashion. Two waist-length braids flew about her with each of her disciplined movements.

*She's beautiful.*

"Is that a Pyrona warrior?" Juniper's heart fluttered, and her temperature dropped as the prince circled the woman with large, sweeping movements.

"Yes, the Royals train with them so they may practice fighting without wielding ice. The female Pyrona specialize in neutralizing our powers."

"Why does she wear a mask?" Juniper's eyes wandered back to the woman's lips.

"To protect her nose and eyes from ice needles and wind." Violet clapped her hands as the prince parried a blow. "Isn't she fascinating? We have two at court this summer."

A groan escaped the boy as a red line bloomed across his shoulder. "Enough." Alder Troms jumped back. He caught Juniper's eye, his pale cheeks pinking. He lowered his weapon. "I have a guest."

They bowed and sheathed their swords. He touched his wound then looked at the blood on his fingers.

The woman remained at attention, her chest heaving as she caught her breath.

The prince glowered at her, wiping his fingers on his shirt as he walked up to the Pyrona. Standing toe to toe, he stood a foot taller. His head bobbed as he traced her breasts and hips with his eyes.

"Filth." He spits on the ground. For a moment, Juniper thought he would walk away. Instead, he pulled his arm back with the speed of a snake and struck her, his fist landing on her mouth.

Juniper flinched at the sound of his ring meeting the woman's teeth. Blood splashed down her tunic, but she held her stance.

Juniper's hands covered her mouth.

"You cut the Prince of the Cryoky." He tilted his chin up. "I don't know how you do things, but we are civilized here." Her blood joined his as he cleaned his knuckles with his shirt. "While in my castle, you will not draw blood during a sparring match." He straightened his shoulders, folding his arms. "Well?"

"Yes, Your Highness."

"You're dismissed." The prince waved the woman away.

The Pyrona joined the guards, blood dripping from her ruined lip. She gathered her jacket and other weapons which waited on a stool.

*Alder does not act like he's fifteen-summers-old.* The boy smirked at Juniper as her eyes returned to him. *He acts like my father.*

The prince pulled off his shirt, and Juniper spun around. Her body trembled. She'd never seen so much skin in her life. The way it moved over the muscle refused to leave her head, even as she stared at her governess.

Ivy mimed breathing. Her hands fluttered to her belly, reminding Juniper how low to pull in her breath.

"Cousin," Lady Violet said, "you have no manners. There's a lady in your presence."

"Right." Alder had the baritone of a man.

Ivy made a circle with her finger and pointed forward as if to say: *June bug, turn around.*

With a gulp, Juniper nodded, turning back to her prince. He drank from his goblet, pulled a fur-lined robe over the lines of his torso, and tied back his black hair.

"Better?"

Juniper's eyes remained low.

"This is Lady Silverneedle, your future princess."

Alder crossed the room, a smile on his face.

"Lady Silverneedle." He took her hand. Instead of a chaste kiss on her knuckles, he leaned in and pressed his lips onto her cheek, leaving a smear of sweat behind.

It took all of Juniper's willpower not to pull away. Her lashes kissed her cheeks as she itched to wipe away the wetness he'd left behind. Her lady's maids would faint if she described this kiss. Their giggles would fill the room, but Juniper experienced no such elation.

Alder's bigness and the heat radiating from his body turned her stomach.

"I'm so glad you've come for the summer."

"Your Majesty." Remembering herself, Juniper curtsied.

Alder held her hand captive, taking the other to help her stand; his head ducked as he met her eyes.

"Come, come, no need for niceties here. I want us to be the best of friends." His moist hands dropped hers. "Now, tell me about your trip. Were there any delays in your travel? I always hear gossip of bandits during these warmer days but have yet to see any."

Juniper resisted his enthusiasm and charm. Her shyness and his boldness became their game. They painted their first summer with watching and waiting. He gave her pieces of his world, and she handed them back with trembling hands.

On their last day together, they stood shoulder to shoulder as General Silverneedle spoke to the king and queen.

"I made you a parting gift." Alder spoke so low only she could hear. He leaned closer, his eyes still facing their parents, and lifted a braided ring of sweetgrass.

*A crown*, she realized. "Thank you, my liege."

"Of course, Princess. One day, I'll give you a real one." He placed it on her head, his hand pausing on her cheek. "And then I'll put some babies in your belly."

She pulled away, her breath catching when his finger slid down her ribs and poked her stomach.

He laughed.

"Lady Silverneedle, our carriage awaits." The general waved his daughter forward.

Alder caught her wrist before she walked away.

"I'll see you next summer, Juniper."

She spent her ride home praying to the Mountains she would never come of age.

Four summers and four sweetgrass crowns later, Juniper dreaded her trip as she packed to see Prince Alder.

"I don't understand. He's so kind to you. Why don't you like him?"

"It's just, I can't fight him off anymore, Ivy. He's always flirting and trying to make me laugh."

"What's wrong with laughing?"

"Nothing, but his jokes aren't funny. He scares me. The way he speaks. The way he touches me."

"Touches you?" Ivy's chubby fingers stopped midway through folding Juniper's chemise.

"You know. Touch me." Juniper tightened her grip on her cape, the fabric growing stiff with cold as she twisted. "Sometimes..." She heaved a breath.

"Sometimes he'll..."

Her teeth chattered.

"Sometimes he will..."

With a crack, the frozen cape broke in half, and pieces fell to the ground, shattering. Her eyes widened as her body shuddered. Static crackled in the air.

"Ivy?" Juniper watched the color of her hands change to blue, crystals forming along her skin. "It hurts." She couldn't move.

"June bug?" Ivy's breath formed clouds. "Juniper, you're all right." The governess retreated. One step. Two steps. Her hip met the window sill. "Look at me. Take a breath."

Agony filled Juniper's chest as her ribs buzzed. Her jaw popped, and her mouth gaped. Her head and eyes rolled back, back, back.

And then she exploded, like a true Silverneedle descendant.

Her governess put up her hands, blocking her face. Ice tore through Ivy, shattering the glass behind her. Her motherly arms and kind smile erased in an instant. She died before the ribbons of her body splattered on the ground two floors below.

Wind slashed like a whip as it spun around the castle. From the ceiling fell fist-sized clusters of snow. They swirled about wildly before meeting the ground.

Frozen in place, Juniper stared at the window where clumps of Ivy hung from the stone.

"Blasted Mountains!" General Silverneedle shouted as he shoved his way into the room, inches of snow encumbering the door.

Her father's hands flew as he conjured walls of ice around her. Trapping her and her storm inside.

"Someone send a rider to Pyrona!" the general shouted. "We need a warrior."

Between the efforts of General Silverneedle and his best men, they moved Juniper to the north tower and sealed her inside.

A day passed before she could move. She fell to the ground. Her limbs stuttered with pain as they broke through their stiffness. The layers of ice enveloping her tower muffled her screams. Tears froze to her face, fracturing as she called for her governess. Ivy's wide-eyed fear imprinted on the back of her eyelids.

On day two, she found the strength to wander her ice prison. Traversing the spiral staircase once before crying herself to sleep. On day three, her body thawed enough for hunger to grip her. That and boredom sent her experimenting with the constant release of the power rushing beneath her skin.

The mice of the tower grew brave on day five. A whole family scurried across her room. Anger sharpened her senses, and she glared at them. *These little beasts have freedom while I am trapped here,*

267

*starving to death.* She pointed her finger, and cold jumped from her to the rodents, freezing them into a line. She knelt on the ground. Her face lowered as she studied the little ears and whiskers. The closer she looked, the more she regretted her actions.

Juniper closed her eyes and pulled her cold out of their little bodies. Her hands went to her chest when she discovered what she'd done. Their abdomens had burst open, their organs spilling out. They'd exploded from the quick temperature changes.

Juniper fell back, dragging her bottom on the icy floor. Snow flurries filled the room, and Juniper succumbed as her power exploded from her. The tower moaned, the foundation rumbling. An additional layer of ice spread over the floor, covering her mess.

On day six, she woke to the sound of boots in the snow. The gait carried the measured rhythm of confidence. Juniper lay on the floor, her eyes studying the stalactites covering the ceiling. A face obstructed her view. Even upside down, the face she saw struck her with its charm. Skin the color of pine tree bark covered a broad nose and wide brow. The woman wore her hair in the Pyrona warrior style. Two black braids fell past her shoulder and tickled Juniper's ear.

"Rubies," Juniper said as she reached up and rested a finger on the white scar bisecting the woman's bottom lip. It turned down as her brows rose. "Or cherries. My cold has colored your lips red. You're so beautiful. Are you real?"

"Cryoky." The woman blew out a puff of air. "They don't know how to keep their hands to themselves." She batted Juniper's hand away.

"Wait." Juniper blinked as the face vanished. "Come back. Please."

She planted her elbows in the snow and pushed with all her strength. Her body didn't move. Hunger and exhaustion left her too weak to sit up. She closed her eyes to a rush of dizziness.

"The problem with your people is their greed." Her voice reminded Juniper of the reed instruments the commoners played during celebrations. "The Cryoky marry for power, so they give birth to monsters."

A drop of water splashed on Juniper's forehead, and she looked up. Drips ran down the stalactites as if they were crying. She remembered a story Ivy told her about her great-grandmother, Willow. At her coming of age, her parents brought home a Pyrona warrior to be her bodyguard. The Pyrona used her fire gifts to counteract the Silverneedle's ice. Willow lived a long life. Her bodyguard held her hand as she left this world for God's Mountain.

"What's your name?" Heat entered Juniper's body, easing the terror of the last few days.

"Balance. That's what your people lack." Boots paced through the slush. "Why filter so much power into one person? This never happens to the Pyrona. We share power among our people." The woman snorted. "Can you imagine a Cryoky coming to our aid if we didn't?"

The woman's face returned.

"You are real." Juniper's chapped bottom lip quivered. "What's your name?"

"And why should I give it to you? You're a spoiled princess, throwing the biggest fit I've ever seen." The woman put out her hand. "Come."

Juniper turned away, blinking back tears. "Don't call me that."

"What?"

"Princess. Please don't call me princess."

"As you say." The woman frowned. "You can call me Pyrona."

Juniper covered her face.

"Don't cry."

Juniper convulsed with a sob.

"Please."

"Pyrona, I... I killed her." Juniper's fists curled with her body, grief spilling from her lips.

"Let's go." Arms wrapped around her back and under her legs, lifting Juniper from the ground. The Pyrona's glow filled the cracks in Juniper's heart as her head lolled against her breast.

"Daughter." General Silverneedle woke Juniper by tossing a heavy robe on her bed. "Get up."

Juniper pulled her robe to her chest, sitting as she blinked sleep from her eyes.

"I said. Get. Up." Her father came around the bed, his hand locking around her arm like a bear trap. He dragged her to the ground.

Juniper knew better than to struggle. Her back screamed from the impact. She reached for the bed to drag herself up.

"Dear Mountains, grant me patience." Her father clapped her ear, and a ringing exploded in her head. "What did I do to deserve a daughter? Now stand."

She found her feet. Her eyes strayed from the ground to see if the Pyrona watched. The warrior stood at attention, facing the door.

"We are a moon cycle late for our trip to the capital. You should not leave the Prince of Troms waiting." Her father turned on his heels, facing Juniper's bodyguard. "We leave in the morning, Firestar. I expect her to be ready."

"Yes, sir. Thank you, sir."

Her father grunted, and the Pyrona saluted, holding the stance until the door closed behind the general.

"What, am I a babysitter now?" The Pyrona came around the bed. "Don't cry." She grabbed Juniper's chin, tilting her head and inspecting her ear.

"I wasn't going to." Juniper wiped her nose.

"Good." The Pyrona ran her thumb along the girl's cheek.

Juniper smiled.

"What?"

"Firestar?"

The Pyrona's hand dropped, and she frowned.

Juniper's smile became a grin.

"I'm surrounded by fools." The bodyguard ambled to the door, swinging it open hard enough to slam into the wall. She hung around the corner. "Aye-oh, you." Her irreverence rang down the hall. "Yeah, you. The Lady needs her lady's maids."

"Firestar." Juniper winced as she sat at her vanity.

The Pyrona returned to her chair, flopping into it sideways, leaving her legs hanging over the edge.

"Yes, Firestar."

"I want to know your first name."

"You're spoiled enough without me giving you everything you want." The Pyrona closed her eyes, leaning her head back.

"Yes, I've been told that I'm spoiled."

"Good."

"I've also been told I'm a waste of space. Unwanted. A murderer. Evil. My father tells me regularly." Her voice cracked, and she pulled her hair out of its braid. "These 'fits', as you call them. I have no control over what happens."

"Sweet Mountains, what else should I call them?"

Juniper's fingers wrapped around the handle of her brush. "I had my first 'fit' the day I was born." She brought it to her hair, her delicate hands shaking with a slurry of emotions. "I shredded my mother to pieces." The bristles ran through the golden locks. "If I were my father, I'd hate me too. But you are my guard. I know how this works. You've sworn an oath. And now you are all I have."

Juniper brushed her hair in silence, watching the Pyrona, who lounged in her chair as if she'd fallen asleep. Juniper pulled a ribbon from her drawer, no longer expecting a response.

"My name is Ruby Firestar, but my friends call me Star."

"Star?"

"If I can't call you princess, I'll call you June." The Pyrona crossed the room to stand behind Juniper. Their eyes locked through the mirror. The charcoal gray of the Firestar's met the grass green of the Silverneedle's. "Juniper is so pretentious. So Cryoky. Plus, I think of spring when I think of you." She gifted Juniper with a smile.

"If we get to pick, I'll call you Ruby. It reminds me of your lips in the cold." With bravery burning in her belly, she caught Ruby's hand.

Fingers intertwined, and eyes strayed shyly away.

The prince greeted General Silverneedle and his daughter as they entered the castle.

"General, may I escort Juniper to her rooms?"

"Of course. As long as it's not a burden, Your Highness."

"Your daughter is never a burden, General." Alder put out his elbow for Juniper, and she took it. Once out of earshot, the prince squeezed her hand. "I heard you came of age. Are you well?"

Juniper's heart raced as it always did when the prince pulled her too close. She opened her mouth but could not speak.

"Princess, you know what this means?" He dropped her hand, his arm coming around her shoulder. He left a slow kiss on her cheek.

Juniper froze, but instead of the ice coming, as she flinched away, she felt Ruby's warmth.

"Juniper?" His hands cupped her cheeks, and his lips came crashing down on hers. His facial hair scratched her, his breath smelled of dead animals.

Her arms went loose at her sides, her eyes squeezed shut, and she clung to the heat at her back, telling her Ruby would not abandon her.

*Please, make this stop.*

Alder jumped away when the sound of metal on stone clambered through the hall. He pulled Juniper behind him, preparing for an assault.

"Who are you?" The prince had frost in his eyes.

"Lady Juniper's bodyguard." Ruby stood at attention, her dagger

 272

glinting on the floor before her.

A strange sense of familiarity filled Juniper's chest as Alder sneered at Ruby. She squinted at the scar on the Pyrona's lip.

*Did Alder's ring leave that scar?*

Juniper rested her hand on Alder's shoulder. It buzzed with discomfort as she touched him of her own volition. "She is dear to me, Your Highness." She infused her words with every drop of persuasion she owned.

"You're dismissed." Alder's angry voice made Juniper's arm hairs stand.

"Sorry, Your Highness, I can't leave her." Ruby's face remained placid.

"That's an order, Pyrona. She is safe with me."

"I am not here to keep her safe, Your Highness. I'm here to keep you safe. You and your family, and everyone in this castle. She could turn this place into a blizzard if I step away."

The prince's face grew red, his eyes narrowing.

"Bloody Mountains, then give us your back, soldier. And put that damn dagger away. How incompetent are you? Who drops a dagger?"

Ruby bent down for her dagger, acting as though she'd forgotten where the blade belonged. She tried her pant leg, her back, and then—*it's from your sleeve.*

Ruby slipped it into her sleeve, and only Juniper could see her guard's half-smile as she turned away from the couple.

"You will not dine with us tonight." Alder's glare turned to Juniper. "I don't want to see her again today."

"I will retire early tonight. I am weary from our travels."

"Yes, yes." His icicle eyes studied her. "We will try this again later. Sleep well, Princess."

Alone with her bodyguard, Juniper fell into bed.

"*'Sleep well, princess.'*" Ruby plugged her nose as she spoke, imitating Alder's accent. "Mountains, that man is insufferable."

"That man is your future king."

"He is your future king and my current headache. I've disliked him since we were children. He's spoiled and disrespectful, like the lot of you." Ruby took off her sword, leaving it by the door. "And you're welcome, by the way."

Juniper sighed. "What do I owe you for now?"

"I'm not clumsy. June, you know this." Ruby checked her daggers.

"Sure, sure." Juniper touched her lips, her mind elsewhere.

"I didn't just drop my dagger for fun."

Juniper sat up. "You mean you distracted Alder on purpose?"

Ruby nodded as she circled the room, checking the windows and the tapestries.

"That was dumb." Juniper hugged herself. *And so brave.*

Ruby stopped at a chair and pressed against the cushion, testing for softness. She nodded before dragging it next to the bed.

"Did you hear me?"

Ruby rolled her eyes as she circled the room again.

"He has no patience for the Pyrona."

"Trust me, I know."

"Then why pull such a stunt?"

"You should have seen your face, your body." Ruby bit her bottom lip. "You looked like you were having your teeth pulled."

"Mountains, you are rude." Juniper pulled off her slippers. "It was my first kiss."

"I could tell." Ruby spoke with her back to Juniper. "You didn't like it, either."

"What is there to like?"

"I'd show you if you weren't such a child."

"What did you say?"

"You're a child."

"And you are a low-born Pyrona who has no right to advise me." Juniper climbed under the covers and rolled onto her belly, too much of a coward to meet Ruby's eyes.

"I'll call your lady's maids. You can't sleep in that."

Juniper felt the room cool as Ruby stepped out. Her body wanted to freeze the world, while her heart begged for Ruby's warmth to return.

Juniper couldn't sleep. *Low-born Pyrona.* Her words woke her every time her eyes fell closed. She didn't think that way.

*No! I have to make this better.*

She slipped out of bed, her heart pounding. Looking at Ruby, she paused. She lay slumped in her chair with closed eyes. Her bound breasts rose and fell under her tunic, pulling it tight with each inhalation.

*You didn't like it either.*

Ruby understood her. Juniper did not like the feel of Alder's breath on her face or how his lips insisted on a response she couldn't give him. She didn't like the hard lines of his body pressed against hers.

She looked down at Ruby's natural pout. *But these lips.* She didn't let herself finish the thought as she stopped herself from touching Ruby's scar.

Juniper knelt before Ruby, resting her hands on her knees.

Ruby's body stiffened.

"I'm sorry." Juniper sat on her heels and waited for a response. "I know you're awake. You're always awake."

"Then you also know my job is easier when my ward is asleep." Ruby didn't bother to open her eyes.

"Can you hear me rolling my eyes?" Juniper's hands dropped.

"Why aren't you sleeping?"

"When did you last sleep in a bed?"

Ruby's lips flattened as her eyes opened. "What does it matter? Get back to sleep, Princess." She gestured to the bed.

"You promised you wouldn't call me that anymore."

"Did I?" Ruby raised her brows, tapping Juniper's nose.

"When was the last time you slept in a bed?" Juniper slid her hand onto Ruby's thigh.

"A long time ago." Ruby squeezed Juniper's fingers with her calloused ones. "Now, go to sleep. You have a big day tomorrow."

"I want to give you something. To show I'm contrite." Juniper scooted closer, emboldened by Ruby's touch. "Take my bed. I'll take the chair."

"You're ridiculous. Go to sleep."

"I won't."

"You must."

"No."

"You're such a..." Juniper stopped the insult with her mouth, her tongue finding Ruby's scar. Their lips fit together like the God of the Mountains cast them at the same time.

"June." Ruby lifted her, pulling the girl into her lap. "Mountains, June."

The breathless way Ruby said her name sent Juniper's innocent lips exploring. She wanted to be the answer to her prayer. Their bodies found a rhythm.

"This is how a kiss is supposed to feel." Ruby wrapped her arms around Juniper's waist, her lips finding Juniper's neck.

*This is what heaven feels like.*

Juniper's staccato heartbeats set a tempo for their hands as they wandered.

Breasts and belly.

Hips and thighs.

Ruby was soft and hard in all the right places. Juniper wanted to taste the junctures between them.

"We should stop." Teeth on earlobe and suck.

 276

"Yes." Juniper's back arched, and snow fell. A glittering flurry surrounded them. "I mean, no. I'll die if you stop."

Ruby rested her face on Juniper's chest, her shoulders rising and falling, rising and falling. The flakes swirled around them, evaporating in blinks.

"This." Ruby squeezed her. "Is punishable by death."

Juniper's thumb rested on Ruby's scar. Her breath hiccupped.

Ruby carried Juniper back to bed, tucking her in and laying atop the covers.

"I'll hold you until you fall to sleep."

Ruby's resolve melted over time, her tender touch highlighting the summer. The dangers forgotten when their passions peaked. Juniper recognized the risks and deemed them abstract. Secret kisses peppered her nights, and careful evasions ruled her days. Alder's pursuit became impossible to deflect. He grew ever more creative and unpredictable.

"A sleigh ride, truly?" The vanilla scent of the sweetgrass wafted through the air with each step, their boots crushing the blades.

"He is to show me the view at the east peak." Juniper covered her smile with her hand as Ruby's warmth caressed her.

"More like he wants to show off his money." Ruby gestured at the sleigh servants horsed on the other side of the courtyard. "Spoiled Cryoky princeling."

"Oh, you're just mad we won't be alone." Juniper's smile widened as she looked up at her bodyguard. The sunlight revealed much about Ruby, like the auburn undertone of Ruby's hair or that her full lips were more coral than dark amber. *She has freckles.* Juniper hugged herself, resisting the temptation to kiss them.

"You're just figuring this out?"

"I learn something new every day." Juniper giggled.

"What's so funny, Princess?" Alder strolled through the grass, his cheeks ruddy from the cold, his hands pulling up the tallest blades as he went.

Juniper stiffened, curtsying. "I'm sorry, Your Highness."

"Don't be. I've never seen you laugh before." The prince ran his hand up her back and frowned when she flinched away. His eyes lifted to Ruby. "I've been meaning to ask. Have we met before this summer? All the Pyrona look the same."

Ruby bowed again, lower this time. "I'm sure you don't remember, sire. We used to spar when we were fourteen summers." Ruby pulled her leather mask from her cloak and put it on, her gray eyes staring out, a smug set to her jaw.

"Yes, I remember you." Alder shrugged his shoulders, adjusting his jacket. "Well, I hope you can ride. You will follow on horseback with the other guards. This way, you're close enough to do your job, but I won't have to suffer the blight of your visage." He turned away. "Now, get out of my sight."

Juniper's fists tightened as Ruby bowed and pulled up her cowl. Her bodyguard strode away; chest held high.

"Lady Juniper, let me show you the workmanship of this sleigh." Alder's alabaster fingers braided the blades of grass he'd collected, unaware of the hatred in the eyes of his betrothed. "I commissioned it as a coming-of-age gift for you."

"For me?" Her breakfast threatened to return to her mouth. "You're too kind."

"Anything for my future queen." Alder took Juniper's gloved hand and leaned in close. "How else am I going to get you alone?"

"I-I don't know what to say, Your Highness."

"Say nothing." He lowered his sweetgrass crown onto her head. "There are other ways to repay me with your mouth."

"If you move further away from me, you'll fall out of the sleigh."

"Sorry, Your Highness." Juniper clung tighter to her armrest as their ride slowed.

"Whoa." The driver pulled his reins as a man stepped into their path. "Whoa." The horses whinnied as a second and third man joined the first.

"Who are these fools?" Alder's hand rested on his sword.

A guard rode to Alder's side of the sleigh.

"Sire, we must return you to the castle."

Juniper slid to the edge of her seat as dirty-faced men materialized from the thick woods lining the road.

"Sire, you must take my horse."

Alder's crystalline eyes darted about.

"We'll be taking this sleigh." The man who first blocked their path unsheathed his sword, pointing at Juniper and then the prince. "And the women."

The men laughed.

Blades slid from their homes, and the temperature dropped as the bandits and guards eased their powers out.

"What do you think, men? How much will the king pay to get his pretty little daughter back?"

"A lot less after I'm done having my way with him." More laughs. "Look at him blush."

An arrow landed in the man's chest with a hollow thump. His smirk froze on his face as he fell. The world flew into action, Ruby's heat ripping away from Juniper as the sounds of fighting commenced. Juniper turned to the prince, wide-eyed.

Alder took the reins. "I'll be back for you." He spoke over his shoulder as the guard dismounted. The prince climbed atop the horse and locked eyes with Juniper. "Show them what you can do." He drew his sword, guards flanking him on both sides. He smirked at her before standing in his stirrups and riding toward the castle.

Juniper slid off her seat and onto the floor. Her head tucked into her lap. She squeezed her eyes shut. Cold spun around her, picking her hair off her shoulders.

*Keep it in. Ruby is out there.*

*Keep it in.* She held herself tight and her magic tighter.

*Keep it in.*

Male hands grabbed her arms and dragged her back. Her heels slid against the wood as he pulled, and she bit her tongue. The iron taste of blood filled her mouth. She screamed, her hands grabbing hold of anything they could find.

"Yes, sweet thing, scream for me." His hot breath burned her ear, and the control she clung to snapped.

Her heart paused as the monster inside her clawed its way out.

*Pain. So much pain.*

Male screams joined her own as her silverneedles tore through flesh. Shredding the man who supported the top half of her body. She fell into the snow, landing on her back, her head bouncing off a rock.

*Is someone holding me?* Heat calmed the diffuse ache that came with wielding ice. Juniper's lashes fluttered as her eyes adjusted to the sun.

*Ruby's face.* She looked at Ruby's face. Juniper gasped as she saw the bloody lines marring her forehead, neck, and shoulders.

"You're awake." Part grimace, Ruby's smile shined with affection.

They stood at the bottom of a hill, trodden snow before and behind them. Pines lined their passageway.

"Put me down."

The guard winced as she lowered Juniper to the ground.

Juniper's hands went straight to Ruby's face and then searched her body.

"I'm fine." Ruby hissed as Juniper's fingers found gouges in her sides. "We're safe."

"You're hurt."

"Nothing a few stitches won't fix. You should see the man who stood in front of me." Ruby shook her head. "No, you shouldn't. You're not a murderer. I'm sorry, I couldn't fight and keep your powers at bay." Ruby pulled Juniper to her chest, resting her chin on the girl's head. "We are a few miles out. I didn't want you to see…"

"Lots of people died today?"

"They did."

"We could have died too?"

"We could have." Ruby pulled Juniper closer.

"Let's run away." Juniper didn't wait for a response. She rose onto her toes and pressed her lips against Ruby's. They melted into each other.

They didn't hear the lone man crest the hill above nor see his ire as he took in the scene. Alder, disheveled and wet, broke into a run.

"Unhand her."

They turned at the words.

The prince smacked into Ruby, sending her stumbling back.

"Alder?" Juniper whimpered as he gripped Juniper's shoulders, a scowl on his face.

"How could you?" He shook her. "I told you I'd come back."

"And you." He whirled on Ruby, his teeth gritting as his uniformed men crested the hill. Adler held out a hand. "Fall back!" The men did as commanded.

"It's not what it looked like." Juniper took hold of the prince's sleeve. "She saved me. You left me, and she saved me."

Alder ignored her, baring his teeth, his eyes locking with Ruby's.

"Kneel!" Spittle flew from his mouth with the word. He drew his sword.

Ruby nodded. "Please, don't blame Juniper." She held up her hands and took a knee.

"No!" Juniper pulled the prince's arm. "Please, my liege. Please." Tears streamed down her face.

Alder's elbow crunched into Juniper's nose.

She fell to the ground, blood gushing into her hands. She ignored the pain, crawling toward her guard.

"Ruby! Fight back, I beg you."

Alder lifted his sword.

Firestar gray met Silverneedle green.

The blade found its mark, cutting clean through Ruby's neck.

*Thud.*

*Thud.*

A small impact and then a big one. Her head and then her body. It went rigid when it landed, a leg kicking twice. Ruby's head rolled into the trees, her eyes forever staring into Juniper's.

"This is your fault." Alder wiped his sword on Ruby's chest before sheathing it.

Juniper fell forward, blinded by tears and wretched.

Alder wasted no time. His boot smashed into her ribs, and she fell flat into her vomit. "Get General Silverneedle," he yelled to his men. The prince's knee landed on the center of her back, his weight pressing her into the ground. "I would have given you the world, Princess." One of his gloved hands plugged her nose. The other covered her mouth.

Juniper's muffled cries died as darkness found her.

Juniper awoke in the dungeons. Complete silence choked her.

*Alder!*

She jerked to a sitting position. Her hands came up, blocking her face.

When he didn't materialize, she shook the buzzing from her ears and blinked into the dark. She pushed back the hair that fell from her braids, her fingers tangling with her crown of sweetgrass. She crushed the gift in her fist.

Her father's magic surrounded her, radiating from the glimmering ice walls.

*He must be my warden and... Who's that?*

Her eyes strained to understand who stood in the room's center.

*Ruby?*

She moved closer.

*Ruby?*

Her chest emptied, expelling hatred and sorrow in a shuddering breath. Ruby's head stared up at the ceiling from a pike. The scar Juniper once loved blended into Ruby's now white lips.

*And her forehead—Mountains, her forehead.*

Hailstones pelted the ground with a deafening fury. Juniper reached forward, tracing her finger over the letters carved into Ruby's skin.

*Traitor.*

The gashes oozed under her touch.

"Alder." She squeezed her sweetgrass braid as tears trailed through the dirt on her cheeks. "I will kill you for this."

The thick walls of ice cracked and moaned, answering her rage. Her surge of power reflected her grief.

She destroyed her prison with a wave of her hand, shattering the ice. Her father and his men ducked behind glacier-like structures they'd fashioned to use as shields.

"Juniper," the general roared. "You will stop this now! You are a noblewoman and a Silverneedle."

"Get out of my way."

"If you can't control yourself, you will never leave this dungeon."

"I said. Get. Out."

She sent the ice shields flying back at their creators, crushing the men against the stone walls behind them.

*I will not be obedient.*

The men howled, their bones grinding. Juniper forced the ice to meet stone.

*I'll shatter the silence.*

"Fall back!" General Silverneedle's voice echoed down the stairwell. "Hold the stairs!"

Fury guided her feet as she advanced. She glowered at the ice rising before her, unimpressed by the barricade the men patched together.

It blew apart with a boom. Men flew back as fragments pummeled them.

Screams.

She lifted a finger, and a freezing wind howled, cutting the air as it picked up sheets of ice from the ground. Like blades, they sliced men in half and relieved them of their heads.

*I'll take their strength.*

As she came to the landing, doubt flashed in her mind for the first time. Soldiers clogged the grand hall. Snow fell around them.

*I'll have to kill them all to get to the prince.*

Armored men loosed arrows. One hit. Blood ran down her arm and over the braided grass still fisted in her palm. Her doubt fell away with her blood.

Splashes of snow rose from the ground in waves, solidifying in time to deflect the projectiles. The swells landed on the soldier's feet, cementing them to the ground.

Madness etched lines across Juniper's face as she reached into the soldiers with her cold, dropping their temperature so fast their blood and organs expanded. She pulled her powers back, and their armor creaked as their innards burst out from their abdomens. She stalked to the throne room, dispatching each rush of men as they came, leaving death in her wake.

*There is no balance.*

Her father now stood before the great doors. He sheathed his sword and rubbed his hands together.

"I knew you were evil." His stance widened. "I knew you were evil from the day you were born."

Nothing could stop her now. She sucked in an icy breath, pain burning through her as her skin lined with frost. She didn't slow. She

284

didn't block. She walked straight into her father's attack. The silverneedles ricocheted off her body and fell to the ground.

Her hand clamped on his shoulder. He cried out as her fingers dug into his flesh and froze his blood. He fell to his knees, panting. His body solidified.

Juniper stepped past him without a second glance, pushing the doors open.

The queen sat on her throne. Her eyes closed in concentration as she lent her power to her king. King Troms stood beside his son. Their shoulders touched.

Juniper locked eyes with Alder knowing she had something inside her that they didn't. She smiled through the power rolling off of the royal family, unphased. A frozen wind, as sharp as a razor, whipped through muscle and tendon.

*Thud.*

*Thud.*

Heads rolled.

The tinkle of crystalized blood striking stone rang in the silence.

The prince lowered his father's body to the ground.

Wild-eyed, he howled, staggering toward Juniper and drawing his sword. Both youths released their power at once. The Mountain trembled. The conical roofs of the castle screeched as they threatened to lift. Juniper's exposed skin became the color of Alder's eyes.

They wielded their icy powers with blows that sent shock waves through the land. Glass broke. Animals fell over and shattered. Blackened frost burns covered the lungs and hearts of their people, sending them to God's Mountain in mass. But neither the lady nor the prince could see past their hatred.

Hail and snow and icicles swirled around them. The projectiles grew ever closer to their targets until Juniper's ice drew a line over the scar Ruby gave him four years before.

*Ruby.*

Alder's brows rose. He looked at his wound and then raised his sword. With a roar, he ran at her.

Silverneedles hit him from the side. Strips of the prince scattered on the ground.

Juniper stumbled, a moan escaping her lips as the cold fell away.

*Is it over?*

She looked down at her hand where the sweetgrass braid dripped blood. She shook her head.

"I don't need your crown." She dropped it on Alder's remains and returned to the dungeon, where her lover waited.

# THE GRUSEL WOODS
## *A Pied Piper Retelling*
By Jessica Julien

## 1 – MILA

I SCREWED UP.

I let him go.

No one comes into the woods without being possessed. *No one*! But that boy with the eyes the color of acorns and messy hair... he woke something inside me. It fluttered through me like a thousand butterflies.

I couldn't draw the knife across his throat or drive it into his chest.

So I tell him to run. I shove him away and demand that he *run*.

What is this boy doing in my woods? Would he make it out alive, or would the spirits capture him before he reached the other side of the forest line? I shake the worry and wonder from my mind. It doesn't matter. I've never let anyone live. Spilled blood is the key to holding the enchantment in place, and now...

Trails of darkness seep over the frosted ground, warming the white blanket and bringing chaos with it. Snowflakes mingle with hazy spirits that claw and reach. Eager to possess.

I'm paralyzed, stunned by the fear of the enchantment loosening around me.

The boy's presence surprised me.

A *stranger.*

A *handsome* stranger.

A handsome, *unpossessed* stranger.

The crunch of his heavy steps draws my attention as I patrol the trees, so I trail him to the giant oak. It is the oldest, most precious place among the woods. I watch as he places his hand against the bark, feeling the carvings in the trunk. He traces them curiously; the marks of the many spirits the women of my family have captured—etched proof of generations of protection long forgotten by the villages.

The boy bends, filling his hands with snow. I watch as he studies it, bringing it to his nose and then licking it as if it couldn't possibly be real. As quietly as I can, I step across the snow, inching my way to him. He may appear to be unpossessed, but I have to be sure.

Brushing his hands on his pants, the boy pivots, facing me. His movement wakes me from my prowl, and I pounce, shoving him against the tree. My knife against his throat.

A branch cracks and the snow piled on its limbs drops to the ground with a muted *thunk.* It's enough to startle me out of my daze of the boy.

I turn, cursing as the snow beneath my boots grows slippery, and race to my cabin. Mother Shutz will know what to do.

My shoes become saturated as the snow turns to slush, but the numbness in my feet can't stop me from racing down the path. All my life, I've run in these woods. I know every root and rock hidden beneath the white powder, every tree, every shadow... and I use it to my advantage.

A spirit rises before me, blocking my way with a silent scream and reaching fingers, but I don't slow my pace. Barreling through the figure, I feel the staticky cloud wisp away. It makes me sneeze like too much pepper in a stew and leaves behind the smell of a fire recently doused.

The pinch in my side eases as the cabin comes into sight. It's a tiny wooden square among the white covered forest, with smoke billowing from the chimney and windows lit with candlelight.

I shove the front door open, not bothering to pound the slush from my boots, and slam it behind me.

"What is it?" Mother Shutz asks from beside the cauldron in the fireplace. Her eyes are wide as she stands to assess me for wounds or damage. I can't seem to catch my breath so I can apologize for the wet floor and then beg for mercy when she realizes it was me who shattered the spells. Instead, tears fall against my cheeks and then my mother is there, wrapping me in her arms in a waft of rosemary.

"Shh, it's okay," she soothes.

With a shake of my head, I confess, "There was a boy, Mama. He-he came into the woods and I... I let him go. I'm sorry. I-I couldn't..." A sob escapes me, and I clutch the patched fabric of my coat over my aching chest. "Mama, I *couldn't.*"

She wraps her arms around me again and squeezes. "My little Mila. This day was always meant to come." I lean back in shock. I'd been expecting a reprimanding or a thorough scolding, however, she is smiling.

"What?"

"There is always one for every Shutz sorceress."

I frown. "What do you mean?"

"There is one that comes to our heart-call. One unlike the others. One filled with hope and promise and life. *He* always comes." She's beaming.

I can't help but furrow my brows. "Mama?"

She shakes her head and a single, frizzy curl drops from the pile of hair on her head. It brushes her shoulder like a curling flame.

"Mila, I swear I'll tell you what is happening and why that boy was there, but right now," she pauses, tucking the loose hair behind her ear before peering out the tiny window in the door. "We must recast the protection spell."

Mother Shutz holds out her hand, but I hesitate to take it. I want to know more of this story. I want to know why I couldn't kill that boy. I want to know that he made it out of the woods safely and why I *care* about his safety... I huff because she is right. We can't do anything until we bring back the frost and conceal the spirits.

With a deep inhale, I slip my hand into my mother's. Together we retrieve the box of matches and light the candles within the selenite holders. We start on opposite ends of the mantle, then we light the tallest one in the center together.

We exit the house and a breeze hits my face, bringing pungent scents of death and wetness with it. My mother appears beside me, the *Opfermesser* ceremony blade made of black obsidian in hand. She draws the onyx blade across her palm then clenches it to ensure the crimson droplets fall against the earth. As the air fills with the scent of copper, I wait for her command. When she gives me a curt nod, I extend my right hand to her. Mother Shutz pricks my thumb. A bead of blood appears and I wipe it down the center of my lips and chin, feeling the warm satin smear smoothly. Then, I withdraw the small flute from around my neck and hold the collection of wooden pipes to my bloodstained lips.

## 2 – AUGUSTUS

I ran.

Like a terrified fool, I ran away.

I'd only been in the woods because I wanted to prove to my father—to *everyone*—that the stories weren't true, that the evil witch

was just a bedtime story to keep us scared of whatever they were truly hiding in there.

But that tree.

And that girl.

A mysterious girl with tangled hair and a patchwork coat who frightened me more than any girl I'd ever met.

I didn't hear her move across the snow, but when I turn to leave, there she is, shoving me against the trunk of the tree, a blade at my throat. Her pale face sits inches from mine, and I swear she is about to cut my throat. Rather, she cringes in confusion. In an instant, she presses the tip of the knife to my heart, one that hammers and skips harder than I thought imaginable, still, she hesitates.

"Who are you?" she demands. When I don't answer right away, she digs the point of the dagger deeper. "Why are you here?" she says louder.

"I-I..." I stammer, unable to tell her I am here because I once believed in bedtime stories of Pied Pipers and deadly sorceresses, but now I want to prove them wrong.

"Who. Are. You?" This time she enunciates every word through her teeth.

"A-Augustus," I manage. As if my words punch her in the stomach, she steps away with a gasp. "Who are *you*?" I wonder, rubbing the spot on my chest where the dagger had sat. "What are you doing in the woods?"

The girl merely blinks at me like she doesn't understand how I couldn't know all the answers to my own questions. Perhaps I *do* know them, but I'm not ready to confess that yet. One word escapes her lips instead of revealing her name.

"Run."

My eyes widen and I swallow hard. If I *did* believe in the stories, then I wasn't meant to leave the woods alive. No one ever returned from the *Grusel Woods.*

Somewhere deep down, I knew I might not make it home for

dinner. I knew it was stupid and childish to run off, but something drew me to this place; a pull... a *knowing*... that this tree with the intricate markings was exactly where I was meant to be.

I was told the woods were cursed to be frozen in time; a place to keep the sorceresses contained. My sister and I listened to the bedtime tales of ugly hags who lured men into the woods with the enchanting melodies of their fluted pipes, only to slaughter them and eat their flesh. My father told me the witch used the leftover bones as wind chimes and sharpened them into tools.

The stories gave me nightmares that still haunt me.

But this girl couldn't be older than me—seventeen, if not younger—and she was frightfully beautiful with pale freckled skin and eyes that seemed to shift from blue to green when she blinked.

She was no hag.

She was no witch.

Her strong fingers grip my arm hard, and she shoves me away.

"Run!" she repeats the command, and this time I don't hesitate. I spin, launching myself across the snow-covered ground.

I slip as my feet hit a pile of slush. Snow drops from the branches all around me in heavy, pounding *thunks* like a slowly rising heartbeat. One collides into my right shoulder, sending icy shards down the collar of my shirt. Shivering, I keep walking because the edge of the woods is within sight.

As I cross the barrier of the frozen prison, I collapse onto soft, warm wheat. Rolling to my knees, I watch as the trees shudder and stretch as if waking from a long slumber. Shadows twitch between them, filling the quiet evening with chittering notes of sardonic coaxing, begging me to come back. Wisps of pale blue and smokey gray emanate from the treeline, creeping through the wheat in hushed whispers. The stalks bend with their slithering.

Pushing to my feet, I race to the village. It's not far, and I'm grateful that the noises behind me lessen. I can already see the thatched roof of the church; a sharp point against the other flat buildings we all inhabit, and I urge my achy feet to keep going.

Muddy water splashes onto my trousers as I slip between the church and the dressmaker shop, round the village center where a well sits surrounded by mothers chatting and filling buckets for their evening meals.

"Augustus?" my mother calls to me, her voice laced with panic. I give her a quick wave and continue to cross the grounds.

Behind the butcher shop, down a little slope, sits a fresh spring where four people sit playing a children's game with rocks in the low grass. Stumbling over my own tired feet, I barrel toward them.

"Auggie?" Ada, a girl with two yellow braids, gasps in surprise. She stands and the three others grapple to their feet after her. "What happened?"

I bend over, hands on my knees, trying to catch my breath.

"Is someone after you? Maybe that old hag from the woods?" Niles chuckles, making his round belly jiggle.

"He didn't go into the woods, Niles, you idiot!" Ada snaps at him, hands on her hips.

I spit in his direction. "I *did* go into the woods."

All four faces pale.

"Y-You did *what?*" Ada exclaims in horror.

"We were only joking!" Niles shouts. It was his idea for me to go into the woods in the first place, telling me my father would think it brave of me to face the villains who steal our men and possess our families.

"Augustus, father will—" Adrina, my younger sister by five years, stares at me with wide brown eyes. Her chestnut hair is a mess of curls around her shoulders, loose and unruly; mother will be furious.

I shake the thought of the oncoming scolding that I'll get for letting Adrina ruin the perfect braids she'd worked so hard on that morning.

"I saw the witch," I interrupt with a shaky voice. Sweat drips down the side of my face and I feel too hot to breathe because the reality that I *had* entered the woods, and I *did* see someone, cascades over my body in a wave of terror.

"That's not possible," Gregor, the seamstress' son, claims. He's too thin and short for his age and always follows our group around like a puppy. Rarely did he have a comment of his own, so his outburst takes us by surprise. "But the stories... my ma says—"

"That was no witch I saw," I cut in. "It was simply a girl."

"But... how?"

I shrug at Ada. "The stories must be wrong! I saw a girl and she couldn't have been older than me."

"But you're alive!" Adrina's gaze trails over my body. "She didn't kill you?" She covers her mouth and I see tears welling in her eyes. I shake my head and she closes the space between us, throwing her bony arms around me.

Patting her warm hair, I say, "She let me go."

Niles snorts. "I don't believe you."

"No one ever comes back from the woods," Ada comments, but she's staring at me as if she does believe me, but she doesn't want to. "*No one*, Auggie."

"I don't know why she let me go. To be honest, she looked as terrified as I was to see another being in the woods."

Suddenly, the ground quakes, sending us all toppling. I pull Adrina down and place my body over hers protectively until everything stills. When it does, an ominous silence fills the air. No birds dare to chirp. No voices echo from the village. Not even the creek seems brave enough to trickle.

"We have to go." Ada springs to her feet, then helps Adrina stand, drawing her from under my grip.

I stand on trembling legs. Is this my fault? There's only ever been a few recordings of quakes in our village history and all happened because someone angered the witches. That girl, though... that girl didn't look mad. She seemed shocked, terrified, but not upset.

Adrina grabs my hand and tugs. "Auggie, we have to go."

My sister drags me through the town center, now empty except for a few people snapping shutters into place in their shops. Our feet

pound up the stairway to our tiny home above the candle shop my parents own, and we throw the front door open. Adrina shoves me inside, then slams and bolts the door. I stare at the crackling fire, where a pot of stew is boiling for dinner.

A buzzing fills my ears.

"Mama? Papa?" Adrina calls, but her little voice is muffled. The pounding of my pulse batters against my eardrums and my vision hazes. The girl's face appears before me like a ghost. Her eyes draw me in, and I want nothing more than to drown myself in their swirling hues.

Mama shakes my shoulders. I blink and her image overshadows the girl's. Her brown eyes wash out the blue and green, her olive skin darkens the pale pallor, and her long dark braid tames the wild red curls.

"Augustus!" she shouts sternly.

I focus on her flushed face. A grunt behind me draws my attention and I turn to find Adrina struggling with the barricade on the door. I hurry to help her. As the heavy beam snaps into place, Mama takes our place and spreads salt across the threshold, then moves to do the same across the windowpanes and any openings to the outside.

Papa hurries in from the washroom. His gaze bounces between our quick movements, ensuring we are all doing our tasks, then he begins lighting the candles on the mantle and strapping daggers to his waist.

Everyone knows weapons provide no protection against the spirits, but they are good for slowing down the bones... at least, that's what I'm told. I've never witnessed any escapes from the past, as the witches have since kept their haunting demons caged inside. It didn't matter; the weapons are of no use. But I know my father finds safety in their weight; the idea that he has them within reach, just in case. To me, they're merely hapless devices.

Adrina brushes by me on her way into the kitchen. She grabs a wooden chair from the table, dragging it behind her like a huntress.

It screeches against the floor, making me wince. I snatch it from her hands and reach for the box of sage bundles from the cupboard easily.

"Here." I hand her a thatched bundle, then replace the box. Mama brings a candle to light it, then Adrina flutters around the room, ensuring the smoke has touched every inch. The scent of sage, vervain, and lavender wafts around as she spins by me to complete her circle.

Goosebumps rise over my body, and I shiver. As I exhale, my breath forms a clouded wisp. I turn and lock eyes with Adrina, and that is when the music drifts to us.

## 3 – MILA

The sound of bones penetrating half frozen earth sounds like thunder breaking. The first time I heard it, I couldn't help but cover my ears. Now as they burst from their graves, sending quakes outward like rippling tides, I merely await my cue to begin. I watch as limbs break free, fingers tearing at the melting snow, trying to find a hold to draw themselves to the surface—bone by bone—filling the air with the scent of rot and soil.

Spirits appear in clouded fragments. They draw themselves together in a *whoosh*, like a rushing gale through the trees, until they're one hazy apparition. As they piece together bit by bit, the aroma of sulfur and wormwood mingles with the rotten scents. Together, the combination is abrasive and intense. It's overwhelming and makes it hard to breathe, hard to think. It takes everything in me not to gag.

I close my eyes to hold focus on my task—to bring the notes to life—but instead of a melody, I see his face. *Augustus.* My heart races and I hope he's made it to safety because once the spell begins to weave, it will be too late for him to escape.

Taking a breath, I steady my thoughts, but I find it hard to shake his image from my mind. Something about the way his eyes took me in has me breathless and my body aches for him to be near once more.

"Mila!" Mother Shutz's voice is harsh, but it's what I need to force my concentration.

I wet my lips, tasting the metallic notes of my blood and the wooden edge of my flute. With a deep inhale, I do my best to ignore the pungent aromas and sounds of the dead coming to life, and hold my breath.

There's a static in the air, like a storm approaching. In a way, there is a sort of storm happening, a turbulent mix of soul and bone and blood and music.

When a tingling sensation creeps down my spine, I know it's time to begin. I exhale slowly into the flute, sending hypnotic notes into the darkness dotted with the bones and souls of those once trapped below. I trill the melody with practiced grace. Every shift of the instrument across my lips, every pause and breathe, every rise and fall of chords, was taught to me by my mother and her mother before her, and so on and so on, until the first soul was ever captured by the first Shutz woman.

The sorceresses of my family have long been tasked with protecting the villages outside the *Grusel Woods* from unhinged souls and possessed bones.

Before they cast us into the forest, they once knew our family as saviors. Praised among the land! One twisted word of bewitchment and disloyal love ruined it all, though.

It's a story every Shutz daughter is raised on. The story of Tia and her betrothed; a man who, driven by jealousy, turned the closest town to the woods against them, creating a ripple effect through the land. A drunken man who one night beat another to death because he made a passing comment about Tia's beauty... or so they say. The betrothed confessed to the murder but blamed the Shutz name. He claimed Tia cursed him that his actions were not his own. Knowing he would be hung, and not wanting anyone else to lay claim to Tia, he swore to take her down too.

Tia and her mother, for there can only ever be two Shutz women of age at once, made a plea with the village. In exchange for Tia's life, her mother swore an oath to continue protecting the people for as long as their line continued. The village would provide a male every generation to ensure the Shutz family lineage never ended. As long as the family stayed true to their banishment, the town agreed to their terms. And thus, the endless life among the frosted woods began.

At the time, Tia didn't know she was with child. My grandmother, Beatrix, was born seven months later and brought up in the way of the Pied Piper. When Beatrix had a daughter of her own, she too taught her the ways of the Shutz women, passing the playing pipe from generation to generation.

I learned to play the small flute at the age of five, quickly memorizing the notes and placement of my lips against the instrument. Day after day, I sat repeating the few songs our family needed to ensure the safety of the village.

One for the souls.

One for the bones.

One for the blood to trap them below.

A trio of melodies that wrapped around the trees, froze the ground, and sent the wandering souls back to their resting places. If any *were* to escape or slither from our icy entrapment, they would seek possession. Anyone unlucky enough to enter the woods—or foolish enough—during this time would risk possession. Being captured was almost always a death sentence because the only way to rid the possession was to remove the spirit... and most hosts were not strong enough to survive extraction.

The wandering souls wanted nothing more than to wreak havoc and become whole again.

The more blood they drew, the more solid—more human—they became.

So instead of allowing the bloodshed, we sacrifice a bit of our own and weave our spell once more, and I let the notes emanate from me in a crescendoed wave of trilling tunes.

Already the air is frigid. My breath puffs in plumes with every exhale, but as my breath lengthens, holding notes in a calming adagio, something shifts.

# 4 – AUGUSTUS

We huddle before the hearth waiting for the music to cease. My sister has buried herself under a heavy quilt, and my mother hums a lullaby in her rocking chair to drown out the delicate notes. The two melodies twine together in an uncomfortable sort of way. It makes me shudder and cringe.

"Stop," I whisper harshly. My mother's fingers pause—the knitting needles hovering between stitches—and she stares at me with confusion. "S-sorry," I apologize. Something about the music tonight makes me want to escape. The sound of the rocking chair begins again, and the creaking makes my nerves tighten.

I've never feared the story of the Piper more than I do right now. We haven't had a disruption in months, and even then, it was nothing like the pounding rhythm growing around us.

"Are you feeling alright?" Adrina stares at me with misty eyes.

I blink, hesitating to answer. "I'm fine." She looks at our father. He sits facing the door with a stern expression and a shotgun in his lap. "Don't," I say with a warning.

Adrina's eyes narrow to slits and she presses her lips together to keep my secret from spilling.

The woods are off limits. Not only because it is part of the pact made with the sorceresses, but from what I believe, is the fear of the story of a man being cursed, a sacrifice to the woods. Some say that once one enters the haunted forest, they become a target for any wandering souls. Like leaving a scent for a hound, they'll follow the trail of human flesh in hopes of taking it as their own. Perhaps I sealed my own death today.

But the witches keep the haunts in... the best they can, anyway. And there hasn't been a male sacrifice in almost two decades.

To not draw attention to ourselves, or offer our own bodies as bait, we're taught to stay out of the *Grusel Woods*. I've always been fascinated with it though—a place forever covered in snow, a place of wicked pipers playing their enchanting tunes, a spell-weaving melody that keeps the dead, well... what we hope is dead. Who knows what they're really doing with the spirits and bones?

A single note rings in my ears. A bewitching minor chord. It leaves behind a buzz in my bones. My feet ache to move and a tingling sensation crawls up my legs. The moment I uncurl my limbs, I find myself standing.

Blood rushes to my toes, and I step on pins and needles as I make my way to the door. The buzzing intensifies, drowning out everything around me. Right now, it's just me and this lingering chord. Me and this desire to *run*.

My fingers wrap around the doorknob and the sound in my ears begins to staccato, as if telling me that this was exactly what I needed to be doing.

Before I can turn the handle, I'm jerked back. I spin to face my father, who stares at me with mad, cold eyes.

My gaze flickers to my sister, who is being held back by my mother. Adrina's mouth forms my name, but the noise in my head is so overwhelming that all I hear are her muffled cries. I shake my head, trying to rid myself of the annoyance.

Fingers grip my chin, forcing me to meet my father's stare. At his touch, the buzz begins to fade.

I blink rapidly, trying to focus on his strong jaw and pointed nose, features I mirror, but it's difficult to concentrate. His face morphs from his to mine and back again... it makes me dizzy.

"Augustus!" he shouts, and it snaps me to attention. "I asked what you were doing in the woods today, boy!" He shakes my jaw.

 300

My mouth opens, but my voice catches in my throat, only allowing a single word to escape. "Run."

"He's possessed!" my mother cries, covering her mouth with a handkerchief, and Adrina turns to soothe her manic sobs.

I stare at my father. His features soften before me like he can't believe I'd be brave enough to actually go into the woods. It's a mix of pride, astonishment, and fear that clouds his face, and I'm not sure how to react. I've never seen him this way before.

"You stupid, stupid, boy," he replies with a shake of his head.

Even as I step away, I can still feel the warmth from his calloused fingers. "I did not do it because I am stupid," I remark. "I went because it was the brave thing to do. It was the *right* thing to do."

"Brave?" he spits.

"No one has entered the woods in decades. Not even *you,*" I challenge.

"Because I don't have a death wish!"

"I'm still standing! Heart beating! No soul has touched me." I'm yelling, but I shrug my reply. "I didn't even *see* a living thing beside a girl. She was as surprised as I was to find another human on the *cursed* grounds."

My mother inhales sharply. "A girl? You mean the *witch!*"

"That hag of a piper," my father adds with disgust.

"She was no hag," I reply, a smile tugging at my lips as I recall her flaming hair and round face. "It was merely a girl."

My father scoffs, and the music expands in the surrounding space. I feel it vibrating through my chest and turn to the door. A hand grips the back of my shirt, yanking me back, but I spin and shove my father. His hands slip free as he stumbles. My mother yelps as he collides with her, but they do not hit the floor. Feet scuff behind me as I lift the barrier and swing the door open. The salt line scatters across the wooden planks under the sound of a shotgun being cocked.

I pause and look over my shoulder. My father has the gun lifted. I can tell by the level of it that it's aimed right at my heart.

"I have to." My voice is a whisper; a pleading cry to let me go.

"He's not possessed," Adrina adds softly. "He is right of mind. I know it." Her tone is urgent.

My father lifts his chin ever so slightly. "Do you feel the pull of the music?"

I don't reply, but I don't need to for him to know it's true. Never before had I broken the protective barriers of our house. Never before had I dared to disobey his rules. Never had I turned my back on a loaded gun.

As I race down the steps, I hear my mother cry out for me, but I'm not in control of my own feet. They carry me through the town square, across the wheat field, and to the edge of the forest where I'd so recently ran from. The music has stopped. When? I wasn't sure. But now I stand before the snow covered entrance dripping in an eerie quiet.

# 5 – MILA

Silence creeps around me and I hold my breath, waiting to ensure everything and everyone has settled. There have only ever been a couple of occurrences where a soul lingered too close to the edge of the forest to make it to their resting place before the song ended. When that happened, the soul simply continued their search for possession, but that hasn't happened in a long, long time.

After a pregnant pause, I release my breath and look at Mother Shutz. "I do not sense any others. Do you?"

"I don't—" she begins to reply, but something's caught her attention. Taking a step forward, she closes her eyes and raises her bloodied palm. Her fingers twitch and then freeze. "There is something." Her head sways. "At the furthest edge north. Do you feel it?"

I shut my eyes and take a calming inhale. Shutz women have a unique connection with the forest. Since we weave our enchantment between the trees, we can follow the magic trails like pathways. I let my mind drift until I sense it; a pulse... a vibration... right at the treeline.

"I think it's just one." I peek at my mother; she sways on her feet but nods. "I will go."

"No." Her voice is stern. "I should go."

"Mama," I say, gently. "It is a single soul. I can take care of it and be back in time for stew."

Her pale eyes watch me, flickering over my face, and then she deflates. "Alright. But be quick."

I kiss her cheek. "I promise." And then I'm sprinting through the trees toward the lingering soul. It takes far longer than I'd like to cover the distance, but my feet never falter, and even though the stitch in my side is begging for me to stop and catch my breath, I know I must finish my task, and fast.

I see the edge of the woods. A place where death and life collide. The lingering soul is a hazy, clouded figure of a man. In his life, he must have been tall and strong because his spirit rises far above me. But it's not his size that stops me in my tracks. It's what I can see through him, standing among the wheat.

"Augustus?" His name comes out in a gasp.

His lips turn up in a smile and his eyes flicker from my own to my lips where the crimson track has dried. My jaw tightens as I realize I must look frantic and frazzled.

Others gather behind him, drawing his confused attention away. A man who appears to be an older version of Augustus, dripping in sweat, goes pale at the sight of the spirit. The gun in his grip lifts, aiming at the apparition. It's a foolish move. His ammo will have no effect on the soul other than angering it further.

"What is that?" a timid voice calls and a young girl steps from behind the man. Her eyes are wide, her cheeks red from running, but it's the shake of fear in her tone that reminds me why I'm here.

"Get behind me!" the man commands, but Augustus backs away from him. "Augustus! No! Don't enter the woods!"

I stride forward, hands raised, and call out to Augustus. "Stop!" But it's too late.

Augustus steps onto the fresh snow, then hesitates as the spirit chitters between us.

A woman, Augustus's mother, raises a finger at me. Gripping her chest, her lips press into a line. "She's a witch!" the older woman shouts. "See the blood on her face? She's already drawn blood tonight! Stay away from her. She'll kill you!"

"I'm not here to kill him! I'm not here to kill *anyone*!" I snap back. "I'm not the one drawing the spirits out. You are! I'm trying to *save* you!" My voice cracks.

The woman spits at the ground, then glares at me. "You are nothing more than a demonic witch. I see through your mask! I will not let you take my son."

"Ma, stop!" Augustus throws over his shoulder, but his eyes never leave mine. "Are you hurt?" His voice is soft and concerned.

I shake my head. "I'm fine. Just—" I groan. "Stay still." Slowly, I reach for the flute around my neck. "I can fix this." I feel the warmth of the magic flowing through the instrument, pulsing with my own heart, ready to draw the spirit back. As I raise it to my lips, his father cocks the gun. The spirit haze solidifies into a single being and whooshes forward.

Augustus looks over his shoulder just as the spirit plunges through him.

"No!" I scream, and my feet are moving again. Augustus blinks heavily and looks as though he may topple, but I grip his shoulders and steady him. "Augustus?"

"I'm fine. It's okay," he replies. It wasn't him the spirit was after. Augustus was merely in his way.

## 6 – AUGUSTUS

Adrina's scream shatters everything around me. I turn and find my father on his knees, hands digging into the soil, begging for whatever has him to release itself. A gray wisp hovers around him slowly sinking, sinking, into him. When he lifts his head, there are streaks of crimson dripping from his eyes and nose and as he opens his mouth, it dribbles out the side.

"What have I done?" I stagger at the sight of the bloodied mess. My father coughs and dark ichor spews from his lips. I try to go to him, but the girl grips my wrist.

"You can't. It will only make it worse," she explains, but I don't care. I tug, but she holds steady. "If you leave again, they will *all* rise and…" She bites her bottom lip and her eyes shift to my father. "I will not be able to contain them myself."

I have no idea what she means by that and I know I don't have time to discuss it. So I jerk my hand free and step out of the woods. I hesitate though, one foot pressing into soft earth and the other growing cold among the snow. The hair on the back of my neck rises and the girl curses. From deep within the woods, the sound of a growing storm begins. Thunder echoes through the branches and snow softens.

"Not again!" the girl groans.

"Auggie!" Adrina calls for me. I'm torn between running to save my father and moving back into the woods. I'm not sure which path is safer. Maybe neither. But that spirit has hold of my father, and if everything happening is real and not some nightmare I'm about to wake up from, then the stories must be real, too.

"You have to save him," I plead with the girl. "Please, y-you have to."

She stares at the scene before her, and I see her fingers tighten around a small instrument. The arrangement of wooden pipes fits in her palm.

"The Piper," I say under my breath. Her gaze darts to me and there is panic in her stare.

"My name is Mila."

I swallow hard. "But you can save him. Can't you? The stories are true. You can play to draw the spirits out." I shift my weight on my feet just as another gray wisp gathers behind her in a *whoosh* of colliding mist. She stares over her shoulder and then glances at me again, unfazed by the apparition. "Mila, please. Save him."

Mila stares at my father and gives me a curt nod. Before I can exhale in relief, she's turning away.

"Wait!" I call after her, but she doesn't stop. Instead, she steps over a fallen log and sprints deeper into the woods.

## 7 – MILA

The trees vibrate as I race past them and roots and rocks toss into the air as bones begin to break through soil. I curse, side-stepping a clawing hand that almost catches my shoe. My throat burns and I taste copper as I swallow hard, but I dare not stop. Never before have we had to do the ritual twice in one night, but Augustus... if he'd only listened to me, I could have fixed this on my own.

"Mama!" I shout as the cabin comes into sight. She appears on the small porch, dagger in hand. "The boy—"

"Not now!" she scolds, and I'm shocked by her harshness. Her eyes dart around me, then she grabs my wrist, hauling me beside her. "Quickly."

In a single motion, she unwraps her bandaged hand and tears the flesh apart once more. I thrust my hand at her; she pricks the skin, and I hastily repeat the motions from before. Smear the blood. Raise the flute. Steady breath. Begin.

## 8 – AUGUSTUS

I shove Adrina aside and fall to my knees beside my father. "You can fight this," I tell him. He gags then spits out a mouth full of blood and dark ichor.

"*You* did this!" my mother sneers, tears streaming down her face. "You've killed him." She takes a step toward me and I rise to face her. "You've doomed us all, you stupid boy." Her hand crosses my face in an echoing slap. The sting, like a thousand thorns, burns my cheek and I stumble back. Tears fill my eyes. Never before has my mother struck me. The idea of her hating me so much hurts more than the slap.

"Mila will fix this," I explain, turning back to my father. He's grunting and growling like a wild animal, digging nails across the soil. The sight makes my stomach churn. I notice Adrina has gone pale, almost ashen in the darkening field, and she bites her nail nervously.

"The *witch?*" Mother grabs my arm, forcing me to face her.

"She's not the villain you think she is!" My voice startles both my mother and Adrina, pushing them back a step. "Sometimes the stories are wrong, Ma."

"Take the flesh." My father speaks, but it's not his voice I hear. A demonic croak of a tone seeps from his lips. "Take the flesh. Gnaw the bones. Human life becomes my own," it chants through gargled blood.

I move to kneel beside him, but the music starts again paralyzing me. The sounds of the frantic forest cease. My mother and sister freeze, staring at my father who is now on his back convulsing. Blood spews from his mouth, and this time I drop to my knees in a rush. Instinct kicks in and I roll him to his side to help clear his airways because he's choking on the gore and his lips are turning blue.

Then, as the music fades, a black mist drifts from his mouth, his nose, his ears, and collects into a single form. It hovers over the body, head tilted as if listening to the quiet music, then in a *whoosh* it darts into the forest.

## 9 – MILA

Before the spirits can collect fully and the bones can break free, they're already oozing back into their holds. The ground, still fresh with ice and snow, melts together again and the enchantment locks in place.

My ears fill with a soft hum. My chest vibrates with the grand pause before the final fortissimo. As I purse my lips to the flute once more to end the enchantment, something sparks within me.

I hesitate to finish the ritual, because a new collection of notes drifts through my mind. It resonates around me in a steady rhythm filled with rich, rounded notes I've never heard before until I realize I'm the one playing them. Breathing into the flute, I feel the wooded edges slide across my lips, letting the smooth melody flood from me without thought.

The ground trembles as the new magic drifts over the blanket of snow. Fresh flakes drift lazily from the canopy, drowning any lingering souls or bones with its weight.

## 10 – AUGUSTUS

"Papa!" Adrina cries, dropping to her knees. She takes one of our

father's hands between her own tiny palms and holds it against her chest. "Papa?" Tears stream down her face and snot drips from her nose.

I reach for her, but she scoots away as if afraid of me. Drawing my hand back, I exhale sharply. I glance at my mother; she, too, is on her knees but she's covering her face with her hands muttering a prayer. With a shake of my head, I look at my father. His chest rises and falls slowly.

"He's alive," I announce, standing and brushing the dirt from my pants. I face the woods, feeling a warmth emanating from the treeline. Something shimmers between the trees, and my heart flutters.

"Augustus!" My mother's command stops me. My feet were moving forward without me realizing it. I'm two steps from crossing into the woods. "Don't," she pleads, but then a song I've never heard trills through the branches and shakes the ground. It brushes over the fresh snow, bringing icy flakes with it until it wraps around me like a winter cloak.

With a last glance at my mother, and a smile for my sister, who is watching me with a horrified expression, I proceed forward, allowing the notes to guide my steps.

## II – MILA

Before I close the ceremony, I turn to my mother. She's staring into the trees unblinking, gripping her chest. The cut on her hand is coated in a second layer of dried dark ichor and she is paler than before. "Mama? That song," I begin. "There's only ever been three. What was it?"

"Your heart song," she replies, turning to me with a smile. She sniffs, tugging her thin robe tighter still. "Part of our pact was that the town would provide a male for our daughters; a way to keep our line never ending.”

*Augustus.* My heart races.

“Every Shutz woman holds a song inside them, one to help draw the boy to them and protect him as he travels through the woods. Once he hears the song, he will come.” Her eyes survey the forest. “You must finish the cast.”

I nod once, grip the flute, and close my eyes. “One for souls. One for bones. One for the blood to trap them below,” I recite.

“And one to call a loved one home,” Mother Shutz concludes. I peek at her. She’s smiling. Before I can utter a single question, footsteps crunch in the snow.

As a precaution, I hold my breath and place my hand on my flute. I hope I’m not wrong and a lingering possessed soul isn’t skulking toward us.

Between the trees, a figure emerges.

“Augustus,” I burst, unable to contain my smile.

He approaches, eyes flickering to the flute. “You *are* the Pied Piper.”

“Yes.”

“Mila?” His voice is filled with questions and I stare, wide-eyed, waiting for him to continue. “You saved my father.” I nod. “You’ve been saving us all.” I nod again. “You really aren’t the villains we think you are.”

I laugh then, because I never thought of myself as a villain. “I’m just a girl.”

“You’re everyone’s protector,” Augustus affirms, stepping forward and placing a tender kiss on my cheek.

# ABOUT THE AUTHORS

ANDREW LI VECCHI is an adjunct professor, writer, and video game composer. Since childhood, he has been obsessed with all things medieval, leading to the completion of an English PhD from Western University in 2020. His research focuses on elements of nineteenth and twentieth-century medievalism. "The Kelpie" is his first published work, and readers can expect to see more of Connal and his world in future stories. Andrew lives in southern Ontario with his wife, Elizabeth.

E. SENECA is a freelance speculative fiction author with an affinity for horror and dark fantasy. She has written original fiction since 2008, and her stories have appeared in various horror and fantasy anthologies and magazines such as DeadSteam, The Sirens Call, Through Other Eyes, Slashertorte, and Sherlock Holmes & The Occult Detectives.

ELISE BERENSEN MEYER is an avid fantasy reader who resides in the wooded lands of Virginia with her husband and four children, but will always be a California girl at heart. She has a Bachelor's in Mathematics Education, a great interest in her Viking heritage, and a deep love for chocolate chip cookies.

BENJAMIN SPERDUTO is a fantasy and horror writer who combines the visceral action and weird stylings of the pulp tradition with a gritty realism drawn from historical research. He is the author of several novels, including *Blackspire* and *The Walls of Dalgorod*, and has published over twenty short stories spanning the horror, sci-fi, and fantasy genres.

ARWYN SHERMAN is a cottage-dwelling swamp goblin with a toad familiar who, despite their obvious best efforts, has yet to meet a cryptid and must content themselves with writing them into their life. Their work has appeared in various anthologies, on a few stages, and is probably tucked away in a chapbook you forgot you bought at a late night poetry show.

J.D. TREBMAL has always been a daydreamer and lover of a good story. She grew up on an island in the cold Pacific Ocean where she pretended to be a mermaid in the water, in her mind, or even on the swings and her favorite fairytale has always been Hans Christian Andersen's original *The Little Mermaid*. She eventually got a BS in Fisheries Sciences and still loves the beach, water, and a good aquarium.

LILY MANNING is a teenaged writer and fantasy enthusiast, born and raised in Chicago, IL. She spends her time adventuring with her younger siblings and thwarting her cat's plans of world domination, sneaking in time to write as often as she can. Elemental is her first published work.

TINA CAPRICORN was raised in Western North Carolina, and grew up on a small farm nestled in the Blue Ridge Mountains. When she is not writing she is busy doing dishes, or laundry in an attempt to avoid editing. She also enjoys spending time with her husband, and snuggling her emotional support cats Captain and Peaches. To check out her other books or what she is up to, visit tinacapricorn.com.

JAN MARIE REYNOLDSON was born on the central plains of the USA but has been living in the mountains of central Italy since 1987. She lives in a national park with her Italian husband and daughter and enjoys writing fantasy stories in her free time. When she is not working or writing she enjoys walks in nature and drawing.

KIMBERLY GRYMES loves being sucked into science-fiction, fantasy, mystery, and paranormal worlds. After many, *many* years of reading books and watching other people's stories on TV and film, she finally took the plunge and started writing and sharing her own stories. Besides storytelling, Kimberly enjoys crafting and designing worksheets and checklists on her Etsy shop and taking bookish photos for her Instagram page. She and her family live on the outskirts of Wichita, Kansas.

PAUL WILLIAMS is a writer of fiction and non-fiction from the UK, now living in Australia. Paul has written books on Jack the Ripper, Mystery Animals, and wolves. This is his 66th published story.

WILLIAM RIGSBY is an author writing science fiction, fantasy, and dystopian fiction. When not writing William spends most of his time reading, hiking, gaming, building worlds for TTRPGs or daydreaming. He lives in his home in Lexington with his wife.

MARIA CARVALHO is a multi-genre author whose short stories have appeared in a wide array of publications, including several titles in the Owl Hollow Press Anthology Series, Edgeheart Press' *The Shadows We Breathe* books, and *Falling into the Five Senses* (Ree-Imagined Worlds), a collection she co-edited. Maria also wrote the popular children's book *Hamster in Space!* and is a regular contributor to *Woolgathering,* a nature-themed magazine. She lives in Connecticut with her husband and son.

CHERIE LYNAE CABRERA SUSKI is a Labor and Delivery nurse from Washington state. Her experience competing in slam poetry and studying Anthropology at the University of Washington has inspired her writing today. She has published poetry and short stories with Dragon Soul Press, Fifth Wheel Press, Dark Rose Press and more. She recently published How I Crave You, a book of erotic poetry. Today, she displays her creativity through her blog DarlingLynae.com, as she works hard to publish her debut novel, I Am Armageddon.

JESSICA JULIEN is a stay-at-home-mom, wife, co-owner of a small bookish shop, and avid wanderluster. When not curating book boxes or folding laundry, she spends her time penning YA novels inspired by her love of all things dark and twisty. She loves dark roast coffee, dark chocolate, watching The Office, and is obsessed with pumpkins, pie, and pandas. When the weather is right, she can be found road-tripping with her husband, son, and two dogs.

# About the Editors

LIZ DELTON has always enjoyed the backstage life of storytelling, considering her degree in Theatre Management from the University of the Arts.

She reads and writes fantasy, especially the kind with alternate worlds. Liz is the author of the Four Cities of Arcera series, the Realm of Camellia series, The Everturn Chronicles, and the steampunk series Seasons of Soldark. She also publishes notebooks for writers. World-building is her favorite part of writing, and she is always dreaming up new fantastic places.

She loves drinking tea and traveling. Visit her website at LizDelton.com

BENJAMIN THOMAS is a multi-genre writer from New England who unequally balances his time between hiking, writing, and quoting seemingly random movies. His short fiction has appeared in a variety of publications including *The Lascaux Review*, *Flash Fiction Online*, and *The Lost Librarian's Grave* while his medical thriller *Jack Be Quick* is available from Owl Hollow Press. He can be found online at benjiswandering.com or on social media @benjiswandering